Tales of Earth and Leaves

XANDRA NOEL

This is a work of fiction. References to real people, locations, events, organizations or establishments are intended for the sole purpose to provide authenticity and are used fictitiously. But, if you do happen to walk into a forest and find a fae prince, you need to message me immediately!

DEDICATION

To my husband, who supported me every step of the way

Hie vaedrum teim

To the stars and back

DEAR READER

Publishing this books was the scariest thing I've done in my life. These characters lived in the back of my mind for years, popping out every now and then and urging me to gather the courage to write.

I decided to tell their stories and invite you to join on their journey, discover new kingdoms and adventures and why not, fall in love.

I sincerely hope you enjoy reading this book as much as I enjoyed writing it!

Thank you for choosing to have a read.

Prologue

"Find it, Anwen." He stopped to inhale a breath, so abruptly that it seemed dirt had entered his lungs rather than fresh air. "You have to find it. Tell no one…" His hold on my wrist twitched, the struggle of keeping me in place taking a toll on his remaining strength, but he gathered enough energy for one final breath. "Evigt."

As soon as I nodded, my brother's hand fell limp after the exhaustion of the words. His mouth closed, dragging his soul away with the last remaining traces of light from his eyes. That was it. The last time I would hear his voice, wasted on a delirious phrase I did not understand.

Winter scattered by, and the request remained as untouchable as his presence. I missed the noises he used to make in the corridor while secretly sneaking someone out of his room. They fell as silent as his grave. Erik, we used to call him. Now we barely say anything at all.

No one knew how it happened, or even had an answer for it. No sign of health problems. He smiled on the cover of magazines, charmed the press and investors, frolicked his way to success and travelled across the world. When he fainted, his friends dismissed it as the conclave of too many emotions stuck in a single young man. Erik did too. How could he have known?

I fell asleep thinking about him every night. I had no life of my own; I gave up a master's degree and a boyfriend, neither of which brought me the speck of happiness they used to.

The fear of doing him a disservice clawed me from sleep and shook me awake, forcing me to do something. Anything in my power to at least be able to understand my brother's dying breath.

.

Spring

Anwen

Chapter One

The smell of freshly cut gardenias tickled my nose and forced me awake. It floated from the vanity right next to the window where dark blue curtains remained shut. Footsteps slowly backed away towards the door when I shifted in bed and opened my eyes.

"Good morning, Marissa," I barely muttered, my brother's face lingering on my eyelashes.

"Good morning, Anwen," she replied with a curt nod. "Apologies for startling you; Mister Jason insisted you wake to fresh flowers today."

I nodded and forced a smile. Like this was explanation enough, the woman who used to be my sitter closed the door, leaving me to bathe in the fresh smell that claimed my bedsheets and every corner of the room.

I breathed deeply, keeping the air in for a second longer than usual, and the thought squeezed my bones. The day I had been waiting for had finally arrived. I would go to Evigt and find whatever Erik needed me to.

To let the realization sink in, I buried my face in the pillow, allowing my slightly wavy hair to form messy branches on the white silk fabric. It must have been later in the morning, the sun was pushing through the curtains, and the room glowed around them, like a magical door opened behind the fabric, expecting to be unveiled. As though nature itself was pushing me into action, afraid that a second longer might convince me to reconsider.

After a long stretch and a few more minutes lingering in the goose-feather duvet, I pulled the covers away. By the time I reached the vanity, the gardenias almost shouted at me for attention, so I admired them for a moment and snatched the note attached to the vase, "For my adventurous daughter." I didn't have a chance to react as another noise creaked from the entry, this time missing the initial subtlety Marissa had. There was no care in the movement, only urgency and tempest-like energy when Cressida appeared in the room, after kicking the door open, the hinges squeaking in pain.

"Are you planning to sleep all day and just ignore us all?" she stared at me with an expression that mimicked both extreme happiness and the wrath of all the gods on a single beautiful face. Her blonde hair rested neatly tied in a bun, dark blue eyes sparkling with tiny stars across her eyelids, perfect makeup as usual. My friend made a stunning entrance wherever she went. Black eyeliner elongated the corners of her eyelids just enough to create that immaculate almond-like shape.

"And you are still in your pyjamas?" she sighed with annoyance.

"I'm having a lazy morning," I raised my hands defensively and smiled at my friend, hoping to calm down the hurricane of tension that followed her in.

"The hell you are! It's your last day here, girl; we need to do it

8

all!" Cressida replied as she raised her hands as well, not to mimic my gesture but to rave to a silent music only she could hear. There she was, by my side as she'd always been, my best friend. One of the most sought after influencers in New York City and the sister I chose for myself, ever since the day we were sat next to each other in French class. We'd been through everything together, boyfriends, sleepovers, graduations and losses. With one glance, she knew what haunted me.

"He would be proud, Anwen," she encouraged. Her long fingers traced my arm soothingly.

I sighed, grateful for Cressi's presence. She had shared every moment of my life and now, she tasted Erik's passing as bitterly as I did. I never knew what went on between them, I faked not noticing the hidden looks, the innuendos they sculpted for years into that column of possibility. She remained by my side every step of the way, through dark nights and depressing days, and here she was again, seeing me off to an unknown place, without understanding my reasons. Still, she supported my choices.

"There is still time to change your mind; we can ask the driver to take us back home," Mom gestured with a circular wave of a hand, ready to give the silent order.

"I will not change my mind," I replied for the millionth time. "I want to explore this forest, and Dad worked so hard to get me there," I continued while lowering my head to rest on his shoulder. It was a theatrical approach, but an effective one.

"I still can't believe you two," Mom replied with a huff, "bothering the Swedish royal family with such petty things, like you couldn't rent a villa somewhere else. We had to use a favour with them," she shook her head in disapproval.

"Only the best for my daughter," Dad said, his attention shifting towards his phone. Something important, as usual. "If she thinks a secluded place will help her find a tiny shred of happiness, then she shall have it."

I remained silent for the rest of the journey, glancing out the window and getting as far away from the conversation as I could within a moving car. They started arguing again.

In the past year, their favourite activity became running away from each other. Dad buried himself in work and came home at very late hours, if at all, and Mom had nothing left to do but to find company in clubs and charity events, make friends where she could and become the peaceful face everyone recognised: the wife of Jason Odstar, the powerful family leading a cosmetics empire. They moulded themselves perfectly in those roles, and even though time passed, they could not escape the fortresses both of them had built around their hearts.

"What about the company? When will she learn the business?" Mom repeated the same reasons we'd been hearing for the past weeks against my departure, ever since I gathered them at breakfast and told them about my plan.

I laid out the proposal and my wish—I needed to go away for six months to a quiet place and heal. To be alone and far away. I had found the perfect place: Evigt Forest, a place where no one could enter without special approval and the only location I had found after months of research that might be remotely similar to the promise I'd made. I convinced them I wanted silence, to learn how to be on my own, to go someplace where I did not have to fake a smile or mind my words for fear of hurting someone or raising ghosts.

At first, Mom started crying her heart out, but after analysing and listening to my points, Dad agreed. He understood what I was going through.

After a few weeks of preparation and Jason Odstar putting in a favour with none other than a royal family, he arranged for me to spend six months in one of the natural world wonders of the globe, in a cabin so large it could fit an entire sorority party, fully stocked with everything my little heart might desire. I had six months to discover whatever Erik needed me to find.

"What more can you ask from her, Elsa?" It was dad's turn to partake in the bickering. "She's been doing everything we've asked her to, she helped with campaigns, she attended my meetings and your events, she throws pretty smiles at the press and dresses how you tell her to. If my girl wants some time alone, then I will damn well give it to her."

An hour later, we reached the airport and passed through the VIP passage, where one of the family's private jets waited with the luggage already stacked inside. I paused for the first time. I was really doing this. My arms acted on their own accord and wrapped themselves around my parents as I struggled to keep tears in.

"I will miss you so much," I sighed, feeling a small drop escape on my cheek.

"Take care of yourself, darling, and call if you need anything. Call your father anytime," Dad pulled me in for another hug.

"And you can always come home," Mom teared up as well and joined our embrace.

"Promise." It was the only thing to say as I wiped tears away, my eyes now filled with them. "I'll call you as soon as I land."

We stood there another few seconds, hugging and crying. I finally took a deep breath and walked towards the jet. My legs wobbled, but step by step, I gained control and forced them to take me up the ladder.

"I love you," I shouted to make myself heard over the wind, waving both my hands, until they disappeared from sight. I took a seat by the window and waved some more until my parents got back into the limo that drove them away. Half an hour later, I was in the air, alongside two pilots and two air hostesses, who were checking every few minutes if I needed anything; the perks of having an entire jet to yourself. I ordered pizza and a can of coke, then took out the laptop and started googling my new residence.

"Evigt Forest," I typed as tiny strands of mozzarella spread from the slice and onto my chin. It was part of my daily routine, scouring the internet for any clues. I still had no idea what I was supposed to find, if anything, or if whatever Erik had told me in his delirious state simply matched a forbidden location, but I was determined to spend each day of those six months researching, until I either gave up or found what my brother needed me to.

Evigt Forest is one of the few remaining natural marvels. It became a Biosphere World Wonder in 1865 when King Karl XV ennobled the woods and built a summer residence for his Queen consort, Louise of Netherlands.

No wonder Mom was so upset when Dad wrote to the King of Sweden and asked if his daughter could live in such a place; it must have cost him a lifetime of favours. I took another bite and continued reading.

The Eternal Forest, as per its name, is host to a multitude of unique species that never shed their leaves and supply the land with its own ecosystem. Amongst the natural species of fauna and flora national to the Swedish country, the Evigt is home to unique breeds that can only exist in three other points of the globe.

By the time I finished eating, I'd re-read all the articles I had saved during my research. The rest, my lazy self decided I would learn on my own once I arrived. Checking the weather, I found out that the average temperature of the Evigt Forest was 32 degrees Celsius, which meant that even in April, I could live in a bikini if I felt like it. I couldn't wrap my brain around the fact that the forest looked like a tropical island, yet it was nestled inside a cold country.

I opened another tab and clicked on YouTube. The first videos to pop up were some of Cressi's, followed by Odstar ads and the Avicii song we played in the morning while getting ready. I went to the search bar and typed in 'Evigt Forest'. Most of the videos were a collection of the images available on Google, others comprised of documentaries from Discovery Channel or National Geographic about the unique plants, and some conspiracy theories about the Swedish King selling his soul to the devil to gain immortality for the forest. No one could explain why the phenomenon happened, and very few people could visit and research.

The forest's perimeter was encircled from every direction and had guard posts at every mile to protect it from unwanted visitors. Only members of the royal family and their acquaintances received permission to visit, along with famous biologists and other scientific parties who had to get funding and get an escort every minute of their stay. Why on earth had my brother sent me here?

In the weeks ahead of my departure, I found many theories about the late queen, each more surreal than the other. A research channel did a two-hour report on her every visit and suggested she was bewitched or that the forest was an enchanted place who trapped the ruler inside. Others suggested that this forest was a remnant of heaven, from when God destroyed the Garden of Eden and a tiny piece fell on earth.

People believed those rumours and while the queen attended business at the palace, they ransacked the place, wanting to get their own piece of heaven. They went into the forest to steal whatever they could, leaves, tree barks, even animal carcasses. The destruction was so great that the land suffered for a long time. During those years, the Queen passed away. Many believed she died of a broken heart after seeing her beloved forest destroyed.

After the funeral, the King ordered guards to be dispatched to protect it and build a high brick wall around. He did not live long enough to watch the ground renew but, before his death, he passed a law demanding all future rulers of Sweden to dispatch guards for Evigt's protection. Even though a hundred and fifty years had passed, the tradition remained. The more I researched, the more surprised I was to know how I received permission to live in the queen's mansion for such a long time.

As always, Dad had managed the impossible. I had to sign a dozen non-disclosure agreements, and my entire trust fund had to be placed as insurance should something happen during my stay. I could not post my location on any kind of social media, and neither I nor my family and friends could alert the press about this journey, at any point of my stay.

I could only have video conversations from inside the mansion and couldn't bring in a mobile phone or any kind of recording device other than the laptop, which was bound to the house. All video communications had to happen for an hour a day during 10 to 11pm Sweden time, and a copy program had to be installed on my laptop so the Swedish Security team could connect for verification.

On arrival, my luggage needed to be checked to ensure I brought nothing that broke the rules. I had one delivery a week where one member of the guard would travel up to the mansion and bring the requirements on a Friday, items which I had to email to a secure address by Wednesday.

In case of emergencies, there was a landline phone available, which was only connected to the Forest Guard Quarters, to call for medical assistance or any emergency. It was the modern version of signing away my soul, but I agreed to everything eagerly, desperate to make it official before anyone reconsidered.

And here I was, only seven hours away from landing in a place that would separate me from the world and bring me a step closer to my brother

Chapter Two

"Are you waiting for another wave of applause, brother, or are you ready to get your seductive bottom in here?" Vikram appeared in the entryway.

I remained still, analysing what I had to do, what faeries from the entire city gathered in the palace gardens, had come to witness. I had seen the palace door open and close a thousand times throughout my life, each one marking significant events: when my older brother Damaris wed the kingdom's healer, Takara; when my other brother, Vikram, entered wearing his Commander of the Realm newly earned shield; or when our parents, the King and Queen of the Earth Kingdom, appeared through them at every new year celebration to bless the realm and bring offerings for another flourishing season.

It was my turn to take an important event through those doors, my coming of age. After twenty-seven years of studying and training, this night forced me to leave behind youth and become an eligible male. Today I would become a keeper. The blessing and duty all young males eagerly awaited on their coming of age. I would be allowed to fulfil the goddess' will and use my power to help life grow.

"Seriously, brother, are you alright?" Vikram insisted, reviewing the state of me.

"I am," I snapped away from the trance and answered. "Just taking it all in."

"Go get your assignment, then I assure you there will be a queue of females who will want to take it all in as well," he laughed, folding his arms across his wide chest, their reflection shining from his breastplates. Ever since he'd become Commander, the second born of the royal family did not miss an opportunity to show off his uniform. Or to let the females of the kingdom take it off.

I nodded to my brother and took another step towards the doors. The sculpted battle scenes I loved to admire when I was a youngling greeted me. There was the Battle of Brumarys, where our ancestor defeated the Wind King, and the Peace Act of Tramerse, where the Water Queen offered the Earth Queen a set of pearls as a wedding gift. Mother had them stored away in velvet trinket boxes, because they were so precious to the family.

Peeking through the battle scenes and family history across the door was another memorable moment, one that I had yet to witness, and with a little push from my older brother, who had to shove me through the door, I found myself forced to step out and see the entire Earth Kingdom court waiting for my appearance and cheering in celebration.

Our father, the King, stood alongside them, and as soon as they saw me, the fae started cheering even louder and exclaiming my name. "Long live Prince Ansgar!" resounded from every direction, and all my ears wanted to do was to shut down the noise and escape through time to the end of the evening, when I could go back to my chambers and prepare for the mission. A shiver shook my body with the acknowledgement of what was to come, its own way to wake up the muscles and force me into alertness.

"There he is!" the King shook the ground with his voice. He shone above all others, his presence overpowering the image of the entire kingdom holding flower arrangements and blessed tree branches. Just one glance at the man standing tall, his long silver hair floating around his shoulders, and everyone fell captive to his power.

"Earthlings, join me in welcoming Prince Ansgar to his coming of age celebration," he continued, raising a hand in my direction, as though to point me out to the crowd. The faeries started acclaiming even louder, their voices bursting my name in the atmosphere. As they did, a wind of petals rose in the sky, held in the air by the echoes and fluttering of wings, some of them energetically rattled.

I let loose a smile, finding my pace. These were our people, childhood friends and teachers, the fae that knew me since I was a youngling and watched me grow up and go through the aging changes. They gathered here, ready to join in the celebration, their joy piercing the sky. I nodded in greeting, and when the ovations grew, I raised my dagger in salute, the highest form of respect amongst soldiers.

After a few minutes, the rest of the royal family joined the spotlight with Queen Bathysia in their lead, her dark skin shining so brightly she could have easily been mistaken for a star. Our family made their way across the rose ornate path to reach the king, who'd already taken his place on the webbed high chair, carved from the first tree roots that had grown in the kingdom. Each ruler added a new branch to be solidified into the union with our ancestors.

As we arrived on the celebratory podium, the Queen took her seat alongside the King, while we three brothers and our sister-in-law remained standing. We took turns to greet and bowed to the King and Queen, approaching them to place a gentle kiss on their cheek and occupy a seat to their left. The first to honour the tradition was their firstborn and my eldest brother, Damaris, heir to the throne and Commander of the Royal Guard, along with his wife, Takara, the healer of the Earth Fae. The couple took their places and joined hands, Damaris letting his arm rest on his wife's lap. What a sight to behold, Damaris was the tallest of us, and his shoulder length hair only elongated his features, making him shine as the king's replica. Silver hair tied neatly at the nape and agate-like eyes, reflecting the water of the lake with green and blue flashes.

Vikram followed with his long dark hair and amber eyes. The Commander of Realm Defence radiated in his polished armour, and alongside Mother, they weaved moon and starlight. He was the only one to inherit her adamant features and would always find opportunities to wear silver accessories to make their beauty pierce even through the cloudiest minds.

I was the last to join them, passing all the members of the family and greeting each before occupying my seat at the right side of the king. In normal circumstances, my throne would be situated to his left, next to Vikram's, but as I was the guest of the banquet, the King honoured me with the laudatory position. Once we sat, and the cheers diminished, Father rose from his throne to address the audience.

"Earthlings, dears and darling fae and faeries, we join this evening to celebrate yet another outstanding event of peace in the glorious history of our kind, the coming of age of our beloved Prince Ansgar. I can remember the night of his birth as if it were yesterday, and I expect most of you do as well, when our Queen brought to us yet another male heir in the blessed tradition of three. As we celebrated for three days then, we will celebrate for three nights now. Without further ado, I invite Prince Ansgar to come forth and perform the Binding Ceremony. To help us perform this rite, Princess Branwyl of the Water Kingdom has good-heartedly taken residence in the Seedling Lake," he finished announcing while bowing towards the water to greet the princess.

"Son, your turn," Father said as he returned to the throne. I took a deep breath and rose to my feet, the crowd absorbing my every movement. Even the wind carrying the petals seemed to stop and listen to my words.

"Thank you all for joining me tonight in celebration. As my twenty-seventh birth anniversary is fulfilling tonight, it is my duty and joy to receive a Keeper Assignment. I am grateful for all the advice and lessons you all taught me, for the stories and anecdotes of your own experiences that prepared me to receive such an honour this blessed night. In front of our King and Queen, our Commanders

21

and our Healer, the Realm and all of its peoples, I swear to protect my assigned district with knowledge and sword and the blessing of our kindred kingdom, the Waterlings. I shall now join Princess Branwyl to accept this great honour bestowed upon me. Until my return!" I raised my right arm in salute, and in an instant, all the fae raised theirs, praising my name.

I nodded to Father and walked from the podium and onto the path that took me to the lake. There were no flowers this time, but a heavy strain in the air as I headed towards the water where the princess waited. Although we hadn't officially met, I'd heard of her ruthlessness and lack of mercy. Unwillingly, I swallowed a hard lump in my throat, knowing I was about to be judged by her. If deemed worthy, I would receive a parchment with the assignment, and if Branwyl considered I was not the right person to guard one of the sacred districts, she had the power to kill on sight. The fae law was rigid with the unworthy, and this was the one moment of our traditions that I did not look forward to.

Even though I had been preparing for so long and a ruler almost always proved his worth, a shadow of a doubt carved its way inside. What if I was the exception? What if I would be the one to disgrace the family? The fae I passed by looked at me benevolently, but their vision had a twinkle of bleakness. No one was a hundred percent safe, and this might be the time where I would see my family last.

"Come, come, young prince, don't be shy," a sweet melodious voice whispered into my ears.

I stood a few feet away from the shore, but Branwyl's magic slashed through. She could ensnarl without moving a finger. I sensed the pulsing of her heart, the movement of her curls in the soft swirls of the lake, and my insides twisted as I imagined her hips alongside mine, moving together to produce waves of pleasure.

There was nothing a mermaid couldn't do to a male with an empty heart. The water reached my ankles, and I kept going, captivated by her presence, hurrying my steps to meet her. By the time it reached my knees, I had completely forgotten about my training and mission.

"Come to me, my prince," she sang.

That voice! That blessed voice. A goddess was opening up for me alone, I had the duty to ripen every fruit she offered. The water reached my hips, and I kept going, utterly trapped in her magic.

"That's it, my love, come to me," she purred, filling every part of me with want. It was unbearable, the thought of not having her immediately, of not being able to bury myself in her and remain conjoined for eternity. I increased my pace, taking bigger and more determined steps, the water up to my shoulders. My heart convinced me to carry on and meet with her, even at the cost of my last breath.

"One more step, and I'll be yours," she moaned like a female trapped in pleasure. Breathing seemed unimportant upon hearing her gasping voice; I had to reach her and unite with her. So I took that step, the one keeping me afloat with air in my lungs, the one separating me from the female of my dreams. I dived underwater.

All the preparation and exercise had been for nothing. My tutors and I practiced this moment, and I knew exactly how many steps I needed to take to be able to hear the princess but not dive deep enough to fall prey to her will. Even my boots were designed so that

I held my grip in the mud better. I knew which phrases I needed to use to block her interest and the spell to counteract, but it had all been in vain upon hearing her voice.

That is when I saw her, floating so serenely underwater, her locks of hair cascading around in rainbow-silken-like rays, her beauty exuding throughout the waves.

"There you are, my prince," she murmured, swimming towards me and touching my cheek.

Oh, that caress. The gentle hand upon my skin, like a fading comet preparing to sleep. My lungs hurt, the need for air suddenly striking as a necessity.

She blinked in surprise, offended that such a minor necessity distracted me from the beauty she had to offer.

"A kiss for your troubles, my beloved?" she purred in offering.

Yes! Yes, a kiss. Just the one to keep me afloat, I thought. To give me the strength I needed to possess her, just one time, find my rest inside her and die. What else was there to live for?

"Yes," I answered, bubbles escaping my mouth as I begged.
She swam closer, her tail swishing through the clear water and reflecting the moon.
The moon. Outside. Life. My mission. It all came back in a single image. Branwyl pursed her lips delightfully and approached mine, her long eyelashes fluttering to leave tiny bubbles of air. Only an inch separated us from the seal of a kiss, and for a moment, I wanted to give in. Did I want the assignment so much that I was refusing such beauty?

Yes, you do, the last shred of life in me shouted.

24

Finding a knife at her throat, Branwyl gasped. I was barely alive but had escaped her magic. She grimaced and waved a hand in disgust, visibly offended by my rejection, and a brown piece of parchment popped into my hand. "Thank you," I mouthed while grabbing it and swimming upward, kicking the water hard, hanging by my last string of life. The mermaid huffed and waved her tail, diving deeper into the lake.

As soon as I reached the surface of the water, I gasped for air, my lungs agonizing in pain. I inhaled profusely and vomited all the lake filth that filled my stomach until breathing became second nature again. I was immune to the cheers and shouting from the shore; the crowd celebrating my safe return. All I wanted to do was breathe, breathe, and keep breathing until there was no bulk of air my lungs hadn't enjoyed.

"You had us worried for a second, little brother," both Damaris and Vikram came to help me swim out of the lake. My body clung heavy with water, face red and eyes wide, mud hanging onto my robe and boots. I nodded, relieved to enjoy deep breaths.

"Come, let's get you changed," Damaris urged, placing his hand on my shoulder.

Around us, hundreds of fae celebrated and cheered while we passed them and stopped in front of the podium where the King and Queen awaited. They both rose from their thrones when I returned, taking turns in hugging me.

"There he is! Our beloved prince with his assignment. May the Goddess guide you, my son, and bring you a fruitful district!" Father wished me with pride.

My only means of communicating was a nod of acceptance, still shook by the realisation that my life had almost ended minutes ago.

"Thank you, my King and beloved Father," I bowed my head as the release of words from my mouth ripped pain down my throat. "My Queen," I bowed towards my mother. "If you would excuse me, I would very much like to change robes," I said, smiling as widely as my mouth allowed me.

"I think it would be for the best; it looks like you had an eventful encounter," the Queen replied with a knowing smile.

"Please, let the celebrations continue!" I echoed to the crowd, who started singing and dancing the instant I burst out of the lake, safe and sound.

Alongside my brothers, I sailed across the sea of ovation until we reached the wooden carved palace doors I had admired at the beginning of the evening and sighed in relief, knowing that I, too, added an event into the future carvings of this gate. Leaving a small trail of mud and algae behind, I followed my brothers into the chambers.

When I arrived, they were already searching my wardrobe for something more suitable to wear, and as soon as I spotted them, I knew what was coming. I didn't even have time to prepare myself that the older prince's accusatory voice resonated.

"Will you ever listen to me?" Damaris started. "Didn't I warn you that you shouldn't wear the celebration robe into the lake?" I remained silent, my head about to drop from fatigue. The last thing I needed was a scolding.

"But how epic would it have looked if he'd done it without

getting wet? Get to the lake and threaten the princess into giving it to him? Then make a turn towards the crowd, his cape fluttering in the wind, scroll in hand and hair shivering in the night?"

Both Damaris and I grinned at our brother, who had clearly envisaged the moment several times over.

"Those little romance phrases you tell your ladies have gotten to your head," Damaris laughed.

"Yee of little faith," Vikram scowled. "Have you both forgotten how epic my assignment ceremony was?"

Our turn to laugh profusely had come. "I remember how you wiped your snot on my tunic," I answered.

"And how you were shaking...after you crawled out on your hands and knees," Damaris added.

"Let us all remember for a second that I had *her*, alright? The Queen's sister? The most beautiful siren to walk this earth?"

"You mean swim...the waters," Damaris grinned. "Dear brother, I just realised why you are this way," he added in shock, raising his hands. He just made a monumental discovery.

Vikram only blinked, waiting for him to tell us more.

"You saw the most beautiful siren there is and fell in love. Ever since, you obsessed yourself with finding the same beauty in women. Again, your way of searching is completely and utterly wrong but..." he went on, waiting for us to catch on.

"But?" Vikram asked with caution.

"You are still in love with Eidothea!" Damaris proclaimed victoriously.

"And here I thought that for once you might say something

intelligent," Vikram huffed with disappointment.

"Oh, lest we forget I had the Queen of the Water Kingdom? Otherwise known as the mother of sirens, the one that taught them everything they know about seducing males?"

"She is not the most beautiful though, is she?" Vikram grimaced.

"And you have been in love with Takara since you were a babe, it does not count," I added as I peeled away my wet shirt.

Damaris placed a hand over his heart and gasped, faking a deadly wound. "It doesn't matter if you are in love," he defended himself.

"Yes, it does," we both reacted simultaneously.

"Also, you are the heir to the kingdom; it would have been crazy for her to kill you," Vikram added. "Maybe she should have...drowned you a little more," he offered.

Damaris frowned.

"Alright, alright, you are here to help me get dressed, yes?" It was my turn to cry for attention.

"Yes, let us undress the young prince and put him into something more fitting."

"Like a female?" Vikram snickered.

Damaris stopped to look our brother dead in the eye, and they both started laughing hysterically at my expense.

"Fine, fine, I get it, I shall bed someone soon," I scratched the back of my head, looking away as strands of algae found their way out of my braids.

Both brothers exchanged looks and started laughing harder.

"Bed someone!" Vikram repeated, laughing so hard that his hands grabbed at his stomach.

Damaris fell into one armchair with amusement, still chuckling.

"This one is going to get married a virgin, brother," Vikram shrieked, caressing his abdomen that probably hurt from bending so much laughter at my expense.

"He'll have to, as you're screwing all the kingdom, there's nothing left for him to bite into," Damaris replied.

We continued to laugh for a good few minutes, joking about one another and remembering funny stories from our childhood while rummaging through my wardrobe in search of something befitting the celebration. While changing pants, I picked up the parchment I earned earlier in the lake, which I shoved in my pocket before rising to the surface. It was almost dry, just a few stains on one side.

"Is it ready?" Damaris asked, my other brother suddenly silent.

"I think so," I replied, my voice raspy with excitement.

"What are you waiting for? Open it!" Vikram demanded.

I turned to Damaris. "Open it," he confirmed.

With shaky hands, I slowly broke the seal from the parchment. The paper was almost dry, and tiny patches of ink shone in the candlelight. I unrolled it slowly, every inch bringing me closer to my mission. There it was, my new location, one of the sacred districts I swore to protect and preserve.

"Evigt Forest," I read out loud.

Summer

Anwen

Chapter Three

"Oh...my...god," was the only thing I thought as I walked through the tall entrance door. Luxury beamed everywhere my vision could stretch, set upon the mansion like a cloud of smog from the nineteenth century that exploded inside. Tall statues and unique vases, historical paintings worth more than I could imagine welcomed me into the entrance hall. I was expecting extravagance, but even I did not envision how eccentric a royal setup could become.

It felt like a visit to the museum and the guard who brought me, sensing my thoughts, started talking about the structure and architecture of the "litet palats". I felt either too tired or too excited to pay much attention, so I was happy to follow him and nod politely from time to time. He presented family portraits and sculptures, pieces of history left behind by prominent artists to honour the late Queen.

"As per your agreement, you will work in the Queen's Painting Room and will use the Royal Bedroom for rest. The Sitting Room, kitchen and both the royal bathroom and the servant's one will also be open, the rest will have to remain sealed as instructed." He stopped in the hallway to make the announcement. One of his hands pointed towards a door to focus my attention to the royal seal. Two thick pieces of rope joined in a very sophisticated knot and wax dripped over them, on top of which the royal seal of Sweden, I assumed, lay imprinted. I nodded, keeping to myself the plans to rummage around the whole place in hope to find anything that might be connected to my brother. I had to be careful though, if they were able to access my laptop, googling things like 'how to break a royal seal' were out of the question. So I faked uninterest and showed gratitude towards the rooms I did have access to, reassuring the guard of my happiness to be there.

"Very well," Isak, the guard, continued more joyfully this time, "I am required to inform you that either I or one of my men may organise an unannounced search of the premises to ensure all rules are complied to," he insisted.

"Of course," I said.

"Thank you," he replied and continued down the hall. I could not deny the obvious. The uniform on this man made him look sexy. He wore a long dark green overcoat with an attached belt to hold a sword and black knee-length boots. He looked like he just escaped from one of the paintings. He wore a cap too, made from woven wool. How was he not bursting out of his skin from this heat?

"We have to wear the uniform at all times," he replied. Clearly what I thought to be a discrete look turned into a very blunt stare.

"Sorry, I didn't realise I was that obvious," I grimaced in apology.

"Not at all miss, I am happy to answer your questions. After all, my men and I will look after you in the next half a year, so it is best to get to know each other. Please ask me any question you might think of," he voiced with untroubled grace.

'Do you know what connection my brother has to this place?' The only question I truly wanted an answer to was the only one I could not ask. I smiled in thanks and gestured for him to continue the tour. Following the blond-haired guard into the kitchen, I found two fully stocked fridges with absolutely every kind of food, including frozen pizzas and several types of ice cream. A wide door at the side of the drinks fridge opened into a spacious cupboard storing vegetables, fruit, herbs and hundreds of cans and pasta.

"Of course, if you need anything, you must let us know by the Wednesday of every week and we will bring it to you."

"If I need anything? I think I'll eat for the rest of my life and not finish all that's in here," I responded in awe.

"It is stocked to last a person eighteen months," the man announced with pride.

"I will only stay six months, and I'll be by myself. I cannot possibly eat all this," I replied as my eyes scanned the myriad of foods stacked in the cupboard. "What do you want from here?" I asked excitedly.

"Miss?" he expressed his confusion.

"There must be something you want to eat from here."

"Thank you miss, I assure you, there is no need," the guard quickly pointed out.

"Come on, I will eat alone soon enough, do me a favour and pick something?" I pushed, not taking 'no' for an answer.

"Cherry cake," he replied so eagerly that my mouth instantly watered at the thought.

I opened the fridge to look for said cherry cake until Isak told me it is a food best found in the cupboard. We both laughed and when I finally found the tray, I placed it on the kitchen table, pulling up two forks, two chairs and brought two cold drinks from the second fridge.

At first we ate in silence, enjoying the taste. I even escaped a barely audible moan as I took my first bite of that amazing dark cherry, sweet and slightly sour, wonderfully covered in vanilla frosting cake. After a few bites, the taste tickling our palates seemed to unite us a bit more and conversation started flowing.

"Are you sure you do not want to take off your hat, at least?" I asked as a drop of sweat found his brow.

"Not at all, miss."

"Anwen," I corrected. "If you want me to call you by your name, you must do the same."

"A beautiful Swedish name. Very well, Anwen. I do not mind keeping on my uniform at all, on the contrary, I am soaking up as much heat as I can. When I return to my post, snow will be my companion."

Of course, another phenomenon no one understood. The inside of the forest was a permanent summer, unaffected by climatic changes within the surrounding areas. Even the sun reflected longer in the sky, sunset arriving hours later than the rest of the country. What the hell was happening here?

"How long have you been captain of the guard?" I asked

curiously.

"Two years. My father was a captain, and the royal family likes to maintain tradition. After I finished the training and served in the military, I joined the guard," Isak replied proudly.

"Do you come here often?" I supposed the guards were free to explore the woods since they were the ones protecting it. Maybe he could tell me more about the forest.

"We receive permission for a day's walk once a year. As captain, I can request three days. And we also need to do maintenance for this mansion, which sometimes can take an entire week."

"So you stay here for a week every year?" I asked.

"Not at all, we are not permitted to sleep inside the litet palats. It is only for the royal family and guests. Though, to tell you the truth, Anwen, no one has stayed here in the past seventeen years. We were all surprised when we heard about your arrival," he said as he took another bite.

"Why is this forest so protected, Isak? What's in here?" I could not delay the question any longer.

"It is heaven, miss," he replied with a smile and continued to enjoy his cake.

As soon as my feet started running, my muscles awoke with a jolt of energy. I could not help but be proud of myself. This was the tenth morning in a row I was out for an early running session. I enjoyed discovering new trails every day, and my amazement with this place only grew more each day. The routine I had created proved relatively ineffective within the week and a half of my stay. After about an hour in the forest, I returned to the mansion and checked every single thing in sight, googled the artists of the paintings, the decorators and designers, the king and queen, the royal family, the history of the palace and the recorded visits. I even asked my brother's former secretary to give me access to his work emails, where I checked for notes and any trace of his connection to this place.

I thought I was going crazy two days ago and almost decided to return home until I discovered a plane ticket in his old emails. A ticket to Lund, the nearest airport to Evigt Forest, the same one I had landed in. Had Erik been here? Had he entered the forest or the mansion? The guard had confirmed no one lived here in seventeen years, but knowing my brother's ability to sneak around, I would not be surprised if he had surpassed security and came here. The question was, what for?

As I traced a new path, the forest became alive, like it found its spirit overnight; the foliage seemed to dance with the light breeze; it felt as the gleaming leaves performed a celebratory chant of some sort. Even the trees seemed to move, their branches lingering wider and more proud while the insects and birds crooned and hummed. The symphony tickled my senses and made me soar deeper into the forest, not taking precautions to mark my path. I couldn't shake the feeling that the woodland had caught a life of its own and it attracted me into its structure.

On this fresh path, I found unusual steps, marked by soles that were not mine, movements that did not belong to me. I shuddered. The place was presumably uninhabited. I'd heard a few noises during my trek and decided to not pay attention, thinking they might be caused by the new trainers making a fuss in the fallen leaves, but now I was not so sure. The ground fizzled. Somewhere from the trees the sounds of another person made their presence known. Someone had been following me, it seemed. To what end, I did not know. *Calm down, Anwen, it's probably nothing.* Another step came from behind a big old willow, this time a shape crept from its branches.

"Who's there?" I pushed. Nothing. Only the wind rustling between the deeply contorted branches.

"Show yourself," I demanded, this time slowly spinning to gain a better visual. I forced my sight to pierce as deep as it could. My breath deepened, heart pulsating at a higher pace. No one should be in the woods, I was the only one allowed in here. None of the soldiers in the Forest Guard could take morning strolls, yet I sensed someone here. I looked around once more, unable to see or hear anything, but I found my feet burrowed deep into the ground, heels ready to push for a sprint should I need to run for dear life. My calves shook with tension, holding for the signal. I had nothing on me; I realised. Nothing to protect myself with in case of an attack.

"Reveal yourself, I order you," I tried as if the potential serial killer lurking in the woods would just jump out because I asked them to. It was such a silly thing to say. Yet, within a mere moment, the wide trunk of the willow turned darker and more steps sounded from inside.

"How dare you order anything in this forest," a heavy voice resonated. It startled me to the point of a heart attack. I'd been right, there was something, someone out there, following me.

"Who are you? What do you want?" I demanded, trying to keep my composure as much as possible. I could start running, but my curiosity spiked, and I needed to know who the man was. I felt attracted to that voice, something deep inside me twisting with need, an urgency to know it, to know of it. As though some kind of connection linked us.

"Do not concern yourself with my name, or my desires," the man responded from the willow bark. Dark clouds covered the roots of the tree and hovered over the moss at its base.

"Why are you here?" I questioned.

"I am playing a game," the voice whispered. "And I seem to be winning," it added.

My breath caught. I sensed danger coming from that voice and wanted to take a step back, when I realised my ankles were caught in the mud, keeping my feet grounded with unnatural force. I tried to twitch and pull one of my legs out, but the dirt kept clawing at me with heavy pressure. It felt like someone's arms were pulling me down, keeping my soles forcefully docked.

"Release me!" I demanded. "Let me go!" I cried as panic overwhelmed me, grabbing one of my knees from behind and trying to pull my right foot up.

"And what would be the point in that? What predator would release their prey?" the voice purred with wickedness.

"Please!" I cried again, trying desperately to get myself out.

40

"Please, I beg you, just let me go!" The pressure in my ankles was causing so much pain, if I tried to move even an inch, the tension could snap my bones like a straw.

"Just a doe in a snare," the voice echoed, pleased with my entrapment. "The more you struggle, the more you will hurt yourself," he announced.

With tears running down my face, I stopped pulling. The stranger was right. The more I moved, the deeper my legs sank into the mud. And he seemed to take a psychotic pleasure from my situation, as though causing me pain just made his morning.

"I don't even know you. Just let me go back home," I tried. My brain pulled out the information from somewhere. I knew I had a higher chance to be released if I didn't recognise my attacker.

"You are my pawn, dearest. I am waiting for someone else to join this party, and when they do, you will have to fulfil a purpose. Do not bore me with your frivolous begging and crying, I do not care for it," he replied with contempt.

"Just tell me what you need me to do and I'll do it. I'll help. Just please let me go." I sobbed, trying to bargain for what was at stake, which at this point seemed to be my own life. Heaven my ass…this forest of wonders might become my burial place.

The voice fell quiet for a few seconds, contemplating my offer.

"There is something you could do for me. It would save us both some precious time."

"Yes, I'll do it. Anything," I agreed.

"I need you to scream," the voice whispered.

"What?" I froze.

"Scream," the whisper commanded.

Instantly, intense pain poured into my body, the sharpness of a thousand blades penetrating into me. I howled in agony, like a wounded animal that gasped its last breaths. In mere seconds, it stopped as abruptly as it appeared. He was doing this to me.

"Very good," the stranger echoed from the tree. "Again," he said, and the blades pierced once more, my throat broadcasting wails into the atmosphere.

I was in so much pain that my lungs stopped and air refused to enter my body. I drowned in my own screams, the sensation so unbearable that every muscle shrieked with torment. As my nervous system struggled to keep the pain afloat, my vision became blurry, dark spots slithering inside my pupils, darkening my eyesight.

"Release her!" a different voice materialized from nowhere and a tall man appeared in front of me, blocking me from view, trying to protect my body from the drive of pain striking from the darkness of the tree. It was all I saw until it stopped.

The pressure in my ankles softened, and I finally took a breath before falling to the ground.

Chapter Four

"Why was I assigned to an island and you get to live in paradise?" my brother protested when we reached the other side of the portal that transported us between realms. A dense forest presented itself to us, with vivid emerald green leaves that sparkled in the sunlight. I admired it and smiled with pride. A whiff of wind fluttered my hair, bringing a hot gust along. The warmth caressed my bare arms and cheeks and I inhaled deeply, filling my lungs with the new atmosphere.

"I love it when it's hot like this," I exclaimed cheerfully. "Let's go find the burrow."

As we walked, a deep carpet of leaves sang under the soles of our boots, to create a welcoming marching band. The tall trees embedded amongst newly growing firs and from the smooth barks, vines brimming with vibrant flowers sprouted in all directions like a waterfall of aromas.

Mellow sunshine beams passed through the foliage, piercing the leaves and casting an unearthly green-gold luminescence across the ground. Tiny creatures emerged from their homes and leapt about in joy and nonchalance, showing no sign of fear.

"I think this is it," I stopped and checked the map I had stored in my satchel to confirm the exact location of my new home.

"After you," Vikram sat on a sizable rock next to the cave and made himself comfortable, like he was expecting to sit there for a while.

"Et missus est ad auxilium crescere, me domus vestra in nos animo et una vivunt," I exclaimed, my echo sending penetrating pulsations into the stone.

The cave mirrored my voice and started crumbling, tiny pieces falling apart as the glue that held them together melted. The strands of rock craved to escape the scrimmage and revealed an entry sized opening.

"You did it on your first try..." Vikram muttered. "How impressive," he skirted at me. "Took me about two hours to remember that damned incantation."

"That is because your pronunciation was always off," I mocked him.

"Get inside already, can't you see your commander is tired?" my brother ordered.

I entered the cave and almost cried with joy when I saw the inside of my new residence. It displayed an embodiment of my living chambers back at the palace, the bed exactly how I left it and my full library, desk, reading chair, writing materials and bathing pool, just as they were back home. Vikram dropped the two satchels he had been carrying and threw himself on the bed, yawning. "I'm hungry. And please tell me you have wine, I am drying out in this heat," he gestured dramatically, waving a hand in the air. Commander indeed.

Vikram chose the guard path, preferring to renounce a family and dedicate his life to the kingdom. The males who did not find a mate had to swear their fealty to the Human Territory or the Earth Kingdom and become part of one of the guards, assigned to either walk the earth amongst the humans, keeping the peace or protect our kingdom and become realm defence. Even though Damaris mated and chose Takara as his future queen, he was also appointed Commander of the Royal Guard, according to his firstborn duty. Vikram joined the Realm Defence and from the first day he became commander, he started behaving like the world belonged to him.

I returned with an assortment of dried meats and cheeses, a goblet of wine and waited on my brother who made himself very comfortable on my bed and appeared lost in thought. I knew what memories this day stirred in him, and I appreciated him even more for joining me.

He had confessed that during his time in his keeper district he enjoyed the many pleasures of human women and felt so enchanted that he became unwilling to give up their company. The males who entered Realm Defence travelled and lived in the Human Territory, but since it was forbidden to copulate with humans and waste the healing energy flowing through our veins, they had to sterilise themselves by drinking nigrum cassia essence. Once a year, during a ceremony, the males gathered and shared the potion, much to the discontent of the females. However, the fae race had to remain pure to insure continual revival. Everything there was, everything that grew on the planet, lived through our shared energy and an offspring with a human would be considered a waste of such power.

As I chewed on a piece of cheese, I contemplated my options. I was not excited about either, but in the past few years, after Vikram became commander and Damaris' attempts at offspring were met with defeat, the Queen monitored me more than usual. Sometimes, when I trained, one of the female helpers suddenly appeared to bring an unrequested refreshment or visited my bathing chambers to offer help. When I pointed this out to Vikram, he confirmed his suspicion. Since the middle prince became sterile and the first born possibly found himself unwillingly in the same situation, I would be the primary source of heirs for the family.

"Did Damaris have the talk with you?" my brother awoke from thought, and with it, dragged me back to the present.

"He wasn't very helpful," I groaned.

"What did he suggest?" Vikram asked.

"You just feel the connection," I imitated my older brother's voice as I mimicked him.

"But what is it exactly that you feel?" Vikram insisted, showing as much curiosity as I had.

"He said it's impossible to explain, it's like you discover an unknown part of yourself that you did not know you had before."

Vikram huffed. "That is the same speech he gave to me when I left to the island. Look how good that did," he laughed, more to his own benefit.

"It's an unknown part of myself that I didn't know I had," I mumbled unhappily. "So is a tumour."

My brother choked on his wine, laughing.

"I can't believe you managed to abstain. Not with Mother's constant meddling," he took another sip of his wine.

I sighed. Even though our mother felt that the responsibility of heirs belonged to me, I chose to wait until I met a female who truly interested me. Unfortunately, when I did, they were too forward and intimidating for my inexperience or they hoped I would be the one to start up a conversation and woo them. Other times, I remembered her and every sexual desire I might have felt collapsed into rubble. She haunted me, sometimes late at night, when moonshine enveloped the realm and silence fell. I still heard the fading heartbeat, flickering, struggling to fight, clawing onto survival. I knew it then. I would not be responsible for such an atrocity. Either I found a female to love and protect until my last breath, or I would remain alone. There was no in between.

"Do not worry, brother, I will make sure the darlings in the kingdom will be too occupied to miss you much," my brother exuded a proud smirk.

"Amongst all the worries in the world, Vikram, this one is my last priority, I assure you."

"Don't trouble yourself, little one. You have three years to find someone. And the guard is always recruiting," he smiled slyly.

After having a bite and a few glasses of wine, my brother said his goodbyes and stepped out of the cave, wanting to find his way to the portal that would transport him back into the kingdom before nightfall. I bid him farewell and offered him another carafe for the journey back, then closed the cave door and prepared for bed.

The forest welcomed me; I felt it as soon as I opened my eyes to the new home. The creatures sang about my arrival, while the trees chanted the old hymns. The sun blessed the morning with healing light, and every seedling would become stronger from my presence by the evening. A rhapsody of wonder entwined with my power, growing from my spirit and feeding from the fresh energy I had brought along from the Earth Kingdom.

This was it. My new home. The place where I would live, where I'll be bound to for the next three years. Not in my wildest dreams had I expected to be assigned to the goddess' burial place, the honour was beyond belief and I stood decided to execute a flawless season, nurse the forest to health and with it span the energy throughout the earth and help the plants around the world come to life.

I pushed the covers from the bed and rose with a long stretch, preparing for an endless day. I needed to measure the length of the district, walk all the pathways and find the species that needed urgent treatment, then I would summon a meeting with all the resident faeries and assign responsibilities and duties. But first, a shower and some sustenance. I plucked my hair from my face and wrapped it tightly behind my nape with a strand of leather to keep it out of the way, then picked up the weapons, which I stored in a leather bandolier, similar to the one I used to carry back in the kingdom, during training. Before I finished getting ready, I heard an unnatural noise coming from the kitchen, a shuddering tension shook the walls. I was instantly there, dagger in hand. In front of me stood a tall male, dressed completely in black to match his ebony hair, making himself a cup of coffee and staring at me.

"Reveal your identity," I ordered.

"Now, now, tree princeling, there is no need for that so early in the morning," the stranger snarled, his voice tinted with disgust.

"Who are you?" I insisted, pressing the dagger forward to reach the man's back.

"You know me, young prince," the voice purred. "You have met me many times, in different stories."

"I will not ask again. Reveal your identity or I'll send you into chaos!" I commanded, my hand pressed tightly to the hilt.

"Sending me home so soon, are we?" The male murmured and his voice sounded harsh, pressing for memories I did not know I possessed.

This male, this invader into my new home, wanted me to become aware of his origin. So I let him know exactly how much I understood.

"What is a fireling doing here? How did you reach this district?" I growled, not letting go of the dagger that rested an inch from penetrating the stranger's right kidney.

"I am everywhere, boy, as long as humans live, so do I," the fae bragged, his voice heavy. His behaviour burst with contempt and the fireling acted like he had a right to claim the world and everything inside it, as though his age pierced through time and tradition.

"Who...are...you?" I almost spelled it to the male and pushed the dagger slightly deeper, piercing skin and muscle.

"Enough!" the fireling shouted and with a wave of a hand, threw me into the wall cabinet, plates and cups falling from their place onto the floor with a shout.

"You earthlings are so smug, so full of yourselves and sure of your victories everywhere you step foot. Tell me, princeling, did you even bother to announce your presence on your arrival? Did you visit the other faeries? No, of course not!" he raised his voice while pressing me into the wall with his power. As a member of a royal family, I stood as one of the most powerful fae in existence, yet my energy was merely a flicker compared to the sheer strength this one possessed. I barely drew breath under the pressure of his impact, forced to listen to whatever he had to say.

He continued. "What did you do instead? You stayed in your comfortable little cot and drank with the barren one until silly couldn't do it anymore and went home to mummy and daddy. And after? Went to bed, probably. This door hasn't moved all night," he admonished in disgust.

"Who are you? What do you want?" I called out, blood dripping onto my lips from the sheer force of energy that pressed into me like a cliff ready to desolate a lake.

"I am death, boy, I am hunger and destruction, I am the one you shall see before you close those pretty grey eyes. I am..."

"Fear Gorta," I interrupted him.

"I go by Gordon now as a surname, makes me more approachable, don't you think?" The male announced as he returned to his cup of coffee, acting like nothing had happened. I could finally draw breath, the power disappearing as suddenly as it came. "And this century I think I will go by Rhylan, a pretty name I picked up in Macedonia. So, Rhylan Gordon," he smiled, pleased with himself.

"What do you want?" I repeated, wiping my blood-stained face.

"What do I want?" the male threw me a malevolent smirk as he took another sip from his cup of coffee. His eyes were terrifying to stare into, a deep black that sucked all the light away. "Why do we do the things we do, boy? Why do you linger in comfort instead of tending to your duties?"

"If you are referring to last night, it is customary for the keeper to be accompanied by a member of the family and summon all the fae-like creatures the day after their arrival," I replied, aware that I did not owe an explanation. "Which is what I am planning to do."

"Earthlings and their traditions," Rhylan huffed. "So used to having it all that you afford such luxuries, acting as owners of the land and the living."

"We do!" I countered. "We are the descendants of the three goddesses and our duty is to continue cherishing their legacy. We are here to—"

"To do whatever the hell you please while my kingdom rots in darkness!" the fireling shouted. We both kept silent for a second, each staring into the other's eyes, darkness facing shadows, trying to guess the other's intentions.

Fear Gorta, one of the most dangerous creatures of the Fire Kingdom, buried inside the surface of the earth, found its way into my district. When Belgarath fell entombed by the two goddesses,

Marynnah and Zaleen, his court was banished alongside him and multiplied within darkness generation after generation. They could not linger outside their realm, and if other fae found them, they were imprisoned or sent back to where they came from. Some of the stronger firelings succeeded in various escapes, most of them volcanoes or during earthquakes, and scoured the realm provoking destruction and chaos. Fear Gorta, one of the strongest, a direct descendant of Belgarath himself, had escaped centuries ago and relished in summoning destruction and famine into the world.

During many of my classes, I had to memorise all the information we held on firelings, how to capture them, weaken and imprison them, but there was one who was always mentioned as indestructible—The Fear Gorta. He could be wounded and slowed down, but his regenerating capacities connected to the forces of the earth, therefore, even injured, he could still regain health.

"I am asking again, why are you here?" My words echoed the fight in my stance.

Rhylan looked surprised. "You didn't ask me that before, you asked me what I wanted."

I sighed. "Forgive my semantics. Why are you here?" I repeated the question.

"To welcome you, of course." Rhylan dropped the cup of coffee and raised his hands, faking an embrace.

"I do not need a welcome from you," I growled.

"Of course you don't, but you are getting one, anyway. Consider me sentimental, but how could I not welcome the third son of a kingdom with a present?"

"Very well, hand it over and leave."

"Hand it over?" Rhylan scowled and shook his head in disbelief. "You earthlings and your vanity. Who said anything about an *it*?"

I remained silent, piercing the male with an angry stare. My patience was thinning, and I did not know where this conversation led. Every shred of me, every nerve ending prepared to run into battle.

"No, dear prince, my gift to you is…much bigger," he grinned. Seeing how I kept silent and started losing restraint, Rhylan continued. "As his future majesty, Tree Princeling of the Kingdom of I-am-the-best-kind-of-fae-there-is could not visit the district immediately after his arrival, because tradition and such, I, your humble servant," attend my mocking tone here, Rhylan insisted as he lifted a finger, "scouted the grounds and found the perfect welcoming gift for the prince of the Kingdom of I-am-the-best…"

"That's enough," I commanded.

"Fine," Rhylan frowned. "There is a human on your grounds, did you know?"

It took me a heartbeat to understand what he was saying. Then I murmured, "You are lying."

"Am I?"

"This location has been forbidden to humans for over a century," I insisted. My mind scoured all the information I had about the goddess' burial place, the history with the queen, and how the place became prohibited territory to the outside world.

"You are correct. Yet, this one got permission somehow. I heard her last night talking to some other humans on those machines they are so obsessed with. She lives in the queen's mansion," Rhylan smirked.

"And what of it?" I tried not to sound worried.

"I thought..." Rhylan cleaned one of his fingernails with a kitchen knife and slowly blew the dust away. "That there would be nothing better to welcome a prince than with a human sacrifice?" He turned and displayed a terrifying smile.

My heart stopped. It would destroy everything, the blood curse would doom the district for centuries and damage any energy source it possessed.

"Just imagine, the harvest! Picture the trees, the earth, the leaves, even the river, all feeding on innocent human blood. Oh, the delight," Rhylan licked his lips with excitement

I grabbed the dagger and attacked the male who invaded my home, but he vanished into darkness only to appear on the other side of the kitchen, sipping from a fresh cup of coffee.

"I never had a brother," Rhylan sighed theatrically. "I never knew what it is to play games or have competitions, I never experienced the joy of winning something and celebrating a victory against someone who wanted it as much as I did. So let's turn this into a game, shall we?" he smiled in delight.

"I do not want to play your games," I answered through my teeth, jaw tight.

"I will play either way. The first one who gets to the human, wins," he uttered nonchalantly.

"Like I said, I am disinclined to play."

"Suit yourself, tree princeling. I'll set the rules, in case you change your mind. If I get to the human first, I kill her, rip her open and drag her across the district until there isn't a drop of blood left. If you get to her, she is safe... for now."

"She? A female?"

"Oh yes," Rhylan relished. "A beautiful, young woman," Fear Gorta licked his lips. "Enjoy the race, princeling," he purred and disappeared.

Anwen

Chapter Five

I woke up on the dark blue velvet sofa in the sitting room, arms stretched, covered by a warm blanket. It took a moment to realise where I was. My vision lingered, blurry with dreams and confusion. I removed the cover and stood, or at least tried to until soreness reminded me of the incident in the woods. My mind struggled to understand what happened, pieces of information not compiled vividly inside my brain. When I managed to stand, balancing onto the nearby wall and stretched, muscles and bones still cramping with pressure, I realised I was wearing my day clothes.

I tried to remember what happened and trudged into the kitchen to pour myself a glass of water, but the banging headache objected, making me pick a cold ready-made coffee from the fridge. There was a sensation I could not shake, like my memories were blocked by some kind of trap, and no matter how hard I pushed to rescue them from that cage, I lacked the strength to do it.

Eventually, reason convinced me I dreamt it. I found some ice and poured the drink in the blender, mixing it together and dumping it into a tall glass. I opened the laptop and clicked on the series I last watched. My brain needed some rest to process everything, and I had to oblige. Halfway through the episode, an engine rumbled, disturbing the peace sprinkled around the mansion. I paused the series and immediately rose from my cosy nook and ran into the kitchen to grab whatever weapon I could find. The footsteps approached and I heard fizzling, then keys shoved into the lock. I hid behind the door and waited, ready to jump the attacker as soon as he entered through the sliding door. It pushed wide open, and a man made his way nonchalantly inside.

"Stop right there," I threatened his back, a wooden rolling pin at the ready.

"Miss, stop," the man demanded in shock.

I paused a heartbeat, just enough to take in the deep green woven coat he wore. Forest Guard. I relaxed and climbed down from his back, apologising under my breath.

"I am truly sorry for scaring you, miss," he said. "I am here to make your weekly delivery."

"Who are you?" I enquired, with a slight suspicion.

"My name is Erik Van Strofler," the man introduced himself.

The sound of his name made my heart skip a beat. "Anwen Odstar," I nodded in greeting.

"Pleased to make your acquaintance, miss," he nodded back. "And once more, my sincerest apologies for causing you a fright, I assumed you were expecting the delivery."

Without delaying his task, the guard headed back to the car to return with three bags and brought them along, setting them onto the kitchen island.

"Here are the books you ordered," he pointed towards a big brown bag, "and the bath salts and other necessities you requested in your email." He meant tampons. The big unit of secret services and guards lurking around since my arrival had forgotten that I am a woman, therefore have a vagina that required chocolate and sanitary products. He continued with a tad of embarrassment, "The third one is from Captain Isak, he left a note inside," he directed my attention towards a yellow bag that contained a lot of tupperware.

"Thank you," I replied with a smile. I was most excited about the books. I ordered a lot of biology and local history ones, hoping to expand my research and with it, find more information about the forest and the surroundings. I still didn't know what I was searching for, but each passing day convinced me that my brother's last words were not delirious at all. Erik had known something and rested his last hopes on me.

"Is there anything else I can help with while I am here?" The guard asked as he purposely stepped closer to the door, marking his way out.

"No, thank you, that is all I need at the moment."

"Anything else, please put it in an email in the next five days and we will sort it out for you," he nodded.

"Seven days," I corrected. The objection escaped my mouth before I could stop it.

"Miss?" the guard looked confused.

"I am to send you an email by Wednesday, or that is what I have been told. Have things changed?"

"Yes, miss, that is correct. Every Wednesday night we go into town to do our own shopping so we can add yours while we are there," Erik agreed.

The image of a forest guard looking lost in the tampon aisle almost made me chuckle.

"Has the delivery day changed?"

"No miss, we will still bring the products on a Friday, as agreed." This conversation took a tedious turn, yet none of us understood each other and for some reason, we kept insisting. As much as I wanted the guard to be on his way, I could not let go of his silly mistake that confused me even more than my spinning head needed to be. I already turned and tossed, unsure of what had happened, and now, this man was getting his days mixed up and me, along with it.

"Sorry, I am confused," I retorted, a little more aggressive than I intended. "Why are you here on a Wednesday with the delivery?"

"A Wednesday?" the man scanned me like I suddenly started speaking a different language.

"It is Wednesday today, isn't it?" I returned the confused look to the guard.

"Today is Friday, miss." His response raised all the alarm signals I had struggled to keep at bay.

Isak arrived an hour later, summoned by the other guard who witnessed me have a full on panic attack and asked for support from the captain himself. He found me sitting on the sofa, wrapped in a blanket and holding a cup of tea. He approached and took a seat by my side, all the while listening to what Erik had witnessed before his arrival.

"She is convinced that today is Wednesday and when I showed her the date on my phone and she checked her laptop, she started crying and shaking, insisting that she was attacked in the woods and kidnapped for the past two days," the guard summarized the events.

I shuddered as he spoke, and Isak positioned himself closer to me on the sofa, then took the hot mug from my trembling hands and set it on the table. With a calm and understanding tone, he asked what happened.

"I don't know," I felt my voice break as I forced the words out. "I was jogging on a new path and suddenly a voice came from the tree, an old tree, a willow, I think. The man said he was playing a game, and I needed to scream. He started hurting me and then he took me to his house and attacked me," I continued as tears dripped into my tea.

"Can you describe him?"

"Maybe…" I frowned, forcing images back in front of me. "Tall, young, well built, longer hair, shoulder length I think, he was…" I stopped to think and remembered the man holding me tight in his arms and asking me to calm down. "He had soft features," I finally answered.

"Where was he? Where did you see him last?" Isak asked.

"It was dark when I came out, I didn't really see, I just started running," I shook my head.

"When you came out from where?"

"The house… There was a bedroom and a kitchen. That is all I saw." I shook my head, forcing the memory to stay, but it faded into thin air right before my eyes.

"In the woods?" Isak insisted.

"Yes!"

"Anwen, there is no other house in these woods except the one you are occupying. There isn't even a cottage for maintenance or anything like that."

"That is what he said, but I know what I saw," I insisted and nodded towards Erik.

The two men looked at one another in confusion, until Isak replied, "Very well, we will search the perimeter and find out more."

He stood from the sofa and headed towards the kitchen where he took the phone and started talking to the other guards in Swedish. When he finished the conversation and hung up the phone, he announced: "We will patrol the woods and let you know if we find anything. Twenty men have divided territory and will report by nightfall. Erik will stay with you until I return," the commander announced before vanishing in a hurry through the door.

At nightfall, Isak and two guards returned to find Erik watching Netflix on the sofa while I made pasta. We both stopped our activity as soon as the three men made their way into the sitting room. Erik raised and greeted his colleagues. Throughout the day, the remaining guard calmed me down, and we started talking about different subjects. He told me more about the household's history and maybe it was his name that made me feel safe, because I settled and started looking at him with a kinder eye. Something about pronouncing the name 'Erik' several times in a day without feeling guilty put me at ease.

"Nothing to report, commander, it's been a quiet day," Erik reported without being asked.

Isak noted the tension in the room and started speaking. "We searched the entire perimeter, along the river bank, into the caves, checked all the willows we could find..." he shook his head and gave me a defeated look.

"And?" I questioned, although I already knew the answer.

"Nothing. Not even a footstep, no blood anywhere, no muddy dents and no sign of another human being."

I lowered my head and sighed. "I know what I saw..." I insisted, though my voice barred the mark of defeat.

"It can happen," Isak said, stepping near me into the kitchen. "People who are not used to so much solitude, especially this suddenly, can experience vivid dreams and..."

"I know what I saw!" I interrupted.

"I am sorry, Anwen, there is no one out there," he insisted.

"But..." I tried to contradict him, only this time, Isak did the interrupting.

"Think of it this way, isn't it better to be safe and know there is no one out there to attack you?"

"I suppose..." I nodded.

"Just take it slower, get to know the forest bit by bit, don't venture so much all of a sudden. You've barely been here a few days. And always stay hydrated, it's easy to have hallucinations when one's having a heat stroke."

"Okay..." I replied.

"Do you need one of us to stay with you tonight?" he asked.

"No, don't worry, I will be fine," I insisted, although part of me wanted to take him up on the offer. I went for bravery as my dominant feeling.

"If you change your mind, we are one call away."

I nodded and thanked him, then took a big tupperware and emptied the pasta I had cooked into it, added the marinara sauce and poured a ton of parmesan on top, passing it to Erik.

"As promised," I said. He threw me a grateful smile.

After a few minutes, the men disappeared into darkness, not before checking one last time that I was fine to be on my own. I locked the door and strategically placed kitchen knives around the house, ready to be used in case of an attack. Grim, I was aware, but it would help me sleep through the night. I dimmed all the lights and went into the bedroom, taking the laptop with me. I closed the door and moved a small chest of drawers in front of it to block the entry, then ensured that each window was sealed shut. Finally, I went into the bathroom and ran a bath, lounging in the enormous tub and trying to rub off the mystery of the day.

Ansgar

Chapter Six

I struggled to carry the woman back into the cave after getting stabbed in the leg. Fear Gorta, or Rhylan, whatever name the fireling chose for itself, had kept her submerged in pain until I arrived. Her screams turned out to be a better guide than my intuition, since they sank so boundlessly, all the faeries must have heard them and known her location instantly.

As soon as I arrived, Rhylan released her and kept himself amused with torturing me instead. But after fighting and stabbing each other, he surrendered and disappeared, much to my surprise. I expected the bastard to wreak havoc, as he'd done many times throughout history, but he seemed satisfied with letting me save the woman and making his presence known. A threat to be lived another day.

Focusing on the urgent task at hand, save the human, I ripped one of my shirt sleeves to use as a tourniquet, applying pressure on the wound and tying it up so tightly that I lost most sensibility in my upper leg. With it, the pain gave a halt, allowing me to limp long enough to reach the cave. I took the girl by the waist and placed her on my shoulder. We travelled together in silence, the human moaning in pain from time to time in her unconscious state while I cursed myself for not visiting the Cloutie trees earlier; I did not have any energy to appear, so I had to walk and drag the hurt human along.

As soon as we reached the cave, I set her onto the bed and looked at her properly for the first time. She was young and quite beautiful, a fine example of a female. My sight lingered longer than I wanted to admit on her legs and the visible part of her breasts. Her dark brown hair was pulled in a bun, many wide strands had escaped the knot and lingered loosely on the pillow. Her face was turned, displaying only her profile and part of her neck, which I took a second to admire. She bared a strange mark, a dark drawing, its location protected by the shell of her ear and hairline. It looked intentional, possibly meaningful.

The woman grumbled in pain, shifting her arm to hang loosely on the bed frame, and opened her eyes just enough to let me see their hazel shimmer before closing them again. She swallowed deep, puckering her lips and barely opened her mouth, though no sound escaped.

I took in her features, her forehead, her slightly crooked nose and rosy lips, the lower one just a bit larger and plumper than its sister. I listened to her breathing, slow and drained, chest barely moving. She had been in a lot of pain. It was normal for her muscles to strain and not function at full capacity. My eyes passed to the arm she had unknowingly extended towards me, still hanging from the side of the bed frame. The other rested tucked under her, so I had to slide her form onto the side, fully facing me.

I continued scanning her neck and torso, my attention once again dropping onto those breasts, pulled tightly inside a very short garment, her abdomen bare. Thankfully, everything looked unharmed. Lowering my gaze from the upper legs, I passed her calves and reached the ankles that throbbed purple and swollen from the torture she had suffered. I pulled her shoes off, along with the socks, leaving her feet bare. On her left ankle, creeping from the purple mess of intertwined veins, another mark appeared. Ancient Germanic runes. This human suddenly became fascinating.

"Why do you mark yourself with such things?" I asked, knowing perfectly well she could not answer, nor she ever will.

Once I finished with her front, I turned her onto the bed to analyse her backside. A few minor scratches on the lower back and her right upper leg, no signs of deep cuts or pouring blood from any unsuspected wounds or cavities. I allowed myself a breath, relief flushing over me as I collapsed on the floor next to her and rested my back against the bed frame. Rhylan failed. No human sacrifice or blood spilling claimed this day.

Placing the human back onto the sheets, I adjusted the pillows to make her neck rest more comfortably and once she was set in place, occupying the side of the bed I usually slept on, I stepped into the kitchen. I returned with two vials, clean cloth and a glass of water. I had knowledge that humans die quickly from lack of hydration, so I had to keep her alive to be able to heal her. I brought a chair and positioned it next to the bed, close enough to reach her from my seat, and gently touched her arm.

"Human," I urged. "Awake and drink."

There was no response.

"Human female," I insisted once more, "I have water."
Nothing. I sighed in frustration. "One would think you want to put some effort in saving your own life," I huffed at her.

"I urge you to wake," I tried again, tone harsher, shaking her shoulder. Her head bobbed to the rhythm of my force, yet her eyes remained closed and breathing torn. It was basic anatomy, muscles needed to regenerate with sustenance, yet this human remained unwilling to wake up and help.

I still hadn't explored the district grounds, or summoned the faeries of the forest into a huddle to assign their roles because I found myself stuck with this headstrong woman, unwilling to help her own healing.

"Very well, if you are not going to help yourself, then help will come to you," and with this, I sat next to her on the bed, supporting my back against the headboard for balance and grabbed the woman to drag her across my chest, splaying her on top of me, head leaning on my clavicle. Her arms dangled still. No sign of waking up.

With one hand, I balanced her head to rest on my left shoulder and pulled her up to position her. Then I opened her mouth and with a spoon, I took a few drops of water from the cup I brought from the kitchen and pushed past her lips, emptying the contents into her mouth. I repeated the action three times until her tongue had enough water to wake up the senses and made her throat react and swallow.

"Good," I urged and continued to feed her liquid until the cup was half empty.

After swallowing the last of the water drops, the woman tilted her head, brow settling on my neck. I felt her breathing. Her chest raised slowly, at a steadier pace. Keeping her in place, we remained connected for a long minute, breathing each other's air until both our inhales became steady, following the same rhythm like an unspoken dance.

My energy awakened, burning through me, and I jolted at the feeling. My heart pounded, as though it wanted to escape and reach the woman's breath. Something felt different, out of place, and my instinct forced me to remove the threat.

I dragged her down and slid her across the sheets, placing her head carefully onto the pillow before rising from bed. I couldn't be in her presence, everything in me struggled for contact, parts of my body begged to touch her again. I needed to leave, so I stepped away and packed the knife and daggers, the sword laying abandoned at the entrance, full of Rhylan's blood.

Pain forced me to remember my injury, and I headed into the bathroom to apply a healing ointment and use proper dressing before changing my clothes. I could not introduce myself covered in bloodstains.

When I returned to the bedroom, I found the woman lying on the bed, with no visible intention of waking or making any movements other than minimally twisting her neck from time to time to get into a more comfortable position. I ignored the drumming of my heart at the sight of her. Whatever this was, I did not have time for it.

Canotilas, eilians, gwillions, heltijas, hongas, portunes and sjorkas, I mentally checked while all the faeries of the district gathered around the oldest Cloutie Tree, the one underneath whose roots the magic of the land laid buried. A Cloutie Tree was the most important living being and a blessing the goddess granted us after her passing. Any damage to them would become a death sentence for the offender. They created the energy portals that allowed us to keep the world alive.

"I am called Ansgar, native of the Earth Kingdom and will be your keeper for the next three years," I introduced myself to my new subjects. "I live in the cave by the river and I cast a spell on my door to help anyone in need, whether or not I am inside. There is no entry password or enchantment. As long as you are earthling derived, what is mine is yours," I announced in greeting.

"Is it true you are a prince?" one of the hongas asked.

As soon as I turned towards the voice, her hair changed to purple and she buried herself in the ground instead of hearing the answer.

"I am the son of Farryn and Bathysia, King and Queen of the Earth Kingdom," I confirmed.

"Are you the young one?"

"Indeed," I nodded.

"Are you mated yet?" An eilian asked and disappeared from sight, only to reappear a second later in front of me. She wore a light blue dress and her hair neatly fashioned to look like a flower. Were it not for her miniature structure, she would be a lovely female.

"I am not," I responded, and she appeared on my shoulder this time, using my loose hair as a hammock. "I am flattered," I looked towards her, only able to see part of her dress and her tiny legs, "though I think it would be appropriate for my future mate to be slightly taller."

The faerie huffed, offended, and disappeared in an instant.

"Now that we have established my origin, residence and sexual preferences, can we continue with this meeting?"

Successively, the faeries educated me in their lives and roles, what the healing priorities were, and any events worth mentioning since the last keeper's visit. After listening carefully and taking notes, I asked if they had any preference regarding their new roles and started assigning missions. The canotilas, the original tree spirits, were assigned to old barks and roots while the eilians, tiny winged creatures that could appear and disappear as they wished, would be in charge of messages and outside protection. The gwillions, tall mountain faeries with dark and rough skin continued to survey the caves and river banks. The heltijas and the hongas, small stature older folk, were in charge of surface and underground healing energies, the portunes had to grow new flowers and sprouts, while the sjorkas, the original protectors of the forest, took the guard role alongside me.

Every morning, I had to accompany one group to be presented with their territories and locations and establish a new maintenance and growth design. After which, I had to prepare the potions and healing powders each group needed to perform their duties for the next moon cycle.

"And what about the pixies?" a small winged creature asked sweetly.

"You have fun ladies, keep the spirits high," I said smiling, and suddenly thousands of winged particles of light started bouncing with joy. I always liked pixies. They were so small they could not even help with mending a dying leaf, but their spirits recited energy and enchantment.

By dusk, all earthlings were joyous about their new keeper and plans, discussing excitedly through their vision for the district and swapping stories and ideas.

"Are we not going to mention the visit of the dark one?" One of the sjorkas raised his voice to make himself heard over the crowd. Silence enveloped the area. No one dared breathe too loudly. After a few seconds, the same questions repeated, creating a never-ending loop of inquiries.

"The dark one?"

"Is it true?"

"Was it here?"

"How?"

"When?"

Small voices talked in low tones, none of them able to give an answer, and so they sent the questions forth until some of them reached me. I had kept silent until then.

"It is true, Fear Gorta was here," I confirmed.

I heard shock across the forest as the earthlings escaped held breaths.

"He provoked me to a game, using the human living in this forest as a pawn, an intended blood sacrifice. He vanished, and she is safe," I explained.

"How can you be sure? Where is she? What if Fear Gorta comes back?" the heltijas asked all together.

"I do not expect him to come back soon. He left the district badly injured. The human did not bleed onto the soil. There is no spilling or curse, I can assure you. She is sleeping in the cave and I will return her once I make sure there is no danger of remembering," I appeased them.

After a few more questions and concerns, which I eased, the faeries seemed satisfied with the meeting and started heading towards their homes for the night. Once the last of them left, I started walking back towards the cave, fatigue finally clawing into me.

By the time I arrived, the night sky flickered with colourful light. I looked up to see shades of green and pink dancing into the dark clouds, forming waves of luminescence, and smiled to myself. At the end of my first day, I stopped a fireling, saved a human, and successfully held the first keeper meeting. Then my stomach growled so deep it might have summoned all the wolves around the district. I had taken care of the human's needs, yet with all the events lining up, I forgot to feed myself. Silly beginner's mistake, my brothers would say.

Upon entering the cave, the first thing I did was check on the woman. I came in covered in mud; weapons dragging down my tired shoulders and begging for me to release the tension. Yet, when I spotted her resting, her position unchanged since I left, I felt light. All the fatigue had disappeared just by knowing she was safe and sound asleep. Even my stomach relaxed and briefly filled itself with a warm sensation.

It lasted little; the muscles tightened to demand food and after removing the weapons and changing clothes for the third time in a day—this time into my loose sleeping trousers—I headed towards the kitchen to prepare the sustenance I had been longing for almost twenty-four hours. I scanned the cupboards and found nut filled pasties, some blackberries, cheese and onion jam, perfect for a quick sandwich. I sat at the table and chewed calmly, stopping from time to time to butter another pasty or to take a sip from the orange blossom tea.

While I ate, I mentally reviewed the events of the day, thinking about how Rhylan could have entered this home, how fortunate I had been to arrive in time to save the human and tried to remember all the names and faces I laid eyes upon during the meeting. When I finished, I took another mug and poured boiling water over a jasmine bud, cut a fresh slice of bread and spread butter on it, then laid apricot jam on top and sprinkled a bit of ground cinnamon. I also took an apple from the basket laying on the table and went back into the bedroom.

She was still asleep, her torso raising and lowering along with her breathing, splayed out on my favourite pillow.

"I will need that back," I told her in a whisper. She made no sign of hearing me, caught deeply in sleep. "Ahem, ahem," I tried, though it sounded more like a theatre action than anything else. The cup was hot in my hand, so I placed it on the nightstand, over the thick leather cover of the book I had been reading at the palace, transported here alongside everything else. I sat on the bed, positioning myself close to her feet and touched one of her calves, shaking it gently. The woman moved. It was hardly noticeable, yet her muscles tensed and one of her toes wiggled. I tried again, repeating the gesture with more tension, pulling on her calf harder this time.

"Mmm..." she moaned, moving her head to the other side of the pillow.

"Wake up," I murmured.

"Mmm…" her answer hummed again. I pulled on her leg, lightly pinching her skin.

"What?" she replied.

"Wake up," I repeated.

"No, it's too comfy here," the human grumbled. Her hands adjusted on the sheets.

"I'm glad you enjoy my bed, but you need to wake up."

"No, I don't want to, five more minutes," she said, hugging the pillow.

"You slept all day, I brought food."

Clearly she had no intention of rising from the bed, which I now wanted back, and lingered in some kind of dream. With my patience diminishing from tiredness, I rose from the bed and renounced any trace of a whispering tone.

"You need to wake up immediately!" I ordered in my commanding voice.

For a few seconds, she seemed to have no intention of moving, then her entire physique tensed and jumped awake. She looked at me with enormous hazel eyes as the portrait of shock sketched her face. Then the nightmare started.

"Stop, just stop, you are breaking my eardrums!" I begged, hiding from the possessed being behind the wardrobe door. The damned beast was making an infernal sound, screaming from the top of her lungs, loud enough to awaken the dead and was throwing everything she could find in my direction, including the mug of scalding tea I had prepared for her just minutes ago.

"Human, stop!" I demanded, but the demon I had awoken kept attacking me with everything she could find, the plate of food, my book, the oil lamp, pillows and sheets from the bed, the blanket and boots from the chair, the chair itself and then…

"Oh no, don't you dare use my own weapons against me," I shouted as she gripped my most precious dagger.

"Let me go!" the barbarian threatened.

She waved the dagger in the air, as if she could block my approach from any direction, so I pulled one of the shirts from the floor and threw it towards her head. She was so preoccupied to block the dangerous cloth attacking her that she lowered her hand and I saw an opportunity. Reaching her, I knocked the dagger away and grabbed both her arms, squeezing tightly, keeping the human trapped. She struggled to escape, shaking with effort.

"Calm down," I told her and kept her squeezed tightly, hoping she would relax. Who was I kidding?

"Mother…" I roared as I felt her teeth sinking into my forearm, hard enough to draw blood. My tight pull loosened enough for her to escape, but after two steps, I took hold of the beast again, my chest pressing on her back, left arm restraining her shoulders and the other keeping a tight grip on her abdomen. I had her trapped.

"Human, may the Goddess save me, if you do not quiet down, I will hurt you myself."

She struggled for another minute, until her strength abandoned her and she remained limp in my arms, whimpering. She had given up. I felt her sighs pushing into my front, head leaning forward in defeat.

"Listen," I whispered, trying to find my least threatening tone, "I will let you go if you promise not to attack me again."

She cried louder as a response. "Promise?" I insisted.

A nod of her head was all I needed as I loosened the tension and allowed the woman to withdraw from the forced tight embrace. She dropped to the floor, sobbing loudly, her spirit broken, and I immediately kneeled with her, ashamed of what I had to do to calm her down.

"It's alright, I mean no harm," I insisted and gently caressed her hair.

Suddenly, the monster inside of her came into power. Searing pain gushed from my abdomen. During the second I took to show her kindness and offer my remorse, she lunged and stabbed me.

"Demon!" I hissed as she made her escape through the kitchen. The vile creature had used the dagger to hurt me. *Stabbed twice on your first day. And the Keeper of the year award goes to...* Trapped in pain, I headed into the bathroom, found a small vial of dracaena essence and shoved it into my pocket, then headed outside, leaving a trail of blood behind me as I disappeared into nothing.

I heard the woman's steps struggling to feel the darkness around her and find her way. She was as subtle as a tornado, making tons of noises and waking up every single creature in the woods. Maybe it would be best to leave her to fend for herself and be torn apart by a wild animal. I analysed my options for a few moments until I remembered that she had been promised as a human sacrifice so her blood could not be spilled until the next moon cycle. "There you go with that goddess damned noise again," I uttered while the human retook her shouting streak at the sight of me.

Running out of patience and gentleness, I secured her by the neck and leaned her backwards, forcing her mouth open, then reached for the vial in my pocket and poured the entire content into her mouth, covering it to make sure she swallowed.

It took her two seconds to faint, her shape falling into my arms, and I used the last of my energy to walk with her to the old mansion. Some pixies and heltijas awaited around the house, awakened by the horrid noises of the human. I placed her onto the entrance steps, grabbing my stomach, surprised to find it leaking dark blood.

"Can you make sure she is inside and safe?" I asked, grimacing in pain as I pressed a hand over the stab wound.

The faeries nodded and took the woman, carrying her inside. I thanked them and started limping back home, the human now safe in the hands of my subjects. Good riddance.

Anwen

Chapter Seven

"Release her!" the voice echoed in my dreams as I shook with memories of lingering pain. "Release her!" he had said. I hazily recalled the man inside the old willow and his dark, menacing voice. Different from the one who stood in front of me and used his own body to protect me from harm. Had I got it all wrong? Did the man try to save me? I forced my mind to recall as many details as I could, but my brain refused to connect the images and sounds. As I struggled through my memory path, I could not resist the fatigue claiming my muscles and fell asleep, unable to piece the events in cohesive order.

The next morning, I woke up recovering from the soreness of the past few days.

"It is Saturday," I confirmed with the laptop, an action I would do for the remaining days I had to spend in this place. What in the name of all the saints was happening here? The sun took its own path. Nature seemed to stop working only inside these coordinates and strange men lurked about, in a place that was supposed to be protected and safeguarded from the outside world. As the day passed, every hour added to the strangeness of the place, one that I found myself trapped in, incapable of understanding my purpose or mission inside these woods.

Two hours later, I stood in front of the door, ready to go outside and confront the possible abuser, decided on finding the man. I got ready this time, I packed cold water and a small hunting knife I had found abandoned in the cupboard, the pepper spray my dad insisted I brought 'just in case' and a smaller knife, wrapped in a sheath which I kept closely stored inside my legging's pocket. Summoning an urge of courage through a few deep breaths, I closed the door, making sure I locked up and placed the keys in the other pocket. I tried to remember which way my steps took me last time and instinctively headed towards the path I would have taken then, walking at a steady pace, looking around for any signs of... anything.

I searched until dusk claimed the sky, and I did not find a sign, not even a footmark or a willow. It looked like the forest completely changed. New species had regrown overnight, covering anything I might have left behind. It was pointless; I felt like I had been running around in circles and unfortunately; I did not think about packing food, so I was starving. The cold water I had at midday turned into a mild tea, impossible to satiate me in this hot weather. Accepting defeat, I decided to head back home, excited for the icy cold water, frozen drinks and ice cream waiting in the fridge.

An abrupt noise pierced my ears. It sounded like a whisper at first, but the closer I got, the clearer it became. Some kind of stream must be nearby, I heard the sound of running water tinting the air. Excited, I hurried my pace towards the sound; I knew rivers filtered water, so they were safe to drink from, and I couldn't wait to refill my water bottle and indulge in the refreshing liquid.

As I approached, a deep line of trees materialised, different from anything I had ever seen. Impossibly tall with thick trunks, these trees carried their leaves in undulating shapes. Each part of the foliage was a snowflake and had its own identity and memory. The stems looked atypical; they glimmered a shade of turquoise, as though the light pouring in the nearby water had been absorbed and reflected onto them.

I stepped closer, surrendered in admiration when I spotted an odd shape that caught my attention. Something hung from one of the wider branches. Clothes. A man's clothes. My body tensed, I immediately grabbed the backpack and opened the zipper to seize the pepper spray and pulled the small dagger from my pocket. A weapon in each hand, I stepped closer to where the clothes were splayed onto the tall branches.

I did not understand it, yet my stomach twisted at the scent. It felt familiar. Orange and a fresh smell of rain filled my nostrils. A primordial memory, which part of me unconsciously carried, made my heart palpitate at the recognition. Whatever feeling my inner self experienced, I did not recognise.

I sensed his closeness, the trail of the unknown, yet familiar scent he left behind, drifting from the river. Following the calling that pulled on my senses, I walked toward the stream, weary of making any noises, and froze. There he was, the man I had seen earlier, bathing in the river without a care in the world.

Ansgar

Chapter Eight

I loved the sanctuary of Cloutie trees; I had discovered the blooming ones by the river earlier in the morning and, after performing the duties of the day, I invoked their healing powers and had a swim in the river while my wounds healed.

The first time I needed a Cloutie tree was when I broke my leg at age five. Damaris tricked me into thinking that I could summon wings if I swallowed a butterfly. I held vague memories of climbing in the tower with both my brothers and being handed a jar with a pink butterfly struggling to spread its wings inside. Then I remembered flying, but only for a moment before harrowing pain overtook one of my legs and prevented me from standing on the ground, where I had been splayed out by the fall.

The Queen arrived shortly after, and both my brothers wore solemn faces. She carried me into my bedroom and ripped away all of my clothes, leaving me completely exposed to the squeaking laughs of the two accomplices who had crept inside the room. The garments immediately passed to one of the guards that also appeared in the bedroom, who pressed them tightly to his chest as if they symbolised a prized possession, and hurried outside. I did not understand what happened and kept crying and asking my mother for help until she explained the clothes had to be taken and hung onto the big Cloutie tree in the royal garden.

"It is the first living thing that grew after the Goddess Catalina's death," the Queen explained. "Even in her eternal sleep, she cared for us and sent us power to heal our wounds. It is in her honour that we are healers of the living things. The Cloutie trees are sacred and they only grow naturally in the burial places of the three life giving goddesses," my mother explained.

"How do they heal us mama?" I had asked as a boy.

"With their energy, in an exchange. You hang the clothes you wear when you are injured onto the branches and the magic of the Cloutie trees will feel the pain and sense where your form needs help to heal."

"Just like we do with the plants?" I had asked.

"Exactly, my son, just like we do with the plants," my mother replied in a soft tone, kissing my brow as sleep laid a blanket of silence over me.

By nightfall, I was jumping up and down again with my brothers, broken bones healed, though the event made me grow a distaste for butterflies.

As I basked in the water, a crack claimed my attention, a dried branch split with a cry, and my attention moved towards the river bank where I spotted the damned woman.

Our eyes met, and I stopped swimming, frowning at the human. Why was it that in a hundred and fifty-six years this district remained uninhabited, but when I arrive, a demon lurks about in my business? She maintained her position on the bank, a few steps away from the water and glanced at me, not shifting. A territorial battle?

Fine, if you want to play this game, let us start. I pretended not noticing her at all, and if I did, her presence did not bother me one bit. I faked feeling more relaxed and changed into a few swimming styles, dived a dozen times and started floating on my back, revealing my silhouette completely to the woman.

At the sight of me, all of me, another twig snapped. And another. When I looked in her direction, I saw her hopping into the forest towards the safety of the treeline.

That's what you get for spying, beast.

"I will need to come out eventually," I announced towards the treeline where I knew she remained hidden. The wounds healed a few minutes after she disappeared, but I enjoyed dragging out the swim. I felt her behind the trees, waiting for the opportune moment.

"I am not leaving," her tiny voice replied, barely audible from behind the branches.

"Fine with me," I shrugged and swam back towards the river bank, embracing my nakedness.

I walked slowly, allowing the sun to dry my skin before getting into the treeline where I sensed she lingered.

"Oh my God! Are you crazy?" I heard her squeak, her eyes on me for an instant then backing away to hide behind a thick tree, knife gripped tightly in hand.

"I fail to see the problem," I replied, standing close to her.

"Get dressed, nobody wants to see that!" the woman's voice

protested. Yet her gaze lingered a while longer than necessary. I couldn't help a proud smile as I replied. "I can assure you, there are many females willing to see this, some have."

"Please put on your clothes?" she grimaced with embarrassment.

"Ah... politeness. I can respond to it better than to your threats," I chuckled, more to my benefit than hers.

She waited for a while, then peeked from her safe zone behind the tree and backed away as soon as her eyes met me.

"You are still naked!"

"I assume my clothes were the ones that attracted your attention, you must know they are in the branches." Was she playing a game or did this human possess less intelligence than I'd initially suspected?

"Go get them," she answered in a breathless tone.

"And leave my back unprotected to the one who stabbed me? Not a chance," I huffed. I did not trust her and had to get rid of her at the closest opportunity. I could not have a human lurking about, interfering with the energy or accidentally encountering one of the faeries. From the reports I'd received, she always stayed in the southern part of the district and never crossed the river, preferring to keep close to her home. This must have been the farthest she'd gotten to our area, and I suspected it was in search of me.

"I don't plan to stab you again." Her voice lingered. "I just..."

No answer came. "You just...?" I pushed.

"I just want to protect myself in case you try to hurt me again," the voice added, almost broken.

Hurt her? Is that what she thought?

84

"I have no intention of harming you or any other female," I replied, more by instinct than thought.

How did she dare accuse me of such things?

She did not answer, but I felt her exhaling in relief.

"As a sign of peace between us, I will climb the tree and retrieve my clothes," I announced, "as long as you make a promise too."

"What promise?"

"Promise not to stab me again while I am vulnerable and naked, climbing a tree."

She chuckled a bit. "I promise," the voice replied, sweeter this time. The smile on her lips made me forget the world for a mere second until it disappeared as suddenly as it had arrived.

While I climbed, several things popped into my mind. The woman planned to stay in the forest. If she lived in the old queen's palace, she must be royalty or on some kind of mission. I needed a plan. Obviously, the human could not find out about me or my duties, severe punishments ensued just for unwillingly being sighted by humans. I did not want to think what splaying out my form and chatting with the human could mean.

A fae revealing themselves to humans was a rare happening these days. It belonged to memories of the past when our ancestors found it a sport to hunt humans down into fairy rings. They either brought them into their kingdoms or used them for experiments. Most of these customs stopped two centuries ago because the Water Kingdom suffered attacks from sailors who wanted to avenge their lost comrades. The mermaids had enjoyed the flesh of men for millennia, yet, as the human population grew, it became difficult to remain unsighted and safe.

In this case, revealing myself to a human twice, voluntarily maintaining conversations and displaying my naked body to the woman would cause at least a good flogging. I could argue that the initial contact was to prevent a blood sacrifice, yet I had no excuse for what I was doing now: toying with the human, deliberately making her feel uncomfortable, just because I was enjoying it.

I found her intriguing, and quite beautiful. The rivers of chestnut hair falling on her back, her big hazel eyes and curvy form. She looked like temptation itself, and part of me was ready to take a bite. I knew I had to end this, let the human be, find out her purpose in the district and make sure we never met again. And above all, have a believable explanation regarding my presence in these woods.

Once I dressed and climbed down from the tree, rehearsing the story I formed while putting my clothes back on, I made a throat-clearing sound to attract her attention.

"I am presentable enough for you to look," I announced.

Reluctantly, she shifted her head from behind the tree trunk and scanned me quickly to make sure I told the truth before she stepped away, letting herself appear in front of me.

"I apologise if my presence offended you, today and the first time we met. I only wished to come to your aid, and I am pleased to know you are faring fine," I took the reins of the conversation.

She continued to glance at me suspiciously, not saying a word. I raised my brows, but did not break the silence.

"What happened the first time you saw me?" she asked, gripping the dagger in her small hands.

"I will tell you if you stop threatening me with that weapon. Put it down and I will tell you what you wish to know."

She hesitated a long while, her view shifting towards the dagger, then back to me, only to fall towards the weapon again, until she finally, slowly, lowered it, her hand relaxing.

"Now, tell me," her voice demanded.

"I was walking through the forest, and I heard screaming. I hurried to the place where the cry came from, following the sound, when I found you, trapped in the mud, trying to get your ankles free. I helped you release your legs, then you fell to the ground and fainted. I didn't have the heart to leave you there, so I brought you home and placed you on my bed so you could rest. In the evening, I came to bring you food and tea and when you woke up, you started attacking me and tried to stab me. The end," I said, trying to look unaffected or annoyed, though both feelings threatened to tense my jaw.

I also did not feel the need to tell her she actually took me by surprise and stabbed me in the gut, forcing me to seek the Cloutie trees for an unplanned two hour healing session. It would raise more questions I had no interest in answering.

"That's not how it happened," she contested, taking the dagger once more and making her tiny wrist shake in pain.

Human, put the thing down or you will end up hurting yourself.

"You asked me to tell you what happened, and I did," I insisted, still focused on her shaking wrist. She was so obviously unequipped to use any kind of weapon, her frail bones could barely support the tension, but she compensated with bravado. I admired that. "Now if you please, throw that dagger on the ground or I refuse to continue this conversation."

Immediately, she crouched with a slow motion and placed the weapon by her feet, close enough that she could pick it up with one quick movement.

"You will not be needing it," I insisted.

"Tell me the truth," the woman folded her arms, as if that little gesture made her more fierce and threatening. If anything, it made her cute in her naiveté.

"I already told you my part of the story, I do not know how you ended up trapped in the mud or why you were screaming so hysterically." How could I tell a human that destruction incarnate tried to use her as a sacrifice and drain her blood to curse the forest?

"What about the other man?" she insisted.

I froze, shock striking me like a block of ice. Had the fireling revealed himself to the woman?

"What exactly did you see?" I asked quickly.

"The man from inside the tree, he hid in the willow. It was like smoke or something, but I clearly saw a man there. Also, he spoke to me, and I think…" she paused, recollecting her thoughts, then continued, "I think you spoke to him too. Asked him to let me go."

Oh, my goddess. This human could see Fear Gorta! I hadn't heard of a single instance where humans were able to see old fae in their natural form. What the woman saw, the way she described it, was so accurate that it couldn't have been a flick of her imagination or visions caused by pain.

When I arrived, I found Rhylan using the energy of an ancient willow tree to cast his power into the ground and keep her trapped. And he had spoken to her!

"Well?" The woman demanded, shaking me from thought.

"I know nothing of whichever willow or man you are talking about. As I told you, you got stuck in the mud and cried for help. I found you alone, no one else by your side," I insisted.

Giving the woman a potion to forget just became a void option. If Rhylan found out about it, he had every reason to return and finish the job. And if she could see the Fear Gorta, what else could she see?

She stared at me quietly, analysing my gestures and deciding on whether I was telling the truth.

"Look," I continued, "I know it must be strange for you to find me here, I assure you I mean no harm to you. The first time we met, I was just trying to help."

"What are you doing here, anyway? The forest is supposed to be uninhabited," she puckered her lips, pleased with herself, knowing fully well I needed a good explanation.

"No one knows I am here," I admitted.

"And why are you here?"

The best lie is to tell the truth, I remembered. "To care for the forest."

"As in, the plants?" she questioned.

"Yes," I nodded.

"Are you a biologist or something?" The woman enquired in disbelief.

Or something. "I am."

"The guards don't know you are here?" she continued her interrogation. I stored this information for later. There were guards patrolling the district. Of course, someone had to care for the woman. They must have used the southern routes to reach her, but it added another point on the list of things we had to keep hidden from.

"They do not know I am here. I did not enter the forest the usual way," I admitted, since I hadn't found a good enough explanation about my presence in the woods.

"So you snuck inside, basically," she reprimanded.

I chuckled. "I did."

"Where do you live? And where is your equipment?"

This woman would make a fine tutor. She ambushed me with ten questions in less than a minute.

"My equipment is at home. The one I am using during my stay here. I will tell you where I live only if you do the same." I had no intention of doing so and hoped she wouldn't either.

"I won't tell you that!" she immediately answered.

"In that case, expect the same privacy from me." I struggled to keep in a smile at the small victory.

"And what do you want?" she pushed.

"I want to conduct my experiments in peace and undisturbed. I am assuming you want the same?" I asked, careful to plant the idea inside her head.

"As a matter of fact, I do," she crossed her arms again. Her eyes widened as soon as the words made their way out. Pure instinct had forced her to utter them, just as I planned. She had spoken them only to spite me, and they gave her no turning back.

"Then we agree. I will not disturb your presence in the woods as long as you respect my privacy and do not tell anyone I'm here."

She thought about the proposal, and before she had a chance to reply, I added, "I am conducting many experiments that will help the forest regrow and regain health, I promise it is for the good. I could not come here through the normal ways, so I had to take matters into my own hands."

After a long minute, she nodded. "Okay."

I smiled in thanks.

Anwen

Chapter Nine

By the time I arrived home, night wrapped the woods in a tight purple embrace. I didn't have time to settle and analyse what had happened, because as soon as I entered, the laptop started buzzing; a sharp dinging slipped through the stillness of the mansion. I ran towards it and saw the screen inundating with notifications, they had been accumulating for hours. I popped the browser open and clicked on the tiny icon with a rainbow camera background.

@Cressidaofficial: Hey sexy

@Cressidaofficial: Are you online?

@Cressidaofficial: Don't let me bother you if you're doing something nice

@Cressidaofficial: Anwen?

@Cressidaofficial: If I don't get a reply from you in two hours I will call the police haha

@Cressidaofficial: Seriously, you are supposed to be stuck to your laptop all day watching series or something

@Cressidaofficial: What is up with you? You never not answer.

@anwenodstar: I am here!!!!!

@Cressidaofficial: Where were you??? I was getting worried, I almost called your parents!!

@anwenodstar: No, you did not!

@Cressidaofficial: I did not, but I was about to.

@anwenodstar: No need, I'm back.

@anwenodstar: What are you doing online all day, anyway? Don't you have a fabulous runway to walk?

@Cressidaofficial: The better question is, why weren't you online?

@anwenodstar: I was out. The whole point of coming here was to get out and search for things, remember?

@Cressidaofficial: Yeah, I got that.

@Cressidaofficial: But where were you? All day?

@anwenodstar: I needed to investigate something.

@Cressidaofficial: Hmmm… that sounds intriguing.

@Cressidaofficial: Please tell me the problem is male :)

@anwenodstar: It actually is

@Cressidaofficial: NOOOOOOOOO

@anwenodstar: Don't get overly excited

@Cressidaofficial: Tell me everything about these sexy men

@anwenodstar: It's just one… And how do you know if he is sexy or not?

@Cressidaofficial: Is he?

@anwenodstar: …

@Cressidaofficial: He is!!!!

@anwenodstar: I didn't say that.

@Cressidaofficial: You didn't have to. We know each other since we wore diapers

@Cressidaofficial: Tell me. Aren't you supposed to be alone in there? Is he one of those guard guys?

@anwenodstar: I was, in theory, I still am.

@Cressidaofficial: So how can you be out with a sexy man? Are you messing with me?

@anwenodstar: Not at all. I said that I was SUPPOSED to be alone in the woods. Apparently I am not.

@Cressidaofficial: Ok, now you really have to tell me

@anwenodstar: He's some kind of biologist

@Cressidaofficial: Aha....

@anwenodstar: He snuck in here, passed the guards and has an apartment somewhere in the forest. That is all I know.

@Cressidaofficial: What's his name?

@anwenodstar: No idea, we didn't exchange passports when we met.

@Cressidaofficial: How did you meet?

@anwenodstar: It's complicated...long story short, he saved me from something. Still not sure what. Then I attacked him thinking he wanted to hurt me. Turns out he only wants to study plants.

@Cressidaofficial: Maybe he will want to study you as well in the near future :)

@anwenodstar: In that case, I will remind him how very uninterested I am.

@Cressidaofficial: Yeah, yeah...

@anwenodstar: How is everything with you? Where are you?

@Cressidaofficial: I'm in Greece, nice and warm weather for once! I'll tell you about the two very sexy Greeks when you tell me about Mr Sexy Biologist.

@anwenodstar: There is nothing to tell...honestly

@Cressidaofficial: I'll be the judge of that

@Cressidaofficial: Tell me the oddest thing from this whole secret meeting you guys had

@anwenodstar: Possibly that saw him naked...

@Cressidaofficial: WHAT????

@anwenodstar: It was an accident

@anwenodstar: He was swimming in the river, I just passed by

@Cressidaofficial: And?

@anwenodstar: And nothing. I asked him to put his clothes on, he did, end of story

@Cressidaofficial: If you were close enough to ask him to put his pants back on, then you were close enough to see his dick

@anwenodstar: Your point?

@Cressidaofficial: Is it big? Or is it biiiiig?

@anwenodstar: I am NOT talking about that, I don't even know the guy

@Cressidaofficial: More description, please

@anwenodstar: He's freakishly tall. He has golden-brownish hair, shoulder length. Everyone seems to have longer hair around here.

@Cressidaofficial: Pretty eyes?

@anwenodstar: Grey, though sometimes they are green, like the sea when it's agitated. And before you ask for a full description, here it is: he has soft features, the curve of his chin is delicate, really muscly and he has a very straight nose, like a Greek sculpture, since you are there, you should know best. He is pretty hot; I'd have to be honest.

@Cressidaofficial: Giiiiiirl, get me some of that! How big?

@anwenodstar: I don't know, he's over six feet for sure

@Cressidaofficial: I am talking about his D! :)

@anwenodstar: Urgh... I don't know Cressi, I honestly don't care...

@Cressidaofficial: I'm sorry. You know I love you, right? I just want you to start being yourself again and forgive my silly horny way of trying to get you back.

@anwenodstar: I know, love you too. But the last thing I need right now is sex. It won't fix anything. And Jonathan is still roaming around like I'll change my mind any second or something. It's all too stressful and I really don't need to think about some new guy. Who is trespassing, by the way!

@Cressidaofficial: I know... How are you? Is that place helping?

@anwenodstar: I'm ok, getting used to it. I cried the first few days, then I debated going home. I really like the forest. It's nice and hot around here and keeping silent for days helps. I don't have to think about what I am saying, how I say things.

@Cressidaofficial: I'm sorry I've been so busy lately, I'm going back home in two weeks and we can chat more

@anwenodstar: Don't worry about me, if I need anything I'll message, I promise.

We chatted for about an hour until my friend had to get ready for the show and I walked into the kitchen to make dinner. This place helped, saying it to Cressida made it true. I had slept through the night for the first time in what seemed like forever; I took the time to linger in bed; I didn't stress about going to meetings or appointments, learning speeches by heart or forcing smiles when all I wanted to do was cringe and bark at people.

And I felt closer to Erik, even though I still had no clue of whatever I was supposed to find, this place, my presence here, gave me peace. Whatever the queen felt when she was here, I started to experience it as well. Like I reached some kind of milestone, bringing me closer to a purpose. All around the forest lay a cape of stillness, the only sounds penetrating through were birdsong and rustling leaves. It offered a calming environment that gave my heart exactly what it needed: stillness and harmony.

I could not find it in me to relax and forget today's events. Everything happened so fast that I did not have a chance to even think properly. I had seen a man naked, unwillingly that is. Even so, he had been naked in front of me and my traitorous eyes had lingered, my disloyal stomach dropped at the sight of him, fully exposed. My thoughts flew to his sculpted body, that abdomen that would have made any model jealous, the triangle of muscles of his pelvis... *No, Anwen, no, stop!* I forced my imagination back and tried to remove the image that remained tattooed into my mind.

He may have been the most beautiful man I'd ever seen, more beautiful than I ever thought it possible, but the twisting in my gut and that surge of excitement at the sight of him suggested trouble. I did not come here to chase men, and meeting him was a mere coincidence. We each had a reason to be in the woods, and that had to be the end of it. With that thought forced into my head, I went to bed.

I need to investigate. The man's image became my wakeup call after spending the night twisting and turning in bed, barely sleeping for a few interrupted hours. He had entered the forest undetected, which meant there had to be a way. And maybe Erik had followed the same route, maybe they even met through a mere accident or coincidence, just like the two of us had. Maybe he knew what my brother wanted from this place.

Deciding that it would be impossible to rest, I hopped out of bed as soon as dawn broke and had a quick shower, barely taking enough time to dry and apply sunscreen. I pulled my wet hair into a messy bun, changed into a new set of leggings with a matching top, and ran into the kitchen to prepare some food.

I formed a plan to take one of the old maps discarded in a drawer in the study desk and follow it, until I found the man's home. Peanut butter and banana sandwiches ready, two bottles of water and the dagger, which became a habitual addition to my list of necessities when leaving the house. Not that I had any intention of using it, but it raised the scale of my bravado. After a hurried breakfast and a few emails I had to reply to, one of them was Dad's daily check in, I went on a mission to find and isolate the stranger.

I followed the various pathways I knew with no success, so I decided to go towards the river and follow the stream, walking along the bank until hopefully, I would find him or at least some tracks to follow.

An unknown urge pushed towards this, towards finding him again; as inexplicable as it was appalling, I had absolutely no reason to show even the most remote interest towards a man who had entered a protected place illegally. Yet I could not help myself, I felt excited to be in his proximity again, but this time I would gain better control of my senses and force out whatever information he had to offer. In order to do that, I had to find him first, and the task seemed to render itself problematic.

Two sandwich breaks proved my lack of success. I walked miles along every side of the forest, but found no tracks, no equipment left to check plants or heard any zooming drones or beeping cameras. If the man was still here, he was as quiet as the forest itself, which seemed to be less noisy than usual. No animals ran around, no branches fizzled, no birdsong. The woods covered him in their ghostly silence.

The sun would set soon enough; it was already making its way towards the warm embrace of the mountain. It shone bright, joyous to go back home after a long day of brilliance and floating away in the sky.

I decided to head back home after the disappointing venture that made my ankles swell and my feet ache. As I turned back, my attention pointed to a colossal cliff, hanging over the ledge, preventing the river from advancing. It posed beautiful and beetling, nesting an agonizingly high steep far into its heart.

It called to me, forming an alluring halo at the top from the setting sun, so I started walking towards it, pulled by curiosity. When I arrived near enough to see the top, I spotted the man casually hiking over the sharp peaks as though the extremely dangerous fall was nothing to be afraid of.

Chapter Ten

The woman searched for me all day and I enjoyed making a sport out of leading her through the most difficult paths and leaving tiny trails in all the wrong directions. Every time she wanted to stop, I kept her interested with a noise, making her believe she was just a few steps away from finding me. It amused me for a while until she was on the verge of giving up, her legs probably cramping with the effort of the day. I surrendered and climbed the cliff by the river, ensuring to make myself blatantly visible in the setting sun.

When I reached the top, I glanced downward and saw her following the trail I left and coming closer to the cliff. She did so while trying to be as quiet as she could, not obvious that she had bitten the bait I had laid out for her. By the time the human reached the cliff, the sun was setting and her ragged breathing, which I and all the animals around could hear, got more and more accelerated. She tried to follow the exact route I had taken to reach the top of the cliff, even though she was evidently unequipped for such an effort, her upper body already giving out. I debated my two options. I could amuse myself further and watch the stubborn human try to hike the impossible route, or help her find the easier option, dismissed by her impatience.

"You could always take the stairs," I announced from the top of the cliff.

She looked up, her face squirming from effort.

"You are telling me this now?" she huffed, her breath shaken.

Why did it feel so good to tease her? Why did it feel so good to look at her?

"You beast, I could have injured myself!" the woman shouted.

"You are only three metres from the ground, worst case you break a leg," I disregarded her fright.

She pierced me with rage, then proceeded to sluggishly come down from the cliffs, holding onto the rocks for dear life. When she came close to the ground, she jumped and fell on her bottom. I started to laugh, my giggles floating away into the river. I barely remembered the last time I laughed with such full breaths, but it didn't last long. My loud laugh halted abruptly. The woman was not moving.

I descended from the sharp peak onto the stairs, climbing down four or five at the time, until within a matter of moments, my feet touched the ground and approached the unmoving human figure. I knew of human fragility but I never expected her to be hurt from such a small fall. I approached her, worry and guilt cascading over me, only to see her shift abruptly, one of her legs raising high enough to kick me in the right calf, trying to make me lose balance and fall to the ground.

When I remained immobile, she frowned with disappointment, suddenly completely fine.

"Did you just try to trip me to the ground?" I asked with disbelief.

"You must admit, if I'd managed to do it, it would have been epic," she laughed while I extended my hand to help her up. I didn't hold back a smile, the sheer nerve on this woman was a thing of legend.

"Come on," I stated, not letting go of her hand, "you are going to miss it," and dragged her up the stairs I had just used when coming to her rescue.

"Where are we going?" she managed to ask before being pulled away and guided up the stairs. Within seconds, her panting returned. I continued to climb, slower than usual for her benefit, towards the top, not bothering to explain or stop for her breathing advantage.

"You know," she uttered between gasps, "I walked all day and then climbed a rock and now I am climbing stairs."

"I know." I didn't bother to explain how.

"Then, can't we just stop for a second to catch our breaths?" she insisted.

Cheeky too, I added mentally to the ongoing list of qualities. "We can't stop, and my breath is perfectly even," I added.

"Why can't we stop?" The woman complained, her body shifting, dragged by my force rather than helping towards the climb.

"We'll miss it," I kept my response short.

"Miss what?" she insisted, calling out for an explanation between abrupt pants.

I did not bother to answer and seeing how she truly was incapable to continue, I stopped and pulled her in my arms, holding her torso with one hand and her legs with the other, then continued to climb two steps at a time. She shrieked with surprise at first but once in my arms she remained quiet, muscles tense. She looked around, possibly for the first time, and saw the precipice below. The human gasped and tied her hands tightly around my neck, securing herself, making sure that even if I wanted to drop her, I wouldn't be able to.

"Miss what?" she whispered from my arms when we were almost at the top.

"This," I replied as soon as I took the last step and arrived on the plateau that reflected the naked rays of sunlight. I had marked the place as my favourite in the district and came here almost every day to watch the sun go down.

The top of the cliff had been corroded by time and the peak demolished by nature, finding its resting place on the river bank. In its stead, the cliff produced calcites to cover the wound of the rock and the wind had polished it into a white mirror-like plateau that shone golden-purple from the emanated glimmer of the sun.

Still in my arms, the woman kept quiet, stunned by the beauty around. Her head moved from side to side, trying to take in this much splendour at once, her mouth still open from what had once been a gasp. Realising I still held her, I let her feet touch the ground gently, allowing her legs to find balance on the glossy surface before letting her go. As soon as I did, my chest sank a little from the lack of touch.

We remained silent, astounded by the eternal yellow-purple canvas that engrossed the horizon, clouds swiftly moving towards their homes to make room for the night sky and its heralds, which started to radiate on the Northern side of the sky.

"This is the most beautiful thing I've ever seen," she exclaimed while crouching into a sitting position, hugging her knees.

"It is," I smiled, my vision fixed on the woman who found comfort on the crystal plateau. She breathed deeply, taking in the image through all her senses. The human caressed the smooth calcite of the plateau, drawing out the clouds that reflected onto the surface and smiled.

If there was ever a moment that would be remembered as pure peace, this was it. I took a seat next to her and shifted my field of vision from her to the sunset, then back to her. We were the only two beings on earth and time had stopped, her smile and the sun's reflection in her hazel eyes, the only things I needed.

While I was admiring her beauty, she turned to me and smiled broadly, her left cheek forming a dimple by the side of her curving lip.

"My name is Anwen," she introduced herself.

"Ansgar," I whispered, focused on the new reveal her face had made.

"It's nice to meet you, officially," she giggled, the dimple materializing again. *What in the goddess' name am I doing?*

"It is," I replied, forcing myself to turn my gaze towards the sun, even though all my eyes begged to see was her smile.

Five hundred push-ups did not manage to take my thoughts off the woman. Anwen. I remembered her soft voice whispering it like a secret I hadn't been aware I wanted to know so badly until the moment I found out. The sound of her voice haunted me, her beautiful expression admiring the sunset as though she had never seen the sun go down.

You know better than this! I criticised myself as I started a new round of push-ups, planning to go for as long as my muscles were able to produce lactic acid or until the pain became unendurable, enough to force me to pass out and remove the woman from my mind. I deserved the pain, I had merited it since the moment I allowed myself to feel whatever this putrid feeling was. How could I be an honourable member of the kingdom when I only brought dishonour? How could I make Father proud, when I acted like a stupid, reckless youngling?

'Anwen,' I heard her voice as I continued to push my body towards pain. Not only had I broken the laws yet again, I had grabbed the woman in my arms and carried her to show her my favourite place, to reveal a part of myself.

Another hundred push-ups went by and my senses leaped towards the memory of her skin caressing mine as we sat on the plateau, wordlessly sharing the same astonishment towards the beauty hanging in the sky. We watched the movement of the sun in comfortable silence, lingering on the last ray of the orange-purple horizon, until the celestial depiction of the heavens became separated by twilight. Only once it got dark, night enveloping the forest and all with it, had she moved to thank me, her features barely visible in the crepuscule.

I nodded, not knowing what to say or why I had decided to bring her there, the only thing I knew how to do in that moment was to stand up and seize her yet again in my arms to climb down the stairs back into the woods. She accepted the touch without protest, making herself comfortable and cuddling my shoulders as she had done previously, only this time softer and more determined, her gestures sure and unashamed. I walked with her slowly, making sure to drag each step only to prolong the closeness we shared.

Only when we were on the ground and the terrain evened, I let her climb down from my arms. She did so reluctantly, as though she accepted her rightful place and would have stayed there for a longer period of time.

Another moment of silence, which had become an unspoken conversation between our gazes. I managed to speak.

"Would you like me to accompany you home?" my voice a whisper after long unspoken passages stopped in my throat.

"I am..." she swallowed, convincing herself of what she was about to say and forcing the words out, "I am... not ready..."

I looked at her in confusion, not understanding how the mention of readiness had any place in the conversation. Until I grasped her meaning and a penetrating breath escaped me. She thought the offering was for me to...

106

"I meant to make sure you arrive home safely. It is dark in the woods and you are alone. I have no intention of entering..." I stumbled upon the words.

As I was going over this, I continued to push my body to the limit in hope that somehow the embarrassing memory disappeared from mind.

I shut my eyes and shook my head from side to side, as much as my sore neck muscles allowed me to, waving the thought away.

Well done, idiot. Who the fuck says that to a woman? I have no intention of entering.

I cringed, forcing another push-up, triceps crumbling in pain.

If she felt embarrassed, she didn't show it, her only reply a soft, "Oh..." and again the damned silence covered the moment. Luckily, Anwen managed to break it.

"I live in the queen's mansion; they call it the small palace. Do you know where it is?"

"Of course," I replied, hopeful, and started to walk into the woods, not before extending a hand for her to grab and follow. She unhesitantly did. Part of me wanted to stretch out the way back for as long as I could, enjoying the warmth her palm formed on mine, tiny strands of sweat blending our union, but I did not want to risk a surprise visit from Rhylan, especially at night when I had no weapons at hand. I walked decisively towards the old mansion and only stopped once we were close enough that the electric lights illuminated our faces.

I turned towards her, still holding her hand. "Here you are."

"Thank you," she whispered, not letting go of the hand yet, the

107

comfortable touch lingering onto our skin, welding us.

I raised it towards my face and placed my lips on her skin, kissing her knuckles and abruptly, letting go. As soon as I did, a pull of energy broke away from me, my heart heavier.

"Good night," I replied before disappearing into the forest.

Anwen

Chapter Eleven

Back at home, the frenzy of the encounter prevented me from thinking clearly and gave me a specific flutter in the stomach that I remember feeling last when I was thirteen and Alex Ramirez had asked me to be his girlfriend. Our relationship only lasted two weeks, as Alex went and kissed Martha Johnson because she had boobs. After this, I refused to have another boyfriend until college and spent a few months with a few guys, but nothing as serious as stomach butterflies.

They did not arrive during my relationship with Jonathan, my ex-boyfriend, either. I thought they had migrated elsewhere until further notice, which appeared to be this night. Or maybe the butterflies only responded to men whose names started with the letter A. 'Ansgar,' I remembered his smile, his eyes, his soft lips pronouncing the name I had waited to hear.

After arriving home, my hand chivalrously kissed for the first time in ages by someone other than my father, fatigue and soreness punched, causing me to fall instantly asleep on the sofa. The sensation of him, of his skin and embrace lingered, allowing me to rest every single muscle in a sweet relaxation, dreaming about colour and sounds. I had witnessed the most beautiful display of natural light the sky could possibly produce, in the company of a beautiful man. Sometimes, during the half hour we spent on the plateau, my gaze shifted from the sky towards his face and back again, amazed at every turn with the beauty I found. Although eager to learn more about him, we were both so humbled in the presence of the marvellous miracle of nature that we remained silent, words vapid during this moment. Our non-verbal communication had shared emotion instead of sound.

It was only when I fully woke up, my skin harassed by the lukewarm water pouring out of the shower, that I saw the previous night's events under a new light. I had forgotten my promise, the reason why I'd been there in the first place. My aching insides at the thought of Ansgar confirmed what I already knew and what really gnawed at my conscience.

I held hands with the man, allowed myself to be cradled in his strong arms and enjoyed the hell out of it. Worst of all, I connected with him on a more profound level than just a physical touch. If I didn't know better, my new feelings sounded very close to teenage love—that ravenous passion that could split the world open for a lover's caress I had only read about in the books that remained abandoned on my shelf.

My heart sank, I felt awful and wanted to kick myself for allowing something like this to happen. I completely missed the point of being here, and at the closest opportunity I had to discover something, I'd ran around watching sunsets and holding hands with some guy, completely missing the point of asking him the questions

I was so desperate to know answers to.

Involuntarily, I bit my lip whilst remembering his nakedness, a hand forcing its way down my abdomen. Yes, maybe that is what I needed, a way to relax and expel the want building up. It had been a year since I last had sex, longer since I last orgasmed. Maybe that's what my body tried to tell me, why it reacted the way it did, searching for comfort and passion.

I decided to listen and I allowed my hand to caress down until my fingers found my ache, already wet and wanting. I slipped the middle finger in, caressing myself while moving up and down, warming myself up, the water pouring down onto my tense physique. Adding another finger, I pressed deeper inside of me, a leg propped against the edge of the bathtub for better support and found that spot that desperately sought attention.

I scraped at it until my breathing became quicker, my inner muscles tensing. Closing my eyes, Ansgar's image inundated me, my hands becoming his. I thought about his large palm cupping my breast while his hand pumped into me, fast and deep, his lips biting my neck and whispering dirty things into my ear. An explosion of relief escaped my inner thighs as a moan parted my lips, a moan carrying his name.

After breathing a few times to allow myself to come down from the hype still pulsating between my legs, I felt relief, my bodily needs sorted, the deep emotion rippling the centre of my body satiated for the time being. I got out of the shower and went straight into the sitting room, landing on the sofa, still in the bath towel. Opening my email, I typed a new address in the box:

cressidaofficial@gmail.com and started typing frantically.

Cressi!

I've done something really stupid!

Remember the guy we talked about? The biologist whose name I didn't know. I found it out. It's Ansgar. And do you know how I found it out? Because I chased the whole day after him in the woods and found him up a cliff. I tried to climb after him and I fell, so he pulled me into his arms and climbed with me—while I was still in his arms cuddling the hell out of his pecs—onto this magical plateau to see the sunset and it was the most beautiful thing I have seen in my life. As in really, it was fascinating!!!! And he just sat there, next to me, watching, we shared this moment, like our souls were fucking each other or something. And when night fell, he grabbed me in his arms again and I freaking nestled there like I was a duckling with the mother. I even smelled his hair, which smells amazing by the way, like orange and fresh earth. You know, right after the rain stops and there is that smell of fresh?

Anyway, not only that I cuddled the guy. After that, he asked if I wanted him to take me home and we HELD HANDS all the way to the house! And you know what else? He kissed my hand! Yeah, like I was some kind of princess or something and then he just left.

I can almost see you reading this with your 'you go girl' face, so change it immediately!

I don't plan on seeing the guy EVER again! I won't even get out of the house for the next month until my stupid brain settles down.

Don't make any snarky remarks please, just give me some advice, I'm going crazy out here on my own and masturbating at the thought of the guy. NOT A WORD ABOUT THIS IN YOUR EMAIL! Just write back to me soon and tell me what to do. Love you.

Once I sent the chaotic email to Cressida, another dash of tension faded away. Putting my thoughts into words helped me dismiss some of the emotion.

I went into the kitchen and found some frozen raspberries and spinach to prepare a smoothie when an unexpected knock stopped me in place. At first, I did not know where it came from, it sounded like a knock on wood, dry and echoing across the kitchen, until I realised it resonated from the front door.

I checked the calendar where I started crossing out the days since the last delivery incident and confirmed it was Tuesday, then slowly walked to the door, just when another knock pierced across the hall. Picking up one of the knives I had placed around the house for safety, I opened the big carved wooden door, peeking my head to see who it was, leg propped up against the door to help me push it back if I needed to.

"Ansgar," I breathed, relief flooding me and allowing my heart to relax and occupy its rightful place back in my chest.

Ansgar

Chapter Twelve

Anwen glared at me through the cracked door, eyes wide with surprise and a smile illuminated her face, the door opening widely. I took a moment to breathe her image in. Her hair was wet, small drops of water dripping onto her breasts and diving towards their death into the towel she held wrapped around her. I did not blame them, who wouldn't want to dive into that gorgeously round chest? My vision dawdled, lingering onto the plumpness I mentally caressed, until she became aware of her minimal clothing and wrapped a hand around the towel to hold it in place. Only then I noticed the knife in her hand.

"There always seems to be a weapon involved every time we meet. The towel is a nice addition though," I put forward my best smile.

To my surprise, she blushed, her cheeks adopting a reddish-peach colour that made her look even more seductive.

"There always seems to be a smirk involved as well, most of the time on your behalf," she replied perkily then pushed her lower lip slightly through her teeth, biting at the touch.

Damn! This woman, I thought as my lower abdomen set on fire with this minimal gesture, my insides calling onto her touch.

"I... you forgot your pack," I mumbled, trying to act normal around the temptress.

None of the distraction mechanisms had worked and I did not understand why it was her and no other that made me feel like a lost puppy begging for crumbs. I had been passionate with other females, some of them I had kissed, caressed and enjoyed their bodies in different ways without fulfilling the complete sexual act. I had seen, touched and bitten breasts before and dampened my fingers and tongue in the sweetest places but I had always been able to stop, mind overpowering my want.

"Ansgar?"

I heard my name and snapped back to reality, thoughts buried in my already troubled head. She stared at me waiting for an answer, unfortunately, my eyes lost focus of the conversation and started wandering along her body, my brain spinning around, trying to memorise each part of her.

"Hm?"

"You can give me the backpack now," she said, obviously having to repeat herself.

Without saying anything, I removed it from my shoulder and passed it to her.

"Thank you," Anwen replied as she took back the object she left discarded on the cliff a night ago.

"You are welcome," I nodded and took a step back, eyes trying to grasp their full until she shifted to close the door. Another step and a part of me started aching, like something precious of mine was pulled away from my reach. She was still in my line of sight but the distance I created between us already started to hurt.

What was this? Why couldn't I let go? Why was my energy tied to hers?

Another step, and another as I forced myself to turn my back at her and put more distance between us. I heard the door pushed into its frame, leaving a screaming creak behind. Even the wood understood my pain and tried to shout for my return.

"Ansgar?" I heard my name and immediately stood back, surprised.

Anwen was still wrapped in the towel, her hair dripping on the entry porch as she stepped out of the house, walking to me. I approached her in a heartbeat, a wide smile setting itself onto my lips.

"It may sound silly but I…" the woman hesitated, stopping to think about what she wanted to say, analysing the effect her words would bring. "I don't know much about the forest. I came here to spend time on my own, I am not a scientist." With that she waited, her eyes scanning mine, trying to communicate the unspoken meaning of her phrase

"Would you like me to show you around?" I sprang at the opportunity.

"Yes!" she exclaimed joyously, the murmur of her heart beating a little faster.

"It would be my pleasure," I smiled widely and she replied with a tiny giggle, her excitement evident.

"I plan to go for a walk, after my shower," she added hesitantly, yet with boldness.

"I'll wait until you are changed and ready to go," I answered.

"Great, I won't be long," she breathed and ran back inside, door snapping shut behind her.

Within minutes, Anwen walked out the door again, this time wearing tight trousers and a longer t-shirt that caressed her curvy hips. No dagger or any other visible weapons, I noticed, just the backpack I had come to return. Her pink shoes left small marks on the fallen leaves as she hurried her steps to approach me.

"I brought some snacks in case we get hungry, and coke. I didn't know which one you like so I brought vanilla."

"Thank you," I replied, pleasantly surprised by the joyful attitude and without thinking about it, extended my hand to her, waiting for her to reattach to me and unbreak the severed connection the night had formed between us.

Anwen looked at my palm and dropped her gaze all the way to my fingers, inspecting my skin and potential touch, analysing the decision she was about to make, her lips puckering with the weight of the thoughts.

"Ansgar I…" she breathed, pushing the phrase further and forcing her lips to pronounce the words she clearly did not want to say, "I made a promise. I do not intend to break it."

I remained silent, examining her features. They had turned rough, unrelenting. She continued, "My brother died a year ago. It was sudden, unexpected." Her throat bobbed and she fought a dry noise threatening to escape. Tears inundated her eyes. "His name was Erik."

"I am sorry," I spoke sincerely. "I can't imagine the pain." I didn't even want to think what kind of feelings would torture me if anything happened to my brothers.

"Did you know him?" Her eyes pierced mine with determined inquisition.

"I did not," I replied immediately, a bit surprised by the question. "How could I?"

"Because he was here, in the forest. Looking for something." She shifted, distancing herself from my closeness, her steps cold. Anwen scanned me, my body language, trying to decipher something that was not there.

"I did not know your brother, Anwen. I am sorry he passed away, but I did not know him. I only came here a half-moon ago. For the first time," I added, deciding there was no harm in telling her about my arrival. Since she could easily piece that together with her attack.

"He was looking for something. Something in this forest. And I'm sure you might know what I'm talking about," she pushed, focusing on my eyes, tracing any sign of knowledge.

"How am I supposed to know what your deceased brother wanted?" I defended myself, but I had my suspicions. And if humans knew about it, we were all doomed.

"I promised him I would find it. And I will not rest until I do." Her words protruded with force and I sensed her determination. I also knew I had to shut it down.

"How can you make such a promise? How can you decide such a thing, without even caring what it might do?"

"Because I am decided," she replied with coldness.

"You shouldn't be doing this, Anwen. you are too young and you are punishing yourself...for what? People die. You are chasing ghosts around here."

It was the wrong thing to say. She erupted, a tornado of rage and hurt overcoming the sweet woman I had come to know.

"You don't know me! You do not get to tell me what I am supposed to feel! You do not get to decide. Do you know why I came here? Because I was sick and tired of men who think they know best. My dad, my shrink, my ex, my professors, a bunch of silly men who think they can decide what women are supposed to feel. What I am supposed to do." She stopped to take a breath.

"I didn't mean—" I tried to defend myself, to calm her down, but her monstrous rage turned beyond salvaging.

"To what? To assume you know best? To think that a poor defenceless woman in a forest needs a man to take care of her? Is that your assumption?" she screamed, her voice resounding in the woods.

"Please let me speak!" It was my turn to raise my voice, if only to make myself heard over her reverberating accusations.

"No! You do not get to have an opinion on my life, and you do not get to bring your sexy self in here and frolic in this forest like it belongs to you. I loved my brother. I owe this to him! If I see you again roaming around, I will call the guard and report you. And if you interfere with my search, I will make sure you get arrested." The wind scattered her threat as she turned and, without another word, went back inside, slamming the door.

I remained grounded, immobilised by what had happened and the sheer force of this woman, eyes wide and too shocked to move a muscle. No one had scolded me in such a way in my entire existence and I did not know how to react. At least one of the words she used to describe me was *sexy*, I consoled my wounded ego.

Anwen

Chapter Thirteen

The utter nerve on that man! I rushed back into the house, abandoning my pack by the door and regretting my poor lack of judgement. Not a mistake to be repeated in the future, I promised myself. Huffing with anger, I took the laptop from the kitchen and removed it from the cloud decorated cover, then flipped it and glared at the desktop image.

A notification beeped and an email from Cressida popped up on the screen. Grinding my teeth with anger, I clicked it open and started to read.

Girl, that's what I want to hear!

Kudos my love, you finally became a woman! Masturbating at the thought of a guy you just met? Who are you and what have you done with my friend?

Just kidding, don't freak out. DO NOT FREAK OUT, seriously, you didn't do anything worth telling. You held hands with a guy and he carried you up and down the stairs, big deal! If you were eighty and a young gorgeous man held your hand and carried you up and down the stairs it would be considered civic duty.

It is what ten year olds do and they don't tell their parents! So a twenty-five-year-old woman doing the same thing is a cute vanilla moment and nothing more.

Love you, text me if you want to chat tonight!

If only I had waited another hour to send this to my friend, I would have known what a liar Ansgar was and could have avoided all this mess. He was hiding something. I knew it even though I couldn't prove it. The only thing I believed from our conversation was that he did not know my brother. So any hope of finding out more about Erik vanished, along with any trepidations my heart had felt in Ansgar's presence.

I clicked the reply button and typed:

All sorted.

He turned out to be a prick. He came to see me this morning to return something I left in the woods and we went for a walk. Ten minutes in, he started judging me and telling me what I should feel. Honestly, he may be freaking sexy but he seems to be living in the middle ages.

I'm fine, I'll keep busy, no need to chat tonight, I know you have a thousand things to do, the last thing you need right now is to virtually babysit my silly self.

Love you too.

After pressing the send button, I scrolled through instagram and checked new photos and the company socials, lingered for a while on pinterest and searched youtube for curious things. When I checked the time, I realised that part of my bad mood was because I hadn't eaten breakfast and it was 3pm already, so I stood up and headed back to the kitchen, flip flops trotting as I walked.

The fridge brimmed with choices, as always, there were all kinds of fruits and veggies, cheese, marmalade, delicatessen, even Jell-O. None of them caught my attention since the void in my stomach had persisted even at the thought of food. I regretted walking away when he tried to explain his meaning, a part of me regretted not giving him a chance to speak, to defend himself and his point of view, yet I was proud with the rush of adrenaline that had pulsated through me in that moment of pure passion. One very silly part of my brain, the one that I was trying to shut down the most, worried about hurting his feelings.

In the end, all he wanted was to enjoy a walk and ended up with a crazy woman defending a crazy mission her deceased brother might have sent her on. It must have sounded mad. I must have sounded like a lunatic.

My stomach twisted again, trying to choke down the guilt that creeped up into me as I closed the fridge door and opened the freezer. Another frozen pizza it is. Lately it had become my food of choice and even though I knew it would make my mother furious, I did not care. I had always been proud of my curves and every time I had to pose for a magazine, they would use photoshop and adjust my figure anyway. So what was the harm in another frozen pizza with garlic dip? Nothing drowned sorrow better than melting mozzarella.

I chose a mushroom pizza and placed it in the oven, setting the timer, then I opened the second fridge and started rummaging for any kind of cold alcohol. I never had anything straight, except for tequila and caramel vodka, but those didn't count, so I tried to find something refreshing and alcoholic, settling for a can of ready mixed cosmopolitan. It would not get me drunk but maybe it would give me the slight buzz to help me relax.

Waiting for the oven to sound, I went back to the laptop, the only constant companion I had these days, and opened my research file to check some of the information from the videos I had previously watched about the forest. Another knock interrupted the quiet and made me startle. This time, choosing curiosity over caution, I leaped from the chair and ran towards the entrance, losing one of my green flip flops along the way.

As soon as I opened the door, the flow of oxygen returned into my body and gave me lightness, allowing me to fully breathe since I had entered the house. On the porch, Ansgar stood with a bouquet of wild flowers and a basket of mushrooms, looking embarrassed and wary, possibly expecting another rage attack. When I opened the door, he took a step back and extended the bouquet, trying to signal his peace offering before I started criticising him again.

His view set on me, body tense, taking a defensive position, his other hand holding tight onto the basket of mushrooms. I looked at him from head to toe, taking the time to properly analyse him. He was wearing boots and grey trousers that hung low onto his naval, a long sleeved shirt covering his torso, lax enough to let him move comfortably but tight enough to embrace his muscles and force his biceps to stretch the sleeves. His hair draped his shoulders, as always, strands hanging free with only a few braids that seemed to be strategically created to keep it out of his face.

"I came to apologise," he took the reins of the conversation, stretching the bouquet so much towards me that the flowers practically tickled my nose. "I am sorry, I had no intention to make you feel like you had to explain yourself," he stuttered. "Please forgive me," he bowed his head apologetically.

The oven decided to finish cooking the pizza at that exact moment and started beeping so loudly that we both flinched at the noise.

"Sorry," I said and went back into the kitchen to turn it off. I allowed a smile to shape my lips into a new form. As soon as I stopped the noise and opened the oven door, I returned towards the entrance where Ansgar still waited, surprised by the interruption.

"I am sorry too," I replied while grabbing hold of the flowers he kept extended, his hand relaxing and enjoying the new freedom. "I probably exaggerated and did not give you an opportunity to defend your point of view."

He nodded in acceptance, shoulders relaxing and chest falling slightly, like he had been holding in a breath since he first knocked.

Another smile crept up on my lips and I made no effort to contain it. "Why do you have a basket full of mushrooms?"

He looked down at the crate, at the fat mushrooms arranged deliciously inside, forming different shapes and sizes.

"They are my favourite, I thought you might enjoy them. I brought them as an alternative to the flowers in case you decided to throw them at me." His lips curled into a smirk and that damn fluttering in my stomach almost raised a storm at the sight of it. Of him. "I hoped you would at least accept the food," he turned towards the basket, admiring his arrangement.

"What am I supposed to do with wild mushrooms?" I chuckled. He looked surprised, not understanding my point and checked the basket in his hand, then extended it to me as he did the flowers moments earlier.

"Make a stew?" he replied, the expression of innocence portrayed across his beautiful features.

"I can't cook that well," I raised my hands defensively.

A provocative grin replaced his innocence. "Do you want me to teach you?"

"I do," I replied without hesitation, more out of instinct than a rational decision and moved away from the door to allow him to enter. He did so wearily, looking around and taking in the grandeur of the place, like a deer walking in the open field.

What the hell was I doing? I had barely been allowed to stay in this mansion, in this protected place, my dad had to pull all the strings in the world to offer me the most exclusive peace and quiet ever known to man. And here I was, inviting a stranger in a home that was not mine, whose illegal walks through the forest I hadn't reported to cook mushroom stew?

Not only was I disrespecting the mansion and its history, I was hiding a trespasser and allowing him to enter the small palace, a place almost as protected as the forest around it.

My face must have been a reflection of my thoughts because he stopped in place and looked at me with concern, then took a step back towards the entryway.

"Do you want me to leave?" he murmured, an offer he clearly did not want to make, judging by his barely audible voice.

"Do you have a phone on you?" I scanned him, his pockets, looking for a mobile phone.

"I do not," he chuckled at the ridicule of the question. "Why would I carry a phone?"

"This place is very precious, a gift from the King of Sweden to his Queen, almost nobody can enter. I was allowed here because of the friendship of the royal family with my own." I took the time to explain it in detail, all the while giving myself a minute to reconsider the invitation. "I had to sign so many NDAs just to be able to step on these grounds and I cannot risk it if you are going to publish anything about this place or even photograph a single painting. I could be kicked out," I bit my lip with concern.

"You can blindfold me and I will dictate the recipe to you," he offered with dead seriousness, his face still and pure. I wondered if he would be willing to do it, if it was not just a joke and my lower belly twitched at the thought of a blindfolded Ansgar, with only his lips available for the taking.

"That's ok, we'll leave the blindfolding for another time," my flirtatious-self replied. "Just please don't tell anyone you've been here, not even on instagram and don't take any pictures. Promise me." I paused, my entire body still as I looked at him with seriousness. He had to understand how important this was.

As a response, Ansgar raised his right hand and placed it over his chest, then intoned solemnly "I, Ansgar of Sylvan Regnum, vow to you Anwen..." he stopped and looked at me inquisitively, until I realised he wanted to know my surname.

"Odstar," I answered, to which he nodded, adopted the solemn features once more and started again.

"I, Ansgar of Sylvan Regnum, vow to you Anwen Odstar that I shall not reveal my visit to this residence to anyone of The Instagram nor will I take photographs of the interior of this mansion." He finished with a reassuring smile.

Ignoring the kaleidoscope of butterflies swarming through my stomach, I grabbed the basket he had left on the floor and walked into the kitchen. The oven emanated heat from the pizza I had planned to eat, now abandoned on the countertop.

"You were already eating?" Ansgar asked as he followed into the kitchen and sniffed around, his eyes finding the pizza that was still hot enough to expel a little steam.

"It's just a frozen pizza, I can reheat it later," I said as I opened a drawer to find aluminium foil to cover the plate and save it for dinner. I did not want to waste food, but I couldn't refuse a reason to spend more time with this man either. As I ripped in the foil, stretching it enough to cover the plate, I noticed that his sight lingered on the countertop, a lustful expression accompanying a barely perceptible bite of his lips.

"Would you like some?" I asked, discovering how the plate had his full attention.

He nodded, possibly an involuntary gesture, then immediately added. "No, thank you. I shouldn't."

"Are you worried about the calories?" I chuckled. "Through a happy coincidence, it's a mushroom pizza, so not as many."

"No...thank you," he confirmed, eyes still lost on the plate.

"Do you have dietary restrictions?" From my experience, guys were all over carbs, it helped them build muscle. Erik always had about three servings of pasta with every meal. I did not know what kind of carbs, only that everyone I ever met at the university gym was 'bulking up' and all the boys ate every few hours. Judging by Ansgar's physique, he must need at least three or four thousand calories a day, especially if he was working out to maintain that fully toned body of his, so a pizza shouldn't present any inconvenience for a man of his stature.

"I don't know if I would like it," he continued, staring at the plate as if the pizza would grow legs and start running around the kitchen.

"What kind of pizza do you enjoy? This is just sauce, cheese and some kind of mushroom, I didn't add any dips to it."

He remained silent, his gaze shifting to face me and I stared at him, expecting an answer. He looked tense, shoulders raised in discomfort. At last, he confessed, "I never had a pizza before," and frowned a little when my mouth dropped to the floor.

"How is that possible?" I exclaimed in disbelief.

"My family prefers more natural food," he clarified quickly, though it didn't seem like a subject he wanted to get into.

"Oh, gluten free, no preserves and all that?" I remarked while opening another drawer to find the pizza cutter.

"Sure..." I heard him say while slicing the delicious plate in eight fairly even portions.

"I promise, you are going to be having the time of your life with this," I announced and placed the plate on the kitchen table, close to where Ansgar leaned against one of the cupboards.

At first, he looked at it wearily as if considering his choice but the smell must have overpowered his indecision because he stood straight and his hand reached a slice, holding it and gently moved it towards his mouth. He sniffed it a few times and looked back at me for confirmation, then took the world's tiniest bite, chewing only with his front teeth.

One moment he was his normal self, as far as I knew from our little time spent together, and the next his eyes were wide, scanning the food with rapid movements to help his brain process the taste. Then he took another bite, this time, his mouth opening fully as he got as much of the slice in as possible and chewed eagerly.

"Good, huh?" I said with satisfaction while Ansgar smiled at me widely, proud of this new achievement. Letting him enjoy a second slice, I went to the fridge and brought more sauces. If I was the one to make him lose his pizza-virginity, I might as well do it right. It turned out that we had the same preference, first garlic dip, then barbeque, with ketchup and mayo on the third and fourth place, not as relevant in the life of a pizza. I also wanted a slice, so I poured on a generous amount of dip and shoved it into my mouth.

"That is delicious," he smiled at me widely. "Thank you. I will look into getting some for myself."

"You can take anything you wish from my fridge, I get a delivery every week so I am always fully stocked," I offered as curiosity about his living arrangements popped into my head. How was this man getting his food? How did he find the house where I first woke up? Was he sneaking around town and popping back in past the guards every time he felt like it?

"Now it's my turn," he announced and grabbed the mushroom

basket he had brought, walking towards the sink and opening the tap to wash them. He asked for a bowl, a knife and a cutting board, which I provided wordlessly, then started to take each mushroom out of the basket and wash it, placing it in the big wooden bowl I had set by the side of the sink.

"Tell me more about yourself?" I tried to push the question directly but casually, making it sound like it just popped into my head and wanted to make small talk while I searched through the spice cabinet without even knowing what we needed. I figured salt and pepper at least, so I tried to appear busy searching for them.

"What do you wish to know?" he asked with the same casual tone, turning from his task at the kitchen sink. The way he towered over it, how his sleeves were raised on his massive forearms and his stance made him look like a diamond in a pile of coal. He had such a commanding presence, as though he was born to be regal, every single movement he made elegant, spreading drops of flair all around him.

Anything, everything, I thought but said, "When did you come here? How? Where are you from? What is your full name? Why are you studying plants? Where do you work and live when you are not foraging for mushrooms? You know, just the general things."

He turned his head in my direction, then raised an eyebrow in surprise. "Are those general things or an interrogation?" Ansgar glared, his eyes scanning mine inquisitively.

I blushed, yet pushed. "Excuse me for wanting to make sure you are not a serial killer," I defended myself.

"Especially since we already ruled out that I am not a rapist," he added, not taking his eyes off me. Heat exploded in my cheeks and I could not take it any longer, so I turned back to the spice cabinet, trying to hide as much of my face behind the door.

"I come from further away, I was not born in this country," I heard him speak and managed to escape a quick look to see that he had returned to his task washing the mushrooms in the sink. "I have two older brothers, Damaris and Vikram, the first one is married to a...doctor. My mother and father have important administrative duties over a lot of...beings."

It was evident that he measured his words, sometimes stopping to find the most appropriate ones. I did not dare interrupt him, not when he was opening up to me. I assumed he was translating in his head from whatever his native language was, even though most of the time he spoke perfect English. I knew better than to ask about his nationality, judging by his tanned skin he was not Swedish. So I continued to bang jars and glass containers, trying to look busy and listening to whatever information he offered. A lot more than I ever told him about myself.

"Both my brothers are soldiers, but I love plants. I have studied them since childhood and I am very good at it. So here I am, at my twenty-seven years of age, in a place far away from the world, peeling mushrooms for a stranger living in the house of a queen."

I did not see it but I knew he grinned under his breath, as he pronounced the words. Provoking me.

"My father," I defended myself. "He managed to secure six months in this place for me."

"Oh?" It came his turn to ask for details.

"My father owns Odstar Cosmetics," I sighed at the big reveal, knowing full well what was about to happen. Every time I told someone about my origin, they automatically assumed I knew everyone, asked about my fabulous supposed-to-be-lifestyle and always ended up with them asking for tons of products free of charge, which I didn't mind most of the time, but did not want people to identify me with the glamorous lifestyle we were advertising, especially Ansgar. I knew full well that I was not the ideal image for a cosmetics company, I did not have the perfect shape and owned a few kilos over. I had breakouts on my period, oily skin and big pores.

Ansgar's face remained utterly blank, moving his head from side to side with an apologetic shake. "I am sorry, I don't know what that is," he replied. I took in a long breath of relief.

"It's just a business," I waved my hand and continued, more relaxed. "He had a long connection with the royal family and he asked them if I could stay for a while, since I needed some time to myself. At least that's what I told him."

"Again, I am sorry about your brother," he added quickly. "Please do not feel forced to talk about it if it causes you more harm than good."

I swallowed the urge to cry, which came every time the thought of Erik found itself in conversation. "It's been hard...harder even lately." He paused and gazed at me, his grey eyes absorbing my feelings, and I felt strong enough to continue. "It's so difficult without him. When I was back at home, I kept expecting him to pop up from his room, walk to the dinner table, or post a video from whatever fancy location. But he is gone, and there's nothing I can do." He paused and gazed at me and I felt strong enough to continue. "It's so difficult without him."

Ansgar took a seat on a nearby chair, hands resting on his shoulder, vision fixed on me. He didn't say a word, allowing me to find my pace.

"After his death, I went back to campus. Tried to live, but everything was grey. Meaningless. So I returned home. I hoped that the closeness to the place where we grew up might help. He was such an amazing big brother. We grew up building pillow forts and he read me all the big boy stories about Pokémon and whatever cartoons were in fashion that mom wouldn't let me watch. He always supported me, no matter what. He dragged me with him to all the parties I could not go to on my own, and he stayed far enough to let me enjoy myself but always close in case I needed him. When I got into his room and found it empty…that was when it truly hit me. The realisation. That he would never come back. That I've lost him forever."

Half an hour later, the stew was boiling at reduced heat on the stove and Ansgar had listened to my story, barely muttering a word and nodding from time to time to let me know he understood. He had two brothers, and by his reaction, they seemed close. I don't know why, but I told him Erik's last words. I had only confided in Cressi about that. I confessed the meaninglessness I felt, not wanting to carry on, knowing I was the worthless half, the one that no one wanted but was stuck with. As I said it, I could not contain the tears and let them escape down my cheek.

Ansgar was by my side in a heartbeat, cupping my face with calloused palms and brushing the tears away.

"You are worth it, Anwen." The shadows in his eyes danced, sending waves of light into mine, some sort of connection that was weaving between us. I raised my hands to his chest, resting them over his heart. Its steadiness made me feel at ease, at home. I had finally found the place where I needed to be. He shivered, awakened from a trance.

"I must go, there are projects that require my attention this afternoon," he declared, not moving his gaze from mine, as though he too wanted to prolong the touch.

"Would you like to go on another walk tomorrow?" I blurted out, surprising even myself at the impulsive invitation. "Without a fight this time?" I felt the need to add.

He smiled and shifted, his lips on my own, placing a surprisingly gentle kiss. Which ended as abruptly as it began. The next second, Ansgar headed out the door.

Ansgar

Chapter Fourteen

What in the Goddess' name had I done? For the entirety of the afternoon, I cursed my stupidity and selfishness. I was constantly breaking the rules, had other faeries witnessing my encounter with the human and I even notified the creatures under my command to stay hidden so I had undisturbed time alone with Anwen. Whatever I was thinking, or wasn't, needed to stop immediately. I pleaded a grateful prayer to the sky for displaying a full moon that night. It allowed me to return home and leave the district, and with it, my obsession with Anwen.

Making sure the sjorkas had everything under control and nothing major required attention for the evening, I anointed my bare feet with galanthus powder and walked in a circle around the roots of one of the newly flourished Cloutie trees until the powder my tracks left behind loosened from my soles and formed a white ring into the moist ground.

Once the portal opened, I leaped inside and touched one of the extended roots, whispering the name of the fae town I grew up in.

Within a flash of light, I found myself in the forest back home, the familiar smell of baked pumpkin seeds floating through the air and tickling my nose.

During a full moon, the fae always served seed bakes to celebrate the cyclicality of the Earth. It was a way to connect the planet with its night guardian that had been celebrated for centuries, in which the men returning from their districts to visit family members and future mates received their welcome back into the realm with honour and cakes. Since childhood, I loved the tradition and when my older brothers fulfilled their keeper assignments, I would wake up at dawn, picking seeds and planning the bakes, tasting each one to insure deliciousness until my tummy hurt.

At night, with the moon hung in the sky, I would accompany the other children and females to receive the keepers and offer them a seed baked goodie from a tray so big and heavy I could barely carry it. Damaris was more preoccupied with his future bride than with me, but Vikram always made sure to take the very first cake from my tray and to enjoy a big bite.

As I walked out of the forest, the line of children and eligible females was already forming, each holding a tray of baked goods. Some of them did not wait for a specific male and only wanted to be noticed and show their relationship availability. The trays and baskets were decorated with flowers or honey, making the cakes smell and look incredible.

A gasp of pride captured my senses, all problems left aside. I became part of something bigger, I was one of the fae in charge with the protection of the realm and for better or worse, I had managed to get to the full moon and returned home safely, without any destruction or incidents within the district, apart from the first day when Rhylan decided to pay a visit.

I made a mental note to report it to Vikram, but did not have to wait long to see my brother again, as I spotted him standing in the first line, alongside other women and children, accompanied by the entire royal family. I smiled widely and forgetting all dignity and grandeur, I ran directly into my mother's arms, causing her to drop the tray, cakes falling into the grass.

The Queen gasped in surprise, then placed her arms around me and squeezed me tightly. As I finally let her go, I turned towards my father, who patted my shoulder with love, an adult form of greeting I did not receive many times. I bowed to the King, who returned the gesture and reached for one of the cakes he held on a small silver platter.

With a smile, I took a big bite and escaped a moan at the peach filling that inundated my mouth. Peach had always been my favourite, present in all major celebrations, birthdays, name days, award days. My first return home should have been no exception. With my lips covered in sugar and a second mouthful preventing me from speaking, I looked at my brothers, who towered at the other side of the Queen, each holding a tray and giggling.

"Baby brother's worthy of his own cakes!" Vikram exclaimed as a form of greeting and extended his tray, forcing me to take another cake while Damaris bit his lips shut, making sure no sound exited his mouth. Vikram insisted, enticing me to take a bite of the cake I had just grabbed from the tray, so I did. It took less than five seconds

138

for my entire face to turn crimson, eyes wide and lips purple.

Damaris couldn't hold it anymore and started laughing hysterically, his shrieks echoing through the woods, where other keepers constantly emerged from. Vikram started laughing too, while I choked and spat as much as my mouth allowed from the fire that had inundated my mouth with a vile taste.

The Queen peered at us, petrified, while the King turned towards his sons, perplexed, wearing a serious expression that demanded an immediate explanation.

"We made a special cake for our brother," Damaris offered innocently.

"With capsicum chinense," Vikram added, laughing so much that he had to grab his belly. Father looked shocked for a split second, then started laughing alongside his boys, while Mother offered me another peach-filled cake to take away the burning taste from my mouth, while scolding her two oldest.

"You two, I can't believe it! Making fun of your brother on his first return home!" she disputed.

"It's the last chance we get, Mother!" Damaris argued. "After this, he will be too busy chasing females," he defended himself while pulling my still coughing self by the shoulder and patting me affectionately on the back. Vikram followed and they proceeded to walk towards the town square, guiding me through the gathering crowd.

After taking care of some of the administrative duties, where the King made a speech to welcome all the keepers who had travelled back home for the first time and asked them to report any incidents to one of the members of the guard in charge, displaying me to the population yet again and mentioning my assignment location, just to make sure everyone knew that I was caring for the Evigt Forest, we headed back to the palace to have a late family dinner.

The table lay arranged as per usual, with the King and Queen occupying their places at each end, with Vikram and me on one side and Damaris and Takara on the other. It was a cosy and familiar setting, during these family dinners we could forget about all titles and duties and become a family, casually dining and celebrating the return of the youngest son.

I asked about events in the past few days and the queen gladly talked me through the changes in the gardens, the new species some of the masters worked on and the preparations for my marking ceremony which was only three months away. In turn, Damaris told me about the situation in the guard and how they prepared a different assembly, while Takara remained quiet and only raised her shoulders, all the confirmation I needed that there had been no advancements with the creation of a nephew.

The King ate and listened, adding some information from time to time and asking only specific questions that affected his dealings with the other fae in high positions. When Vikram's turn came, a wild grin possessed my brother's face. "Four earthlings, a waterling and two women," to which the Queen scoffed and threw her napkin into her son's soup, splashing liquid all over his shirt.

I chuckled, along with the rest of the table, then adopted a more serious posture.

"There is something to report with regards to the realm

protection," I added gravely and all the family quieted, facing me in wait for more details. I looked at the King, then at my brother and added: "Fear Gorta is back." The King bashed his knife into his plate, creating a sharp ring, while Vikram growled in disgust.

"Where?" was all the King said.

"In the district. In the cave," I carefully added, trying not to create more urgency than I needed to. "The very first morning."

Father stood abruptly and pushed his chair back with a thump, making Takara sitting next to him skid with a fright.

"It was in your home?" he roared and started walking across the room, taking big, angry steps. I maintained my calm and replied, "It adopted the figure of a male, tall, dark hair and eyes, sharp features. It calls itself Rhylan Gordon, apparently he took the name in Macedonia."

Vikram shifted towards me, any fraction of a smile long disappeared from his lips. "Do you need guards?"

"No," I quickly added, "there is no need, I wounded him with the opal sword and he disappeared, for the time being."

"What was it doing there? What sort of business does Fear Gorta have in Catalina's burial place?" the King enquired bitterly.

I raised my shoulders. "He tortured a human, a woman living in the forest. He wanted to use her as a blood sacrifice on my first day."

"This is outrageous!" the furious King exclaimed, this time supporting his balance on Mother's chair, who was looking at each of us, stunned.

"What is the state of the woman?" Vikram asked.

"She is fine, did not bleed, only a few bruises and a scare. I

141

monitored her for a few days to make sure she was alright," I announced while the thought of Anwen made my stomach twist and pulse accelerate. I hadn't just 'monitored' her, I had touched her, held her and found any excuse to spend more time with her. And kissed her.

"I had to make myself visible a few times," I looked down at my plate, then threw a quick gaze towards the Queen, awaiting her reaction. She waved it off and relief ran through every muscle of my tense self.

"We'll deal with that later," she disregarded and I caught another breath. The Queen was the one who commanded over the magic of the realm, whatever and however it was used and she had the supreme authority to impart judgement over any offences made, whenever they were not located in one of the fae territories. She could have very well asked for one of my arms to be cut off just because I had revealed myself to a human, but she was too concerned with the presence of the Fear Gorta to care about what seemed, in comparison, a minor incident.

After convincing the King and my brother that Rhylan had not returned in the following days of my stay and the event was dismissed as an isolated incident, we continued to dine and eat more of the seed cakes, though none of us truly relaxed.

A few glasses of wine, some tense jokes and we prepared to retire for the night, not before the Queen made sure that I had all things necessary at the cave and asked me to make a list of whatever food and equipment I needed restocked. She kissed all three of her sons and grabbed the King's arm to accompany him into their chambers. Vikram lingered a while longer, then excused himself, wanting to speak to his men and ask for reports of Fear Gorta sightings in other districts. He bid his farewell and offered some battle advice, then went over the protocol of sounding the alarm in the district and made a joke about the spice cake coming down, then disappeared from the dining room.

"Other than that, how are things?" Damaris asked when just the three of us were left in the room. Takara chuckled and placed one of her hands comfortably on her husband's shoulder. The familiarity of that single gesture was enviable, I had always admired the relationship between the two.

"What my insensitive husband means to ask," she intervened as she affectionately flicked Damaris' cheek, causing him to giggle, "is that we heard many young eligible females talking about how they plan to come greet you on your return."

I smiled and took a long sip of wine, guessing where this was going. The perfect couple wanted to form another couple, and seeing how Vikram had gone his own way, their directions turned towards the youngest of the family. I wanted to immediately dismiss the conversation, but the feelings for Anwen stopped me. There was no better way to find out exactly what was happening than asking these two.

"Basically," Damaris took reins of the question and stopped dodging his intentions, "we want to know if you already like someone or if we should start to casually invite females over so you can meet them."

"There goes the tact we discussed earlier," Takara raised her hands defeatedly and sat on her chair after choosing another cake from the table.

"There may be someone," I said and the two immediately stood straighter on the chair, giving me their full attention and absorbing my words and gestures. "I am not sure yet."

"Who is she?" Damaris enquired but Takara patted his arm to calm him down. She adopted a sweeter tone and turned to me, "Is there anything we can help you with?" she asked gently.

I scratched the back of my head, arranging one of my small braids. "I don't really know," I admitted with a frown, "what I am supposed to be feeling."

My sister nodded, barely breathing from fear of losing any details I might divulge, so I continued. "She is beautiful, very, very beautiful," I felt the need to emphasize, "and very attractive. She is smart and determined, very funny when she wants to and snarky at times, especially if I say something she doesn't like. She makes me feel…" I paused to think for a while, "happy when I am with her, and restless when I am away," I tried to explain. Before I was through analysing my own feelings, the two shifted, barely managing to remain seated, fidgeting in their chairs.

"That's your mate!" they both exclaimed the phrase in perfect synchrony.

I only looked at them, expressionless, my eyes bouncing up and down as they were fixed on the happy couple.

"Who is she? Are you going to see her tonight?" Damaris asked and took a celebratory drink from his cup.

Here came the part I dreaded to mention, knowing fully well the effect it would have on the moment.

"Tonight is the only night I *can't* see her," I emphasized, making sure my words were clear. Not clear enough it seemed, as the heir to the throne and his mate looked at me with confusion painted on their serene faces.

"She is the woman I mentioned earlier, the one in the forest," I added and immediately the two broke their hug and relaxed their bodies, taking back their respective seats. Takara looked disappointed while Damaris uttered, "That's not your mate then, it's just a woman you want to have sex with."

"How can you be sure?" I insisted. "Do you think Vikram feels this with his...everyone?" It was easier to say that than enumerate the number of species my brother had proudly joined with.

"You are young and inexperienced. In a way, it's normal that the first woman you see sparks curiosity."

"She is not the first woman I saw!" I pointlessly defended myself, but Damaris dismissed me. "Just fuck her," he casually advised, just as his wife bit into another cake, causing her to choke on the sugar drizzle.

"Damaris!" she reprimanded.

"What?" he defended himself. "Humans have protection measures and he can gain some experience, have some fun and not be punished for it. You've seen how Mother didn't care that he revealed himself to a human."

My brother turned to me, "Let him reveal himself completely," he smiled slyly.

Takara shook her head in disapproval, then intervened. "You do

145

not need to do anything, Ansgar. The right female will come and you will find happiness with your mate."

I nodded in thanks, then finished the wine and rose, bidding the couple a good night. Before I was out the door, Damaris stopped me with a hand on the shoulder and whispered, looking me dead in the eye, "Go have some fun with the human, get it out of your system, then focus on finding your mate and come back home. You have a duty to this kingdom."

I bowed my head, acknowledging the truth of my brother's words.

Anwen

Chapter Fifteen

Rest did not call on me that night. I twisted and turned under the satin bed sheets that were supposed to offer relief and comfort, instead they felt like pins and needles around me. I didn't want to speak to anyone and sent emails to my family to notify them that I needed to go to bed early and could not be around for our daily chat. I hoped that the night would be a good companion and offer some clear thoughts, but the only thing the stars did was remind me that morning was a few hours away.

Ever since Ansgar left, I craved for him and lingered in the kitchen until late afternoon just because I did not feel prepared to get away from the scent he had left behind. Whatever perfume that man used, it was driving me crazy. *Be honest, Anwen, it's not the perfume.* There was nothing to do to stop thinking about him. I tried reading, writing in a journal, eating the damned mushroom stew that turned out so delicious it made me moan with delight, watching one of the shows I had followed for several seasons that always seemed to get my mind off things, and even went jogging at 1 am. Nothing worked and I was too afraid to take a shower or a hot bath because I did not trust my head or my fingers anymore.

The way this man made me feel, it was not normal. Whenever I was with him, the world stopped, I only focused on our interaction and that connection we were building, stretching and growing stronger with each gaze, each touch. I'd seen him only three times, but recognised what was happening. To my body, to my mind. I decided not to allow it. I did not have time for it, I could not lose myself to him and I had very limited time in this place. Nor could I allow any distractions.

I knew exactly what needed to be done and what the right decision was: stop seeing Ansgar altogether. I could not lie to myself anymore and hope to only be friends, because one does not want to devour their friends and come back for seconds.

Knowing full well that I would not be able to find rest, I pulled the sheets away and jumped out of the bed, walking into the drawing room which I seldom used. It was equipped with everything I needed to write a letter.

Ansgar,

Thank you for everything, for taking care of my wound that day, for having the patience to explain what happened and sharing a wonderful sunset together, for the mushrooms and for teaching me how to cook a stew.

As you know, we are both here with a specific plan and I have to focus on mine. Unfortunately, I will not be able to make today's walk and I do not think I can spare time on other days either.

Best of luck with your projects and I hope the research goes well.

Take care,

Anwen

I found an envelope and wrote *Ansgar* in big letters, then folded the paper and shoved it inside, licking the borders to stick it together.

I felt like a coward, an immature girl, incapable of balancing my feelings. All the more reason to stay away. I went downstairs and found some tape in one of the drawers, opened the entry door and stuck the letter on the outside. Then closed it and locked it. The next logical step was to go into hiding and I chose the only windowless room I had access to, locking myself inside at the first fracture of light in the morning sky.

There were 1037 tiles in the bathroom. I had counted them three times over, making sure to always start at a different one. Each time I carefully placed a marker, to avoid over counting or doubling up. The most difficult stop had been under the skirting, as some of the tiles were cracked by the pipes that had been replaced several times. I decided to count the ones that still held over seventy percent of their capacity as one and the tiny corners and cracked ones I ignored, as they did not hold sufficient material to be considered a full tile themselves.

Once I finished with the tiles, I scrubbed the sink and the bathtub twice, using the lemon descaling solution I found in one of the cupboards in the far corner. Then I continued with the large mirror. I first scrubbed it with what had now become my old toothbrush since I had already used the only available brush on the sink and bathtub, carefully going over every square inch of the surface with surgical precision.

I rearranged the towels, did a load of laundry while relishing in the wild noise that covered everything else and when the wash was finished and ready to hang, I decided it didn't look clean enough so I shoved the clothes back in and set the longest program, then sat on the floor next to the noisily vibrating washing machine and remained crouched by the wall until, two hours and a half later, it started beeping.

After what seemed an agonisingly long time, I mustered the courage to crack open the bathroom door just wide enough to spy into the bedroom, which I insured had fully covered windows and nothing could be seen inside the house, just like the drawing room and every single window in the sitting room and kitchen.

I relaxed when my eyes spotted darkness, which meant it had to be past eight in the evening and my mandatory self-exile could come to an end.

Ever since I wrote the letter, my heart palpitated with terrifying abruptness and the best option turned out to be self-isolation from anything that might make me change my mind or force me to have contact with Ansgar. I'd locked the door three times and closed the drapes on every single window to prevent anything inside the house from being seen. As if that weren't enough, I barricaded myself into the bathroom, to make sure I quarantined every sound he could possibly make when finding the letter.

If he knocked on the door to ask for an explanation, cussed me for wasting his time or shouted my name at the entrance, I did not want to know, so I kept myself locked away until the night offered me protection. Relief flowed over me as I opened the door wider and stepped out into the bedroom that was enveloped in darkness.

Feeling grateful for the cover of the night, I removed some of the pillows splayed on the bed, making enough room to fit onto it. The anxiety that shadowed me throughout the day turned into sweet relief, the throbbing relaxed and I let myself fall into a deep sleep.

Two weeks passed since I placed the letter on the door and during this time, I had barely left the house. One of the days following the letter, still in my bedroom, I heard a loud knock and my heart skipped a beat, until Isak announced his presence and I hurried to the door to unblock it and open it for him. The guard pushed the door wide open to allow himself to enter with all the bags he carried, along with the printer I had requested to have installed. I allowed myself to peak outside long enough to notice that the letter had disappeared from where I left it taped to the door and hurried to seal it shut after the commander made his way in.

We chatted for a few minutes while I unpacked and he installed the software, just like he'd done during my very first day with the laptop. He told me about his wife and made small talk about the weather and the difference in climate in the woods. After he left, I barricaded myself once more and stayed there until the next delivery day, when another guard dropped bags into the kitchen and quickly made his way out. At first it was hard to focus in complete solitude, heart still trepidating at every outside noise, but after a couple of days, I got used to living indoors and started planning my days, like a routine that turned out to be very beneficial for my state of mind. In the mornings, I woke up late and did several workouts from youtube videos, then showered and made some breakfast that I carried back into the bedroom, where I researched for most of the day. After a very late dinner, I either video called my parents or Cressi and fell asleep to a movie or series.

My main project remained my brother. I had to recognise that I did not know what I was doing, but with each day that passed, with each unnatural event or article I found on the internet, I was more and more convinced that I was in the right place.

Deciding to go back to the source, I emailed my brother's former secretary again and requested access to his work computer, to his bank statements, emails and all the passwords and accounts she could find. I spent hours and days tracing Erik's movements, the pictures he posted on social media, the meeting calendar he had kept and all the travel he had done. My entire bedroom ended up plastered with maps, notes, photos and post-its full of information and big question marks. I established connections to work events and focused on the leisure days, the trips he took, sometimes on his own, in his spare time. I even messaged some of his friends who had accompanied him on travels and asked questions that might have seemed inconspicuous to them, but directly connected to whatever I needed to know.

With the help of Google and Mastercard, I connected four places: Lund in Sweden, Mindanao Island in the Philippines, St John's in Canada and Goa in India. Four airports Erik had visited in his last year of life. On several occasions, he had abandoned important business conventions and meetings to travel urgently to those places. Curiously, all four were located near points with phenomena as inexplicable as Evigt. Places as protected and restricted as the forest I was living in. The question was why? There had to be a connection and I intended to find it.

Ansgar

Chapter Sixteen

As soon as my lips touched the peach filled cake, I felt at home and offered Mother a wide smile of gratitude. She returned it and motioned for me to take another bite, which I did, enjoying the discovery of poppy seeds at the centre of the cake. The king and princes were nowhere in sight, in fact, not very many males attended this second visit of the keepers. The time for family had been replaced by the game of hide and seek for mates.

I registered that most of the holders of trays were young females and they all wore their finery, hair arranged in buns or small braids draped around their shoulders, wearing broad smiles and sharing cakes with various males. *Let the game begin*, I exhaled, relieved that the Queen made time to welcome me and didn't let me fall prey to the many females who casually tried to make their way across the crowd.

"Is everything alright, my son?" Mother asked as she observed me, her dark skin making her light blue stare reflect into my soul.

"No events," I immediately responded, my grey eyes pouring into hers with the same intensity. I knew how worried she must have been. "Excellent!" she replied, cheer making its way onto her face and I relaxed at the image of my contended mother.

"In that case, my son, let me introduce you to Lady Amara," she said and immediately waved a hand, changing position to unblock the image of a blonde female who straightened a few steps behind the Queen. She smiled and bowed deeply and slowly, holding my stare the entire time.

She was beautiful, long hair kissed by sunlight flew on her shoulders, with waves falling onto her hips, small braids ornate the curls to create density and volume. Deep blue eyes, shining though like azurite bathed in moonlight with a sparkle of hope, I noticed. Evidently, the young woman had been invited by the Queen, who did not miss the chance to shove my body towards the female with tiny pushes of her elbow.

Lady Amara dressed in finery, a long navy dress floated around her, making her bright skin shine through. I understood what I was supposed to do and extended my hand to allow the soft palm of the female to reach me.

The memory of the last hand I had kissed made my stomach jerk. I forced my mind to push it away, like it did every time Anwen came into my thoughts. It had been a month since I last saw her and each day I woke up with the hope to find her wondering about in the forest. I made a point to inspect the Eastern side of the district with every available opportunity, in case she decided to come out for some fresh air, yet every time I came accompanied by failure.

"It is a pleasure to meet you, Lady Amara," I replied as soon as my lips departed from her delicate knuckles. "May the Goddess bless the moonlight shining upon your path," I uttered the greeting, customary between a male and a female at night.

"The pleasure is all mine, Prince Ansgar. May the Goddess bless your path," she exclaimed, her moving lips the colour of ripe pomegranate.

"Lady Amara is visiting us from the Wind Kingdom," the Queen announced, "and is honouring us with her presence at dinner tonight."

Great, the one night I get to come home and I need to play the prince.

"We are delighted to have you, Lady Amara," I announced instead and extended my arm for the beautiful female to take. She smiled, delighted, and immediately sprang into action, squeezing my biceps with a broad smile and walking proudly alongside me, her head high. I barely managed to extend my other arm to Mother, who swiftly seized it and hurried the pace to catch up with us. With the Queen on my left arm, I looked at her and an internal sigh transmitted through my gaze, to which she puckered her lips to contain a grin. Royal duty first, that had always been the understanding the entire family had accepted and followed throughout their lives.

It was an unspoken agreement that I followed since childhood, with little exceptions when breaking the rules had either been a trap set by my brothers or a demand of the heart. I adopted my princely demeanour, standing higher, stretching my back and neck and smiled at the lady clutched to my right arm. I swallowed and prepared my tongue and mind-set for what was to come and started conversing with the lady, telling her about the history of the forest, showing her some of the main monuments and landmarks of the Sylvan Regnum along the way, making sure to keep the stories light and entertaining.

When we reached the town square, the Queen excused herself, explaining that she had to make the final arrangements for dinner and kissed my cheek as she let the words sound only into my ear, "She is the Queen's niece," and threw me a very suggestive *don't screw this up* look before she made her way through the crowd, smiling and waving at her people.

Fuck. I knew what this meant: a mating instigation. How convenient that the Wind Queen's niece happened to wander around our kingdom just when I came home and what an unexpected turn of events that she was young and beautiful and her aunt had always hinted to an alliance between our territories.

The Wind Kingdom had been forced to abandon part of their armies a few centuries back and had not been able to recuperate from the loss. The newest solution of the Queen it seemed, was to find ties to the stronger kingdoms by way of a marriage alliance. Unfortunately, I was the only eligible candidate to make this happen and judging the way the lady caressed my arm, grabbing my muscles up and down and 'accidentally' placing her head on my shoulder from time to time while admiring some of the monuments, she was open to the possibility.

"Lady Amara, if I may ask, what fortune brings you to honour us with your visit?" I decided to investigate, taking the opportunity since we were alone and unsupervised.

"My aunt wanted me to visit all the regnums, enhance my view of our magical world," she replied with a rehearsed precision, her honeyed voice caressing my eardrums.

She was very beautiful. Tall and slim, with elongated features and a precise beauty, a sharp chin and gorgeous long hair, she shone like a ray of moonlight, her light skin igniting against my tan and her posture so mild that a breeze could effortlessly fly her away.

"My prince?" she claimed back my attention. I turned to her and found her smiling, fully aware she had been admired.

"It is a beautiful kingdom, indeed," I said something that would partly fit whatever ideas she might have expressed.

The windling smiled again, lowering her head and caressing a strand of hair with her long fingers, then setting it back into place so her hairstyle remained perfect and glamourous. Her lips pursed for a second. She wanted to say something, then decided against it and turned, continuing to walk in the town square. As we made our way through the alleys, some of the shopkeepers spotted me and started to invite us into their shops or offered gifts for 'his highness' companion'. I wanted to wave them off at first and clarify, then thought better of it and allowed Lady Amara to receive flowers, chocolates and sweets, much to her delight.

It was the wrong thing to do, to let myself focus on her features and imprint her image into memory, willingly replacing the one that troubled me.

Why not Lady Amara? She was trained to be a princess and act like royalty and it would benefit the kingdom greatly. The only thing I needed to do was learn to love her and judging by the sweetness with which she shook hands with the people and smiled at the children who formed a circle around us, pointing at her long dress and hair, it could become a possibility.

After passing through a few more alleys, the gifts piled up so much that I had to carry about thirty bags of chocolate and Lady Amara was barely able to hold the enormous bouquet of flowers, we decided to return to the palace as the time for dinner approached. When we arrived, I passed the gifts to the lady's helpers and kissed her hand again, announcing my pleasure in seeing her at dinner. In just a few hours, she made a strong impression, her smile and sweetness making me forget the royal duties and actually enjoying the walk and informal chat with a female.

When I reached my chambers, my brothers stood from the bed.

"So?" Damaris asked as he approached to welcome me with a short hug.

"You bastards! You knew and didn't tell me!" I complained and shoved him away, making Damaris slide into a wall. Ignoring Vikram, who occupied his position on the bed again, I went into the bathroom and ran the shower.

I lingered under the hot stream for a long time, trying to piece together the events and make the best decision under the given circumstances. It was not as if the lady suddenly decided to visit the kingdom, she had been invited by someone in the family, which meant that my parents were already in favour and had brought the best candidate forth without feeling the need to discuss things first with their son. I had expected my brothers to notify me, until I remembered confessing to passionate feelings towards a human, so deep they initially thought I had found my mate.

Amara was a classical beauty, one that painters across the ages would sell their soul to just to be able to recreate her features on the easel. The least I could do was give the evening a chance and see how it developed. She had already made a surprisingly pleasing first impression as we walked the alleys and had proved that she could be kind and generous to the people. If I managed to fall in love with her and mate, it would do wonders for both kingdoms, securing a strong alliance and maintaining our leadership position.

Many other thoughts crossed my mind as I carefully scrubbed myself immaculately clean and after I dried with a towel, I took the time to make myself look presentable. I arranged my hair half up in a braid, allowing the rest to flow freely on my shoulders and chose a light green tunic with a grey shirt underneath, to enhance the colour of my eyes. After all, Amara was not the only one that could be rejected. If the lady did not like me after tonight, she could easily refuse a second meeting. All females had the possibility to do this during the mating process. The males were the ones doing the courting, but in the end, females had the power and could very well choose to refuse a male until their thirty third gathering, as the law dictated.

When I stepped out of the bathing chamber, finding my brothers still in the room, both their jaws almost dropped at the sight of me, eyes wide with surprise.

"You...brushed your hair," Vikram breathed out.

"And your clothes shine. Are you wearing a tunic?" Damaris exclaimed.

"And your scent is really strong," Vikram added, waving a hand around his nose for emphasis. "Are you planning to court her, brother?"

"Isn't that what I am expected to do?" I replied dryly, irritation making its way back onto my face, remembering the lack of messages and warning received from them.

They sensed it and immediately started to defend themselves. I found out that the lady arrived only two days before I did, without a letter of invitation and with a message from the Wind Queen, announcing her niece's travels across the land and asking for the Earth Kingdom's hospitality. The Queen has been beyond excited with the arrival and treated Amara almost like a daughter in law, telling her everything there was to know about me and bragging about everything I ever did in life.

"She talked about you so much, that windling could write an anthology about your favourite foods," Vikram mocked.

"Why is Mother so keen on this?" I asked and searched for some adequate shoes.

"Considering my lack of heirs and Vikram's choices, she is counting on you to produce offspring, I suppose," Damaris' voice tried to remain casual, although a hint of pain lingered at the mention of his mating problems.

"Why not Vikram?" I shifted my head outside the wardrobe to point at the middle brother who was cleaning his nails with a small dagger.

"He's Mother's favourite, you know that. She would never ask him to do something he didn't want to, that's how he managed to become commander. The bastard," Damaris threw Vikram a sharp look to which the middle brother blew him a kiss and continued with his manicure.

"Are we going already? My stomach is creating a soliloquy," Vikram asked from the bed, still concerned with the cleanliness of his fingers.

"I don't want to know where those have been, if he is cleaning himself so obsessively," Damaris chuckled and we started walking towards the door.

The dinner presented a traditional earthling feast, containing several dishes that were only supposed to be cooked during specific events, yet at the request of the King, they had been prepared and brought out for the enjoyment of the guest, who seemed cheerful and delighted to experience such a treatment. After the first course, mushroom milk with roasted pea puree and black seeds, the conversation about politics and military situations held mostly between the king, Vikram and Amara, faded in favour of more relaxed and cheerful subjects, such as solstice traditions, river bank dances and childhood memories.

The second course, lamb marinated in truffle oil with purple carrots and Romanesco roots, found us giggling and making fun of one another, enjoying the company. Amara made a point in trying to guess the flowers in the surrounding decorations, much to the delight of the entire family.

For dessert, the lady insisted on bringing some of the chocolates she had received earlier during the walk and we held a tasting contest, guessing the exact composition of each chocolate and cleansing our palate with various wine fragrances.

At midnight, the King and Queen gave up, failing to keep up the drinking and eating with the young and retired to their chambers, bidding me farewell. The Queen lingered a moment onto my cheek and whispered how much she liked our guest. In retort, I whispered softly, "I do too."

Not too long after, Damaris and Takara, the ones that usually stayed up until dawn during every family reunion decided to take some chocolates to enjoy privately in their chambers and left, with the heir to the throne winking at me and nudging Vikram with an elbow to the head who, for once, took the hint and said his goodbyes not long after.

The lady smiled knowingly as Vikram closed the door, leaving us alone in the dining room, surrounded by wine, chocolate and flowers, with a full moon throwing a curtain of rays onto our faces.

"I believe we have intentionally been left alone, Prince Ansgar," she chuckled.

"I believe we have," I agreed and bit into another chocolate, chewing slowly and moving the piece around my mouth, rotating it onto my tongue and through my teeth to find all the aromas.

"Dark chocolate, cinnamon, lemon zest, a touch of spice and lavender," I confirmed as my companion checked the ingredient list for the particular truffle I had selected and released another chuckle, before throwing the handwritten note onto my dessert plate.

"How are you so good at this?" she lamented with a playful smile.

"As I am sure my mother has told you, I have a thing for plants."

We both started laughing at the informality of my answer and as we did, Amara extended her hand across the table to touch mine. It was sudden and urgent. As though she had just managed to raise the courage and was afraid that if the moment passed, she wouldn't have the strength to do it again. She pinned me with her dark gaze and did not allow me to shift outside her vision, until I quieted, returning her glare, unsettled sea waves crashing into silver clouds.

She moved closer to me, maintaining my hand in hers and squeezing slightly, grabbing me like a stag in a vine, not too strong, but firm enough to prevent any attempt at escaping. Her fair face rested inches away from me. I had no intention to disturb the steady pace she created, I squeezed my lips shut and moved my tongue across, releasing them moist and rosy, prepared for what was to come. Amara copied the gesture and licked her lips with a visible slide.

It made me grin a little and without waiting for her to complete the courageous race towards my lips, I pressed mine first, finding her mouth with a straight shot. Our lips touched and greeted each other, not in a lover's caress but in a courteous movement, almost a formal presentation. We remained immobile until the very last necessary movement, when we both felt comfortable and I pushed my tongue towards her lips, caressing them and moving to open her mouth. She allowed me to inundate her with my taste. Her tongue jumped in motion and greeted mine, performing a slow dance, touching and releasing, changing directions and stopping. The kiss was long and honest, my hand finding its way towards her neck. I clutched her nape with my fingers, pulling her head towards me, supporting her while my tongue explored deeper and deeper and after a while, both her hands were tangled in my hair.

We rose from the chairs we had been occupying and stood, in need to be able to touch each other, our kiss only interrupting for a second until it reburst, more openly and passionately. My hands wandered on instinct, wanting to touch the windling and feel more of her, which somehow, ended up with Lady Amara pressed against the wall while I caressed her neck. The other hand was situated on her hip and dangerously moving towards her lower back. On her end, Amara lifted herself on her toes to be able to reach me and kissed me eagerly. Her fingers pulled hard on my hair while the other navigated on my abdomen, gently scraping with her nails.

A door snapped open and an immediate "Apologies, my prince," interrupted us. Parting my lips from hers, I shifted towards the door to find one of the servers bowing his head low and avoiding any possible eye contact. Sensing that the attention in the room had shifted towards him, he burst out an explanation.

"A thousand apologies my Prince, we didn't hear any noises so we assumed you and your companion used the double door to exit the room. We only wanted to start cleaning," he apologised and bowed so low that his chin touched his uniform.

"Please continue, I will escort Lady Amara," I replied. I heard a disappointed breath from the lady who must have wanted to dismiss the cleaner and continue our activities. Part of me did too, but the open door snapped me to reality and cut off any desire for the night.

I extended my arm to Amara and she snatched it without saying a word, then walked outside the dining room and into the corridors.

We remained silent until we reached the staircase, her hand on my arm, just like the first time we met, a few hours back.

"I must bid you goodnight, Lady Amara and thank you for a wonderful company this evening," I bowed almost as low as the cleaner did and kissed her hand for a third time in the evening.

"Thank you my prince, I would ask you to call me Ama from now on, that is how all my friends know me," she threw a suggestive look, her eyes flashing images of what had just happened between us.

"Then I must insist you call me Ansgar. No short name, I am afraid. It was never a tradition here." I returned her smile.

"Ansgar it is," she curled her lips and started to climb the stairs. I watched her take each step, waiting for her to arrive at her floor so I could go to mine as per protocol. Before she took a turn out of my vision, she smiled, her voice almost purring.

"Ansgar?"

"Yes?" I released a breath.

"Should I visit on another full moon?" she turned her head gently, posing for a portrait that she knew would remain carved into my memory until the next time we met.

"Please do, Ama," I returned the smile.

Anwen

Chapter Seventeen

I woke up with an urge to go for a run, and for the first time in a week, I decided to listen to my instincts. The investigation on my brother's travel led to the conclusion that he wanted me to find something inside the forest. Something that possibly connected with the other three territories in the world, whose magnetic resonance and natural phenomena differed greatly from their surrounding regions. Four unexplainable places on the globe. And I was in one of them.

I did not find an exact map of the forest, the history books I had ordered offered very little information of the inside of the location, so the best course of action was to take advantage of my privileged position and make the most of my time here. I printed the satellite mapping of the territory and knew the overall shape of the district, so the next step urged for exploration and discovery.

After half an hour, I felt ready to conquer the world, comfortably wrapped in my usual attire, leggings, a matching gym top and pink trainers, with a backpack fully packed with water bottles, doritos, sandwiches and a notebook and pen. I planned to walk towards the river and follow the bank, in hope to find the place where Ansgar and I watched the sunset together. I wanted to climb the cliff and spread my yoga mat, also nestled in the backpack, along the plateau and spend the day tracing every path I was able to sketch on my map.

I packed the keys in one of the zipper pockets and started frolicking around the forest. Everything felt new and magical to my eyes, a wave of wonder washed out over the woodland and gave it a newer, shinier appearance since last I saw it. The past month had done wonders for the development and growth of the place. The trees stood taller and greener, the paths I used to take completely changed and alleys of flowers replaced the dark leaf corridors. Even the birds sounded happier.

After taking a few breaths and clearing my senses, I started walking towards the river. On the way, I discovered many new plants, flowers and new animals and stopped so many times to watch them that an hour's walk turned into several. By the time I got to the river, it was already midday. Trying to remember which way I went last time, I followed the stream upwards, hoping memory served me correctly. The flow of water echoed melodious, in perfect symphony with the chanting of parrots, a new addition to the forest.

I felt drawn by the sounds and wanted to participate, so I took off my trainers and socks and took a few steps into the river, the cold water caressing and reviving my calves. I enjoyed the feeling so much that I continued to walk by the river, following the stream and splashing around with every step, giggling at the tickles and whistling from time to time to encourage the birds to start a new song.

Finally, the conglomerate of cliffs materialised and I stepped out of the river, put the socks and shoes back on and walked around the big cliffs, trying to find the stairs Ansgar used the first time I visited this part of the woods. It didn't take long to find a carving inside the cliff with abrupt etchings placed systematically across the surface, leading all the way up. I did not remember climbing them the first time, since being in the man's arms had taken a toll on the rest of my memories from that night, but this was not what I expected. Judging by the way he had so leisurely stepped on these up and down carrying me, I hoped for even terrain. Instead, I found a very serious climb that forced me to use both hands and knees to be able to make it safely up.

Taking a deep breath to encourage myself, I started climbing onto the rough carvings, up, up, up, using my feet and arms as balance when the height proved too abrupt or I made the mistake to look down. I wasn't afraid of heights and enjoyed the views from a helicopter or a plexiglass floor, but going alone in a forest, without a safety harness or someone to at least know where to find me, made me wary and insecure in my own abilities. I took the climb slow and rested as often as I needed, making sure to be safe at every moment.

That was, until I reached the plateau above and the secure feeling I tried to impose onto myself during the climb went off the window. Or in this case, went off the cliff. I hoped that all the feelings and confusion I had experienced were due to my solitude, but no, it had everything to do with Ansgar.

Ansgar, who was lying on the plateau, shirtless, with his pants rolled up above his knees and dishevelled hair, sprawled across the shiny platform. My stomach dropped so low it almost touched the ground and my pulse started racing, breath uneven.

What was I supposed to do? I ducked away from sight and crouched on the last stair, bending to make myself disappear from sight. I considered climbing down, but if he moved or wanted to get down himself and saw me running away, I would look silly and childish.

I decided to be brave and face him, maybe muffle an apology, stay for a minute and leave, making an excuse about forgetting sunscreen or something trivial enough that he wouldn't even pay attention. I retreated a step, making it seem like I just arrived and released a stretching sound, like I grew tired from the effort to reach the top. I even took the final step with a full palm, splaying it across the plateau with a snapping sound, making sure to pant. A deep breath and my head popped up with rehearsed surprise, only to find him in the same position, not making a single gesture to acknowledge my presence.

"That was a long way up!" I heard myself say before even thinking, pushing fully on the platform, but he remained immobile.

Is he giving me the silent treatment? Rage rose inside of me at this childish behaviour. Sure, I wasn't the nicest neighbour out there and I did cancel plans and basically told him I did not want to meet with him ever again, but I deserved at least a 'hello' or a nod of the head, something to acknowledge me. I frowned and started walking towards where he lay stretched on the crystal surface, deciding to make him at least look at me.

"Generally, when someone arrives somewhere, the other person greets them," I huffed as I continued to walk towards him. Ansgar had the nerve to keep ignoring me, as though I wasn't even there. *Fine, I'll just ignore him too.*

I removed my backpack and pulled out the yoga mat I had carried for half the day. I did not know how he could stretch on the hot crystals bare skinned because I touched the surface with the palm of my hand and instantly felt the burn. The sunlight had been warming the lucent top of the cliff all day and it was piping hot, yet the man looked perfectly comfortable just lying there. I sat on my mat and drank a sip of water, by some kind of miracle, it was cold and refreshing.

"Care for a drink?" I scoffed more than offered to the shirtless man stretched close. No answer again. *That was my last try, screw you.*

I pulled out my map and a pen, opened it and looked around for inspiration. The scenery beamed absolutely gorgeous, so beautiful I had to stop and observe for a few moments, humbled by the marvel decorating the horizon. The sun shone high up in the sky, hanging effortlessly like a king reigning over the artistry of the universe with the forest and the river mixing together in perfect harmony. For a while, I forgot about everything, about my own plans and just stopped and admired. Until I was rudely interrupted. I almost forgot he was there, taken away on the currents of air along with the wings of the birds I had been following with a curious eye, until a heavy hand fell on me and made me tense.

When I arrived on the plateau, Ansgar was facing the river, with his back to me, but now he had twisted, facing my direction if I didn't count all the hair that fell on his face, covering most of it. His head rested on his left arm, twisted in such a way that it formed a pillow supporting his neck. He was asleep, I realised and all the anger immediately turned into tenderness.

I watched his chest rise and drop, slow and relaxed, his ribs expanding with each breath, making his muscles even fuller. His golden-brown hair gleamed in the sunlight, positioned perfectly to protect his face from the hot rays, making only his lips and part of his nose visible. I wanted to see his eyes, watch his long lashes curl up inside one another and enjoy the peaceful look on his face. My crazy self-decided to do just that.

Before moving, I blew some air towards him and coughed once or twice to see if he would wake up, but he seemed to be soundly asleep so I lowered myself on the yoga mat to be at the same height as him, turning to one side, making our faces almost touch. I had no idea where this nerve came from, but the impulse weighed stronger than reason.

Ready to make an excuse if he suddenly woke up, I made very slow movements, taking a strand of his hair and pulling it away, revealing part of his nose. He did not move or react. *Good*, I thought and repeated the gesture over and over again, until his entire face remained free of any wild hair and completely uncovered for me. He looked peaceful and absolutely gorgeous, his face relaxed and mouth slightly open, those long eyelashes that I put so much effort into seeing casually resting, nestled into one another.

My brain lost control over my fingers as they traced along his cheekbone, feeling his soft skin, then, seeing it lead to no reaction from him, they continued onto his cheek until they reached his chin and rested there, afraid to sever the connection of their touch.

Fully aware that I played with fire, I urged my fingers to repeat the movement backwards, sliding upwards towards his cheekbone. Gaining more courage, I allowed my palm to caress his face. Then grey eyes opened wide, boring into me.

I froze, hand halting the movement but maintaining its position on his face. Ansgar looked startled at first, a deep breath accompanied his awakening and looked around a few times, studying my face, the sky and the hot crystals he stretched on. They returned back to me, penetrating and questioning.

He seemed to realise what I had been doing and a sly smile appeared on his face, to which I snapped back and moved to withdraw my hand. Too slow, as his own palm cupped it and forced it to maintain its place onto his face. I stopped pulling, there was no point in denying what I had done and part of him did not seem to mind, as he continued to cup my hand into his and moved under my touch, until his lips placed a kiss on my fingers. My thumb resumed its usual movement along his face, by instinct more than anything, and he smiled widely, his eyes glinting.

The next moment, his lips were on mine, pressing onto my mouth with gentleness, enquiring and delicately, until a soft moan escaped me. That was all he seemed to need, because he pushed his tongue through my lips and into my mouth, playing and discovering, allowing me to taste him and open my lips effortlessly to him. His free hand found its way to the back of my neck, thumb caressing skin while the other hand remained intertwined with mine, resting on his cheek.

Ansgar expertly danced with my tongue, inundating the roof of my mouth and licking every portion of my lips. He wanted to make sure his taste would remain with me long after his lips parted. They didn't, not for a while. A clash of lips and tongues kept us joined together for more than a few minutes, only interrupted by his low breaths or tiny moans that escaped my throat without permission.

Chapter Eighteen

I couldn't stop devouring this woman. She laid in my arms and I held her so tightly that I barely allowed her to breathe from fear of letting her slip away again. It was not a possibility any longer, I would never let her go from my arms again. My chest ached for her and the closeness, the touch and feel of her inside my embrace, her soft lips entwining mine and tongues in perfect harmony exceeded my wildest dreams.

Neither of us wanted to stop, even as our mouths went dry and needed a rest. We merely paused for a few seconds, eyes travelling to one another, before starting another kiss, as desperate and full of desire as its predecessor. We remained joined together in a grasp until Anwen's knees slipped and grazed the heated surface, causing her to wince in pain.

I parted my lips abruptly from hers, awoken from a trance and jolted down to where her hand had initially moved to cover the pain.

"Let me see," I whispered and she sat on the mat she had brought and tilted the injured knee towards me, still holding it under the cover of her palm. I placed my hand over hers and removed it slowly, then inspected her skin to find the red mark of a burn, no doubt caused by the piping hot crystal that baked in the sun all day.

"You need healing cream," I announced as I stood up and looked around the plateau, trying to find the shirt I removed in the morning.

"I have some at home," she replied with a low voice.

"Mine is closer," I said and put my shirt back on. I took a swim in the morning and after climbing onto the plateau, I let it dry while I laid on the surface and mentally planned changes for the Northern side of the district. I did not recall falling asleep, but awoke with the smell of her perfume, surprised to find Anwen startled, caught in the act. She seemed different, more sure of herself and her desires, almost daring. I prepared for a push or worse, a smack across the face and was surprised to be received with the same passion and ardour that haunted me for the last month. She fully opened her lips and let me in, caressing my tongue with hers until our tastes combined to create a new aroma.

My body tensed and every part of me wanted more, especially my lower abdomen that jolted with desire. Trying to deflate the situation, I started talking about her need of healing balm and indirectly offered an invitation to my home. Why that sentence escaped my mouth, I did not know, except maybe for the fact that my brain did not do any thinking at that particular moment.

If the invitation surprised her, she did not show it and kept the same position on the mat, scanning me, her gaze moving up and down along my body, stopping from time to time to admire the proof of my desire that poked through my pants.

176

I felt a blush rising to my cheeks as a thousand reasons why I should not bring a human into my allocated district home came rushing through my mind. I combated each and every one with the justification of her injury and need of healing. At least, that's what I would tell the Queen at the next family dinner.

As soon as my thoughts rushed to Mother, Amara's face inundated my vision, along with everything we had done. When I was with her, I felt peaceful and relaxed, her company easy to accept and enjoy and her kisses delightful and refreshing. With Anwen, a fire scorched my insides begging for more and I found myself incapable of letting her go.

It was wrong, so wrong and I was disgracing myself, my family, the district and the goddess herself. I felt worthless in comparison to my brothers, and what I did had no excuse nor did it deserve forgiveness. But now that I had Anwen back in my arms, I did not care about anything but spending time with her. And I planned to do just that.

Twenty minutes later, I crossed the hidden bridge over the river and into the Northern part of the district with Anwen in my arms. I carried her from the top of the cliff, following the tradition we had set during our first encounter. This time, with her knee throbbing in pain, she caught herself onto my shoulders and comfortably retook her position. Surprised by a part of the forest she did not have access to before, Anwen kept quiet and scanned every single branch and the road that brought us closer to the faerie-occupied territory.

"Welcome to my home," I said as I moved further inside the cave and made room for her to follow. Once she did, I closed the door, sealing it shut, and allowing light to flow only from the kitchen window. The chaos of the dishes I left the last night made me regret my lazy choices. In my defence, I did not expect company and even though clutter did not have a place amongst the tolerated behaviour for a prince, she could only judge me as a common messy male. I assumed humans had plenty of those too.

Her eyes gleamed wide, surprise making their hazel shine brighter, her head moving around, trying to take everything in. I did not request much when I received my assignment, the only things that replicated into the cave were the ones I knew I could not live without for three years. Everything else I could pick up during my monthly visits. I had a small kitchen and a hallway, a bathroom and a pantry, along with my full bedroom that contained all my weapons, potions and bookshelves. The windows of my bedroom copied as well, which made an explanation even more difficult. How does one explain a window inside a cave?

She visibly struggled, keeping any thoughts hidden and biting her lower lip, trying to stop the questions fighting to get out of her mouth. It amused me how much she wanted to appear calm when her entire form burst with curiosity. One of the things I liked about her most, always unpredictable.

Any other woman would have probably run away at the sight of a home contained in a cave, yet here she was, acting like she stumbled across the most casual thing in the world. The sweetness of that concentration face she made, plus the continuous biting of the lip enveloped me and I gave in.

"Three questions," I offered as I moved into the kitchen where I had some gauze and a marigold balm to alleviate her pain.

She didn't need further invitation and blurted out in a split second, "How the hell is this even possible? How did you find this? How did you move all of these things undetected by the Forest Guard?"

As I searched through the cupboard, I heard her shifting and moving around the hallway, waiting for me to reply. When we first met, I decided to tell her the truth, or part of it, so the answer to her three questions could be summarized in a single word.

"Magic," I answered, wary of adding more questions to her never-ending list. I heard her chuckle, but she did not push it further, more concerned with the objects and decoration around my bedroom than anything else.

When I found the cream, I pointed for her to take a seat on the bed and I kneeled on the floor, placing her foot on my knee to elevate the injury. It was a nasty burn, the blister had popped and left a trail of dry blood and plasmatic liquid across her leg. She needed alcohol and it would be painful. I placed her leg back on the floor and went to the kitchen. I found wine, plum brandy and absinthe. I decided on the strongest so I grabbed the bottle and returned into the bedroom.

Anwen shifted her attention towards the bottle and chuckled. "Are you trying to get me drunk?"

"I'm trying to get your knee drunk. You need alcohol," I replied with seriousness and shifted back to my initial position. Damn it, this woman had me on my knees twice already and it was only mid-afternoon. I uncorked the bottle and she jolted at the sight of the green liquid smeared across the gauze.

"Is that absinthe?" she asked with disbelief and excitement.

I nodded and Anwen immediately gripped the bottle from my hand. I did not have time to protest when she took a big shot and immediately started coughing from the burn.

"That is for your knee," I replied and snatched the bottle away before she could place her lips on it again.

"The last time I had this was at uni, my first year. They don't make it anymore. Where did you get it?" she asked curiously while caressing her throat to relieve the burn.

"My family makes it." Again, telling the truth seemed to be the best option. Before she had time to form another question, I pressed the green gauze on her knee and kept it still with my hand while a cascade of curses escaped her mouth.

"Do you have a girlfriend?" her scan penetrated my face with inquisition. A question I did not expect in that particular moment, it made my grin even wider.

"I do not," I barely contained a smile.

"A wife or any kind of partner?" Anwen pushed.

"Neither," I struggled to remain as neutral as possible as I wrapped gauze around her knee.

Anwen relaxed and as soon as I finished, she laid on my bed, removing her shoes to make herself comfortable over the sheets. I remained immobile by the bed and I watched her swim in the green satin that brought me cold comfort at night. From now on, it would burn like embers after her touch. The message impossibly clear. She wanted me to join her and for a moment, I couldn't care less about anything else, duty and honour be damned.

My instincts raged dangerously, if I were to listen to them, I would find myself buried in this woman in the next instant and forget every worry I ever had in my twenty-seven years of abstinence. I remembered my brother's advice, humans had many ways of protection. She wanted me to.

But it felt wrong, dirty, and I did not want to take Anwen in these conditions. She deserved much more and if we were to become intimate, I wanted to bring her the world along with me and make her scream with pleasure, loud enough for all the faeries to hear. Terrible things crossed my mind, everything I wanted to do to her enveloped in vivid images, my eyes widening with thoughts, positions and moans I imagined the woman in front of me made when she reached ecstasy.

Cutting the wait short, her lips leaped on mine. Anwen was no stranger to my taste any longer, so after a few soft movements, her tongue slid into my mouth. It was gentle and soft, caressing my lips as she did, touching my tongue slowly to feel more of me. I groaned and grabbed her tightly, pressing her torso to mine while I explored her mouth, my tongue twisting hers and clashing onto her lips with eagerness. She moaned lazily, the sound muffled by the kiss, only audible to my ears. Her hands found their way into my hair, pulling tightly as she let herself fall back on her feet, giving into the strength on my embrace. I felt impossible to stay back much longer, desperate for the touch and feel of her, so I stepped towards the bed, forcing her to mimic my movements without breaking the kiss until we reached the bed frame.

I clutched her lower back to support her and shifted so abruptly that she lost her balance, her physique remaining at my mercy as I positioned her carefully onto the mattress and grabbed the pillow that would forever be my favourite, placing it under her head. My body encased on top of hers, crushing her under me, not hard enough to inflict pain, but rigid enough to incapacitate her escape. She did not seem to mind and her hands moved from my hair onto my torso and started pulling at my shirt without breaking the kiss. Muffled sounds escaped us both, the passion and desire we held back during the past month roaming free in a duet of moans. I let go of her lips only long enough to place my mouth on her neck, nuzzling the shell of her ear, my tongue drawing little circles onto her skin.

"Ansgar," she gasped, and my name on her lips was the best sound in the world. It made me lose the last shred of control and I allowed my left hand to escape to the place it had dreamt of touching ever since I met her. I traced the triangle between her legs, enjoying the heat emanating from it. My fingers slipped lower to caress her womanhood over the tight pants she was trapped in. Her entire flesh tensed and I was ready to pull it tighter onto me and start playing with it as she whispered my name again, shifting under me. It drew my attention back to her face, red and wet from kisses and tongues, her lips swollen. Her big eyes questioned, giving the impression that what we were doing did not please her. I immediately removed my hand and helped her raise on the bed.

"I'll walk you home," I barely found the strength to part my lips away from her and cut our connection short. She gazed at me in disbelief, taking in my ragged breathing and the evident want poking at her through my pants.

"Okay…" a barely audible sound made its way from her lips. She followed my lead and stood from the bed, arranging her clothes and hair.

"When can I see you again?" My heart drummed fast while I awaited her reply, I could not bear another one of her requests to stay away. Not now, after what we just did, not after her taste coloured my lips and her smell lingered on my bed. Not when I decided to court her.

"The guard is coming tomorrow with supplies," she answered. "I'm free Saturday," her voice made the announcement, displaying a hopeful smile.

Anwen

Chapter Nineteen

"Hello," I greeted the tall man as I opened the door. Generally, the guards made a habit to deliver around lunchtime or early morning, yet this man had arrived at my door in the late afternoon carrying the bags in one hand as the other carelessly lingered across the door frame.

"Good afternoon," he hummed melodiously, making his way in without an invitation. He seemed to know his way around and went straight into the kitchen to place the bags on the island, then started unpacking and carefully arranging the foods side by side.

I raised my eyebrows, surprised by the audacity and the lack of soldier-like behaviour of the man. But he wore the uniform and he was here with my food. Maybe I got used to the rest of the men in the guard being super respectful. At the end of the day, he was just doing his job, possibly trying to get rid of me quickly and finishing his shift. I decided not to get in his way and walked into the kitchen to help him unpack.

As I approached, I got a better look at him and was left mesmerized. He stood tall and well built, hair dark as the night sky and adamant sculpted stare. Where do they get this kind of men? First Ansgar and now him? Back at home, you could find one in a million to look as attractive, but these two could basically rule the world amongst themselves and make people surrender countries to their whim with just a smile. *Damn*.

I decided not to help so I could take a longer look at the sexy man standing next to me. Whatever my fairy godmother foresaw by my cradle, I don't think even she imagined that I would be kissing the most gorgeous man and also have the darker version of him in my home in less than twenty-four hours. If this developed into one of those romantic love triangle stories, I was in.

No, no damn it, you are not!

My brain screamed as I wiped away images of my mouth being kissed by Ansgar and my neck by this dark haired mystery man while their hands wandered across my body. What the hell was wrong with me?

Lost in my thoughts, I must have done something to catch his attention, because he stopped unpacking and looked at me with such a seductive grin that made me be grateful for my thoughts' ability to stay private. Maintaining that smirk on his face, he stepped closer to me and extended a hand.

"Apologies, I got lost in my duty and forgot to introduce myself." The way he stared at me gave me a shiver. I tried to maintain calm and shook his hand, shuddering at the touch as I introduced myself. If Ansgar was heaven, this man was hell. The kind of hell one would burn gladly in.

"Pleased to meet you Anwen, my name is Rhylan," he nodded and kept my hand in his, without breaking eye contact. I became mesmerized by those obsidian eyes, so deep I saw the layers of my soul in them. I retired my hand and nodded as well, throwing him a quick smile, then I picked up the bags and started unpacking more things. "I am fine to finish on my own if you need to go," I replied, avoiding eye contact. He made me uneasy with every step he took behind my back, even though I tried to brave it out and not look in his direction.

"Please do not worry on my behalf Anwen, I have all the time in the world," he replied nonchalantly and I heard him walk into the sitting room where I liked to spend most of my time lately. Without invitation, he took a seat on the sofa and grabbed one of the magazines my mom insisted I subscribed to. Rhylan flipped through it and one of the articles must have caught his attention because he made himself comfortable and started reading.

"Anwen, could I borrow your pen?" he asked and when I turned to him, I saw him flick one of the pens I left on the table in the air, moving it slightly to catch my attention.

"Of course," I replied and went back to the groceries. I did not remember ordering so much, some of these things were not even on my list back at home. I never even tried okra, yet I had a paper brown bag full of them and the unpacking took forever. Passion fruit, sweet kiwi, chestnuts? Had he just picked whatever he fancied and placed it in my delivery?

I heard him laugh, then he shifted and jumped up from the sofa, finding a pink highlighter and returning into the kitchen with the magazine.

"Are you sure this is my delivery?" I enquired as he sat, uninvited again, on one of the stools and placed the magazine on the table, uncapping the marker.

"I added some extra bits I thought you might enjoy," he said without lifting his attention from the page. I stared at the article, it was one of those women's tests magazines liked to invent that gave you an intricate answer, making it seem that Sigmund Freud himself created them. I never enjoyed them and skipped them most of the time, I didn't care what shade of lipstick would work best for my skin tone and other silly things.

"I'll do you a test," he announced excitedly. "My results were spot on."

"If it entertains you, sure," I decided to be friendly and once he finished, I would politely kick him out.

He smiled and shimmied in the chair to make himself comfortable. "You are on a first hot date and he offers you a ride home, do you: A. Politely decline and take a cab, B. Give him a kiss goodbye and leave, C. Sure, why not? Or D. Think about it but decide to call a friend to pick you up."

I frowned, but he lifted his head from the magazine, highlighter at the ready, searching my face for an answer.

"D," I replied.

A disapproving sound escaped his throat but he circled my answer. "When your partner asks you to do something adventurous, do you: A. Rip their clothes off and show them your wildest side, B. Shove them in the closest room and perform oral, C. Book a safari trip, D. Get tipsy and let the spirits free."

I looked at him in shock and remained silent, surprised by the questions and the nerve he had to read them to me. He scanned me for an answer and when one didn't come, he frowned, uncertain.

"What?" he finally asked.

"What kind of questions are those? I replied angrily.

"Discover your kinky side in 10 questions," he lifted the magazine and showed it to me.

Crimson does not even begin to describe the colour of my face.

"You are in Sweden. People have a threesome a week here. Shy doesn't suit this country."

He actually expected me to answer, but I snatched the magazine from his hands and threw it on the sink cabinet.

"Which is why I am only visiting." I shoved all the bags in one and gave them back to him, then I nodded and pointed at the door.

"Thank you for the delivery, it is getting late." I walked across the room and headed to the door. I was practically kicking out this impertinent prick and I did not care. He could move his sexy ass somewhere else, I already had more sexual tension than I could handle, I didn't need a new man in my life wanting to know how kinky I am.

"Of course," he followed and then picked up another bag that I hadn't noticed before. It looked pretty heavy.

"This is for you," he lifted it and placed it by the door, making it drop with a heavy thump. "It may come in handy someday." Rhylan nodded a goodbye and walked out, throwing me another one of his seductive smirks. I waited for him to get in the car, a polite gesture I made with everyone who came in, but I didn't see a vehicle parked in front of the house.

"I'll walk. I need to take care of something," he read my

thoughts. A deep wicked grin conquered his face as he said it. Whatever he planned, it didn't look good.

"Enjoy," I replied dryly and closed the door behind him. This visit turned into a wild ride and I was not emotionally prepared for the excitement. Curious, I opened the black bag he left by the door to check its contents, but I frowned with disappointment. This man left me a bag full of iron chains. I grimaced and returned to my laptop.

The next morning, excitement woke me up before sunrise and as soon as I opened my eyes, a jolt of emotion passed through my entire body, knowing I would see Ansgar again. I decided to follow my instinct, if it didn't want any more sleep, I wouldn't force it. Plus, it gave me an advantage in my schedule because I had so many things to do until he arrived that I even made a list.

The very first thing on it was me, I had to be at the top of my game. I hurried to the bathroom and turned on the tap of my huge bathtub, letting the water flow freely. After washing my face with a cleanser, I greedily soaked in bath salts and after about half an hour of letting my skin absorb everything it possibly could and washing my hair, I carefully shaved every inch of me that required attention. Then, I dried my hair with a towel and added some foam to make up a few waves. I finished my skincare routine and spent extra minutes in the mirror to analyse some of the bigger pores and applied some extra serums to get rid of their appearance for the day.

I didn't know what he wanted to do or if he wanted to go somewhere, so applying makeup proved a more difficult task than I thought. I didn't want to not wear any, he had already seen my sweaty face too many times, but I didn't want to put on a full face of makeup, with primers, foundations and ten powders for him to take me swimming somewhere or hiking where I could sweat everything off and look like a Picasso. I decided to go for comfortable and cute, a bit of a sixties look with waterproof mascara, eyeliner, just a bit of brow liner, a touch of rosy blush and a dark shade a nude pink. I checked the mirror for confirmation and blew myself a kiss. Cute enough.

I decided on a dress, he had never seen me in one, and ballet slippers. Also, they would give me the excuse to not be able to walk much, so if he really wanted to go somewhere far away, he would have to carry me. A smile cropped up on my face at the memory of him carrying me up and down cliffs and through huge trees, the touch of his skin and his hard muscles. *Mmmhhhmm*, I moaned hungrily. It was official, I would turn into a slut for this man and be proud of it. Perfume and deodorant came next, though I kept the perfume close to reapply throughout the day, just in case we were staying home.

By the time I finished getting ready, it was nine in the morning, and when I looked at the clock, my chest throbbed slightly. He could show up any minute. We hadn't set up a time, but I hoped he was as excited to see me, so I sharpened my ears for a knock on the door. I quickly went down to the kitchen and grabbed a granola bar, I didn't want my stomach growling and ruining the fun, then went back up into the bedroom to air the room and change the bedsheets. My first reaction was to go for crimson, but I was worried it made everything too sexual, so I decided to go with white satin. Classic and clean. Plus, it would make his tanned skin shine even brighter in my bed. A mental image cropped up and made me drop the sheets as my stomach clenched with the thought of the endless possibilities that could unravel in those sheets today.

Nine thirty and I opened the windows to let fresh air in, sprayed a bit of perfume around and on the bed, and folded a few clothes I had left out. As I finished, I looked around the room and I felt proud, it looked and smelled amazing. I went down into the sitting room where everything lay around, proof of my messy living. I snatched the empty plates, mugs and cans of coke I had left there a while back, cleaned the table and the sofa, sprayed some more perfume and once everything was in its rightful place, I went into the kitchen to do the dishes and clean some of the counters, leaving out only a bowl of fruit and a bottle of wine I would 'casually forget about' along with two glasses close by. I checked the time. Eleven thirty-two.

Ok, so he was coming for lunch. I didn't know how to cook intricate stews and complicated recipes like he did, but I knew my way around pasta, so I decided to make spaghetti puttanesca. I checked the cupboard to make sure I had all the ingredients, took out the parmesan cheese from the fridge and placed everything I needed by the cooker to have them at hand.

I planned to start cooking at about half twelve and hoped that by the time he arrived, the room would smell delicious. I brought the laptop into the kitchen and played some music, I scrolled around a few songs and playlists, not knowing what kind of songs sounded adequate.

I decided to take a break from all the mapping and paths I had traced, with three possible ways to access the bridge we had crossed two days ago. There were too many inexplicable things, I knew that I was close to something and Ansgar had access to the information I needed. I hoped that he would start trusting me more, but for today, I wanted to look interesting and not over-investigating, repeating the same things over and over again. If I discovered what my brother needed me to and also get the guy in the process, I was all up for it.

At quarter to one, I placed the pasta in boiling water and started chopping onions and garlic. By two o'clock, I gave up trying to keep the tomato sauce hot, it had been on the stove for so long only scraps remained and the pasta, which I kept in the water, was so overcooked that it turned into a mash. My eyeliner had probably half faded by now and I poured a second glass of wine. I didn't feel like eating my cooking so I just made myself a sandwich and went back to my comfy place on the sofa to watch my favourite show. It was a good thing I knew the episodes by heart because I did not focus one bit on the screen in front of me, constantly shifting my gaze towards the door in hope to hear a knock.

At six, I went back into the bathroom and redid my makeup, then changed my short dress into a boho one and went back into the sitting room, clicking on the play button. Three episodes remained in the season and I damn well hoped I would not finish watching it tonight.

By nine thirty, I finished the bottle of wine and all hope of a visit vanished, it was getting dark outside and even if he did drop by now, I was not planning to be a booty call for anyone.

I turned off the laptop and brought another bottle of wine from the cupboard, heading back to the bedroom, and made sure to close the entrance door. When I reached the bathroom, I cleaned my face and I looked at my reflection in the mirror.

Stupid girl, I reproached with disgust, then threw my dress on the floor and grabbed the long t-shirt I generally used as a night gown. A lump in my throat prevented me from breathing as I watched tears form in my eyes.

I walked straight to bed and nestled into the white sheets, allowing the tears to flow freely on the pillow.

Chapter Twenty

I woke up to the sound of screams and as soon as I gained control over my strength, I ran outside to see where they came from. Fire enveloped the forest. Around the flames, faeries were shouting for help and screaming in an agony caused by their injuries. By impulse, I threw myself into the open flames and seized as many as my arms reached, without caring if I caused further damage to their bodies with my sharp movements. The time to heal would come later, now it was the time to save.

The heltija and kaluks looked the most affected, their powers and energy coming directly from the scorching soil beneath, so I pulled them out first and threw them one by one, then in groups, towards the cave. They squealed under my touch, their injuries deep and difficult, yet none protested as I captured them in my arms. I ordered the skorjas and the portunes to call onto the river and carry as much water as they could over the open flames that I pushed myself towards.

Pain did not come immediately, the adrenaline shooting through me as I jumped from branches to tree trunks, lifting cliffs and digging out faerie remains from embers. By the time the screams stopped, I had managed to rescue all the living, though there was no joy when it ended, when the river stream poured into the ground to extinguish the burn, leaving a trail of pain behind. Luckily, if we could even use the word anymore, only a few younglings and cubs were lost, some buried so deep underground that ash reached them first and suffocated their tiny lungs.

Some beings drew their attention to my injuries, announcing them to me with alarm, as if I couldn't feel the extent of them. They were probably right, the physical pain meant nothing in comparison to the destruction I was surrounded by and from fear of letting it all hit me once I started digging through the remains.

Digging so hard that part of my nails fell off by the time I finished. I had completely lost track of time, my body bursting in pain from the burns, skin covered in blisters. Long fingers found their place on my shoulder, squeezing hard enough to make me pause.

"You did everything you could." I recognized Karem, one of the sjorka elders. He squeezed harder and his grip unravelled the last thread that kept my emotions in place. "It's time to let go." I crumbled down on the ground and started howling in pain, ample tears forming a red stream down my face.

I only allowed them to flow for a couple of minutes, honour and respect for the families of the fallen stopped me from becoming overwhelmed when they counted on me to direct them through the pain. As the district keeper, I was supposed to be the one to arrange passages with the goddess and take care of the bodies. But first, I had to care for the living. The cave became host to the creatures that once lived in the Northern side of the district; most of them tried to find a place into my living chambers and helped each other heal with all the remedies they could find in my cupboards. I went inside and took out all the reserves of fresh gauze and the ointments and potions that I could find, explaining what they helped with and applying some of the more complicated ones myself. I brought all the clean shirts from my wardrobe and ripped pieces to form fresh gauze.

Some of my boils burst as I was anointing the wing of a portune and she grimaced in pain and disgust when some of the liquid splattered her legs.

"Go clean yourself, you are disgusting and a risk of infection to all of us," she grunted but looked at me with soft, caring vision. I nodded and passed the task onto someone else, thanking them for the help. She had a point, I was covered in blood and open wounds, the pain and burnt flesh almost stopped my muscles from working.

I decided to use my last strength and appear by the river, seeking help from the Cloutie trees. After I employed all my energy to bring earthlings back from the fire all day long, I decided to use the last strand to jump into the river and found myself submerged into the cold stream. Excruciating pain shot through my anatomy, the open wounds and pus pulsated at the contact with the freezing water and a few grunts escaped my throat as I dived fully under into the darkness.

By the time I finished bathing, though I still remained covered in open wounds, a spate of light cropped up on the sky, cracking it open. For the first time since last morning, my mind flew to what it struggled to block all day: Anwen. The fact that the second chance she had given me was probably blown away and I didn't find absolutely any logical excuse to make her understand why I had failed to visit.

The only thing that alleviated the pain I currently found my body in was the thought of her. Her face and soft smile stroked my senses and made me forget. A face that I wanted to see, now, more than ever, without caring about the consequences or what she would think or see, the disgust I would probably provoke her at the sight of my injured self.

Not if I remained in the dark, I thought, and within a second, I appeared at her door. I had to swallow hard, vomit threatened to burst out, a sign that my energy was completely wasted. I hoped darkness remained strong enough to cover most of me when I knocked so insistently that the door almost gave out. I heard steps pop down on the stairs. Another frantic series of knocking and Anwen's beautiful face appeared on the threshold.

"What?" she complained sleepily, her eyes barely opened and a sharp frown on her face. Those eyes and her presence, the balm I needed to heal every wound.

"I wanted to see you," I smiled, careful to stay far enough that she would not notice my wounds.

"I am mad at you bastard, you made me cry myself to sleep," she huffed and pushed the door out, wanting to close it.

"Anwen, I am so sorry," I pressed my hand against it and hid my shape behind, letting only my face, most of it covered with hair, visible.

"What do you want?" she asked with a grumpy tone.

I pressed my lips to hers, quickly and smoothly. I needed the contact of her soft lips, the touch of energy I required to gain my strength, and with it, myself.

"Good night," I parted my lips and disappeared into darkness, not waiting for her to answer.

I would visit Anwen again and explain everything. If I was to become like Vikram then so be it, if I had to give up my title or be tortured and punished for the revelation to a human, then so be it, but I was not willing to waste any more time, especially not after today.

When I got back, some of the faeries were leaving the cave to find new nests and homes, others were moving to the Western side while the ones who remained too injured to move or travel either rested on my bed or on whatever pieces of furniture they could find. Some pillaged the pantry for food and more potions. I changed my clothes, finding a few that hadn't been destroyed in urgent need of dressing and distributed more potions and ointments. I would have to get a full supply once I returned into the kingdom, most of what I had now finished or missing key ingredients for completion.

I cooked for them, cared for them and created more bedding, making sure that each and every remaining faerie received the care it needed to get better. As the day progressed, the other regions came in with more healing herbs, food and invitations into their own homes until the forest regrew. They were accepted with kindness and tears while I kept making sure every injured being recovered quickly and safely.

Sleep was not an option but I kept dozing off when I could for the following days. My time wasn't my own and in between changing gauze, making more potions and ointments and healing the affected part of the district, I ended up running up and down, sometimes without eating for a whole day and night.

Within a week and with most of my power spent, I managed to recreate the burnt section to its exact replica, including the nests and newer species that I had barely brought in the past month.

With it, my home started to clear, each faerie preferring the company of their families and friends once they were strong enough to walk and fend for themselves. As they left, we hugged or shook hands, all of them grateful for the care received and showing kindness and gratitude towards my very tired self.

When I finally had the bed to myself, I realized I was too tired and that, if I were to fall asleep I would not be able to wake up for a couple of days. Before I succumbed to my body, I decided to take care of my spirit. I left the cave with the door open should anyone need anything and started walking towards the queen's mansion.

Anwen

Chapter Twenty-One

A hard knock on the door made me startle and abandon my spot on the sofa. I hadn't even realised it was Friday already, I had been so involved in research and mapping that I completely lost track of time. I barely believed that it had been six days since my big-date-turned-deception. My head had been all over the place lately, so much that I even had a very vivid dream of Ansgar cropping up from nowhere in the middle of the night and then disappearing into thin air. Since then, I tried to make myself busy. I discovered some new routes and tried to get back to that bridge Ansgar had taken me, to no avail. It was as though it disappeared overnight. I did start reading about all the supernatural phenomena believed to take part in the forest and tagged a lot of articles.

I had just turned a page to a new chapter when the noise of the knock drew my attention and forced me to head towards it. Any speck of peace I had found till that moment vanished when I saw the guard standing on the threshold.

"Rhylan," I humorlessly acknowledged him and stepped aside to leave enough room for him to enter.

"Hello, Anwen," he greeted back with his usual cold composure and headed into the kitchen to start unloading the food.

"I hope you didn't add any extras into my delivery again, lots of the things you wanted me to try last time are wasting away."

He sneered and froze from the action, glaring at me so deeply that for a moment the darkness in his eyes caused me to feel like I was falling in the pits of hell. I felt scared and happy at the same time, afraid that he could snap any minute and proud of myself for managing to annoy him so much that his brows almost touched his nose from frowning.

"I didn't think you needed more, especially not since you made some special requests of your own," he replied, almost criticizing, as his gaze continued to penetrate into every thought I ever had. I felt exposed, uneasy and somewhat defenceless.

He was a Forest Guard so in theory, tasked with caring after me and protecting me in case of emergency, but Rhylan felt different from any man I ever met. First of all, his looks were distinct from everyone else's, his beauty appeared evanescent, as if he had been created to last through time and his posture so elegant it seemed royal. Every single gesture he made felt classic and dignified and he acted like his presence on Earth, and especially here in the mansion, was a huge favour to all mankind. He looked gorgeous, between him and Ansgar, I would have my hands full till the end of my life, but when Ansgar was making me uneasy with passion and butterflies in places that had been long asleep, Rhylan was curt and cold, making me feel eerie rather than sexy.

I noticed that he grimaced as he searched his pocket, then found a pink small package and placed it on the table, close enough for me to see. At first, I wanted to laugh at the image, a man with dark eyes, hair and everything underneath his uniform—even his sword had a black hilt—carrying around a pink box. Then it hit me.

"Fuck," I let out through gritted teeth.

"I assume that's what they're for, yes, the big question is, whom with?" he questioned as he scanned me, waiting for an explanation.

None of your damn business, my mouth wanted to shout at him, until I remembered that I was the only person who knew of Ansgar's presence in the forest. I mentally reprimanded myself for being so silly and adding birth control pills on my delivery request list the morning I had a hot date. Or was supposed to. With my busy schedule, I forgot to delete the no longer necessary entry when I sent the email to the guards.

"It's to manage pain," I replied without giving it a second thought and hoping to be believable.

He took a step and forced me so close to him that I had to raise my head slightly to be able to look at him.

"You don't like pain, then?" he continued to pin me with his stare until I was so uncomfortable that I shifted and stumbled up onto a chair just to get away from those eyes.

"You wouldn't either if your ovaries decided to behave like little bitches every month," I snarled and grabbed one of the bags just to have a reason to do something and keep myself away from his imposing closeness.

He seemed to relax, though I felt his stare lingering, analysing my every movement until he convinced himself of whatever he needed to. He relaxed and once again occupied a seat on the sofa, finding the exact same position as last week.

"And here I thought," he said as he picked one of the magazines from the table, "that you found one of the fae and wanted to have some fun."

I stopped and stared at him, then I burst into laughter.

"A fae?" I chuckled. "As in Tinkerbell?"

I returned to unpacking a bunch of bananas, still giggling at the thought. I was never a big fan of Disney and princesses, but the idea of a tiny winged faerie needing birth control sounded hilarious. I looked back at him, hoping he would join in the joke but his face remained dead serious.

"They are very beautiful," he continued, "the fae. Especially the males. I thought that you might have found one in the forest and decided to have some fun. That was all."

"You can't seriously believe in faeries? Or you do, you do?" I howled and a tiny bit of saliva forced out of my mouth from the big exhale and laughter outburst. I needed to grab my stomach. Something about making jokes while he remained so serious made me laugh even harder. After about thirty seconds more, seeing that his face remained a sketch of seriousness, I gave up and breathed the last of the laughter out.

"It's curious that you come to stay in one of the four corners of heaven, as people call them, yet you take no interest in discovering the history of the place. Maybe you met several fae already but your human idiocy kept you from seeing the truth." He looked at me in disgust as he uttered the words.

I frowned and wanted to protest but Rhylan raised a hand to shut me up and continued. "Considering that you are here and you are who you are, I would show slightly more respect." He stood and took big steps towards the door, then opened it to say, "I hope that by the time we see each other again, you will take things more seriously. I really hope *you do, you do*" he mocked me and slammed the door frame shut.

I stopped in shock as the bang of the door echoed in my head, then spat a few curses in his direction and returned into the kitchen to finish unpacking the delivery. I had read the legends but seriously, how can he expect me, or anyone for that matter to take them seriously? The way he talked about the fae, with such conviction and in present tense, as if they were truly real, surprised me.

I was aware that many cultures thrived on folk tales and I had read a Swedish anthology of tales before I came here, some of those stories mentioned fae, mermaids and even elves, amongst all the other fantastic creatures to which the ancient Swedes prayed to and left offerings for. Maybe Rhylan came from a family that remained considerate of traditions, but if that was the case, he should have let me know instead of slamming my door and admonishing me in such a rude way.

I was more intrigued by his reaction than anything else, so after I poured myself a tall glass of wine, I returned to the laptop and opened a new google tab in which I wrote one word: 'fae'. Amongst definitions and pictures, the first and most reliable result from a research perspective was Wikipedia, so I opened the page and started reading a twenty thousand words article. They had no official origin, some references described them as fallen angels, others as pagan deities and some stated that the fae were nowadays so advanced that they could appear perfectly human without any distinctive attributes. Apparently there were hundreds of types of faeries but most of them could be classed into elementals, which had a connection to air, water, fire and earth, their magic connected to the original four gods that held these powers.

I scrolled through pages and articles, I probably read about twenty different links and watched an hour of youtube, when one of the suggested links drew my attention. It described the four original faerie gods and their placement in the current world and, I didn't know if it was because of my geolocation or mere coincidence, but Evigt Forest was listed as one of the burial places of the four gods, more specifically the Goddess of Earth.

Ahead of my arrival here I had done some research but most of what I found back at home were articles about the energy from these parts coming from a hidden piece of heaven that the angels hid from God in the hope he would change his mind.

From a romantic perspective, both theories sounded very beautiful and plausible, were it not for science and my complete lack of belief, but since I was investigating the fae, I decided to click it and read more. I discovered that there was a whole theory about the Evigt Forest and I even found calendars on when the fae were expected to visit and with what frequency.

I remained fascinated by all the quotes, references and bibliography the website mentioned. I even found an entire study on the forest alone, and it showed that over eighty percent of all the plants in Europe originated from this place or some kind of spore that multiplied and travelled from the Scandinavian Peninsula.

I clicked on another link that directed me to the connection to the Earth fae or 'earthlings' as the author called them and the Evigt. One theory affirmed that the millions of species in the forest needed a source of permanent energy, so an earthling was assigned to its keeping at all times. Apparently they would change every few years and could only abandon their position on a full moon, though no one seemed to know exactly why.

I read about another half an hour more after I had my wine refilled and started to doze off from information overload. If the Swedes believed these tales and they thought that one fae was always in the forest, it made sense for Rhylan to be upset if he thought I had insulted the spirits his family believed in. I made a mental note to apologise if I ever saw him and decided to go to bed. I cleaned the table and put the glass by the sink to wash in the morning.

As I closed one of the tabs, I recognised a name: Sylvan Regnum. I'd heard that somewhere but I could not remember no matter how hard I tried to. I checked Erik's travel list, hoping I would find it there, then I checked his instagram for a tagged location, but nothing popped up. So I went back into my browsing history and reopened the tab to read the paragraph again.

Sylvan Regnum was the capital of the Earth Kingdom, where the royal family of the earthlings resided. That did not answer my question so I started rubbing my temples, trying to remember. Where have I heard it? I knew I had, I just couldn't place the moment when... Ansgar's voice popped in my head. "I, Ansgar of Sylvan

Regnum." *Ansgar of Sylvan Regnum*? What? My pulse exploded while my fingers shook so hard that I could barely touch the keyboard.

'Characteristics of an earth fae' I typed and many pages digitally rolled down in front of me. I knew I would not be able to read, my body shook too hard, so I clicked one of the videos and skipped the introduction, letting the woman on the screen talk about what she knew best. She wore a costume and looked prepared for a Halloween party, the lunar cycle painted on her forehead and wearing some kind of diadem and a green dress. With all due respect to her, I didn't care about her outfit, all I needed was to find out the information I wanted, so I kept scrolling until some of what she spoke started making sense.

"The fae originated from…" no, that was not it, I clicked further in the video, stopping from time to time to find out what I desperately needed to know. "The Goddess of…" no, that wasn't either. Scroll.

"Many people believe that the fae are still amongst us." Okay, maybe that was it. I let the video play as I grabbed the wine bottle and took a big gulp from it.

"The fae can look and act similar to us, they like to eat and drink, well," she giggled, "Maybe not the same exact food as us, I can't imagine a fae chatting to another over cocktails." *Pizza!* My brain shouted, trying to find all the similarities or whatever I thought fitted the description. He said he had never had pizza before. *Big deal Anwen, some people never had bacon.*

The girl continued: "They do not refer to themselves as man or woman, that is solely reserved for humans and they feel the need to distinguish themselves from us, preferring to use other terms." He once said that he hadn't found a female yet. I had considered that to be a language barrier and never thought about it again. "They can travel into their kingdoms during a full moon, the energy is different due to the solar arrangement and it makes it easier to open gates into other worlds," the girl continued to say, along with other information that didn't seem relevant to me because I did not know that much about Ansgar and he had recently decided to stay away from me.

"The stronger the energy of a fae, the less injuries they suffer and if they do, they can heal very fast." I did not know what to do with that information, until I did. Even though my very first memory of Ansgar remained cloudy and distorted, I could swear I had stabbed him in the stomach. He admitted that to me the second time we met by the river. So how can a person recover from a stab wound in a day or two? I had seen him shirtless, and there was no sign of an injury. And he lived in a cave for God's sake, one that was inexplicably equipped with absolutely everything.

I started shaking feverously, my body reacting violently to the information it tried to process while big tears rolled down my face so fast that my neck soaked within a minute. "The only affliction known to fae is iron, every reference of a captured faerie mentions cuffing them in iron chains as they…" I flipped the laptop closed with a noisy thump. Rhylan had brought me a bag full of iron chains and left it by the door.

He knew. That bastard knew about Ansgar and he didn't tell me.

208

Chapter Twenty-Two

By the third knock, I started to get worried. I heard her moving inside the house, her breathing so rugged it made it impossible not to draw attention, still she hesitated to open the door. A million thoughts passed through my mind, could she have seen my wounds from the other day and gotten scared? Was she so upset about my failing to attend our date that she blatantly refused to let me in? If so, why did she open the door last time, when I kissed her?

"Anwen, please open the door, I need to talk to you," I added in hope that it might persuade her to look upon me with a kinder eye.

I heard shuffling and metal clicking as the handle moved and the door cracked open with no Anwen in sight, so I pushed it and hurried inside. I had visibility into the room and towards the open archway into the kitchen, but she was nowhere near. I took another step and fully entered the house, walking slowly and trying to discover my role in whatever this was.

Unfortunately, the painful discovery came when I turned towards the wall and she jumped at me from behind the door where she had stayed hidden, raising a black object. I was too stunned to react and by the time I realised what was happening, the iron pipe hit me fully in the temple, causing me to fall to the floor where my head hit another hard object. I wondered if she planned my fall or the banging of my head was pure coincidence. I did not have time to develop a full thought when my eyelids gave out and I drifted away while something warm soaked my hair. I felt the tangy metallic smell before I lost consciousness. Blood.

I awoke with a sharp pain, a strong pulsation at the back of my neck squeezed tightly, too tight, causing my head to pump blood into the wound at a fast rate. I needed to release whatever kept my head hostage to the ache, but as soon as I tried to raise my hands, I felt a sharp burn, like molten liquid poured onto my skin. Someone around me released startled noises and with it, I struggled to push my eyes open, my eyelids lead-heavy. I only saw shreds of the person in front of me.

"Thank all the gods you're alive!" I heard a female voice, stepping closer to me. Anwen, I recognised her melodious cadence of tone. She sounded scared. Why was she scared?

"My head hurts," I mumbled through the pain.

"I know, I am sorry," she crouched close to me but remained at a safe distance. Between blinks and turning my head to the side in very slow movements, I realised that I laid on a settee. Laid wasn't quite the right word. I was chained to one. Iron chains, I confirmed as my skin touched them again, releasing steam from the scorched skin.

"You know…" I whispered, words barely escaping my mouth but my surroundings turned dark.

Someone shook me awake, my head bobbing back and forth as Anwen repeated my name over and over, ordering me to wake up. I struggled to obey her command to find her standing over me, hands on my shoulders as she kept jolting my neck from side to side, making my body shake and my wound expel more blood.

"I am tired," I sighed. "Pain," I barely pronounced and my eyes dipped shut. With the iron chains stopping my flow of energy, I did not get enough to heal the wounds, and by the scared look on her face and the wetness on the back of my shirt, I was bleeding heavily.

"No, you can heal this, I know you can, I read about it," she implored. I forced my head to raise just enough to look at her and by the goddess, even when she was trying to kill me she still made me smile. I gazed upon her worried face and saw that she cared, maybe more than she realised, the concern genuine. As I took her in, a slap shifted my face to the side and I heard her say, "Stop smirking you idiot and heal yourself."

"I can't," I replied honestly, my hands fighting the instinct to cover my now sore cheek to avoid further burn from the iron chains.

"Why? Just do it, I know you can," she demanded while her hands arranged the hair on my face, removing it from my forehead to give me a better view of her.

"There's iron against my torso, fahrenor, I can barely breathe," I mouthed and on cue, my lungs wheezed a tortured breath.

"If I remove the chains from your chest, will you heal? And swear not to grow strong and attack me?" her view shifted to mine, analyzing my reaction.

"I promise," I whispered and let my head fall back on the pillow she had placed for me, waiting to either be able to gasp more air or fall back from consciousness. In less than a minute, after I heard chains rattling, release flooded my lungs. They filled with much needed air and I sucked in deep breaths, the pressure fading away. I closed my eyes and laid back, focusing on breathing.

The smell of food tickled my nostrils and made me open my eyes. Most of the pain had disappeared and whatever squeezed my head was removed, my hair tied back in some kind of bun. I blinked several times to take my setting in, disappointed not to find Anwen by my side.

Judging by the noise and smell coming from the kitchen, she must have been cooking for a while. I took the time to look around me and adjust to the new situation. She knew about me and by some coincidence, the woman had iron chains handy to immobilize me on the sofa. Luckily, only my hands and feet remained tied up and she had made sure that neither chain touched directly onto my skin. I looked down to see my feet wrapped in long socks, a weird lavender colour, long enough to cover my skin all the way up to my ankles. I

212

would not complain, anything looked better than open wounds.

My hands were wrapped in the shirt I had worn, which was covered in blood and twisted onto my hands and part of my arms, tied up with various knots along with the iron chains resting over the sleeves. I found myself shirtless and tied up by Anwen, a potentially interesting situation were it not for her thinking I wanted to harm her. By the table, a glass of water laid set for me so I stretched my arms and tried to reach it, but I had no fingers free so I ended up spilling it across a lot of magazines and papers.

I looked to the door where a trail of blood remained smeared on the wall, then followed the stains to find them splayed out on what remained of a small table. That is what must have hit my head. So how did I end up on the sofa, a few meters away from the gory scene? I checked the floor to see a trail of blood smeared across the parquet until it reached the place where I sat in. She must have carried me.

"Anwen?" I called for her, pointing my stare towards the kitchen in hope that she would come out of the room with softer features. I saw her taking slow but decisive steps toward me, then sat on the chair opposite mine, her gaze fixed on the water I had spilt just seconds earlier.

"Are you going to live?" she looked back at me with rough features.

"Yes," I replied.

"Good," she stated and stood, heading back towards the kitchen.

"Anwen?" I called her again. "I am sorry I didn't tell you."

The room lingered silent for so long I thought her answer would never come.

"You are not sorry you didn't tell me. You are sorry I found out," she replied as she came out with the same iron pipe that had wounded me earlier. She retook her seat on the chair, her wrists shaking at the weight of the newly acquired weapon as she squeezed it tight and waved it in the air between us.

"I will ask questions, and you will answer. If you try any magic on me, I will hit you in the head again, I do not care if you die. Do you understand?"

I nodded, deciding it was best to keep silent until she allowed me some time to explain myself and convince her that she had absolutely no reason to fear me.

"Tell me the truth about the first day, why did you kidnap me?" Anwen demanded as her wrists barely sustained the weight of the object she threatened me with.

"You were attacked by another fae, one renowned for its wickedness. On the first day I arrived in the district, it appeared at my home and threatened to turn you into a blood sacrifice. I couldn't let that happen." She looked scared enough already, I did not feel the need to give more details about Rhylan and what he could do to her, to all of us, if he felt like it.

"Why did you kiss me? Why come close to me?" she asked, struggling to process the information I had just given her.

"I don't know," I admitted and shifted slightly, making the chains rattle. By the look on her face, my answer was not good enough, and her gaze pushed me to continue. "When you were passed out in my bed, I had to check you for wounds and I cared for you, made you drink, let you sleep. You were my responsibility. After that, I wanted to get to know you, I made excuses to come closer to you, but when you left me the note, I decided to stop. For both our sakes. After you searched me again, and you kissed me, I didn't care about anything else," I admitted.

"Is that why you abandoned our date?"

I smiled, realising that she had been expectant, probably waited for me for a while and I disappointed her. The fact that she cared enough to ask for an explanation filled me with hope.

"There was an incident in the district, a fire in the Northern area, near my home. I had to help. It took several days," I grimaced at the memory, the sight of the fire and pain making my skin prickle.

"Why are you..." the question was stopped by a noise coming from the electronic device laid out into the kitchen. Anwen rose and ran towards it. At the sight of the screen her face illuminated. She grabbed the device and brought it back to her chair, making it sit on her lap. She released the iron weapon onto the table between us. "If you make any noise at all..." Anwen looked threateningly towards the pipe.

I nodded. "Understood."

She proceeded to make herself comfortable while the noise sounded on repeat from the machine, until she touched something and made it stop.

"Hey sexy," another female voice came from the device.

"Hey you," Anwen answered, smiling carelessly.

They were talking through the machine, I came to understand, and by the way Anwen made faces and played with her hair in front of the screen, they could see each other. I remained quiet and started looking at the paintings displayed around the walls, not having much to do and not wanting to interfere more than I already was, in a private conversation.

The fact that I remained tied up and held prisoner, still under threat, made me feel better about intruding in women's conversation. After all, the indiscretion was not my fault or my choosing. I looked out the window and saw moonlight behind the curtains, I hadn't realised it had been a day since I was here.

I came by in the evening and could remember some bits of daylight throughout the pain in my head. Her hit, combined with the head injury, the iron chains and my lack of sleep in the previous days must have knocked me up completely.

"So how is it going with that Ansgar fellow? Any news?" My attention shifted as I heard my name escape the other woman's mouth. Anwen remained paralysed, her eyes wide as she threw a threatening look at me, reminding me not to make a sound.

"Nothing much to tell, honestly," she replied nonchalantly as if I wasn't even there.

"No more dirty dreams since the kiss then?" her friend pushed and I wanted to give this woman a gift for making Anwen have this conversation in front of me. I laid back onto the sofa, making myself comfortable and awaited her reply.

"No, not really, how's your tour?" she tried to bypass the answer.

"Excuse me, my darling, but I don't believe you," the woman responded. "You touch yourself at the thought of the man, then kiss him and now you expect me to believe it all disappeared all of a sudden?"

My jaw dropped, actually dropped as Anwen's cheeks turned bright red. I needed to make sure that this woman, whoever she was, got rewarded for the precious information she let escape.

Anwen's face did not shift from the device, she didn't even dare lift her stare to face me or even look in my direction as I tried to contain a big proud smile from painting my face. Tried, not succeeded.

"Cressi, I'll call you another day, I'm in the middle of something now," was all she managed to say as she waved at the screen.

"Fine, fine. Go do your thing. Love you sexy." This woman was my new favourite human in existence.

Anwen waved goodbye and closed the device, then hopped from the chair directly into the kitchen, where she remained for a long while. My content-self enjoyed the small victory, learning that she wanted me. Knowing that she touched herself thinking about me made my organs twitch. Even though my limb circulation was very poor with the chains, my body still managed to get enough blood to raise desire in between my legs. I tensed my form and tried to break free from my ties, wanting to run into the kitchen and touch every single part of her, but I was not strong enough to break them. Hopefully within a few hours, my energy levels would improve and I could break free into her arms, if she still wanted me.

"Anwen?" I broke the silence after allowing my body enough time to process the information and release extra blood accumulations. The last thing I wanted was for her to find me like that, especially since she felt visibly uncomfortable.

"Anwen, please," I called after her. "I need water."

A lie, I could go a week without water and several without food, it was part of the training. I even held competitions with my brothers to see who could fast the longest and I won twice, until Mother found out and had us force fed for the following weeks. I heard her shifting and the fridge opened and closed as her steps echoed closer to me. She exited the kitchen carrying a glass of water and a metal straw which, without even looking at me, held close to my mouth, allowing me to drink.

"Thank you," I said after I finished drinking and released the straw from between my lips.

"There is pizza if you are hungry," she barely replied, retreating into her safe area.

"Please, thank you." The smell of melted cheese flooded my nostrils as Anwen approached with a plate of deliciousness which she placed on the table next to me.

"I can't touch anything," I complained, lifting my tied hands for her to see.

"I am not removing those chains," Anwen glared at me for the first time.

"I only need a few fingers," I protested. "How else am I going to grab the food?" I made sure to innocently stare at her. The woman took me in and sighed. She took a seat next to me on the sofa and I shifted my arms towards her, wiggling my fingers through the fabric to help her release them.

She pulled at the sleeve covering my right hand but as soon as she removed it, part of the chain squeezed onto my skin and I tensed in pain. "Sorry," Anwen said, her face grimacing to imitate my pain. A smile cropped up on my lips at the sound of her apology, at finding out that she felt bad for causing me pain.

"It's alright," I encouraged, "maybe if you rip the fabric so my fingers can wiggle through?" I suggested after a few attempts that ended up in more wounds on my wrists.

Anwen went into the kitchen and returned with scissors. Claiming back her seat next to me, she made small cuts into the shirt and pushed the fabric back onto my fingers to allow them through. I thanked her and eagerly took a slice of pizza, excited at the discovery of the new flavour. I was on my second slice when I observed that she remained standing next to me, watching me eat. I stopped mid-bite and offered her the slice I chewed on, not the most chivalrous of gestures. She smiled and declined, her appearance kinder and her face more relaxed.

Dropping the slice, I moved closer to her, adjusting forward so I got to her lips. My rushed gesture broke any tender moment we potentially could have had. She leaped from the sofa and away from me, then back into the kitchen. I did not want to push her, and soon enough I would be able to follow and hold her, so I allowed her the time she needed to process whatever this was.

She returned and placed an empty bottle next to the pizza plate. "In case you need the toilet," Anwen announced and before I protested, the woman started climbing the stairs. "Good night," I heard her say as a door slammed closed somewhere upstairs.

Anwen

Chapter Twenty-Three

I blocked the bedroom door and placed iron chains at the entryway, but could not shut an eye for the remainder of the night. I did not exactly have enough time to process the events, one minute I was reading about the fae, next I was hitting Ansgar with an iron pipe I had found in a bucket of spare parts under the kitchen sink.

When it punched his head, I found myself praying for a bruise, yet his face started to swell and I almost had a panic attack. By the time I dragged him onto the sofa, he was bleeding so much that I had to use a cotton shirt to be able to contain the river of blood that painted his neck. Images of his grimaces while unconscious chased me through the night. I regretted leaving him alone on the sofa when every instinct shouted at me to go and untie him, but I just couldn't.

There was no way in hell that I would keep Ansgar in pain, I could not bear to see his skin crack open at the touch of iron, I had done it once and I must have squeezed so tight that I physically saw his bare muscles prickle underneath what used to be skin.

I fidgeted in bed, from one pillow to another, under the blanket, then over it, pulled my socks off then woke up to put them back on and scratched every single part of my body until I found a position comfortable enough to make me relaxed so my eyelids finally managed to close. By the time I opened them, the sun hung in the sky and sent direct rays onto my eyelashes. I woke up, not knowing the time or how long had passed since I went to bed. I grabbed a long shirt and unblocked the door, moving the chains far enough to allow me to crack the door open and exit on the side, but keeping them close enough to block the rest of the entry into the bedroom.

I took the stairs one by one, stepping on my toes and not making a noise until I was properly able to assess whatever situation awaited for me in the sitting room. Halfway down the stairs, I had a full view of the sofa, but I did not spot Ansgar anywhere. My pulse rocketed and I almost leaped the remaining steps to get into the sitting room, where he should have been. How had he managed to escape? I made sure to wrap the chains tight enough to keep him steady, yet he managed to disappear.

Only he hadn't. There he was, laying down on the couch, curled up in a fetal position to be able to fit next to the wide cushions smeared with blood alongside him. Wanting to make him as comfortable as possible, I went into the bedroom and pulled a pillow and a blanket from the bed, then went back downstairs, almost tripping on the stairs. I stepped next to him, removing the empty plastic bottle and pizza plate to make enough room for the cover.

He was sound asleep, his chest raised with regular and relaxed movements while his hands hung loosely onto the side. He did not look to be in pain.

A soft tenderness conquered my heart as I watched him sleep. I raised his head just barely, with slow movements, pulling from the back of his neck, where just a few hours ago blood poured out of a deep wound. If I still needed convincing of his supernatural abilities that would be enough. It was not humanly possible to receive such a blow to the head and be sound asleep the next day instead of dead. I slowly slipped the pillow underneath and let his head drop back onto the satin pillowcase.

I watched him adjust to the new sensation, the slickness of the fabric and his own skin holding a softness competition. He did not wake up with the movement, so I took the blanket and wrapped it around him, covering most of his torso and long legs, though, even curled up, he proved too tall so his feet remained out.

Containing an urge to cuddle next to him, I checked the time. Seven forty-three. The sun was barely out, Ansgar still slept so I decided to run a bath and give myself time to plan the day before I came into the kitchen to make breakfast and wake him up with the coffee machine.

I snuck back into the bedroom and closed the door behind me, then went into the bathroom and turned the hot water tap to the maximum. I needed a good soak to burn the stress away.

I added some bath salts and an essential oil bath bomb that, coincidentally, smelled like orange. I did not know how Ansgar did it but every time I was close to him, no matter the time of day or the condition he was in, his perfume always managed to outshine everything, leaving a sweet scent of fresh earth and orange. Bubbles started to pop up and dance in the tub, so I decided it was time to get in. I don't know how long I'd soaked for, when my eyes startled open at the screeching door and I saw a free Ansgar entering the bathroom with slow and smug movements, allowing me enough time to process that he got himself free. My initial instinct wanted to jump out of the tub and find something to defend myself with. But I was completely naked, with absolutely nowhere to go and no iron objects near me, so I did the only other logical thing I thought of, dip as low into the tub as possible to cover as much of myself under the bubbles. I had never been more grateful to foaming bath bombs in my entire life than I was in that particular moment. My hands instinctively covered my breasts and I pushed my pelvis low into the bottom of the tub, making sure the foam covered anything that might look interesting.

"Good morning," he murmured and stepped closer to me, deciding to kneel right next to my bathtub. He stood within reach, I could easily hit him if I wanted, though, his strength was far superior and he had managed to escape his chains, which led me to believe that without a suitable weapon, I was defenceless. I decided to keep what remained of my dignity, knowing that I still had the power to dominate the mood of this conversation and decided to use it to my advantage.

"What are you doing here?" I asked harshly, in the best demanding tone I mustered.

"I woke up," he answered with a small lift of his shoulder, like it was the most obvious thing. "Just wanted to come say good morning," Ansgar continued.

His left hand rose upwards to touch the side of the tub, fingers playing with the hot water and making small circles around the bubbles that were not doing such a good job at covering me as I initially thought. "I didn't expect such a warm welcome," he

223

accentuated. His palm moved onto one of my knee caps that pierced out of the water and continued to make the same small circles with his fingers. My insides exploded at the rhythmical movement, the way his finger scraped at my skin triggered waves of sensation in places I was not ready to admit.

"I assume you rested well enough, seeing how you managed to escape and all," I tried to maintain my composure while his fingers started sliding down into the water, dipping inch by inch onto my skin.

"Hmmm..." he smirked, pleased with the discovery of bare skin. His stare remained fixated on my lips as his hand continued its journey downwards with treacherously slow movements. I breathed out a huff when he touched my inner thighs and kept digging deeper with his annoying little circles on my skin. It drove me so crazy I had to resist the urge to bite my lip.

"Thank you for not placing the chains directly on my skin, it would have made the pain of escaping a lot more difficult to endure." Reading my mind, he was the one to bite his lip, attention still focused on me while he reached and stopped his hand right at the bone of my pelvis. One more inch and he would have me fully in his palm.

"No problem," I tried to sound focused on the conversation while feeling my nipples harden under my hands. At this point, there was no use covering them, if he was about to touch everything else, the sight of my tits would not cause any of us further offence, so I decided to release them.

I directed one of my hands over his, catching it in mine.

Whatever movement he prepared to do, it stopped, keeping his hand in place while his eyes did all the penetration he possibly planned in between my legs. He looked at me so deeply, so fully, that I almost felt my skin melt away with the heat those grey eyes raised in me, my breathing accentuating and my entire body dishevelled under that gaze.

"Is it true?" he asked, not letting go of the territory he had gained between my legs, even though my hand pressed tightly over his. "What your friend said?" His breathing burst in rapid fire and his fingers restarted their circling motion, ignoring the pressure I sustained over them. I knew that whatever my answer, they would react accordingly. Even though he was close to my inside, he would not cross the barrier unless I allowed it.

My body begged for him, tense and expectant, demanding more of his touch. Goosebumps scattered onto my skin from the desire to have him continue whatever he was planning to do to me.

"Yes," I murmured and before letting me finish the single word that escaped my lips, his fingers followed their course onto my folds and started caressing my inner thighs with decisive movements, expertly reaching and tantalizing me so deeply that a moan escaped my lips. That seemed to unravel whatever composure was left in him and made him throw himself into the bathtub with me, placing his body behind mine in a swift movement. He made it so that I found myself sitting in between his spread out legs, my back glued to his chest.

Within a heartbeat, I understood why he wanted to change into this position, as he grabbed my breasts in both hands, squeezing and caressing the nipples while his mouth bit and scraped on my neck.

I undulated onto him, curving my body downwards to give him better access to me, angling my neck as one of my hands buried itself into his locks. He kissed and licked from the shell of my ear onto my shoulder, his sharp exhales tickling my skin and sending more heat downwards, into the area that had been left unattended.

Deciding the wait was long enough, I interlocked my fingers with his and dragged his hand downwards, towards where I wanted him to be and touched the area with both our fingers, showing him that he could access it and do whatever he wished. *God, I hope he would.* It only took him a few moments to take control, his long fingers sweeping up and down and in circular motions deep within my folds until I felt slickness on his fingers while heat squeezed into my insides.

I angled more of myself onto him, to give him better access and as soon as I did, his fingers penetrated me, making me gasp with pleasure. "Yes," I moaned while shivers flanked my slit all around where he was touching me. He groaned into my ear as a second finger joined and started to move in and out, deep into me, slightly curving into my core to find the spot that would completely make me shatter.

And oh my god, he did. I felt his fingers scraping at the inside of me while his mouth sent tickles into my ear. The sensation was too much, I quivered all over and wanted to escape, so I moved upwards to force his fingers out of me but, in one quick movement, his other hand tightly pressed around my hips, keeping me in place on top of him, his fingers moving with rapid movements over that soft spot.

"Ansgar," I breathed out in protest and hope, but he clutched me closer and pinned me to him, making me feel his hardness pressing at my back. Pleasure roared through me. I felt him so hard for me and I pressed my ass into him, letting go of the shred of control I had left, relaxing so completely that my entire weight rested on the hand that was pumping eagerly, forcing my hips to move up and down with the push. I let my head fall onto his shoulder and my body onto his, abandoning myself to the pleasure. Ansgar's fingers pulsated inside me so abruptly that they moved me into him, up and down, up and down, while my ass rubbed against his hardness with the same rhythm.

I sensed the pleasure building up, my core barely able to contain it as the pulsations of his movements vibrated through my slit and inside of me. He could feel my rugged breaths and with one abrupt throb, he made me shatter into thousands of pieces with his name on my lips, deep and hard until everything went dark and pleasure was the only thing that mattered. He let me ride it out until my heartbeat calmed and my tense muscles relaxed over him. Until he let go and returned to kissing my neck. His fingers released me and caressed upwards onto my stomach, leaving a trail of slickness on their path.

I turned to face him and found him smiling, the fae threw me a satisfied manly smirk as if what he had done was the greatest achievement of mankind. I wanted to say that I'd had better but it would have been a lie and I experienced a feeling of gratitude for one of the best and most spontaneous orgasms of my life.

So I remained quiet and smiled back. Suddenly, his lips released themselves onto mine and without warning, he twisted me over so that I laid fully on top of him, my weight pressing upon his abdomen and my core rubbing upon his hardness. Were it not for the pants he kept on when he jumped in the bathtub, he was perfectly positioned to enter me. His lips crushed mine, his tongue inundated my mouth with the rich taste of him. I pushed one of my hands over his pecs and dragged it lower onto his abs, making it descend to the line of his pants, excited and ready to grab the hardness that tortured me with delicious pressure.

I did not have the chance to feel it fully under my hand, let alone touch it when he stopped me abruptly, electrified by the feeling. I tried again and this time, his hand gripped mine into a halt.

"Don't," he whispered, though his voice showed more desire than he was leading on. His breath echoed ragged with anticipation, yet he pulled my wrist tightly to stop any movement downward.

"I want to," I clarified in case he thought that I might feel obligated to do it after the dance his fingers had performed inside of me. I wiggled my hand for emphasis, like I could lengthen my fingers and be able to touch the firmness that craved my touch.

"Please, don't," he murmured and shifted back, forcing me to move along with him and changing positions to angle me sideways and block any intent I had to.

"I can't contain myself with you," he moved his head from side to side, taking in the image of me.

Without giving me a chance to speak or protest, he leaped out of the tub, leaving me by myself in the lukewarm water and grabbed one of the towels hanging on the wall. Ansgar dried his skin and hair with the cotton cloth, then proceeded to hang it low on his hips, shimmied his pants down and let them fall to the floor. The towel embraced his muscled ass tightly. I swallowed at the sight and had to clasp my fingernails onto my thighs to avoid the need to jump out of the tub and start mounting him then and there.

"I'll make some breakfast while you finish your bath," he announced casually, picking up his wet pants from the floor and planting a quick kiss on my head before disappearing through the door.

Chapter Twenty-Four

I barely contained myself as her rear slid up and down unto me. When I strode into her bathroom, I expected her to be upset at the sight of me, but there she was, naked for the taking and with an attitude. Whatever possessed my hands to claim the human, I did not know, but the little moans she made along the process were enough to have me surrender to the firelings just to be able to hear them over and over again.

When she tried to grab at me, making her want and desire clear, I knew I had to either surrender to her or escape. I cowardly chose the second and I now waited in her kitchen, staring into the cold box at hundreds of items I understood nothing of, while she probably remained naked in that water.

I needed to force my thoughts away from what had happened, so I started making a fruit platter with the twelve species I found around the house. By the time she came down, her wet hair wrapped neatly in one of the white towels I used to dry and cover myself with, I had managed to cut them into small pieces and decorate a plate.

"Looks good," Anwen exclaimed while she took the seat next to me.

She hovered over the food, taking the arrangement and the colours in, then dived in and picked a handful of berries, shoving them all at once into her mouth. She chewed eagerly, turning her attention to me expectantly so I mimicked her gesture and found a slice of pear, taking a small bite.

"Aren't you hungry?" the woman asked, surprised. She took a slice of mango and enjoyed a generous bite.

"I've learnt to preserve resources over the years, the pizza from last night should last me the rest of the day."

"Huh," she nodded and went for the banana this time. "I did wonder how that muscled shape of yours is preserved so well. Now I see one needs superpowers to do so."

We both stopped and stared at each other after that sentence. There it was, the conversation we had both been avoiding, coming out into the light. Instinctively, I reached for one of her hands, feeling its softness and sensing orange on her skin. I must have looked surprised, because she felt the need to explain that the smell came from something she called a bath bomb and that it had been a coincidence. *A pleasant one,* I thought.

I caressed her wrist with my finger, massaging gently onto her veins to make sure the blood was flowing steadily. I had read in one of the human anatomy books that it could keep them calm in stressful situations and I wanted to be prepared for any reaction she might have.

"I assume you have questions." Not that I expected her to believe me or accept our differences without investigation. We both knew that whatever was happening between us, it could not be explained away.

"I do," she replied gently, afraid to start thinking about everything that had happened.

"There's been a fire in the forest, it started a few days ago and the energy is still recovering." She nodded as though she understood, but it was visible that the information flew over her like a shooting star across the sea. "My role in the district is to help conduct this energy into life," I tried to clarify to no avail.

"Okay..." Anwen replied, expectant.

I took the fact that she accepted information as a positive so I continued.

"There are many others living here, flora, fauna, faeries, all affected by the damage. Lives were lost, homes destroyed, species became extinct. I needed to bring the energy back and help regenerate it. The day I planned to come see you, that's when it happened. I woke up to screaming in the morning and spent the whole day pulling them out from the flames."

"You went into the fire?" she asked, surprised. Concern traced a self-portrait onto her features.

"It is my duty," I explained.

"That night, you came to see me. You were hurt." It was more an affirmation than a question, a dream she thought she had that needed a reality confirmation.

"I did. I needed to see you," I explained. "After all the death, all the suffering, you were the only thing that could bring me a shred of hope. I just wanted to see you, even from afar."

"You kissed me," Anwen murmured, reliving the memory.

"I am sorry." I didn't want her to feel used, especially since she was the one who helped me regain control. "I've never been the sole curator of energy in any place, it was the first time I had such a duty and the responsibility that came with it scared me. I felt lost, weak. Until I touched your lips. You gave me the strength I needed." I sighed and gazed back at her, hoping that what I tried to convey from the tangle of feelings I felt trapped in shone through.

"Then why lie to me? Why not tell me the truth?" the woman demanded, her voice softer this time. My confession had relieved part of her anger.

"It is a very long story, one that deserves a longer time than I have right now. I don't know how you found out, and I don't know what light my kind are portrayed in, but know this: we are the same."

Her eyes went wide and she stopped chewing on the piece of pineapple that kept her occupied. Anwen glared incredulously then frowned, vision penetrating with reprimand, warning me with a single look that I'd better not try to tell her that I was leaving.

"I must, Anwen," I touched her wrist again, answering the unasked question. "I need to continue my work and I already missed a day. There are beings who depend on me."

"What about me?" Her plea was a whisper, one that drilled into my heart. She had a million reasons to banish me from her life but still wanted my company. The realization gave me such joy that if I were a dandelion, I would have scattered into a million pieces from delight and happily faded out of existence.

I cupped her face in my hands and raised her head slowly to

make our eyes connect. "Anwen, if you'll have me, I plan to spend every free instant I have by your side."

She smiled and kissed me softly, gently, like we had all the time in the world to do just that.

"Can I see you again tonight?" I loosened my lips from hers only long enough to ask the question.

"Youbm bemter," she replied through the kiss and caressed my hair as she did.

I kissed her cheek and grabbed a banana from the basket laid onto the table, then headed towards the door.

"Anwen?" I asked as I cracked it open with my foot, stepping onto the threshold.

"Yes?" She jumped up from the kitchen chair and came closer to me in a heartbeat.

"No matter how much I like to be at your mercy, can we please leave the iron chains aside this time?"

She chuckled and the sound of her laugh filled me with ecstasy.

When I stepped outside the mansion, I contemplated the woods and my surroundings with a different perspective, that of a male in love. There was no point in denying what happened between us, and after the confirmation and kisses she planted on my lips, whatever fear I had of progressing and delving into this dissipated.

Thoughts of duty and family chased me back to the Northern

parts of the district but even though it seemed unexplainable, I knew, through whatever emotion announced the calling, that this human woman was my mate.

She was the one I had been waiting for, for twenty-seven years, and I was decided to explore the possibility of us being together. I never abused my role and position within the kingdom, performed my duties most of the time with excellent results and remained a satisfactory member of the royal family, not outshining the heir but offering the comfort of my strength.

If I came home with one request, by reason and probability, I hoped it would be granted. I already foresaw Mother's anger and possible resistance, maybe I would even receive a punishment from Father, but my hope sprouted from the thought that if Vikram was permitted to renounce offspring, I would in turn be allowed to have them with a human.

That is, if Anwen wanted children. One thing at a time.

I spent the rest of the journey back to the cave planning different possibilities and reactions in my mind while stopping from time to time to check any damage to roots or unnatural markings on leaves, breathing easy when no signs became visible. I was desperate to take a shower and change from the wet pants I had to put back on before I left, but those plans needed to be postponed. Two of the elder skorja waited in the cave, sipping wine at my table.

"What happened?" I asked, terrified to find out their answer. If two elders of the strongest race of faeries inhabiting the forest decided to pay me a visit, it could not be for a casual chat.

"Your highness looks to have had an eventful morning,"

Drodjen, the older of the two replied, his long beard moving along with his jaw to leave strokes along the table that almost mixed with his drink.

"I am fine," I sat next to them and took the empty glass, pouring myself some wine.

"We wanted to bring a proposal to you," Karem disclosed as he sipped heavily from his glass, emptying more than half.

"Of course," I nodded. If they offered wisdom, I would be a fool not to accept.

"We are proposing to force the human to vacate the queen's mansion," Drodjen firmly planted the suggestion.

I frowned so hard that I only saw them through long slits, all the muscles in my forehead warped together in a bundle of anger.

"What does Anwen have to do with anything?" I objected.

"It seems that *Anwen*," he pressed, making sure to emphasize that knowing the human's name meant more than just that, "might be a distraction to some of the faeries."

A polite way to tell me they knew about my visits and worried that I was not performing my duties well. I understood subtleties, something that they weren't even trying to do right now, so I decided to drop the politeness and speak my mind.

"How does she affect the faeries to be precise?" I pushed.

"We are concerned that the human's presence might be more disrupting than helpful, my Prince," Karem replied, waving his hands defensively in the air. "There is no need to be upset, the last thing we wanted was to cause you any kind of distress."

Oh, but you did. This is exactly how you wanted me to react.

"I disagree," I answered curtly and stood, pushing my chair so far back that it slammed into the wall. "If that is all..." I raised my eyebrows and planted myself by the door, a silent invitation for them to step out.

"My Prince, please do not understand our intentions the wrong way, we are merely expressing concern about the effects the human might have on the residents of Evigt," Karem insisted. "We were informed of your frequent visits to the mansion and the friendship Your Highness has tied with the human...."

"So it's not the faeries you are concerned about, it's me."

"My Prince," it was Drojen's turn to intervene, "you have such a wonderful reputation, news of your abstinence for a fuller union with a mate is no news around the kingdoms. We would resent it if a mere human would hinder you from such a remarkable goal."

"Drojen," I stepped towards him with rage illuminating my way. By the time I towered over him I observed him shaking with fear, "I am hoping that a *mere* sjorka elder did not just tell the prince of the Earth Kingdom whom he can or can't join with."

"No, no, Your Highness, of course not, I wouldn't dare," he whimpered under my threatening gaze, his aged composure shivering with the tension.

"Then I would kindly ask you to leave, if this is the only reason for your visit."

Before they had a chance to step away, I reconsidered. "Send a message into the district. Tell the earthlings that the human discovered what I am."

They stopped and stared, petrified. "But my Prince, how can it

TALES OF EARTH AND LEAVES

be?" Drojen's shaky voice barely muttered.

"Technology...is there anything they can't do these days?" I huffed, abstaining from showing my pride towards Anwen's achievement. How she discovered it was beyond me.

"Luckily," I continued, my frown harsh, "she is a friend. With no intention to reveal our location. As a gift for her kindness, she is allowed to visit every part of the district and cross the river to our side. Tell the faeries they might see more of her from now on."

I didn't give them a chance to protest and dismissed them. "You are free to go," I responded with a wave of a hand.

Both of them vanished instantly and I was left alone in the kitchen, realising I had just defied two of the district rulers, some of the oldest faeries in existence, because I felt they could be a potential threat to Anwen.

Anwen

Chapter Twenty-Five

I spent most of the day researching the fae, their customs and history until the sun came down. But most importantly, I wondered if this was what my brother wanted me to find. To know. According to maps and websites I wouldn't have trusted before all this, the four corners of heaven, as they called it, were connected to the four deities of the fae.

I stopped in the middle of a video, the same blonde girl with makeup on her face whose content helped me discover Ansgar's identity, when a knock interrupted my activity. My heart startled out of my chest. I checked the time and saw that it was almost ten in the evening.

"Come in," I invited and leaped from the sofa, arranging my hair and realising I wore a long tacky t-shirt and shorts and probably looked disastrous.

"Very funny," Ansgar replied from behind the door while I arranged the small pillows on the sofa, trying to hide my vegetative state for most of the day. The rest of the bloodied cushions I had already thrown out.

"Ansgar?" I checked, not understanding why he wasn't coming in. Meanwhile, my hands moved as many objects around as they could to make the room look a bit more presentable.

"The door handle?" he remarked drily. "Iron?"

I hadn't even realised. I quickly marched towards the door and pulled it open with an urgent movement, as the memory of him kicking the door open this morning made so much more sense.

"I am sorry," I said but my mouth stopped muttering words, too busy drooling at the image in front of me. It was Ansgar, but in a way I hadn't seen him before. He wore loose dark green pants, they had dropped under the triangle of his pelvis, only an inch or two from something I very much desired to see. A knife holstered into a sheath neatly tied onto his bicep, the blade covering the skin up to his shoulder. His hair pulled half up, gathered into a small plait at the back. The rest of him was bare, his tanned skin shining into the moonlight.

"Oh my God," I gawked and made him chuckle with slight embarrassment. In response, his lips touched my head and planted a small kiss, making his way inside. "Is this how you normally look?" I asked, still amazed at the sight of him, my eyes running all over his body.

"I wanted to see you so badly I didn't bother going home to change," he explained and grabbed an apple from the kitchen, enjoying a big bite, then taking a seat on the sofa that still remained speckled with his blood from a day ago. I really should have cleaned instead of snoop on him and his kind.

"Is this how you wander around the forest? Shirtless and sexy? If so, damn, I wanna go to work with you!" Verbal diarrhoea may not be the best way to start the evening, but I was absolutely shocked by how stunning he looked and those pants hung so tentatively low, inviting me to pull down on the string that kept them tied around his hips.

"Did you have a nice day?" he asked, the most obvious question to calm down my agitated self. Before I answered, he turned his attention towards the video I had paused and my notebook that was left open at a page where I had circled ERIK with big letters and green highlighter. He turned to me with a smile, "I see you've been busy," then turned back to the laptop and read the title out loud. "Faerie gods: documented cases."

"It's all just theory and people talking," I shoved the screen away while discreetly closing the notepad that contained all the information I gathered throughout the day. I didn't want him to jump straight into an interrogation.

"You have questions. It's understandable," he nodded in agreement and caught one of my hands in his to kiss my knuckles. "I can answer them if you wish."

I nodded and went straight to the fridge. I wasn't sure if alcohol was the best choice at that moment, but it seemed necessary to get me through the night if this almost-naked supernatural being was to spend time at my side and perform kind gestures on my skin.

"Drink?" I asked as I opened the fridge and checked the options.

His reply came slow and affirmative. "Sure, thank you."

I did not exactly know what fae drank and that was not the question I wanted to start the evening with, so I brought a bottle of caramel vodka and two cans of ready-made cosmopolitan, then opened one of the cupboards and grabbed two tall shot glasses and went back into the sitting room.

"I hope you like sweet drinks, that's all I have." I placed them all atop the table next to where he sat, very comfortably so, on the sofa.

"I'll have whatever you are having," he smirked at me, like he was planning to taste something more than alcohol tonight. My stomach dropped and my insides twisted with desire as his eyes burned on me.

I opened the bottle and poured two shots, silently passing him one. I swallowed mine in a single breath, then poured a second one and did the same thing. I was on my third when he picked his glass up and lifted it to his nose to smell, then slowly, very gently, placed his lips on the rim and took the world smallest sip. As he did, he moved it around his mouth and licked his lips, swallowing.

"I like this," he smiled with satisfaction, positioning himself even more comfortably on the sofa as the drink made its way into his stomach. The hilt of his dagger drove into the back pillow, making his arm shift with the movement. "I apologise, I forgot I had this," he excused himself.

Ansgar untied the leather band that held the weapon onto him, releasing it and placing it on the far end of the table, outside of his reach. I knew he did it for my benefit and I nodded, grateful, taking my fourth shot of the evening.

"I have questions, Ansgar," I finally replied, working up the courage to speak, "but before I do, you must make an oath onto silver," I stated, hoping that I remembered the article correctly. Apparently not, since he started to laugh frantically, shaking his head and taking another sip of his drink. He looked at me with a grin so great that made me feel like some kind of a buffoon, only there for his amusement.

"What's so funny?" I asked angrily, crossing my hands for emphasis.

"There is no such thing as an oath onto silver, it's how my ancestors tricked the humans to make them believe we cannot lie," he continued to grin and enjoy his caramel vodka.

"Then how can I make sure you don't lie?" I asked surprised.

"How can I make sure you don't either?" he retorted. "Is there a magical oath that binds the humans into solely telling the truth?"

"Of course not, that would be ridiculous," I protested.

"I agree," he said as he finished his shot. "May I get another, please?"

Frustrated, I pushed the open bottle towards him. He took it with a soft movement, raised from his seat to fill my glass, then retreated back onto the sofa and filled his own.

"Anwen, our peoples did not always have the best relationship, an unfortunate fact but a reality nonetheless, so I would suggest, rather than listening to everything your device tells you, that you ask me everything you need to know. Since humans might have developed not too pleasant versions over the years, which is understandable and unfortunate. I promise to answer as truthfully as I can and to the best of my knowledge."

He seemed honest and with a true desire to help me understand. Of course, this was his version and I only knew his point of view, but honestly, how many people were able to have shots with a supernatural, a fae being, the stuff of legends and fairy tales and still afford to be picky with the source of the information.

"Fine," I said and leaned back, reaching for my can of cosmo and popping it open with a fizz, taking a few heavy sips before sliding his.

"What is this?" he asked immediately.

"A cosmopolitan."

He smelled the can incredulously, then pressed onto the top, tapping into the aluminium seal with his finger.

"You have to pop it open," I told him and showed him mine. He frowned and then tried to push the hole with his thumb and through some miracle, he succeeded to rip the seal open without using the key. Ansgar took another sniff and smiled, pleasantly surprised by the fruity smell. He took a sip. "I like this too," he nodded and raised the can towards me, imitating a clink of glasses.

"Everyone loves a cosmo, it's human nature," I raised my shoulders with the explanation. "Now, tell me something that is fae nature."

Ansgar took a moment to think, checked the paintings on the walls, from side to side, up and down, dragging his reply.

"We only eat meat at dinner," he stated then took another sip from his cosmo while I drank from what was my fourth or fifth shot of vodka, I did not exactly remember.

"Why is that?"

"Out of respect for the creation. We can hunt them during the day but one meal is more than enough to honour the flow of energy. I don't exactly know where the tradition comes from, it must be from the early times, closer to the goddesses than to my world."

"Is that part true? About the goddesses? That this place is more special than other woods because of some kind of energy?" I tried to remember all the information I accumulated through the day and how it fit with Erik's travels.

"This is the place of burial of the Goddess Catalina, she was our goddess, of the Earth Kingdom. We are descendants from her creation and keepers of the earth as a realm. Everything you see, everything that grows, is flowing from our energy and the connection my fellow keepers establish through their presence around the realm," he explained.

"So what we call Mother Nature, that is you? Your people?"

My head started spinning from the realisation, I took yet another shot, even though my stomach was beginning to burn from the amount of vodka I had forced into it over such a short amount of time.

"Part of it. We are closely tied together in our work with the waterlings and windlings, the two other kingdoms that prevail on the realm. Together, we generate the growing force around the globe through which plants and animals can coexist and flourish. There used to be another one, it still resurfaces from time to time to bring trouble in its wake, the firelings. Every time you hear about natural disasters and calamities, their escape had something to do with it. Any encounter with them is not a pleasant one, most of the time it brings war and death to our people and yours," he sighed and sipped some more of his cosmo.

"Do you have to fight them?" I asked, imagining something like a scene from a fantasy movie, where two bands run into each other on a big field, my heart stopping at the thought of Ansgar in the middle of it.

"We do, depending on which territory they erupt in and how escalated the situation is. Sometimes one kingdom can hold the force within and sort it out on their own, other times there is an entire battle in which all the kingdoms must take part. I've participated in a few battles within our kingdom and two wars so far, the occurrences are more and more frequent these past decades," he explained and finished his cocktail, licking the side of the can to save every drop. He did the same to his lips. I breathed heavily at the sight and automatically went towards the fridge to bring another round, in the hope that I might see the gesture again.

This time I opened his, and instead of sitting in the chair opposite the table, I took a seat on the sofa next to him. As I handed him the cold can, my fingers lingered and touched his own as he picked up the drink. They remained intertwined, and our eyes followed their lead, locking.

"Ansgar, are you planning to hurt me in any way? Is there some kind of revenge on humans or some kind of tradition you need to perform that involves a human?" I asked as shivers travelled from my fingers towards the rest of my body, not from the cold can but from his soft touch.

"Anwen, I swear, I would never hurt you," he murmured as he paused our connection to place the can onto a safe place on the table, before cupping my face with both his hands.

"I did not know you were here. The first time I met you was

when you were attacked and since then, I can't stop thinking about you. There is absolutely no reason why you should fear me, I promise," he reassured as I relaxed onto him.

A smile took over my face and I unconsciously puckered my lips, readying them for what I hoped would come. He smiled and pressed his mouth on mine, his tongue slipping inside and inundating me with an acidic cranberry taste.

.

Chapter Twenty-Six

Her hands grabbed onto me, onto my stomach, everything she could touch, everything she was able to. I held her on top of me, her legs spread wide around my waist and kissed every inch of her neck. She tasted sweet, a mixture of fruit and sugar from the drinks we shared, her tongue moving restlessly, trapped in a waltz with mine, circling and spinning between breaths and caresses.

I held her in my arms, able to touch every forbidden part of her and murmured my desire in her ear, a prayer to her body and heart, one that her mind could not understand, but I hoped her heart would respond to. "Sostja dum lahns menelenth denentum, fahrenor," I breathed into her, my hands imprinting into her skin, holding, touching and scraping along her hips, her back, her thighs.

Her core undulated onto me, making me hard and wishful, barely able to contain myself as she slid up and down with swift and pressured movements, making me feel the wetness that emanated through her short pants. I slid a hand over her bottom and touched her desire from behind, dragging my fingers in the same rhythm as she did, stroking her so that her slickness marked the cotton protecting her slits from my hands. In an abrupt movement, she pushed back and pulled away her shirt, giving me a full view of her breasts. They were positioned so perfectly at the same level with my mouth that all I had to do was move my head forward. When I did, one of her nipples fell captive to my mouth. I used my free hand to cup her other breast, not stopping the circular movements that my tongue drew around her nipple, burying myself into her generously round bosom.

An annoying repeated ringing made her react, forcing my mouth to let go and my fingers to stop stroking. She pushed away from me and gripped her shirt, focusing her attention towards the device that occupied so much of her time.

"It's Cressi," she announced, expecting me to react to the announcement. I remained in the exact same position, my hands spread apart, waiting for her to retake her rightful place inside of them and blinked a few times in confusion. She huffed at me, then turned her attention to the ringing and touched something to make it stop. At the same time, she arranged her dishevelled hair.

"Hey girl," Anwen spoke to the device, taking a seat further from me on the sofa, trying to keep her rugged breathing in place.

"Hey sexy," the device responded and I inched closer, curious about what she saw. I discovered a blonde woman on the screen, but before I could spot any more details, a hand pushed my head back and Anwen got closer to the screen, making the device reflect her like a mirror. Apparently, I was not allowed to be part of that mirror towards the blonde woman.

"Are you okay, do you have some kind of allergy or something?" the woman asked, stopping her action to approach the screen and check Anwen's reflection.

"No, no, everything is fine," she replied, wiping her lips with the back of her hand, trying to make the redness of my biting them go away. Unsuccessfully.

"Anwen," the woman paused and sent a penetrating stare through the device that had the power to make Anwen blush. I had to learn how to do one of those too, they might come in handy in the future and they seemed to have an effect on the receiver. "Tell me what is happening, now!" she demanded and pierced her gaze through the device again. Even I backed up a bit, it was almost as scary as one of Mother's. Must be something females can control better. Anwen sighed defeatedly and grabbed the device in her hands, shifting towards me, so close that she almost sat on my lap. It made me become mirrored inside it and the woman's attention immediately shifted towards me.

"This is Ansgar," Anwen introduced me, caught in the act and forced to do something she wasn't planning to.

"Ansgar," the woman exclaimed, excitement in her tone and wide eyes studying me, or the parts of me that she could see. "It's very nice to meet you, Ansgar. I've heard many great things about you."

I nodded, not knowing what to say to this woman, to which she continued, "I see that you are keeping my girl company. And if she moved over just a bit more, I could see your abs better. Very, very sculpted." She actually licked her lips when she said it, causing

Anwen to find a pillow and cover most of me with it.

"We were just having a chat," she replied quickly. I shifted towards her in surprise.

"Clearly. Your lips are red, your pulse is at a hundred and sixty, your hair is a mess and he's shirtless. If only all my conversations were like the one you two are having," she sustained her face with her knuckles and looked at us like we were something cute, causing us to smile awkwardly at the same time.

"Okay, I'll leave you to it. Anwen, your dad wants to do a new campaign with me, he'll email you tomorrow. You two have fun," she wiggled her eyebrows before disappearing from the screen and leaving the device to reflect the girl talking about fae gods once again.

Anwen placed the tap over it, folding it in half and making it disappear into a cover of plastic. She took a seat next to me.

"She is very different from you," I stated the obvious.

With a smile, Anwen told me about her friend, Cressida Thompson. They knew each other since they could remember and had always been best friends. They grew up together and visited each other every week on holidays. Cressida's job was a complicated mess I did not understand, but it made her bold and direct, Anwen explained. She had to take care of herself ever since her parents died in a helicopter accident.

"She is my best friend, I am sorry if that was awkward."

"Not as awkward as last time," I chuckled, making her relax into me. Anwen rested her head on my shoulder, adopting a cuddling position at my side. "She is right though, we were supposed to talk, not…" she stopped.

"Not fondle each other?" I completed, making her laugh.

"That is one way to put it." She turned to me, her stare locking in with mine. "This is all very new to me. I never felt like this, all the shivers and the want, the urge to touch you. I just need…" she stopped to think for a second, "I need a bit more time to get used to it all," she gazed at me apologetically.

"Is this you asking me to stop visiting again?" Desperation inundated my voice. I expected her to ask me anything but this, not now, when I finally held her in my arms, not because I made her feel uncomfortable.

"No, of course not," she protested and lifted my sorrow. "Absolutely not, you cannot do that to me again, I went crazy that month," she exclaimed and gripped my arm for emphasis.

I smiled proudly and snatched her back in my arms, placing her shape onto mine, holding her across my torso. "No sex," I uttered her thoughts, the message she wanted to deliver but was afraid to, the request she did not dare say. "Until we are both ready."

"Is that okay with you?" she asked cautiously.

"As long as I get to kiss you all night long," I replied and planted my lips on hers yet again.

None of us could remember how we stopped, it was probably when our lips became so swollen from their continuous frolic onto one another that they shifted crimson and pulsated in pain. We'd talked about the fae, about customs, but most importantly, I answered every single question she could think of about her brother.

She showed me documents and maps, tracing his journeys across

XANDRA NOEL

the world. I was stunned to discover how much he knew, how he'd travelled near the location of the four burial places, but I still could not help as much as I wanted to. I did not know what he wanted Anwen to find, though it was obvious it had a connection to the fae. Unless it was… I stopped my thoughts, no human in existence could possibly know about *that*. It was a secret that costed one's last breath.

I woke up in the middle of the night with Anwen's body resting over me, both of us crammed onto the sofa with moonlight shining upon our skin. When I tried to position myself differently, she groaned at the disturbance and pulled my neck closer to make the movement stop. I immediately did and let her rest onto me while I remained awake and listened to her heartbeat so close to mine, her relaxed breathing tickling my skin. I caressed her hair, illuminated by the moonlight and seeded small kisses onto her head, gentle and steady to make her relax and fall back into deep sleep.

About an hour later, a small snore creeped out from her nose and I had to bite my tongue to avoid a laughter attack. Small noises, similar to a hedgehog's, resounded from in and out of her nostrils. I started to shift sluggishly, moving my figure inch by inch from underneath her, until I made myself fall onto the floor with only my hand attached to her. Standing up, I clasped her, leaving the one hand underneath her head and shoulders and the other gripping her legs, then rested her against me and climbed the stairs towards her bedroom.

It proved more difficult than I remembered since I had no light in the upper floor and many doors remained closed with a seal, but

I found the unlocked door at the end of the hallway with an enormous bed attached to the wall, where I let my woman slide into her comfortable sheets. As soon as she touched the pillow, her body recognized her lodgings and spread widely onto the mattress, grabbing the pillow and turning onto her side.

I wrapped her in a blanket and left a trail of kisses along her face and neck, then headed towards the window to check on the time. By the way the moon shone, sunrise would arrive in two to three hours. I stood there, walking over the floor illuminated by silver light, debating whether to sneak into bed with her or return home. The first choice looked wrong without an invitation, I did not want to claim more territory than she was ready to allow and inviting myself into her sheets seemed one of the most intimate gestures a new couple could have.

I smiled at the thought, we were a new couple, our kisses had sealed the promise hours ago. I grew a bouquet of white anemones onto her pillow, removed the roots and left the stems and flowers rest by her side, then kissed her again and disappeared back home.

Anwen

Chapter Twenty-Seven

I woke up with a fresh floral scent radiating around the bedsheets and I lazily opened my eyes to the new day, a wide smile on my lips from remembering last night's events. Shifting to the side and expecting to find him next to me, I was struck by a huge bouquet of flowers that caught roots in my pillow.

I touched the present he left for me, forming a path with my finger along the soft buds, making them tingle and spread clouds of that wondrous scent. I had seen them in a garden somewhere, but could not remember their name.

Ansgar was supposed to come visit me at lunch and having no idea what time it was, I decided to make haste and get ready just in case he would be here any second. After I showered and changed into a boho dress with nothing underneath but a pair of matching thongs— thank you Cressi for insisting I brought sexy lingerie—I brushed my teeth, combed my hair and applied sunscreen. I added some blush and just a bit of liner, not enough to form a cat eye but sufficient to highlight my lashes. Then I went into the kitchen and prepared some cereal, opening the laptop to check the messages from my dad and read the tons of DMs Cressi sent to me after our conversation.

11:43, I quickly answered my dad first while chewing on the cereal, read the report he attached and sent a few opinions about the shooting location. I went back to instagram to read the dozen messages from my friend, most of which seemed to be appreciative towards my boyfriend's torso. I stopped. *My boyfriend.* Was that what he was? Was I comfortable to go so fast with this guy, that after a few kisses—well, okay, a lot of kisses—I wanted to make it official between us? Did the fae even have partners? I decided to leave the question lingering a while longer, scanning line to line of what Cressi wrote.

@Cressidaofficial: Giiiirl, you need to marry him like yesterday

@Cressidaofficial: That is the sexiest man I HAVE EVER SEEN

@Cressidaofficial: Mmmmh... those abs, I would lick them up and down like melted chocolate

@Cressidaofficial: Or better yet, add melted chocolate into the licking

@Cressidaofficial: Damn, so hot

@Cressidaofficial: And he is cute as hell too

@Cressidaofficial: Poor baby, he was so uncomfortable and trying to keep his composure

@Cressidaofficial: You better bring him home with you, don't let a man like that wander around all alone in that forest of yours

@Cressidaofficial: And I better be the first one to meet him

@Cressidaofficial: Me needs to inspect that man up close

@Cressidaofficial: I am officially hosting a pool party for your return...if you know what I mean :)

@Cressidaofficial: Seriously love, you look HAPPY!

@Cressidaofficial: Whatever you are doing with this new sex bomb, it's working

@Cressidaofficial: And tell me all about it when you do haha :)

A couple of seconds later, the knock on the door demanded my attention and I ran towards it, opening it with a wide grin. Ansgar received my gaze with an open smile until he had time to take me in and his mouth fell open. I blushed and made way for him to enter.

"If I knew we were dressing up, I would have worn my gala tunics," he said, grabbing me in his arms and planting a long kiss on my lips, his hands lingering on the curve of my hips.

"And here I was, expecting your shirtless self," I faked disappointment.

"It can be arranged," he smirked, his fingers trailing my lower back.

If that's how our day started, I doubted we would get much done, though I would not be the one complaining. Shortly after, he let go of me softly, releasing my body with a long trail of caresses, until each part of me slipped away from his hold.

"It is proving difficult to control myself around you, especially when you dress like that," he pointed towards the deep décolletage my boho generously showed. I pursed my lips and threw him a dazzling look.

"Is it difficult for the fae man to get used to human fashion?" I fluttered my eyelashes mockingly, making him chuckle.

"First of all, smartass," he replied while flicking my nose affectionately and walking back towards the entrance, "it's fae male, man is the term we have for humans." I followed him out, trailing after him and wondering where we were going and if I would need any supplies but he continued, "And secondly, if you are to mock my proper title, you should say Fae Prince," Ansgar announced, making me stop in my tracks.

"Excuse me?" I wheezed a surprised breath. "Prince?"

He nodded and stepped on the porch, signalling me to follow.

"As in, royal prince? With a crown and stuff?" I remained unmoving from the realisation.

"With a crown and stuff yes, but I will only tell you more about it if you manage to follow me. The pixies will eat our food if we don't get there soon," he pointed, silently inviting me to join him outside. I did, managing to force my legs to listen to my body again. As I stepped out of the house, he grabbed the side of the door, touching only the carved wood and slammed it shut.

I must have waited until we were about ten or fifteen steps away from our departing point when the questions flooded my mouth and I made no effort to stop them coming out.

"What do you mean you are a prince? How many princes are there? Are you super important in your country? What about that crown though?"

All of them made him chuckle but he held my hand and placed a few kisses on my knuckles, then turned towards me and cupped my face in big hands, forcing my stare to meet his.

"Anwen, I promised to answer any question you have, and I understand your impatience, but we are soon to be seated and the conversation will be plenty. Seeing as this is our first official courting, would you kindly parade alongside me a while longer and let me enjoy you?"

His shadow-grey eyes pierced me so deeply I almost forgot my name, let alone all the questions I had. I nodded in answer and he smiled, placing his lips over mine. Ansgar offered me his arm to hold onto, an elegant movement which no doubt came from all that prince training and started walking alongside me. We strolled across the forest, his fingers intertwined with mine in our first official courting, whatever that meant.

I followed him blindly, focused on the touch of our hands, the way he walked beside me, keeping his long steps in place so we could both advance the same length at a simultaneous pace. I relaxed into him and took a chance to admire the surroundings.

Ahead of us, a corridor of white flowers opened, growing everywhere and onto anything, they emerged from between the leaves of grass, spiking upwards and sideways from the tree barks, engrossed in the moss and every possible branch, forming a portal meant to transport us.

"Ansgar," I stopped, my eyes wide from wonder at the beauty pouring around us.

He immediately stopped and took me in, scanning my face for whatever I was not saying. "What is this?" I asked in a shaky voice.

"It is for you. A courting gift," he raised his palm towards the sea of flowers to further enunciate the movement and unnatural flowing of the petals and aromas.

"You did this...for me?" I pressed, looking around in awe.

His reply came with a proud smile.

"Come, we are almost there," he encouraged, guarding my hand tightly into his. I followed his steps, noticing that he walked slower to keep up with me. I was constantly slowing down and stopping to take in all the details I missed, even bending to pick some of the flowers and form a bouquet of them in my free hand. Each time I reached for one, he did not comment or protest, letting me enjoy and take in his gift. By the time I formed a bouquet, I suspected he arranged a crown of petals into my hair, both of us managing to do so without letting go of each other's hand.

We stopped in front of a dome created entirely from intertwined arches, in such a way to form an escape from the surrounding greenery.

Six trees, along with their trunks and branches formed an arch where white flowers of hundreds of kinds continued to pour from the ceiling and grow alongside every space they could find, their leaves and petals interlacing to form a magnificent site, one designed for the two of us. At the centre of this magical snow globe-like-sculpture of trees and flowers waited a table and two chairs, with candles and white roses cradling alongside glasses and a diverse arrangement of food, sorted in several silver platters.

Ansgar kissed my hand for a third time and invited me inside, helping me step across the branches and carpet of flowers until I sat comfortably in my chair.

"Ansgar, this is…" beautiful was not a satisfactory word for what I was witnessing, for what he was able to do with his power, for what he had planned and organised for me. "Thank you," was all I could say, considering the mesmerizing shock I experienced. If only I had a camera to make sure this remained in my memory forever, with the exact details and the intricate sculptures he had created.

Ansgar took the seat opposite mine, while grabbing a glass and pouring white liquid into it. It looked like wine, but smelled of berries. And peaches.

"Why is everything so white?" Even his shirt and trousers of the day turned a white-creamed shade and his hair tied back with a white ribbon. Among all the questions my brain could have produced in that moment, after being in the presence of a fae, doing lots of sexy things with said fae and finding out the same fae is a prince, my brain concerned itself with aesthetics.

"You seem to enjoy white flowers. I wanted to guess anemones this morning, but I see my senses were distracted," he pointed at the bouquet I settled on the table containing mostly gardenias, calla lilies and roses.

"It's gardenias," I smiled, "but I love all white flowers," I added quickly, making sure he understood how grateful and amazed I was with this 'gift', as he'd called it. More like the most romantic thing ever done on this earth, by anyone, ever.

He nodded, taking the information in and as I didn't know what to say, still amazed by everything, I picked up the tall glass and took a sip. The aroma lingered with berries and peach, though it tasted different from any wine I ever had.

"It is called lily essence," he told me when I moved a second sip around my mouth, trying to taste the full palate of the drink. "It's a softer kind of wine, designed for day drinking. Helps one get back to their duties in the afternoon," he smiled. "As opposed to the sweet drink you shared with me last night," he felt the need to add.

"It's funny to see a supernatural drinking cocktails," I almost laughed, remembering what the girl had stated in the video.

"The fae are not very different from humans, we are the ones who work to keep the realm in health and good condition, we have done so for millennia. Calling us supernatural is not only insulting, considering the history humans have in their beliefs, but erroneous, seeing as my kind are the ones who truly work to keep the natural order of all the things you know."

"I am sorry, I did not mean anything by it," I immediately reached for his hand and apologised. "You must understand, this is all very new to me and I am still to wrap my brain around all these events. Is there a 'fae guide for dummies' manual or something I can read?"

He chuckled, relaxing instantly, letting the piece of cheese he had in between his fingers slip onto the tablecloth. "What is a 'fae guide for dummies'?" he threw me a curious expression, and let yet another chuckle escape.

"It's a book that makes things simple for people to read. It gathers all the information and delivers it very easily, so everyone can understand. For dummies," I explained like it was the most obvious thing. I wondered how much of the world Ansgar actually knew and especially...

"How old are you really?" Another wild escape from my mouth. This time, I supported the haste.

"I am twenty-seven."

"No, but really. How old are you actually? In human years."

He looked at me with disbelief and repeated. "I am twenty-seven years old. I have had twenty-seven birthday parties, including the one on my birth," he clarified. For dummies.

"Aren't fae really old? Like centuries old?" From what I read, and my knowledge from popular culture, these kinds of beings did not share our age and were always centuries old or even immortal.

"They used to be, until the human population grew to such an extent that it took a toll on our common energy. My great-great-great-grandfather for example lived to be three hundred and fourteen, he lived in the times of Shakespeare and collected his works. But now we do not live more than a hundred and twenty, some, one fifty. We live, grow old and die, same as humans do," he explained while he filled my plate with fruit, cheeses, vegetables and stuffed mushrooms and peppers. Amongst all the things the human population did to destroy the planet, this new information pained me to a deeper level. We were shortening the lives of those who dedicated their own to protect our world.

"What did you mean by our first courting?" My question took him by surprise. He almost choked on the wine. After a second, Ansgar dried his mouth with his fingers and placed the glass back on the table, suddenly staring into me.

"I would like to make my intentions clear, though I planned to do so at the end of this picnic."

Damn, if this was a picnic with Ansgar, I wondered what a romantic dinner would be like.

"Anwen, I find myself extremely attracted to you, my energy is screaming for your presence whenever you are not by my side and I find myself in need of your company in moments one should not even be thinking about companionship. At my hardest times, your face, the memory of your smile and caresses keep me at ease and I shall like to request the joy of your presence furthermore, should you be willing, of course." He expulsed the long sentence in a single breath, speaking clearly and loud enough, taking certain intonations at specific moments. He had practiced this exact phrase many times over.

"Ansgar," the words didn't come to me nor did I care to make another big speech as he had done. I just wanted to get it over with and make it official. "Are you my boyfriend?" I asked with a swarm of butterflies inundating my stomach like I was fourteen again, in love for the first time.

"Yes," he replied decisively, "if you wish me to be."

I nodded, keeping my eyes on his. I couldn't part myself from those beautiful ashen waves flowing in his vision.

He smiled and held my hand over the table, planting many kisses on my knuckles, my palm, all the way up to my wrist. Suddenly I was not hungry or thirsty for food anymore and I rose from my seat and took the steps alongside the table that separated us, situating myself onto his lap in a determined movement. He shifted his knees to make more room for me and, without letting go of my hand, placed it across his heart, allowing me to feel his heartbeat.

The emotion inside it echoed so great that I did not contain myself anymore. I pressed my lips frantically onto his, parting them open with my tongue. I had never wanted anything more than I wanted Ansgar at that moment. Our tongues caught a glimpse of one another and, immediately recognised the familiar taste.

He groaned when I moved against him, grinding up and down along his growing hardness, making his breath uneasy. His grasp on my hips tightened. Grateful for my wardrobe choice, I lifted my dress in a single movement and uncovered myself to him, throwing it on the ground. I remained in my underwear and reconnected with his groin with only the soft lace covering the last piece of me. His hands and mouth reclaimed their rightful position across my breasts, caressing and sucking and I continued grinding on him, eagerly needing to feel more and more. Whatever plans I had of holding back, they long vanished and I found myself ready to surrender to him fully, then and there, under this piece of heaven that he had created just for me.

Hearing my thoughts, Ansgar stopped his teasing of my nipples for a mere second to hoister me up into his arms, my legs still spread across him. He laid us on the ground where a blanket of petals had magically appeared, perfect for him to stretch over, maintaining my position on top of him and surrendering to my teasing movements.

It was my turn to torture his broad chest. I allowed my tongue to lick across the tight pecs while my hands caressed his abs and started travelling lower, until they reached the waist of his pants. This time, they were allowed to slip under and feel the hardness that had teased me for days. Ansgar let out a groan as I reached for him, pulled him in my hand and started moving him up and down.

My fingers teased the veins that pulsated across the tick length of him. I had only seen it once, but as my hands were allowed to feel it for the first time, my insides twisted at the thought of the union, imagining the pleasure it would bring. I lowered his pants and allowed his length to come out, the sight of it making me shudder as well as awakening desire.

Suddenly, I found my mouth craving it. I was never the type to enjoy placing my mouth on male parts. The few times I had done it had been out of insistence or because I had received oral sex and it seemed only right to return it. But this one, what Ansgar had for me, invited me for a taste. Without thinking, my mouth lowered towards it with excitement and craving but before I placed my tongue on it, it was taken away from my sight. My body shifted into a different position, with Ansgar no longer under me but jumping up and forcing his cock back into his pants, tying the string and shaking his head in disapproval.

"What is wrong?" I touched his shoulder blade, wanting to make him turn back to me, not understanding his hesitance. "I want to…" I clarified, if only to appease any remorse he may feel for some unknown reason.

"I… Anwen… I can't," he looked back at me, panting, proving that his body clearly wanted this.

"Why? Don't you find me attractive enough?" I suddenly became very aware of my naked body and how the position I sat in created rolls across my stomach. I covered myself placing my arms across my tummy.

"What? No! Anwen, don't you ever say that!" He hoisted me back into his arms again, holding me tightly. "I am absolutely enchanted with you, so much so that I can barely contain myself when I am around you."

266

"Then why?" I placed my hand on his upper thigh, unable to stop, remembering that just mere seconds ago he groaned in pleasure under me.

He looked away, pursing his lips, deciding whether to confide in me or not, so I squeezed his arm, trying to reassure him.

"I haven't done this before," he blurted out the words and swallowed drily, showing how much effort their coming out had cost him.

"What, have sex in a forest? It's fine with me, but if you are uncomfortable we can go back to the mansion. I have a bed there," I replied with pride, thinking I had sorted all the world's problems. His expression darkened.

"Not in a forest... specifically, just, generally..." he awkwardly replied and looked at me with clouds in those beautiful eyes of his.

"With a human?" I whispered, feeling even more aware of my imperfections. Were we anatomically different? Was that what he was trying to tell me? I knew sex between fae and humans was possible, he confirmed it himself, yet he looked at me in such a way that I knew something must be wrong. "Is it because I am human?" I pressed.

He shook his head in denial, then took a breath so deep that his eyes closed along with it. Like he needed to disconnect from the world and gather the strength to tell me whatever he needed to.

"Anwen, I've never had sex. With anyone."

Ansgar

Chapter Twenty-Eight

She looked at me for a long while, her face portraying surprise and wonder. It took her a beat to assimilate the information and even longer to process it enough to reply to me. Even then, she looked lost for words, the news supposedly the last thing she expected me to say, especially after she took me in her hand and offered herself freely to me. I wanted to convince her, to explain my choices, the traditions she had no knowledge of that supported part of my decision.

"Fae children are very rare and they must always come as the fruit of a marriage, which is why we have so many laws concerning the fact. A male can only marry after he completes his first keeper assignment, during which he is given three years to court and find a mate, or at least the closest, next best thing. Those who do not find their mate sometimes choose to marry their friends or lovers from their youth."

Anwen settled back on the blanket of petals, listening to my explanation while covering with the garment she had chosen for the day. She sipped every one of my words, so I continued. "My older brother, Damaris, wed when I was only a boy, but he and his wife have not been blessed with any children, whereas my other brother, Vikram chose to become commander of the force that roams the earth to keep the peace. It makes them incapacitated from having children, out of fear that they might copulate with humans and our species would be revealed. So when they take the oath to form part of the guard, they have to drink a large enough quantity of sterilising potion, it changes their anatomy and makes them incapable of siring offspring."

"And you are the youngest of the three, when two of them cannot have children," she voiced her realisation.

"Ever since Vikram took his oath, Mother became adamant to insure the continuation of our family, so much so that she started sending different servants or ladies of the higher classes into my chambers at the most awkward and annoying of times, in hope that I might plant seed in any of them," I admitted. She frowned in disapproval, struggling to understand Mother's motives. I admit, so did I, many times.

"So you've never been with anyone, because you are afraid of having children?"

"Not at all," I hurried back and took a seat next to her, taking her hand, which she blissfully allowed to rest in mine. "I want to have a family and I am eager to find my mate." For a moment I thought whether this was a good moment to tell her more, but judging by her look, seeing how she struggled to understand, I decided not to overflow the information. I had to show her the darkest part of me. Prove to her my inability to let go. Show her how I remained captive in the pain, unable to forget, scarred by what the other males witnessed so often it had made them immune. Demonstrate my weakness to the woman I loved.

"There is something else." I barely expelled the words and unshed tears climbed towards my eyelids, deciding to hang there for this part of the conversation. Anwen spotted them, of course she did, but thankfully her hand remained in mine and squeezed it with reassurance. Telling me to trust her.

"During my first war, in the Wind Kingdom, the firelings managed to put together an army. They had a battalion, more or less." She nodded, ushering me to continue. "Whenever they escape in a large number, we have to join forces. An individual territory can handle a few, but they are powerful and they destroy at touch, so we were summoned to help. It took about a week." Images flooded my mind, memories I had kept hidden, controlled, fearing the reactions they awoke. But I forced myself to continue, holding onto Anwen, a pillar keeping me grounded into the present.

"The battlefield is a difficult image to take in. There are bodies everywhere, smells of rotting intestines and blood, everywhere, on everything. There is no fresh air, just the choking metal on metal, the clinking of lives falling away. I expected that. I was not prepared for the nearby village to be set ablaze by some of the escaped firelings. It was never an agreement, but more of an unspoken decision. That soldiers would meet soldiers and fight for territory.

That females and children had to be spared. The tradition had been followed since the beginnings. That day, they decided to stop." I took a breath, forcing my gaze to focus onto a nearby tree, then continued. "There were so many injured, so many screaming in agony. My warriors and I were the first to arrive and aid, we grabbed as many as possible and summoned whatever water force we found nearby to trample the flames. They engulfed everything, trees, faeries, animals. We saved many, though some more died from their injuries. Along with a pregnant woman. I found her nestled into the barn, she thought that hiding with the pigs might spare her life. It did not. Her skin, once set ablaze, was falling off her bones. She took her final breaths by my side. I wanted to hold her but I did not want to cause more pain." I could not stop the tears from falling as I muffled a cry.

"She had positioned herself on her knees, bending over her belly, head and arms nestling it, trying to protect it from the blow. She could have ran, could have tried to save herself, but by the size of her belly she was due within days and doing so might have risked the baby. She willingly scorched her body, trying to save it. Hoping that I would save it. She died with a smile on her lips.

But I couldn't. There was no way, even if I was a prince. I still did not have enough power. I stood there, holding the remaining pieces of her as I counted the baby's heartbeats, followed as they slowed and barely echoed. Until they stopped completely. Because I was not good enough, strong enough to do something about it," I finished, breathless. I forced myself to continue, even when I wanted to stop and cry, I needed to expulse this memory and make her part of it.

"How old were you?" she asked.

"Nineteen," I replied between cries.

"You were so young," she tried to defend me.

"Had I been a year older I could have saved her," I exclaimed, wiping the last of the tears away. "We connect with the Cloutie trees on our twentieth birthday. If I'd stayed on the battlefield, if I hadn't chased those escaped firelings, I could have…"

"Even more would have died. The entire village and who knows how many. It was not your fault, Ansgar," she replied, caressing my arm and dropping a small kiss on my clavicle.

"I couldn't be with anyone after what I saw. Part of it because I saved myself for my mate, yes, but mostly because I was unable to bear a child destined for the same fate. Not with a defenceless female, and put her in danger. Not until I would be ready to protect them."

When I looked back at Anwen, she shifted in her seat, looking uncomfortable, her hand pulling at a strand of hair that waved its way across her neck and fell over her shoulder, caressing the breast that not so long ago stood nibbled in my mouth.

"Anwen, I never meant for this to happen, just, I find it impossible to control my senses when I am around you." A shiver went through my body, fearing the worst, terrified that she might decide to end this, without even giving me a chance to properly court her, without her getting to know me better and even allow me more days to try to make her feel what my heart shouted since I had first laid eyes on her.

"No, Ansgar, not at all," she rose from the ground and to my surprise, laid herself in my lap again. This time in a soothing movement rather than one filled with desire.

"I should be the one apologising, we both decided to wait and I should have thought that you may also have your motives," she said, shifting onto my legs, both of us fighting the growing sensation our bodies sent to each other.

"Anwen, there is nothing more I—"

"Ansgar, I am really—"

We both stopped, grins popping up on our faces. I caught her in my arms and squeezed her tight, placing my head onto her chest and allowing myself to breathe after a long beat. Her hands kneaded into my hair. She placed her lips on my head, dropping soft calming kisses on my brow. I wanted to shout my heart to her. Tell her that what I felt, in her arms, that her skin onto mine was unequivocally the best I had ever been and nothing in the world could compare with the cadence only her presence could carve into my soul. I had finally found my mate.

"Ansgar, I need to tell you something too," she whispered to me as I rested onto her, refusing to part myself from her beating heart.

"Anything, fahrenor," I whispered. That is what she was, *my starlight*, my guide into the darkness of a life without love.

"I… am not," she shuddered into my arms, squeezing me tightly like she feared my reaction.

"Hmm?"

"A virgin, I mean." She pulled my hair slightly to force me to look into her eyes and I was surprised to see a worried expression on her face.

"What are you talking about?" I huffed, not understanding what she tried to tell me.

"There have been others," she murmured. "Men I have been with throughout my life." Anwen exhaled a long breath.

"Why are you telling me this?" I asked in disbelief.

"Because, I thought you should know. If we are going to be together, if you still want to be my boyfriend, you should know," she insisted.

"Anwen," I found her chin and pushed her face upwards from where she was staring into the ground, forcing her attention to me just like she had done moments ago. "You do not need to tell me anything, it is normal for you to have had a life before we met. You are a beautiful woman and any man should consider himself blessed to have been in your company."

"So, you are okay with this?" she whimpered.

"I am fortunate to have you in my arms," I replied and placed my lips on hers, kissing the worry away. "Now that we have such things settled, may I have your permission to return to what we were doing?" I hummed and licked down her breasts to emphasize my request.

"Shouldn't we have some ground rules, just in case?" she asked as my mouth returned to one of her breasts.

"Yes, let me enjoy all of you," I groaned, placing myself in between her legs as I made both of us appear by the now empty table, laying Anwen on it. She gasped and squeezed me tightly, making my insides jolt with tension and desire.

"How did you do that?" she looked at the flowers we were sitting on mere moments ago, then back to me.

"One of the things I can do," I replied and I caressed her legs upward, bringing the fabric of the dress with me as I went along until I reached the tiny triangle of lace she had the nerve to call underwear. With a smooth movement, I flicked a finger over the lace and shifted it to the side, leaving her bare for my touch. But my mouth was the one who hurried towards her, with the urge to consume her entire core. I did not stop until Anwen's moans filled the forest and my back ended up marked by her sharp nails.

Anwen

Chapter Twenty-Nine

By the time I got home, petals were sticking out of places petals shouldn't stick out from. Ansgar walked me most of the way home, then returned to the duties he had been postponing hours after hours, choosing to be generous with orgasms instead of…whatever he was normally busy doing. He did explain it many times, struggling to make me understand, but the gist of it was that this territory symbolised a very important place for energies, that connected to smaller ones around the globe, and he had to care for every single plant and animal and being out here, because if they died in this forest they might do everywhere else.

I would not lie to myself and say that I understood his role, somehow his energy, converted some kind of fuel for Mother Nature and had a role in the growth of the forest and life on earth in general. That was the most reasonable explanation I could wrap my brain around and I decided that, since I ended up living in a fairy tale, I might enjoy it rather than overanalyse every single moment of this unreal thing happening to me.

I took a shower and made sure to use orange shower gel, not ready to give up his scent from my skin. I'd asked him about it and he said orange was his natural smell, something every male had to make himself remarked amongst females. It sounded very beast-like and primal, but I envied him. Who wouldn't want to smell amazing every single day?

Wrapped in a towel, I made sure to edit the email scheduled for the Forest Guard and make a mention that the iron door handle needed to be changed. I wrote that the door jammed and I remained trapped in the house because rust had gotten all the way in and the key did not twist properly. Expecting a firm refusal and some historical reason that no changes could be made to the home decor, I found a Victorian handle, very similar to the one I currently had, made of bronze gold and offered to buy that one myself in order to maintain the historical and valuable sense of the mansion.

I also added an alarm clock, I would need it to remember to take the pill every day from now on. It would take another month until it became effective and I did not plan to push Ansgar. If he didn't want to go further, I had to live with it, seeing how the virgin fae turned so experienced in giving oral pleasure.

My mind didn't even want to think about how many similar encounters he enjoyed throughout his life to become so well versed in female anatomy. When I asked him about it, while he gave me a break between my second and third orgasm, he replied vaguely that being a virgin did not mean that he did not get to enjoy other things. I didn't have time to enquire more, his tongue started twisting again inside of me in that way that made me shudder. I completely forgot my ideas and my name.

After grabbing a bite, I answered another email from work and messaged Cressi to tell her I could not video chat with her that night and went straight to bed, the excitement of the day, not to mention the various orgasms completely drained me.

I woke up with banging noises coming from downstairs, so I lazily rose from bed and pulled up a pair of shorts and the shirt I left on a nearby chair a few days ago. At first I thought Ansgar decided to make an unplanned visit until I heard drilling, so I hurried my step down the stairs to find the door wide open and Rhylan working on the locks.

"Good morning," I greeted, "wish you would have knocked".

"I'm here on a Thursday," he replied humourlessly. "Isn't that enough?"

The iron door handle sat discarded on the floor and a shiny new one cropped out of a plastic bag, along with hinges, screws, a hammer and other utensils.

"I am sorry, I did not expect Isak to send you so quickly, I thought it would take you at least til next Friday," I replied as an apology.

He didn't want to be here, partly my fault but at this point, I cared only about the handle that my boyfriend could touch and use without getting injured. And since Rhylan had been the one to casually bring iron chains, a conversation about the fae was something I could stumble upon over coffee.

"It's fine," he grunted, twisting some screws into the wooden door with considerate care. "Besides, you are paying for it so I might add my handywork to the total bill."

"Of course," I shared my response without hesitation. "How did you manage to find a handle so quickly? It looks almost identical to the old one."

"It is," he confirmed.

"Hm?"

"Identical. To the old one," Rhylan pressed.

My eyes widened with panic and I almost shifted from my seat on the sofa with the urge to come closer and read the materials from the box that lay ripped on the porch.

"What is this one made of? I emailed about a handle I liked made out of golden bronze." I tried to seem casual enough.

"It does not matter what you like, *sprout*." His tone sounded mocking, almost ridiculing me and that word, calling me a sprout as if I was so young to the world and knew nothing of it.

"But I don't want it to be made out of iron again." The phrase escaped my mouth before I even thought of it.

He stopped and turned his gaze to me, scanning my face. "Is there a problem with iron?"

"No..." I corrected my posture and made my way to the kitchen, leaving him alone with his work. By the time I returned with two steaming mugs of coffee, Rhylan had renounced his uniform in favour of a black undershirt. So low cut that I had a perfect view of his abs and his sculpted form. Both his arms shone ornate tattoo sleeves with such intricate designs it would probably take me an hour to decipher the stories they told. I swallowed hard—he looked very hot—he had the body of a marble-carved roman god, but his entire posture shared the coldness of the stone. That chest was not one to lay your head on, it was one where even the finest of doctors would struggle to find a heartbeat.

"Coffee?" I offered, coming out from my hiding place in the kitchen and passed him the hot mug. He reached for it, placing his long fingers over mine and pressing them onto the steaming mug. My hand twitched from the burning sensation and pulled away, abandoning the mug that was left resting in his hand.

"No tolerance for pain, I see." He threw me a dark look, taking a big sip from the black liquid.

"Black coffee, how did you guess?"

It doesn't take a genius to see it matches your heart, I wanted to say. I settled for, "Just a guess," and retook my seat on the sofa, sipping from my own mug, latte sweetened with two brown sugar cubes, hazelnut milk and whipped cream with cinnamon.

"Do you have the alarm clock as well?

"I'll swing that by tomorrow, I thought the priority was the handle, was it not?" Another one of his dark judging looks penetrated through me.

"No problem." I settled further on the sofa, mending my coffee while I watched him work.

"Is this going to take all day?" I realised that Ansgar might want to make a surprise visit seeing as it was almost midday.

"Why? Expecting someone?" Rhylan huffed mockingly. Whatever his mouth kept from me, his dark gaze projected. He knew I was hiding something and he probably had a few guesses. The way he looked at me sometimes, menace blended with disappointment, made me quiver in my seat.

I fluttered my eyelashes. "I have a queue of visitors every day," I responded sarcastically.

"I presume you will have at least one visitor." Rhylan let the tension fade out in the air, and even though I knew I should shut my mouth, I needed to push him on it.

"What is that supposed to mean?"

He threw me a distasteful look. "Do you really need me to say it?"

I kept silent and pierced him with a sharp stare, trying to penetrate into his skull and find out exactly how much he knew.

"First you mysteriously decide to take birth control and now you change the locks, not because they are not working, as you stated in your request, but because you suddenly developed a distaste for iron. One can only piece the puzzle together."

"Meaning?" I stood from the sofa and placed both my hands on my hips in a threatening stance.

"Meaning that whatever you are doing *sprout*, that fae is one lucky bastard."

There it was again, that mockery of a name, yet I was much more concerned with the fact that he openly admitted the existence of fae. The tension lingered so thick I could pierce it with hot coal and the smoke would still not manage to blast off the visual bond we had created.

"I do not know what you mean," I answered, in the calmest, lowest tone found.

"Of course you don't," he smirked knowingly and returned to his work.

In the half an hour that he mended the handle and screwed bits on the door, I debated whether to leave and try to get a message to Ansgar or stay home and pray that he would finish quickly. When I saw him trying out the new piece and gathering the remaining parts into the box, breath flowed calmer into my lungs.

He closed the door and locked it, leaving me trapped inside, then a few seconds later opened it with the key and did the same thing on the inside, ensuring full functionality. I immediately stepped close to him, passing back his uniform jacket and thanking him for the help.

"The new handle is made out of golden bronze, as per your request," he threw me one last sharp look.

"Excellent," I replied uncaringly, but deep down I choreographed a small victory dance.

"The key," Rhylan handed me a small key, one that looked basic and normal compared to the huge iron intricate design I had to carry around for the past two months.

"I need both," I replied coldly and hoped that he would not comment on it again, though both of us knew that the first time I came in I received only one key and did not complain.

"Of course you do," he chuckled with distaste and handed me the spare from his jacket pocket. "As I said, lucky fae bastard."

Without another word, he turned towards the door he had just fixed and slammed it shut, disappearing into the woods.

I would have to be careful with him from now on and keep conversations to a minimum, but I did not take his knowledge as a threat. After all, there were many legends around these parts and people believed this was a corner of heaven. Even if he went back and reported that I supposedly dated a fae, it would be more probable for him to get demoted than me getting in trouble. And I was too focused on the surprise I had prepared for my new boyfriend to give it another thought.

Ansgar's knock on the door found me cooking dinner.

"Come in!" I invited with a playful voice.

"You may think this is funny, fahrenor, but after the day I had, I promise it is not," he replied with a bitter tone.

"Try it, humour me," I dared him from the other side of the door. I heard his long breath, as he prepared for the pain he knew was coming. For a moment, I doubted my plan. I put him in a situation where he needed to receive pain so he could get to me. My heart sank as I knew he would do it unquestionably.

When the door creaked open, I spotted the surprise on his face. He kept looking from the handle to me, then back to the handle again with the sweetest face of wonder.

"Surprise!" I emphasized just in case his features were not testimony enough.

"How?" he asked, analysing his unburnt hand.

"I had the locks changed," I smirked and stepped into his embrace. "And," I applied my seductive voice and caressed a trail from my breasts to my hips, "there is a key on my body for you to find."

His hands immediately accepted the challenge and started drawing lazy lines across my back, though he surely had an idea of where exactly the key would be.

"And why, pray tell, do I need a key, seeing as I can come in as I wish?" His lips pressed on the shell of my ear. He breathed down on me, leaving a path of goose bumps on my skin.

"It's customary," I barely breathed as I spoke, "in the human world, to give someone a key when you ask them to live with you." I felt weak in the knees and he was only touching my neck and my back. The things this man could do to me...

He stopped to gaze at me, piercing through my soul and making my core throb with desire.

"Do you want to live together?" His eyes formed waves of emotion, though I had yet to decipher if they echoed good things.

"I thought," I swallowed hard to allow myself to gather some thoughts as his hands moved lower on my back, "that since we both live alone, and we spend a lot of time together, we could share a home. If you will. "

Ansgar blinked a few times, still piercing deep into me but said nothing.

"My home does not have a key, it is open to all," he replied in the end, not shifting his eyes from mine, "but consider this the invitation," he said and placed his lips on mine, joining them into an impatient kiss. I parted my mouth to better receive him and his tongue slipped in, caressing mine into the waltz they both practiced so often lately.

"Now," he stopped to grin at me sensually, "about that key".

I barely expelled a muffled moan when his hands hurried at the apex of my tights and started caressing me expertly, locating the small bronze key I had hidden in my underwear. Ansgar placed a finger over it and wiggled it around in my panties. Within seconds, he fell on his knees, sustaining my weight with a hand wrapped around my hips. The other lifted my dress and pulled down my panties with a single, brutal movement, making the key slip and jiggle on the floor.

"Don't you want to eat first?" I murmured as the smell of fried potatoes reminded me that he was supposed to be invited for dinner.

"I plan to," he replied, taking me into his mouth with hunger.

Chapter Thirty

For the past two weeks, I spent most nights at the mansion with Anwen in my arms and the time had been the most blissful moon cycle of my entire existence. It pained me to be away from her tonight, after I had gotten used to her falling asleep on my chest. Since she invited me to stay with her, I spent most nights in her bed, caught in loving embraces and toying with each other with tantalizing wickedness.

We'd wasted hours watching stories on the device she loved so much while she made a habit to make me taste new foods every day. We consumed various kinds of drinks and I even learnt to touch some of the buttons and make her friend appear on the screen to have conversations with.

Cressida proved to be an acquired taste, a very demanding and bossy one. The first time I made her appear, she questioned my intentions with Anwen, whom she called her sister and made me show her my abs and biceps, purring when I did so. Luckily Anwen came back from the bedroom and saved me, but after that, I became invited into their sisterly chats. Another obstacle to Anwen's happiness at times were notes she received into her device that she called emails. She explained that some of them were work related as her family had a body ointment and soap business and others, ones I made myself vanish to give her space to mourn, were addressed to her brother and resent to Anwen to deal with.

Whenever I had a free moment during the day, I helped her map the forest and ran all the pathways we could, trying to search for species of plants and wells of energy that could have been of interest to her brother. I think part of her relaxed after discovering my true nature. She had done as promised, came to Evigt and found something. Found me and my kind.

I did not dare breach the 'mates' conversation just yet, she was barely getting used to me and my courting attempts, but even those seemed to bother her at times because I had once grown a bridge alongside the river made out of roots and transfigured branches in front of her and at the sight of my power, she almost fainted.

I did not think it adequate to unravel both my feelings and my knowledge onto her, she constantly shook in the presence of every faerie she met in the woods. She had made some friends. Faelar, a young female sjorka turned out to be a frequent visitor and accompanied Anwen on walks when I didn't do it myself. In the evenings, my mate would tell me stories of her adventures with Phyrra and Rennyn, the heltija twins. Apparently the three of them could get into a lot of trouble pillaging the pantries of the elders and the twins loved braiding Anwen's hair and showing her different clothing styles.

Not all the earthlings proved as welcoming towards a human. Some of them, especially the elders, showed reluctance and hid or disappeared when she walked nearby, especially after the official introduction during which Anwen took the opportunity to show a portrait of her brother and ask every single one of them if they had seen him. The answer always the same, no.

They had tried to convince me of the absurdity of the situation, the fact that I strongly believed the human to be my mate. Such a thing proved unprecedented in history, a matter I prepared myself to discuss with the Queen. Walking through the portal and into the kingdom, I felt wary and prepared myself for the scarring of her wrath. When I appeared through the tree trunks, I exclaimed a low huff. I had completely forgotten about Amara, who stood casually chatting with the King and Queen, each awaiting with a platter of seed cakes.

I hadn't even spared her a thought from my last visit and the fact that she had *asked me* if I wanted to see her again and I, like an imbecile, said *yes*.

I added it to the list of things that would wake Mother's displeasure tonight. One: her son will not mate with a lady from the Wind Kingdom. Two: her son is convinced his mate is a human; and, three: her son wants to mate with the human and bring her into the kingdom. That third part might instate wrath in my mate as well, especially since she seemed to be very fond of her life and technologies and I did not know how to bring the news that it was tradition for the female to follow her mate into his kingdom if they were born in different places. I pushed a smile on my face and stepped out of the forest.

"Mother," I kissed her and served myself a cake from her tray. "Father," I bowed to the King who nodded to me. "Lady Amara," I took her hand in mine and kissed her knuckles gently. She shifted under my touch and bowed slowly, giving me a better look at the generous décolletage of the green dress she wore. Already adopting our colours.

We walked back to the city grounds, while Mother took it upon herself to give me a detailed report of all the activities she and Amara enjoyed in the past moon cycle, all the while praising the windling for her various talents and skills. Meanwhile, Amara comfortably hung on my arm, pinching and squeezing my muscle with sharp intent. The message crystal clear. After what we did last time, she expected more and had all the right to play with my body in front of my mother.

"Mother, thank you for all the stories, they have been wonderful and very intriguing but now, if you would excuse Lady Amara and I, I would very much like to talk to her alone," I blurted out with determination. I would not prolong this and was intent on being truthful today, the first step had to be to cut this female's taste for the crown.

It was all the Queen needed to hear, since she completely vanished within seconds, suddenly finding another one of the ladies to talk to, leaving me and Amara alone on the stone carved bridge we had been passing.

"Would you like to accompany me for a walk, Lady Amara?" I asked politely though she was already pulling me towards the

289

market. It seemed that she made herself quite loved amongst the people here, many earthlings greeted her by name and bowed their heads to both of us as we passed, their eyes lingering on the wildling more than they did on me. Whatever her and Mother had been conspiring, it moved faster than I'd realised.

As we continued to walk past stalls and flower shops, Amara started telling me about her adventures in the kingdom and how similar she found it to the Wind Kingdom, to home, casually chatting about similarities and traditions that she enjoyed over the past few weeks.

"How is your district faring?" she turned the conversation towards me.

"It is very well, thank you for your concern, my lady," I replied with the most diplomatic answer I found, waiting for the best opportunity to open a very different conversation. I did not have to do it for long, because as soon as we walked out the flower market, which turned out to be her favourite one, Amara dragged me to an alleyway then shifted to the left onto an abandoned open stall and within a heartbeat, she placed her lips on mine with eagerness while grabbing my shirt and pulling it upwards to scratch my abdomen.

I let myself be pulled into the fervent motion for just a second, my body so surprised that I barely reacted in time to stop her tongue from swimming into my mouth.

"Lady Amara," I urged, parting our lips, a request for her to regain composure.

"Ansgar, I missed you." Her reply was to pull on my pants and slip a hand to touch me.

"Wow," I twitched and gripped her by the wrist to stop her digging deeper in between my legs.

"It's okay," she murmured, ignoring my hesitation, "I can show you what to do," and with that, the windling made a motion to get on her knees, her intention overly clear.

"I beg you to stop immediately," I almost shouted as I moved away and pushed her with more strength than I wanted to, causing her to fall on her bottom. As soon as I pulled up my trousers and made sure they were secure enough, I helped her up with an apology, flicking her dress to make sure the dirt left no stains.

"I thought you wanted this too," she whimpered, analysing every line on my face.

"I am sorry," I stated as I took a seat on the stall and gestured for her to occupy the one next to me. "Lady Amara, I cannot apologise to you enough," I continued, knowing I had to hurt her feelings and I hated myself for doing it. For not even remembering her during the time we'd been apart.

"Last time, you told me you wanted to see me again. So I stayed," she looked at me confused, covering her forehead with gentle fingers and rubbing it slightly, as though the massage could help her comprehend my reactions better. "You wanted me. Last time," she clarified, "you were eager to shove me against the wall."

"I am truly sorry, Amara." There was no point in denying it and if she was the first one I had to confess to, I might as well drop the titles. "I have found my mate," I whispered, trying not to let the smile that curled my lips shine all the way through, out of respect for her. She glanced at me with a wide unbelieving stare.

"I did," I smirked a bit, proud of myself. "This month," I continued as she settled onto her seat, still looking me up and down.

"How?" was all she asked.

"I have known her for a while," I did not want to give Amara the exact details, not when even the members of my family had no idea what was happening yet. "At first, I felt confused by the feelings, the need to be around her, to just exist in the same place as she does, but it became clearer and she is starting to accept me."

"Why aren't you with her then? Why come with me at all?" Amara asked with slight confusion but I was not about to confess any more than I had to, so I replied vaguely.

"I want to announce it to my family this evening, after that, we will see..." I drew in a breath, hoping the outcome would be favourable to me.

"I understand," Amara rose from the small chair and started walking back towards the alleyway we passed through minutes ago.

"Lady Amara, please allow me to accompany you back to the castle," I offered.

"There is no need, Prince Ansgar," she accentuated my title with sharp coldness, telling me with it that she wanted nothing to do with me anymore. "I shall arrange my journey back in the morning and I need to buy some late minute presents." She offered an official bow and walked back into the flower market.

Out of respect, I circled out the market and crossed the river through the longer bridge, to make sure I spared her another face to face meeting, since she had been humiliated enough. By the time I arrived at the castle, darkness had fully covered the kingdom like a thick veil and I found it more difficult to guide myself home.

By the time I arrived, the family had already finished their first course. Mother looked at me with disbelief and almost huffed as I took my usual seat at the table, noticing that another seat had been added to my right to accommodate the windling lady that was now missing from us, causing Mother to revolt in her own seat.

"I thought you and Lady Amara would be excused for the evening, so we started without you." It was Father who uttered the words. He found my glass and poured wine into it.

"Lady Amara is arranging the journey back to her kingdom in the morning," I voiced as I nodded my thanks and accepted the drink. Running home in the darkness had made me thirsty.

"What? Why?" Mother turned bewildered by the news. "What did you do?" she raised her voice accusingly, fully coming into her role of a mother and shaking off her queen side.

"I only told her the truth," I smirked at her. "That I found my mate."

I uttered the last sentence with pride and it seemed to sweep the sentiment across the table. Father laughed hard with joy, Mother exhaled with relief and Vikram padded me on the back with a cheerful expression, even the staff who served dinner smiled at me and cheered. The only ones that did not move were Damaris and Takara, the ones that I had already spoken to last time about my feelings towards Anwen. Their faces remained straight, eyes piercing into me. A dash of hope rose on my brother's face. He kept looking at me awaiting more information. Traditionally, when one was certain about having found their mate, she would be invited to dinner and officially introduced to the family, though it was more a ceremony than anything else as almost everyone knew everyone in the city and gossip travelled faster than wind.

"Well, where is she? Bring her in!" Father insisted, rising from his seat to give me a proud hug. Once I became free from his arms and regained my seat, I took a breath, preparing myself for what was to come.

"She is not here," I announced and I felt Damaris shift. "She is in Evigt."

Father frowned. "What kingdom is she from?" I followed his range of sight scanning a point onto the wall, moving from side to side while he probably mapped my district to find traces of the other kingdoms.

"The Realm," I replied. "She is a human." I saw no point in prolonging it and a selfish part of me wanted to get the news free. I had held it inside for so long that just the expulsion of this message lifted rocks from my spirit.

"What?" Mother barely whispered and as I glanced at her, I found tears making their way through her beautiful eyes.

"Ansgar, I thought we had settled this last time," Damaris broke the silence. Both my parents could only stare at me in disbelief. The atmosphere of the room shifted, even the staff remained stiff on the side, pretending to become immobile pieces of furniture.

"You knew about this and did not think to report?" the King slammed an angry fist upon the table, making all the glassware clink and shake abruptly.

"It was not his duty to report it to you Father." I found myself taking control of the conversation all of a sudden, "It was mine. And that is what I am trying to do."

"You cannot mate with a human!" The King rose abruptly from his seat, "Don't you know anything?"

I copied his gesture and stood as well. For once, I would not let Father have the last word and if there was ever a moment to fight him, let this be the one.

"I do know Father," I maintained a steady and decided tone, "that I have found my mate. The particularities of her belonging to a kingdom are unknown to me, nor do I know why it is her. What I am convinced of, *my King*," I made sure to emphasize the words and even bowed my head slightly to him, "is that this woman is my mate. And that I love her."

The King's face coloured red, wrath and disappointment shining brighter than ever before at the sight of me. "Love!" he huffed. "Love, boy?" He took a step closer to me, shifting to face me directly. "What do you know about love?" His upper lip curled, just barely, with a shade of disgust. "Get back in your seat and keep your mouth shut. You are not to see this woman again. Find somebody to fuck from our own kingdom."

"Father…" I remained standing but his hand on my chest stopped any words I planned to utter.

"That's the end of it!" the King demanded.

Anwen's perfume invaded my nostrils. Her smile. The way she giggled every time I caressed her hair.

"NO! It is not the end of it!" I felt my lungs flooding, the new air giving me a push, the one I needed to face the King, to defend my love. "You do not have an opinion on this. I am merely informing you that I have found my mate, not asking for permission. In case you missed it, Father, I am a grown male. Free to choose whomever I want. To establish my own path in life, without permission."

Everyone in the room had kept silent, afraid to breathe or interfere in such an unprecedented situation.

He looked at me in disbelief, no one had ever dared disobey him. Or even contradict the King. Giving me one last chance, shock and disgust now claiming the entirety of his features, he barely spoke. "Don't be a disappointment, Ansgar..." he pronounced my name with a warning tone.

"But I already am, Father. Isn't that what you told Damaris?" The memory I kept suppressed for so long resurfaced. "That I am too soft for war? That I can't fuck anyone because of my stupid little trauma? That you are disappointed by my soft heart?" I accused.

His pupils showed a glance of surprise, it barely shone through his anger. I continued, "I am done! Done doing your bidding. Done living the way you ask me to, like a little saint who can't do anything else but obey you. I have found my mate. I will be with her. And there is nothing you or anyone can do to keep me from her. You have no authority in this!"

As soon as I finished speaking, I felt Father's wrath upon my cheek, his hand remaining still in the air after striking me. His face shook, the gesture dominated by instinct rather than hatred.

Still he had done it. In front of the staff and the family.

I looked at him as I felt my cheek turning red. His face remained surprised, regretful, hand shaking, but it was too late.

"As you command, my King," I managed to say as tears clouded my vision and I turned to exit the dining room.

"Ansgar," Vikram grabbed my wrist to stop me but I pulled away, continuing my journey out of the room. As I passed my mother, I forced my gaze away, not wanting to look at her, though I sensed her pain radiating across the room.

I only let myself shed the tears once I was back in my chambers, door locked and windows barred, making sure no one disturbed my pain. I sat on the bed, the replica of the one back at the cave. Images of my childhood, of my life came flashing through my eyes. I was no longer to be a Prince of the Earth Kingdom, the king had made that clear. I did not know what I expected, but it was not this.

Even though Father had always been proper and sometimes cruel for our benefit, I had not expected him to disown me. That's what he had done. Striking a child in public meant banishment from the family. I could still return to the kingdom, but how was I supposed to come back where I no longer belonged? When my father, the person who saw me grow up, who encouraged my training, the one that I fought alongside for the peace of the realm had made the decision to renounce a son rather than give a human a chance?

Hard knocks shook the door into tremors, someone forced the entrance to my chambers, trying to get in.

"Ansgar, open up!" Vikram's voice echoed from the other side.

"Mother and Damaris are talking to him right now, please come back, we will make him reconsider," he raised his voice to make himself audible, though I did not care anymore. I was not a member of this family. The thought, barely out of my head, made pain ripple through me as I made myself walk towards the door and open it. As soon as I did, Vikram's arms jolted around me, hugging me tightly in the embrace I did not think I needed but once I got, made my knees buckle.

"Brother," I mumbled into his shoulder, squeezing him as tight as he did me.

"It'll be okay, you'll see, just give him a minute, he will reconsider and come and apologise," Vikram padded my back

"It is over," I stopped hugging my older brother, the pain of the slap across my face waking me back to reality. "I must go."

Anwen

Chapter Thirty-One

Going to bed without using Ansgar's chest as a pillow turned out to be harder than I thought. I got so used to his presence in the past month, craved his touch every single hour of the day and I found myself thinking about him in the weirdest, most uncommon situations. Since I gave him a key, he had spent most nights with me, either watching movies and kissing on the couch or skipping dinner all together and enjoying each other in the bedroom, though not in all the ways I would have wanted.

It felt like we lived in a bubble, we even had breakfast together some days, then I would meet him somewhere in the forest for lunch and in the evenings, I found myself cooking dinner for when my fae man returned from his duties, whatever they were on that day. I even made a few acquaintances of my own from the faerie lands, even though it proved difficult at first to get over Faelar's mossy hair and elongated ears. She was a great conversationalist and listened to everything I had to share from the 'Realm', as they called it, with major interest.

She was the first to come out of hiding when Ansgar took me to the Northern side of the district and showed me how to cross the river. He built an entire bridge for me out of nothing, with the power of his mind and a flick of the hand, but that was the least of the shocks I experienced that day.

Hundreds of faeries popped out of thin air, they blended so well within the surroundings that, if they hadn't moved to greet me or nodded in my direction, I would have passed them by without a second thought. Not all showed excitement towards the meeting, but the younger ones came by Ansgar's side and introduced themselves, some carrying flowers or small offers for the human friend. The most amusing ones were the twins, Phyrra and Rennyn, always coming around the mansion to ask for new kinds of food and bringing me some of theirs in exchange. Their skin was hard and shaped like tree barks, so they loved playing pranks on me, calling me to a place and then disguising themselves, giggling as I searched for them for longer than I wanted to.

A creaking of the front door made my entire body shiver with anticipation, feeling Ansgar's steps heading towards the bedroom. Darkness still lingered outside and when I looked at the alarm clock I confirmed quarter past four in the morning.

Even though I felt happy with his prompt return, I also knew that he wanted to talk about something important with his family and I feared it may not have been successful if he returned home so quickly.

'Home,' it sounded weird to say it, especially since I was due to leave in three months and had absolutely no idea what would happen with us, nor did I have the courage to ask him. I felt terrified that the smallest dangling of air could rip our bubble open and cause everything to break. So, today, I would call this mansion home, alongside the man that made my heart trepidate with every closing step.

I felt him sneak into bed and wrap his arms around me, pulling me closer to him and straight into a tight embrace.

"Mmmmh," I slowly moaned with pleasure when our skin connected.

"Miss me?" he asked while planting a kiss on my neck.

"Mm-hmm," I approved and extended my neck so his lips had a better reach. I felt him smirk as he continued down my skin and moved onto my shoulder.

"How was your evening?" I asked, still enjoying the soft trail his kisses left on me, forming tiny goose bumps.

"Eventful, but that's a conversation for another day."

I turned to him abruptly, he had been excited to visit his parents, we had talked about our families many times and we both confessed how much we missed them, so as soon as he said the words, I knew something had gone wrong.

"What happened?" I enquired, scanning his face. He looked tired and his eyes were slightly red, the capillary veins plummeting in the whites of his eyes. He had been crying.

"Ansgar," I stood, my hand instinctively caressing his jaw. "What happened?" I repeated.

"Nothing," he dismissed, but his look was regarded, dark shadows straining his vision that rippled more saddened than ever. "Just had a fight with the King, is all."

Only my boyfriend could come to bed at four in the morning, after having visited some magical kingdom of faeries and say that he had a fight with a king as if it was the most casual thing.

"Was it a fight with the King or an argument with your dad?" I wanted to clarify.

"Both, this time they went hand in hand," he puckered his lips, a shade of regret portraying his features.

"I am sorry," I whispered, taking my turn to plant kisses on his neck. I brushed his unbraided hair to the side and started at the shell of his ear, trailing down.

"Anwen, I..." he stopped, swallowing his words and breathing them out, as though he wanted to send the unspoken sentence away from his mind.

"You..." I murmured, unbuttoning his shirt, sewing small kisses along the way.

He stopped me and cupped my face. I smiled softly at him, but his eyes pierced deeper, penetrating, like they wanted to bare my every thought.

"Hie vaedrum teim fahrenor," he whispered, the words barely allowed to escape his lips before meeting with mine in a pressing kiss.

Yet another phrase I did not understand. He was doing it more and more often, allowing his language to fall through. This time, it sounded different. His words marked me, even though I could not decipher their meaning, they slid from his mouth and into the tunnels of my soul.

I tried to push, but Ansgar was not willing to talk about whatever happened during his visit, albeit he seemed to be more than willing to explore more of my body and after two matutinal orgasms, I fell asleep in his arms. I woke up hours later to the delicious smell of toast and melted butter that came from the kitchen and I heard Ansgar having some sorts of a disagreement with the coffee machine. I admired his bravado, whenever I showed him a piece of technology he would listen carefully to my description, ask a few questions and instinctively start to use it after a demonstration or two. His favourite one so far had been movies and the way the laptop streamed them but something about the coffee machine made him lose his malleable temper and curse through his breath at the pods. Wanting to save him, I hurried downstairs.

"Good morning," I said and touched his back. I glued my lips to his shoulder for an eager kiss. Ansgar relaxed under my touch, a low breath released from him as he turned and kissed my brow, then my nose and finally, my lips.

"Good morning to you too, fahrenor," he replied, then sighed and pointed to the coffee machine. "This devilish creation does not swallow the beans like it should," he accused.

Of course it wouldn't, he had jammed the water filter with ground coffee. I chuckled internally, then asked him to allow me to do it while he finished the toast and bacon. Two minutes later, a latte macchiato and an espresso released tiny steams on the table. We sat in front of our plates. I was very hungry, I realised after the first bite into the toast, and started excitedly chewing on a piece of bacon that smelled and tasted amazing. Ansgar looked at me, not touching his toast.

"Can we talk?" he captured my attention from a second piece of bacon that made its way into my mouth.

"Surmm," I half replied, struggling to chew all that food at once.

He paused, letting me finish and give him my full attention, which, after a huge gulp, I did.

"Remember when I told you about mates?" Ansgar asked, his features too serious for this to be a good conversation.

"Yeah...." I replied hesitantly. I remembered what he said about having to find a mate after he left the forest and get married, like his older brother had.

"What is your opinion on mates?" he asked with the same seriousness lighting his soft features.

I puckered my lips, giving my brain a moment to think. From what Ansgar described to me and what I read on the internet, their version of mates looked similar to our version of soulmates. A person created for another, two souls that would fit together and make a full circle. I did not know what to think of it, I had never seen it in real life, except in books and all the romantic comedies ever made, but not in a real couple because it seemed too good to be true. Two people coming together as one, joining hands in the long journey through life, supporting and caring for one another every second of every day. I wasn't the most experienced person in the realms of love, the only time my insides fluttered, as love is described, was with Ansgar.

"Why are you asking me this?" I startled all of a sudden. *This is it*, my brain alerted the rest of me of its realisation, he was leaving me. To go find his mate. I would lose *him* too. My entire body tensed at once and the food I so eagerly devoured earlier wanted to make its way back, but I swallowed hard, trying to keep it in. Tears came into my eyes but I blinked rapidly and grabbed the coffee to take big sips and push down that lump in my throat.

He looked uneasy, his body language stressed and he fidgeted and made tiny scratches on his toast with the butter knife. *Oh my god, he was leaving me.* My heart started pulsating frantically and I felt bile rising in my throat. Desperation came over me and gripped every muscle. My lungs forgot how to drag in air and pain bloomed in my torso. A clawing pain that was taking control of my insides, rapturing my feelings into nothing. I gasped and tried to allow breath into me but it would not come, my neck muscles squeezed tight and in pain, blocking every inhale I tried to take. I would lose him. I would lose Ansgar just as I lost my brother. Because I'd dared to love again.

"Anwen?" his eyes grew wide on me and when I met them, tears started pouring down my cheeks.

"Anwen?" I heard his voice, worry seeping into it as he pushed his chair back and materialised by my side the next second. "Anwen, what is happening?" He pulled me in his arms and I let myself fall to the ground, his shape the only support I wanted. I couldn't breathe. The air pressed heavy. All around me. Crushing me. On my skin. Touching me and pushing down upon my chest, trying to crush me under the weight of nothingness.

"ANWEN!" I heard Ansgar shout my name, grabbing my face and forcing me to look at him, trying to capture my attention but I barely saw him anymore. The world around me was slowly fading into darkness. All I could do was choke on my breath, my insides hard as cement.

"Anwen, breathe," he commanded and with a swift movement, the fae prince pressed his lips on mine. Not to kiss, I understood as a swirl of air came forcefully pushed down my throat and into my lungs. Then another. It was all I needed, the impulse of a breath, a breath that he had given back to me.

"That's it, slow and steady," I heard him say while my lungs pushed the air he had lent me back outside and took the first breath on their own. "Very good, fahrenor, another one," he encouraged in a trembling voice. I gulped a second breath.

He took my hand and placed it on his chest, his body a pillar for my weight. "Like this," he urged as he pressed my fingers just above his heart, allowing me to feel his lungs heaving up and down. I sensed his heart beating heavily, full of worry and his lungs inflating and deflating, encouraging me to do the same. So I mimicked his movements and forced my body to copy his. Up and down, up and down.

I don't know how long we stood, breathing in silence, until our inhales coordinated. All the while, Ansgar caressed every part of me that he could find. My hair, my neck, my back, every muscle within his reach, trying to calm me down.

"I'm okay," I whispered, not daring to fully voice the sentence from fear that everything might start all over again.

"I am so sorry, Anwen," he uttered almost silently. "We'll talk about it another day."

His words almost pushed another attack down my throat, he would do it another day. He would abandon me another day because I was just a silly human who could not handle her emotions and he was too kind to break my heart after I had a full breakdown in front of him. Because I couldn't handle the news of him wanting to leave.

Because I had fallen in love with the forbidden fae prince.

Ansgar

Chapter Thirty-Two

I held her in my arms, forcing her body to keep breathing. What the hell was I thinking? Of course she would react like this. What did I expect? For her to jump into my arms and accept the mating? Of course she wouldn't, she was scared within an inch of her life and stopped breathing from the fright I caused her.

My mate would rather stop allowing air into her lungs than come with me. Scratches of pain penetrated whilst I re-envisioned her reaction. What in the goddess' name had I been thinking? For such a beautiful woman, who has success and riches in her life to just want to abandon everything and come with me into an unknown world just because she liked me and I was her mate? I huffed at the idiocy of my expectations, making my way to the river.

My marking ceremony remained scheduled for the next full moon and I had everything in my mind but the decision I needed to make. When a keeper chose their mark, it bound them to nature through the respective sign and allowed them to channel energy throughout the realm, enhancing their abilities by using said mark.

Because I guarded this district successfully for the past three moon cycles and was...had been—a crippling twist in my stomach reminded me—a member of the royal family, my ceremony opened the lines of celebrations and all the other keepers in the kingdom would follow in choosing theirs. The marking ceremony was one of the most important events in a keeper's life. It would become a symbol of their house once they chose a mate. Throughout their life, their and their family's energy would be represented and channeled through the mark they had chosen.

I had been thinking about what I wanted to select as a mark since childhood. At first I started with fantastic ideas like dragon's teeth or a harpie's wing until I learnt such symbols had to be real, living things, and the more widespread the better. It meant that the energy surge would be constant throughout one's lifespan. So basically, I had to pick something regal enough which would hopefully still be alive in the next century.

Father had chosen an orchid and Damaris a gloriosa, while Vikram renounced the right alongside his desire for a family. I was the only remaining one, the youngest prince, banished from the family. Great.

I spent the rest of the day healing, sprouting and explaining my glum expression to the passing faeries. Faelar found me just as I dug an old sycamore root to carve new life into the stem and kicked my shoulder to draw my attention. She reprimanded me for over ten minutes about how I left Anwen crying and scared, barely giving me a breath to explain the real situation.

"Are you sure?" the sjorka female asked, more to convince

herself that her elongated ears had received my message correctly.

"I can't explain it, but I know it," I replied in such a firm tone, that she backed away a step. I immediately withdrew my power and apologised, but Faelar didn't seem too upset. She disappeared within seconds, assuring me she would form a plan to help. Before she made a turn out of my view, she asked me to make my home presentable.

It was late afternoon when I finished cleaning the cave and, with Faelar's help, wrote up an invitation for Anwen to join me for dinner, then passed it to the twins who offered to deliver it along with sugared raspberries. I thanked the females and, after their departure, took the time to make myself look presentable. After showering and scrubbing away the dirt of the day, I selected a grey shirt with the purpose to make my eyes brighter. The arms were just tight enough for the fabric to mould to my biceps but not too much so I ripped through it. I wanted her to like me, to feel attraction towards me. I hoped that if she enjoyed my looks, she would not want to break our relationship just yet.

A knock on the door announced her arrival and I sprinted towards the entrance to let her in. As soon as I opened the door, my eyes gouged out with amazement. She wore a red dress, perfectly modelled onto her form, displaying every curve of her body and showcasing her round breasts. Her hair was tightly pulled up in a sophisticated updo, her neck and shoulders bare and lips sparkled, painted in such a deep shade of red that they practically begged kisses.

"Anwen," I stupidly called her name in a husky voice. I remained breathless and my brain stopped functioning correctly from beauty overload.

"Ansgar," she replied, her gaze scanning mine. I pulled her into my arms, my lips devouring hers with urgency and need. I relished in the feeling, her unaltered desire towards me and kicked the door closed, pressing her tighter onto me.

I felt our lips mingling, breaths conjoined and hearts beating together and understood that I needed this woman now.

If I had a limited time with her, I had to enjoy the blessing. Without saying a word, I lowered my hands, pressing one onto her lower back and the other on her upper thigh, pulling her towards my waist. Her legs moved instinctively and curled over my hips, as she continued to taste my mouth, not breaking the kiss. Her hands ran through my hair while I moved us towards the bedroom with hurried steps. I caressed her thighs, her ass, her lower back, everywhere I could touch and lowered her onto the bed while she pulled at my shirt, dragging it from me with desperation. The gesture forced me to break the kiss just enough to take it off, leaving my chest bare for her to scratch and bite. I made quick work of her dress, unzipping the back and dragging it towards her legs and making it fly to the floor. Which left Anwen wearing only a small lacy red pair of panties.

"Red is officially my favourite colour."

It raised a chuckle from her sinful lips. I started spreading kisses on her inner thighs, coming closer and closer to the red lace temptation, her only defence against

my eager tongue. I bit her slit through the lace, announcing what was to come, but instead of the low moan I had gotten so used to, Anwen released a gasp, her entire posture hardening. She instantly covered her bare breasts with her palms. I did not have time to move when I heard a familiar voice.

"If they look this good, I wouldn't mind mating a human either," Vikram's voice echoed from behind me.

I turned abruptly, releasing Anwen's panties from my mouth and tried to cover my brother's field of vision with my body.

"What are you doing here?" I rasped.

He ignored me and shifted to gaze at my mate again, whistling in delight. Like a disgusting lustful male in heat. Rage overtook me and I didn't stop the instinct, nor did I want to. I attacked my brother and automatically started covering his face with my fists, over and over until blood came pouring out of his nose and mouth. The only thing that stopped me were Anwen's terrorised screams, begging me to a halt. *Stop scaring her,* my brain commanded, ordering the muscles to stop pumping blows into Vikram's already hurt face.

"Ansgar, stop!" my mate's cries demanded, so I released him from my grasp. I instinctively went back to her, covering her with the shirt I had just worn and cupping her cheeks, making sure she was alright. Tears gathered in her eyes, her face a composite of emotion I was unable to read. She shifted them from me, they went to my injured brother, then back onto my face.

"That's my brother, Vikram, he will not harm you." I stared at her, making sure she understood and I pierced her with a look until she nodded slowly.

"Why are you doing this to your brother?" Anwen could barely murmur.

"That's on me," I heard Vikram's voice while he probably pulled himself together. "I should have known better than to stare at another male's naked mate."

I turned to him and saw him cleaning up his bloody face, spitting up blood on the floor I had cleaned for Anwen's arrival.

"What?" she whimpered, face still cupped in my hands.

"You are safe," I repeated and kissed her brow, then turned to Vikram.

"What do you want?" I asked with a threat, calming my ragged breath enough to have a conversation at this point. The only thing grounding me was Anwen, held and protected, tightly in my arms. He may be my brother, but he had offended my mate and something inside me snapped with hatred.

"To tell you that Father is sorry and you are not disowned. He will talk to you and apologise on your return. Your marking celebration continues to be scheduled for the next full moon," Vikram replied with frustration, words barely making their way out of his mouth, then turned towards the door. "You both have a good evening," he declared and looked at me first, then wanted to shift to Anwen but stopped midway through. He nodded again and disappeared through the door.

I gazed back to Anwen, who remained cuddled in my arms, pulling my shirt tightly around her. Tears still danced on her face.

"It's okay, he is gone now," I brushed my hand through her hair to capture her attention.

Anwen's eyes pierced mine, and I found pain and surprise in

them. "What the hell was that?"

I stared back at her, not understanding which part of what had happened in the last few minutes provoked the question.

"Mate?" Anwen whispered. "I am your mate?"

Anwen

Chapter Thirty-Three

I stared at him blankly, trying to wrap my head around what had just happened. Within a matter of seconds, Ansgar had switched from wanting to have sex with me to ripping his brother's face off, all because he saw me naked. And I was his mate. That's what he tried to tell me in the morning, when I so stupidly thought he wanted to leave me.

I was his mate.

My brain could not process the information, the meaning it held, the fact that Ansgar had apparently been disowned because of an argument with the King, which I could safely assume had everything to do with me. I did not know what to feel, what to say, how to react to the news, so I thought it best to remain quiet and buried in my thoughts, trying my hardest to grasp into understanding all the events rolling out throughout the day.

"Fahrenor," Ansgar came to my side and wrapped an arm around me, wiping away tears I had not realised I'd shed from my cheek.

"What does that even mean?" I choked at the lump in my throat, the realness of the situation hitting me harder and harder.

"My starlight," he whispered into my ear, his breath brushing my skin as it passed the information. His starlight. That's what he had called me all this time and I didn't even have the nerve to ask him for a translation.

"Anwen, I…"

"No," I rushed and placed a finger over his mouth to cover the half spoken words. "Not here. Not like this."

I pierced him with a pleading gaze and he nodded in understanding, his lips stopping the words. He settled for sketching a kiss on my palm, turning back to the sweet man I had blindly fallen in love with. A wave of happiness flushed over me at the realisation. Ansgar loved me! This beautiful, committed and honourable man had feelings for me.

"I need to go," I said and collected myself, wearing only his shirt and my red panties.

"Go where?" He immediately followed after me as I grabbed my shoes and headed towards the door. "Anwen, where are you going?" He snatched my waist from behind and pulled me close to him, squeezing me in an embrace, my back tightly pressed to his bare chest. I almost melted at the touch and my entire body throbbed for the caresses and pleasure he had been about to give me. I paused for a moment, abandoning myself to his soft skin and massive forearms. He was built like a god and every shred of me begged to worship.

"Ansgar," I murmured. He started to leave a stream of kisses from my neck down to my clavicle.

"Please don't go," he pleaded, his embrace tightening just enough to make his point. There was no place better for me than those arms, and both he and I knew it.

"Ansgar, this morning I had trouble breathing, I had palpitations throughout the entire afternoon, just witnessed you kicking your brother's ass and found out I am your mate." I blurted all my anxiety, making a point to leave out that the attack I had was sheer terror of his abandonment.

"Let me get some rest, think things through and we will pick this up again tomorrow." I paused. "I don't want it happening like this," I admitted.

Ansgar had wanted to go further this time, a raging desire shimmered in his eyes when I arrived. He had claimed me with no reservation, no stillness and care. He wanted to go all the way this time. And for the love of all the gods, I hated myself for not ripping his pants and jumping him, like I dreamed about doing many, many times. But he deserved better.

We deserved better.

"Okay..." was all he said as he turned me to face him and his eyes displayed a projection of his understanding. "Let me at least accompany you home."

I sighed at the thought of walking back in those shoes. I don't know why I thought it would be a good idea to wear high heeled boots in a forest, apart from the obvious fact that I wanted to look sexy as hell. The thought of twisting my ankles in the darkness did not appeal to me.

"Can you do that thing where you magically appear in places?" I asked, my look giddish.

I had asked him several times, especially when he had plans to court me, to keep things as simple and human as possible until I adjusted to the thought of him being who he was, and to his credit, he had limited most of what he did and kept it outside the small palace we lived in. But seeing how my boyfriend had powers and I didn't fancy walking in the darkness, one little bend of rules could be easily passed by in this situation.

Ansgar smirked and kissed me, his lips finding mine, tongue expertly opening my mouth and doing that twist thingy that drove me crazy. I moaned into his mouth and he pulled me closer, tighter, his wide torso covering me in a protective embrace. By the time the kiss finished, we were both standing on my porch and I was looking around like a silly person to convince myself that it had really happened. That in the span of a kiss, we'd travelled about three miles from his bedroom to my house. Ansgar's gaze fixated on me, taking in my every movement. A small smile curled his lips.

"There are some benefits to this, fahrenor," he finally replied with a slight satisfaction.

I had to pull myself away to not be drawn back onto him, so I grasped the doorknob tightly and held onto it for dear life, trying not to fall into Ansgar's embrace. My traitorous body screamed so desperately for his attention that I would probably end up taking him right there on the porch.

"Good night," I said sheepishly, images of what was to come flashing my vision.

"Good night, beautiful, I'll see you tomorrow morning," he whispered and glanced at me one more time, with promise in his eyes before he vanished into thin air right in front of me.

I giggled like a schoolgirl as I opened the door. For the third time that day, I drew a startled breath. Standing on the sofa, flicking through a magazine, was Ansgar's brother.

"What are you doing here?" I tried to look calm but I scanned my surroundings for any kind of weapon. I was in Ansgar's shirt and had nothing iron made on me nor had I kept any of the chains by the door. Damn it.

"I came to talk," he stood from the chair and raised his hands when I immediately took a step back. "I have no intention of harming my brother's mate. I come in peace. I promise."

To prove his point, he took a step backwards towards the table and grabbed the set of knives from his waist, placing them on the marble surface. "They are part of the uniform, nothing more," he stated, then proceeded to remove the silver breastplate and several pieces of armour from his shoulders and forearms. It took him about two minutes and at the end of it, Ansgar's brother presented in front of me in a simple white shirt and leather pants.

"Is my brother coming?" he asked, not shifting his eyes from me.

I hesitated at the question. If I replied truthfully, I might find myself defenceless against a trained fae warrior, but if I told a lie and made him believe his brother would arrive any minute, he might hurt me quicker if that was his plan.

"How did you get in?" I decided to ignore his question.

"The front door was unlocked."

I cringed. Of course it was, I hadn't locked it since Ansgar started sleeping here, there was no point, now that the stranger I had been terrified of became my boyfriend.

"What happened to the old lock? The iron one?" he inquired and when I widened my eyes to him, he explained. "A childhood friend kept here, two rounds back. He had many stories to share about the queen and legends."

"I had it removed," I cut him off. If he was willingly giving out information, I had to do the same.

"Because of Ansgar?" Vikram asked, surprised. I nodded. He sucked in his lips, agreement and admiration flushing his face.

"What do you want?" I asked again, hoping that after the little chat we had, he would give his true motives.

"To have a conversation with you alone. Since you did not answer my question earlier, I assume my brother is not coming." I grimaced at his logical line of thought. "Should you need to change first, I am happy to wait."

That made me snort. As though I would leave him alone in here, free to just pick up a knife and come after me to find me naked and defenceless. Not that my forced outfit choice looked appropriate.

He read my hesitation and continued, "Do you have any iron left?"

"Like I would tell you that," I replied aggressively. *How stupid does he think I am?*

"To prove that I am not planning on harming you in any way, I volunteer to be iron bound until your return, should that make you feel more secure," he offered.

"Seriously?" Ansgar's pain still haunted me. And he'd been unconscious when I chained him. Why would someone voluntarily put themselves through that? "Doesn't it hurt?"

"Like a bitch," he chuckled.

"Okay, I may decide to trust you," I unwillingly replied. If this

320

man would suffer for a conversation with me, I could at least make an effort to trust my boyfriend's brother.

"Give me five minutes?" I asked and started climbing the stairs leaving him alone in the sitting room.

"Ah, excuse me..." his voice trailed.

"Yes?" I stopped midway through the staircase.

"Is it okay if I rummage your fridge and get some ice?" He pointed at his still swollen lip.

"Go for it," I nodded and started climbing the stairs again. I removed Ansgar's shirt and placed it carefully onto his side of the bed, it was the one item of his clothing I had in this house.

Generally, he wandered around the forest in some pants and bare chest, then came to sleep and shower here and he simply removed said pants, but never brought any of his items apart from his so called uniform of daggers and knives he carried around either on his arm or in a bandolier.

I scanned my wardrobe and found a much needed bra, a pair of cotton panties, a long t-shirt and some comfortable wide pants. I did not believe it was possible to make a worse impression on his brother after he saw Ansgar's head in between my legs and most of me naked, so I decided to go for comfort.

When I returned downstairs, the brother was sipping a canned drink, eating a sandwich and watching youtube. *Make yourself at home, why don't you?* All of a sudden, realisation hit me. He watched youtube and used the word fridge. Not only was it curious because of Ansgar's complete lack of contact with technology, but I did not ignore his night sky dark skin. How were they brothers but looked so different?

I coughed to make my presence known and he paused the video to turn his attention to me.

"How come you are so different from your brother?" *Well done Anwen, can't keep a thought to ourselves, can we?*

"I inherited my mother's power, thus, dark skin. Damaris and Ansgar are shaped after Father," he replied.

"Oh," I responded, still accusing my brain for asking such stupid questions.

"If I were to have children, they could be born with any kind of power from the past seven generations, we have no control over it," he explained further.

"I am more surprised by youtube," I confessed.

"Oh," it was his turn to say it now. "I am Commander of Realm Defence," he proclaimed proudly. "I practically live here more than in the kingdom, so I can enjoy the benefits of both worlds," he raised his canned cocktail and took a long sip. "We receive reports on human advancements every year, though not many have the pleasure of testing them."

"So you know how this world works," I continued.

"I do, which is why I would like to have a friendly conversation with my brother's mate." He invited me to take a seat onto the sofa but before I moved he announced apologetically, "You might need alcohol for this."

I went to the drinks fridge and randomly picked two cocktails, then returned into the room and placed one next to him on the table, taking a seat on the opposite side.

"Thank you," his vision sparked at the can and he popped it open. "I love mojitos," he said excitedly.

"Your brother loves cosmos," I replied with a grin and he stared at me.

"NO!" he exclaimed with disbelief and surprise.

"He does," I nodded in confirmation and smiled slowly, making him chuckle.

"I would pay good money to see Ansgar have his first cosmopolitan."

"He had a few," I admitted, "and caramel vodka."

Vikram grinned and took another sip of his drink, grimacing slightly when the can touched his swollen lip.

"I am sorry about that," I heard myself saying. Even though I hadn't directly caused it, my presence in his brother's bedroom created the situation.

He waved it off as nothing. "We started off on the wrong foot and it is entirely my fault. Please, let me make things right. I am Vikram, Ansgar's middle brother, it is nice to make your acquaintance," he said and extended his hand for me to take in a handshake.

"Anwen Odstar," I introduced myself as I shook it.

"Is this your family's home?" he asked.

"Oh, no. It belongs to the royal family; I am just staying here temporarily. Sorry, not a princess," I voiced raising my shoulders apologetically.

"You will be, soon enough," he replied and my face turned blank. I hadn't even considered that possibility.

"What happened on his last visit?" If we were speaking so directly, I might as well get the information I needed first. He had mentioned something about Ansgar's disowning and I remembered his pained face when he returned. Something big must have happened.

"I suspect you know a fair amount about the kingdoms by now so I will talk to you as one of us. If at any point you need details, stop me and ask." I nodded to confirm.

He continued, "Also, for this to work, we need to be truthful to each other. I will tell you the unabridged information you want to know with the request that you answer my questions as well."

"Agreed," I confirmed.

He looked convinced enough because he started speaking. "Last night, Ansgar announced that he found his mate and took us all by surprise. We all believed he would continue to get to know the windling lady better, since he asked her to stay and wait for him. Both our parents were hopeful for a fortified alliance with the Wind Kingdom, so the news took us all by surprise. Especially since you are human."

"I am sorry, what?" My eyes widened with rage and surprise. "What lady?"

"Lady Amara, niece of the Wind Queen?" Vikram said slowly, as if I were an idiot. "She and Ansgar… last month?" His face burst with the realisation. I had not known.

"Did Ansgar already have someone?" I asked him. That would explain his reaction and why he was so angry with his brother when he saw me. Because he could tell me about this lady he had at home.

I bit my tongue to stop tears from falling onto my cheeks, but Vikram immediately waved his hands. I did not know if the gesture was to take back the words or bring my attention towards him.

"I don't know how much he's told you and I honestly don't want to cause any trouble. This female, she is almost a princess in her kingdom and she came to visit. Mother took a liking to her and introduced her to Ansgar. I think they spent a few hours together and kissed a few times but that is all. Then she lingered at the palace, apparently Ansgar said he wanted to see her again but she made a big deal of it and spent the entire month acting like she was the new princess. When Ansgar came home again, the first thing he did was take her for a walk, and by the time he came to dinner she was going home and he announced finding you," he was breathless by the time he finished speaking.

Relief inundated my muscles and my heart started beating normally again. Even though we'd been kissing from time to time, Ansgar and I started being together after the past full moon.

Vikram interrupted my internal monologue and continued, "It is not tradition for one to find a mate in a human, there are severe punishments if fae willingly reveal themselves to humans, let alone..." he struggled to say the next words, "have sex with them."

My cheeks turned red as I remembered Vikram's face when he saw me squeezing his little brother's head between my thighs. I wanted to tell him that we hadn't gone all the way, but seeing what plans I had with Ansgar tomorrow, that subject would quickly be ticked off the list.

Noticing how I remained silent, Vikram continued, "Damaris

had previous knowledge of you, apparently Ansgar talked to him a few months back and asked what a mating bond felt like. It seemed he had his suspicions ever since you two met, but Mother and Father had no idea and to be completely honest with you, they do not approve of your mating bond. First of all, because there haven't been any cases of a bond with a human and secondly, because relationships with humans are frowned upon. Ansgar raised his voice at Father, shouting that he loves you. No one can do that to the king," he clarified for my benefit, "and Father lost it. He slapped Ansgar publicly, which means he is disowned."

"So everything that happened, is because of me?" I asked and lost control of my tears. "Because he is with me?"

Vikram settled for a nod, spearing me the words.

"I am sorry," I replied, now fully sobbing. "I am sorry I am causing him pain."

The brother stood from the sofa and came closer to me, occupying the seat to my right. Without reservations, he placed a hand on my shoulder blade and stroked gently.

"Anwen, this is what I need to talk to you about and I need you to be honest," he remarked while his hand moved up and down my arm in a soothing repetition.

"A mating bond is one of the rarest kinds of energy there is, and it can only be felt between beings who are capable of producing and controlling such energy. My brother is inexperienced to say the least; he has never been in love until now. I chose not to search for a mate, but I have felt love many times, it is easy to confuse a male, especially one who is opening his heart for the first time."

"I didn't plan this, Vikram. A month ago I didn't even know your kind existed. I even mocked one of the guards about it."

"We tend to keep it out of the human world, I'm sure Ansgar already explained it. This and the punishments for human interaction."

"What punishments?" I asked dumbfounded.

He huffed, as though he admonished himself for not realising it sooner. "Ansgar is betting his fate on our parents' love. If the Queen does not accept you as his mate, he is to stand trial."

"Stand trial? What for?" I replied astonished and scared.

"For this." He pointed at me. "For you."

"What? Why?" I asked aggressively, not understanding what I had to do with it. With anything.

Vikram took a sip of his drink, preparing to speak for a long time.

"About two centuries ago, the rulers of the kingdoms decided to install severe punishments for all those who interact with humans. There are lists and hundreds of trials throughout this time to stand as an example. If one is seen by a human, unwillingly, they get a lashing. If they reveal themselves to a human, they are jailed for any number of years the Queen considers fit. If one touches a human, they lose a limb."

"And if one mates with a human?" my voice trembled as I uttered the words.

He shook his head. "It's up to the Queen. If he weren't her son, Ansgar would already be dead."

"But you are here, revealing yourself to me!" I protested.

"I am Realm Defence, it's my duty. I chose to live amongst

humans and protect them. I have already paid for the privilege."

"What are you saying?" I wiped away the tears just enough to look at him through the watery mess pouring down my face.

"I am asking you to do the right thing, if you truly love him."

His piercing gaze told me everything I needed to know. He wanted me to break up with his brother and set him free. He was a fae prince after all, one who deserved better than a human. One that would put his life in danger. That I was not his mate, it was only Ansgar's strong feelings for me that confused him into thinking that. At the realisation, I wailed in pain, Vikram's hand stroking my back with calming movements.

"But I am his mate…" my voice sounded like a coal ready to be extinguished.

"Anwen, if there were any way to prove it… You've seen it for yourself, how he acted, the way he attacked me to protect you. He never crossed Father with anything, ever, but he would gladly lose his family, position and kingdom for you. Because he loves you. And he will be punished for it. My question, Anwen is," he stopped to scan my face, "do you love my brother enough to stop him?"

Chapter Thirty-Four

I'd been up at dawn but decided to perform duties first and let Anwen sleep a while longer. After the excitement of yesterday, she deserved rest. I walked through the district and cared for several roots and healed some barks ripped by the strong winds, I sprouted hundreds of gardenias, enough to make a bouquet suitable for my beautiful mate, then went back to the cave to shower and change my clothes. At about mid-morning, I knocked on the door, heart beating with excitement.

If we hadn't been interrupted yesterday, she would be resting in my arms, just as she did every night in the past few weeks. Only we would be mated, and I would belong to her completely, just like I knew every shred of my heart already did.

"Good morning," Anwen's voice greeted me as she opened the door. I immediately sensed something wrong. Darkness in her eyes, which were red and swollen.

"Good morning, fahrenor," I replied and placed a kiss on her lips. Which she did not return. My mate shifted to the side to allow me enough space to enter and her extended hand pointed me to the sofa, treating me like a guest. I had shared this space with her so many times I practically knew it as well as I did my own chambers. Without protest, I followed her instructions and sat onto the sofa, feeling her stare at my movements, my every gesture watched.

"Are you going to join me?" I asked innocently after I planted myself in my favourite spot, the one that had a leg extension. Whenever we watched stories on her device, I would sit there, with my legs up. She wrapped herself in a blanket and found a cosy position in my embrace, resting her head on my shoulder. Sometimes she fed me popped corn or sweets and I would bite her fingers gently and she would giggle. Now, the person sitting next to me seemed to be a shell of that woman.

"Ansgar, we need to talk," Anwen announced as her bloodshot eyes made a point to avoid mine.

Something was very, very wrong, and it happened after I brought her back to the mansion. In my chamber, on the porch, she sounded hopeful and in love. I knew I shouldn't have left her alone, whatever thought inundated her mind last night, I would make a point to collapse each and every one of her worries.

"Before you say anything, Anwen," I started, needing to take some control of the situation, "I want you to know that I am in love with you." *Time to confess, Ansgar.* I needed to put her worry to rest so I opened my heart and started splurging my feelings for her.

"My heart recognised you since the very first time I held you, I felt the surge of our energies connecting and, even though I could not grasp it then, a part of me knew we were made for each other. That you are to be mine and I, yours." I went back to that first time she was injured in my bedchamber, how my heart fluttered at the touch of her skin. "I can't stop thinking about you, I feel an unyielding need to be close to you and I find every excuse to do so, because I cannot understand a world where you are not by my side."

She shattered, deep shivers passing through her figure, her skin, as tears overrun her cheeks. I rose and rushed to her side in an instant, wiping them away with my thumbs. We sat there, more tears spurting from her red and swollen eyes. I continued, "The first time I kissed you, I felt complete, as if I had found the missing piece of myself. I never knew such happiness existed until I held you in my arms. Every minute I spend by your side is a blessing and I swear to you that I will always be here, loving you every hour of every day, if you will have me." She made desperate efforts to control her grief, but it flooded through her, changing her like the lightning does sand.

She forcefully removed my hands from her face and stood, her posture struggling to put as much distance between us as possible. Her entire body trembled and she turned to me.

"Ansgar, I am sorry," she murmured, her voice rasp as she forced her gaze on me. "I am so sorry," she continued. Sobs were expelled from her rib cage.

"Anwen, my love," I was by her side again, grabbing her tightly to my chest and pressing my lips onto her hair, whispering softly. Whenever she walked away from me, I would come back to her side.

"My starlight." I planted deep kisses over her; her hair, her forehead, her face, her puffy eyes, her lips, all the while she remained unmoving, empty. "Whatever it is, we will face it together. Please, just tell me what is wrong," I begged.

Anwen adopted a statuesque figure, so still that I had to halt and listen to her breathing to make sure it had not stopped. She cleared her throat and pointed her gaze to mine.

"I can't be with you." She stopped to think better of it, then spoke again, "I don't want to be with you anymore."

I sook my head, refusing to take in the information, denying to acknowledge what she had just told me.

"No…" I wavered, vertigo taking hold of me. My knees sank onto the floor. I was begging in front of her, begging for her to change her mind, my head bowed and low in front of her as my shoulders trembled in pain. I hadn't known true loss until that moment. A mate's rejection burnt the spirit. I had heard it before, of unfortunate males whose lives crumbled into specks after the cursed moment. I did not think it would happen to me.

"Anwen…" was all I said, defeated. I abandoned myself into her eyes one more time and saw tears. It was true. She was crying because it was true.

"Anwen, please, don't do this. I love you," I voiced as the rest of my body collapsed to the floor and I found myself sitting on the ground like an unstable child, my back supported by the sofa. She took a seat in front of me, crouching next to where I had landed. A hand touched my arm and I felt her squeezing lightly, as though she was afraid I would break.

"I am sorry, Ansgar," she replied. "I am so, so sorry."

I did not say anything, couldn't even look in her direction

without unravelling, so she started telling me the story I did not ask to hear. "After you left last night," she paused, thinking her words through and taking a few breaths of air, then continued, "I started thinking about everything. About the way you treated your brother. I don't know you, not really."

I growled from the pain built up inside me, her every word drilled into me, but she resumed. "It made me realise that what we have, what we thought we have," she corrected, "is just a fantasy. I am a human and you are fae, we are built differently, we feel differently, we have different needs."

"Anwen, I would give you everything in my power. I am sorry I scared you last night—" I tried to argue but she cut me off.

"I like my life, Ansgar. I don't want to hide and live in a forest forever. And I would give anything to have just another moment with my brother, yet here you are, treating yours with unimaginable violence," she continued.

It was my turn to stop her. "You can have all of that with me Anwen. We can travel, we can have a life. I will make amends with my brother, I swear to you."

"I love my human life. Why would I sacrifice it all for—"

For me. The words remained unsaid but I grasped them. I was not enough for her. What kind of life could I offer her if she would have to follow me into an unknown world, where everyone, even my family was against us? I understood. It broke me, it destroyed every miserable trace of hope I still held, but she was right. She wanted more. She deserved more.

I forced myself up. Anwen followed me, extending her hands

like she wanted to help me get up but I ignored them as I responded, "Anwen, I truly hope you will be very happy, you deserve everything this world has to offer."

For a second, her instincts pushed her to me, as though she wanted to return into my arms and an invisible wall held her back. She held her composure and responded with a nod.

"Thank you, Ansgar, I hope you find another mate and live a happy life too," she said as new tears sprouted.

"There is no other," I murmured and forced my form to disappear. I found myself back into my chambers, the aroma of Anwen's perfume lingering in my nostrils and I finally allowed myself to feel. Pain, desperation, frustration, jealousy, misery and regret formed a nest inside the place I once called heart and transformed every ounce of joy I ever felt... Into nothing. Whatever world was spinning around me, it faded away by the desperation of losing my mate, just when I had finally found her. Nothing else mattered.

My heart pumped so fast that I prayed to the goddess to help it burst and put me out of this misery.

Broad daylight burned by eyes, forcing them open. I felt my throat rasp. I needed a drink, so I reached towards the nightstand where a bottle of absinthe had found permanent residence.

"Looking for this?" A voice echoed from the opposite corner of the room. I saw Damaris casually sitting in a chair, waving the half empty bottle at me.

"Aha," was my only reply. I extended my hand in his direction, willing the bottle to appear in my hand.

"Don't you think you've had enough?" he asked but I replied with an uncaring groan and turned towards the wall, covering my head with a pillow to block the sunlight.

Steps came towards me, then the pillow was forcefully removed from my face and my shoulders were shaken abruptly, forcing me back into consciousness. Damaris' face greeted me.

I smiled widely at him, "Hello, brother. What are you doing here?"

"Ansgar, what are you doing to yourself?" he grabbed my jaw and forced me to look at him. "You've been at this for two weeks, it needs to stop. Now!" he ordered.

"How do you know that?" I reprimanded him for spying on me.

"Brother, we've been receiving reports of faeries seeking aid and finding you constantly drunk. And the palace's cellars are emptying so fast it looks like we're hosting a party of a hundred. It needs to stop," he repeated.

I waved my hand dismissively, "What do you care about a few bottles?" but his firm hands did not leave my shoulders.

"You have been drinking for thirteen days straight and by the looks of it, passing out is a common occurrence for you these days. The district is neglected and your liver will not take much more of this."

"It's fine," I replied as I tried to get back to my pillow but his firm grip kept me grounded. "The goddess is caring for them, they'll live," I said. I did not know if two weeks had passed indeed or if Damaris just wanted to make me react. The truth was that since I last saw Anwen, the only thing left to do was try to drink the pain away and absinthe seemed to be the best solution. After a few bottles, I felt nothing, my entire body left in this floating frenzy that washed away every feeling.

Since I discovered its effects, I had not stopped, selfishly pushing away the return of any possible memory. The drink made me forget who and where I was, whatever purpose I might have had before and it helped my brain block the surroundings. It was only me against the pain, absinthe the guardian against such agony. If I remained constantly away from the world, I could not feel Anwen parting from me anymore.

"What about you? Do you think you'll live long if you continue?"

I waved him off again. "I don't care," I replied.

My brother analysed me for a long moment. I read pity in his stare. That's what I was. That's what I'd become. One of the rejected. I had to form a band and pillage small villages, just like those males who couldn't live in their city anymore because the hurt of seeing their mates with someone else broke their sanity.

Finding one's mate bound the energies of the couple, and rejection left one as scarred as though someone cut them in half and forced them to continue living. Being unconscious dispelled some of the pain, made me forget about that part of my energy that had been lost forever.

"It will pass," Damaris replied in the end.

I huffed. He had no idea what I was going through. He hadn't felt it. The rip. The breaking of the bond, which left me with only half of what I used to be. It was common knowledge that the breaking of a mating bond was the worst pain imaginable. Be it through death or rejection, once a couple had bonded, the splinter of the connection affected our energy so severely that many went crazy from the pain. From constantly seeking what was no longer there.

"Don't you dare tell me it will pass. You have Takara, you bastard. You have your mate!"

"She is with child," my brother breathed the news.

That immediately awoke me and I widened my eyes at him.

"Is she really?" The ghost of a smile wanted to restore on my face.

"Really," he nodded and by the proud shine in his gaze I knew it must be true.

I pulled my brother tightly in an embrace and congratulated him, a small part of me filling up with joy. I would be an uncle. And the kingdom would finally have an heir. A minuscule spark of hope sprouted from whatever scattered remains it could find.

"Ansgar, I am asking you to pull yourself together for Takara's sake. The announcement is to be made at your marking celebration. We are asking you to retake your duties and not screw this up. If not for you, do it for her. For your nephew's sake. You cannot fail this; you know what the consequences are."

I nodded.

"I will be honoured to bless your child, Damaris."

Anwen

Chapter Thirty-Five

I looked outside for what felt like the millionth time to make sure I was truly seeing things correctly. The forest started to retake its natural bright green and the glum clouds and blizzard-like winds had been put to a halt. When Ansgar left, everything went dark and I lost all sense of connection, I did not know the time and place I was in, the only thing that I felt was pain. Pain and anger. I hated myself for what I did, for what I'd chosen to do and his pleading words echoed in my head over and over again.

As I laid in bed, trying to store his aroma in the drawers of my memories, I thought about all the possible outcomes of the relationship we didn't even properly start before it ended so abruptly. I did not know when I'd fallen asleep, probably the headache and nausea from so much crying got the best of me in the end and forced me to black out into sleep.

I was awakened by heavy rain and lightning gusts and for a moment I thought I was back in New York. Until I looked out the window and saw the forest, the trees, plants, grass and seedlings pulled out from the earth by powerful winds. All the while, a rainstorm and mist engulfing the land.

I grimaced at the pain flushing through my entire body. I knew this was Ansgar's doing. I had once asked him how it was possible for the land to be preserved in a permanent summer while the rest of the country got affected by seasons and he told me that the energy of this place was connected to one of their goddesses and to him, as the keeper of the power.

I followed the progress of the weather for the remainder of the day, the surroundings becoming my only connection to the fae prince and was relieved as the storm dissipated at nightfall, followed by a gust of rasp wind.

After that, my existence resumed to sleeping, watching movies without paying any attention to the plot and spying on the forest from my bedroom window. The only time I was forced to move from the room was when Rhylan came in to bring the delivery, even though I hadn't sent an email requesting specific things. He made a few mentions about the forest but when he saw my uncombed, dirty-self coming out of the bedroom wrapped in a blanket, eyes red, he made haste of delivering the cakes he had brought for me.

I didn't expect a nice gesture coming from him but I found myself needing company, even if it came from a menacing presence like his. I pulled two forks and sat at the table, lunging into the cake without looking in his direction. After a few moments of throwing me that penetrating look of his, Rhylan accepted the silent invitation and sat next to me, poking a generous bite of chocolate cake.

"Is this period eating or are we forming a hate club against a specific man?" he asked innocently, his deep voice making even the walls shudder.

I replied with a disgusted gaze. "Are those the only two possible reasons a woman can eat cake?"

"The way you are doing it, yes," he uttered the words just as I was shoving a full slice in my mouth and trying to make it fit.

"It's nice to know you don't go by stereotypes..." I huffed, still battling the giant-sized cake in my mouth.

"From my experience, sprout, women either want to fill their stomach to forget about their empty heart, or they plainly become monsters and require sugary offerings."

I laughed, bits of half chewed chocolate escaping my mouth. To my surprise, Rhylan rose and brought a tissue, then stepped closer to me and used it to wipe my chin. My body vibrated at the touch, at the contact with his skin, and I immediately rose from my seat, startled. He had the audacity to look disappointed, as if wiping my mouth was the biggest gesture he could have made and I owed him gratitude.

"You need to go now." I was being rude but did not care. Something wrestled in me and Rhylan was at fault. His presence, his touch, him. All of it needed to go.

"Come on, Anwen, don't start with this again," he reprimanded, following me out of the kitchen. Each step of his made me want to take a step back. Run from him. Keep him away. But he came closer, so close that my muscles tensed, expecting an attack.

Rhylan stood inches from me and his breath pressed against my face.

"Don't you want a bit of fun?" His fingers pulled a lock of my hair and caressed it. "Or more than a bit?" he grinned.

My breath came out in interrupted sighs. "If you touch me again, I will report you to Isak."

His fingers released me in the next second and he turned back towards the sofa, planting himself in the seat Ansgar used to love, without an invitation.

"You are a faithful sprout, aren't you?" he smiled and a line of pride appeared on his face, fading instantly back into the blackness.

I didn't reply. I only lingered there, pinning him with an angry look.

"Noted, you don't like fun. But honestly, how are you still sane in this depressing place? This forest used to be nice to visit, now it's as glum as the dead."

"Don't worry about me, I'll be leaving soon." I had been debating whether to call this off and ask my dad for a plane ticket back. He was right, what was I doing here? I didn't find what Erik wanted me to, instead I discovered an entire civilization and messed things up in an epic way.

Rhylan's eyes almost gauged out at my words.

"You're leaving?" he asked, almost shocked. "You can't leave!" he interjected.

"There's nothing left for me to do here, and the place is glum, just like you said." I didn't want to get into details and tell him how this entire situation and the appearance of the forest was my fault.

"Just give up then! Of course you would." Rhylan stood from the sofa and stepped closer to me again, although this time, respecting my private space. "Is this all you're made of, sprout? One hardship and you give up? There's so much more to do here, so much more to discover. People around the world are begging for a chance to be here, even for a few hours, and you have two months

341

left and want to abandon it all?"

His words made me feel ashamed. He was right. He was so right I wanted to stop and start cursing myself. I was taking things for granted and I still needed to find whatever Erik wanted me to. I had yet to discover the connection to the four kingdoms and his travels and I could not give up just because of my wounded heart.

I didn't need to give an answer to Rhylan, the realisation on my face must have been enough, because he threw me a satisfied smile. To my surprise, he stayed for a few hours to visit, just as a normal person would, and we talked about the forest, about its history and all the crazy request letters they received from all round the world. It felt nice to see him like that, unselfconscious, free. He truly knew the place, he even talked me back to the queen's visits and the rumours that she had found a fae male to keep her company.

I laughed at the absurdity of the gossip, for his sake, but I knew better. When he left, a feeling of peace had settled over me and I could not believe it was because of Rhylan. The few hours of normalcy he had given me did wonders for my mental health and placed me on the right track. That was until I remembered I had to sleep alone again and Ansgar was no longer joining me. That's when the tears returned.

This morning, however, my eyes remained pierced outside the window and a burden lifted. The leaves turned green again, the plants around them flourished and the grass reflected a bright vivid colour. For the next few days, I debated whether to email my father and ask for a ticket back home or stay isolated inside the mansion's side of the forest, where I knew no faeries would step into, for the next two months.

The girls tried to visit a few times but every time I saw them I would burst into tears and by the third visit, they only settled to wave at me from a distance, when they were passing by the mansion to make sure I was alright.

I spent my days researching Erik's travels and googling so many supernatural theories I ended up with migraines, but nothing seemed to piece together anymore. I reached the conclusion that it was highly unlikely for my brother to know about the faeries, because I couldn't believe he would have kept something like this from me.

My guess, though I still did not know if true or not, assumed that Erik had investigated the magnetic force around the four places and wanted to learn more on it, from a scientific perspective. He had always been the brainiac amongst the two, always inventing things at school and planning research for the business.

When delivery came that day, I was lying in bed, too lazy to react until I remembered that a fresh batch of pain au chocolat would be on the way so I apathetically went down the stairs to see Rhylan already making himself comfortable on the sofa. In the past month, it had become a tradition. Rhylan popped up in the mornings and we ate chocolates together all day long. We talked about life, the guard and I told him the many theories about the forest I found online. His visits became a grounding point in my life and his entire demeanour seemed completely changed. I even dare say he became friendly.

"Hey, busy week?" was my best greeting as I eagerly grabbed the bags from the table and moved them into the kitchen, searching for the frozen goods to save them from the heat.

"Yeah... I've been busy organising things," he replied with a detached greeting as he selected another magazine and started skimming through the pages. What was it with him and these magazines?

"No uniform today?" I had to ask, noticing how he adopted a fully black attire, a tailored suit and black shirt, much too sophisticated for a mere drive into the woods.

"I have plans after this," his vague answer the hint that I needed to stay out of his business.

"Cool," I replied. If he planned to make me jealous, I was far away from the feeling.

"How's the new handle treating you by the way?" he turned his full attention to me, gawking at every gesture, as though he was prepared to commit them to memory.

"Yeah, fine," I replied, not knowing what else to say.

"Did..." he paused for emphasis, "your friend enjoy it?"

I made a full turn towards him, trying to keep my calm. "What friend?"

He sighed, slowly walking towards me as his soles brushed the overly sanded wooden floor.

"Sprout, I think it's time to stop lying to each other," he replied and leaned onto the island board, his face only a few inches away from mine. His stare rippled darkness, intruding into me so fiercely that I had to close my eyes for a second and blink that gaze away. I tried not to think about Ansgar, as though he would be able to see inside my mind.

"Stop calling me that, it makes no sense," I huffed and turned, searching for anything to shove into the fridge and escape his closeness.

"Oh, but it does," he purred. "You will understand eventually."

"Aha..." was my only reply, head still stuck in the fridge. I had come to know the two Rhylans, and the dark one wanted to come and play today. I much preferred the friendly detached guard who liked cake and Kit Kats.

He remained silent a long while, waiting for me to finish storing things away so I didn't have any excuse to dismiss the conversation. After a few minutes I gave up and closed the fridge, turning towards Rhylan yet again. I felt tired and this was probably the weirdest conversation I'd had in the last month, so I involuntarily snapped at him.

"What do you want, Rhylan?" I tensed, expectant of his reaction and hoping it would not be a violent one. Somehow, even my frail muscles knew this was not a man to be crossed.

Surprise lit his eyes and a seductive smile cropped up on his face. "It bites," he murmured, throwing me a pleased smirk.

"What I want to know, lovely sprout, is if that fae fuckboy of yours enjoyed walking in and out of this house to his heart's content."

If there was ever a time for my heart to stop from shock, this would probably be an adequate one. I drew in a slow breath but I didn't say anything. Rhylan continued, "Before you try to offend my intelligence again with your lies, girl, I know about the fae," he confirmed. "I know what they eat, where they sleep, what they do and how they do it. I know everything."

Rhythmic gasps came out of my chest, my mind blocked, not knowing what to say.

"How?" It seemed to be enough to de-tense him slightly because he turned towards the sitting room once more and regained a seat on one of the armchairs, the closest one from the kitchen.

"My grandmother's sister," he announced, suggesting it was all the explanation I would need. When I frowned, he sighed dramatically, most probably at my incompetence to connect information and continued. "She went into the faelands. Fell in love with someone and went along with him."

"She went into their world? How?" I asked, surprised. My curiosity piqued and I moved to take a seat on the couch, making sure to place enough distance between the two of us.

"Mates. None of the family understood but the two of them were convinced, so he came and asked for her hand in marriage and off they went."

My heart started pumping uncontrollably, so rapidly that I was almost dazed from the amount of oxygen flooding into my lungs.

"Your aunt mated a fae? A human?" The words turned into a whisper, so soft that he must have read my lips rather than hearing them.

"Yup," he nodded. "Apparently it is a rare thing back there," he leaned lazily on the upholstered back of the armchair, stretching his neck.

"How..." I barely breathed. "How do you know it's true?"

He raised his eyebrows, not understanding my meaning.

"That they were mates, I mean," I clarified, readying myself to devour his next words.

"She came back to visit, couple of years later. Told my granny everything, her life there, customs, stories. So many details that my only bedtime stories were about the fae."

"Do they keep in touch?" I enquired, needing to know if I could contact this woman and ask her everything I wanted to know.

"Nah, she stopped visiting once she started popping out kids. They had seven the last time my grandma saw her." Rhylan turned back to his usual activity, flicking through women's magazines.

"So your grandma didn't see her again?" I questioned.

"She wanted to, her sister left her some kind of tea for her to drink and pass into the faelands to visit. But Nana had my mother and... life happened," he replied.

"What kind of tea was it?" I eagerly asked.

"I don't know," he replied bored. "Some kind of burnt root of something. I have it at home," Rhylan explained with a sigh, not in the mood for more questions. "I can bring it to you if you want, use it with your loverboy. He'll know what to do with it."

"Thank you, Rhylan!" I wanted to hug him, but he raised his hands to push me away.

"Contain that excitement for your guy, sprout. You'll ruin my suit." He threw me a disgusted look but I did not care and pulled away my fingers from his designer black jacket.

I would be able to tell Ansgar what I'd found and show him the tea, maybe it was a way for me to visit my family whenever I wanted to. My mind bloomed with thousands of possibilities, making plans for the two of us, for a life together. Because if I had even the smallest chance to prove humans can mate fae, and be with the man I loved, I would use every strand of energy I had left.

Watching my thoughts work, Rhylan stood from his seat and headed towards the door, all of a sudden in a hurry. I didn't have time to ask him more questions because he headed outside, then stopped abruptly and looked at me with a curiosity I had never been worthy of before.

"Is this for you?" he sounded impressed.

"What?" I asked but he moved away from the entrance door to let me peek outside, where an ocean of gardenias illuminated the woods. They came from everywhere, growing on trees, lunging from branches, billowing from the soil. Everywhere I looked, rivers of gardenias floated around in big clusters of petals.

I nodded and Rhylan smiled. He actually threw me a genuine smile. I dare say there was even a shred of pride in his eyes.

"I'll bring you the tea now. It's a full moon tonight, the least you can do is go and thank him properly," he smirked, then disappeared into a black SUV and drove away onto the corroded stone path.

I paused, giving myself time to encrypt my surroundings into memory and breathe in the soft perfume that penetrated my nostrils, when the realisation pounded through me. It was a full moon that night, Rhylan had announced and the entire forest became engulfed by gardenias. My favourite flower. A symbol that I was not forgotten to him. His mark.

He had told me the tradition, he even asked my thoughts on the matter and told me about other marks from his kingdom that members of his family or friends had chosen in the past. It was an emblem of his love for me, a motif that will accompany him for the rest of his existence, to remember me by. *My mate.* I trembled at the thought, sending an influx of devotion through my veins.

I paced up and down the sitting room, counting the minutes until Rhylan would be back with that tea and rehearsing a speech for Ansgar, for when I saw him. That is, if I managed to see him again. I had no knowledge of that kingdom apart from what he had told me from time to time. All I knew was that his marking was an important event and the evening would turn into a celebration. Not enough to help me form a solid plan. As he was the prince, and these festivities were held in his honour, I had to think about the possibility that I might not even reach him. Maybe he lived in a palace somewhere with hundreds of guards around.

Maybe it was better to wait until tomorrow, until he finished his marking, whatever that meant, and just go to the cave in the morning to avoid any complications or get him in trouble. Even if it was possible for me to be his mate, I did not know the reaction of his family and those around him if I just showed up, unannounced and uninvited to his big day.

Rhylan knocked frantically on the door and when I moved to open, I found him restless on the threshold.

"Here," was all he said, then started walking back to his car, the black paint of the SUV gleaming in the dusk. He looked shaky and unsure. Like he regretted giving me his aunt's tea.

"It's okay, I decided I'm not visiting tonight after all," I replied and tried to return the small vial back to him. I could not take the woman's chance to see her sister one more time away, just because I felt overly excited.

He stopped in his tracks and turned towards me with a deep frown. "I'm sorry, what?" he reprimanded.

"It's too complicated," I shook my head, "I'll just wait and find him another day." I would not, under any circumstance, tell Rhylan where and how to find Ansgar. His intentions proved noble enough until now, but I did not trust him completely.

He raised a hand, twitching his fingers in an elegant movement as though to make a point. "Excuse me, you made me go all the way back when I had serious plans," he stopped to punctuate, "so you can decide against it in forty minutes?"

His voice echoed rasp and that unsettling darkness flickered in his eyes with anger.

"I don't want to create complications for him. They have a party tonight," I would not do any more explaining than that.

"And you don't want to go to a fae party?" he looked at me incredulous, almost disgusted.

"I'm human, hello?" I used both my hands to point to myself, revealing the information to Rhylan.

"Aha…" That apathetic frown persisted on his forehead.

"How would it look when a human drinks some tea and crashes a fae party to search for her...fuckboy?" My instinct had been to use 'mate' a word still new in my vocabulary but I did not think it safe

350

to reveal something that I barely discovered myself.

"Tiny sprout, are you kidding me right now?" exasperation portrayed his features.

"No, I am not," I defended myself, skipping the fact that he continued to use that term on me when I'd specifically asked him not to.

"They won't know you're human. That's what the tea is all about," he glared at me like I was the village idiot.

"You didn't say that before," I defended myself. "So I would look fae?"

He huffed, drawing in a big breath. "You boil whatever it is in that thing and drink it," he stated, pointing to the vial still in my hand. "Then you find something close to the one you want to see, something that belongs to them or a place they stay a lot in or whatever strong connection. Then you will feel sleepy and doze off, wake up in their world, boom."

"How do you come back?"

"How am I supposed to know? Ask your lover to bring you back," Rhylan waved his arms around to show that he grew tired of my hesitation and questions.

I paused, debating whether to return the vial or keep it. My hands remained clenched around it, holding it tightly and I took a moment to analyse it. It was small and its contents looked dark and dry.

"All I'm saying is," Rhylan drew back my attention as he opened the car door, "if he can do all of this for you," he paused to point at the gardenia-snowed surroundings, "the least you can do is go to that party and surprise him. What's he going to do? Hug you too tightly?

Spread your legs and eat you at the grand table of the faeries? Maybe you'll get a chance to see how kinky you truly are," he winked and disappeared inside the car, driving away in the next second and leaving me on the outside porch, with magic tea in my hand and a decision to make.

But I had already made it. If Ansgar was willing to claim a symbol of myself for life, the least I could do was show up and stop wasting time. Time that we had already lost, time that we may not have too much of. I had only a month remaining of this visit, before I would probably be escorted out by force if I refused to leave, so I was not willing to risk even another second away from the man I loved.

Selfishly, I did not want to waste any more pages from the story of our life together, so I sprinted to the wardrobe in search of something suitable for the party. If I was to go to a fairy-tale celebration, I might as well dress the part.

I was never more grateful for my mother's insistence to look good and prepare for any situation as I grabbed the ornate silk box underneath the cabinet drawer where I had stored it after my arrival. The always elegant Elsa Odstar had forced her daughter to pack an evening gown should any encounter or invitation with the royal family happen. And here I was, getting ready to meet a prince.

I curled my hair and pulled a few strands together in some kind of elegant hairdo youtube suggested, while I bathed myself in perfume and lotion, aiming to smell good enough to eat. After about half an hour, I looked in the mirror with pride. The dress was a strapless light green A-line cut made of georgette sink with

Swarovski crystals that ended up with a Paris chiffon finish. A beautiful designer piece that had been exclusively made two years back for the Milano fashion show. I adorned myself with diamond earrings and an emerald bracelet, combining the radiance of the dress between the two colours of the precious stones.

Pleased with the way I looked, I made my way back into the kitchen to prepare the dreaded tea which already rested inside the teapot, awaiting boiling water. When I'd opened the vial, I almost vomited from the disgusting smell emanating from the root and decided to place it in the pot and cover any trace of that awful scent until I was ready to face it.

I boiled water and poured it over the small black root, holding my breath until steams started spiralling out of the liquor. The dark root, which looked like it had been burnt and preserved into the small flask, spread out its colour across the mug, creating a black, disgusting-looking substance that smelled so bad I wanted be sick all over my dress.

I did not know how much I needed to drink and I was aware that this might very well be ending up with me in an emergency room with food poisoning, but the hope pushed stronger than my hesitation. I pressed my lips on the cup and drank big sips, all the while holding Ansgar's shirt, the one he had left on the bed, tightly to my chest.

Rhylan said I'd go to sleep and wake up near the person I wanted to see, but what happened turned more violent. As soon as the first sips reached my stomach, uncontrollable pain flushed through my body, making me fall to the floor and contort with pain, my muscles convulsing with murderous pulsations. I spent minutes in agony, barely able to breathe, my mouth foaming until blissfully, everything turned dark around me and I faded away.

That was such a stupid thing to do. That first thought came to mind as I slowly pushed myself back to consciousness. I tried to prompt my torso up from the wooden floor, but when my palm reached the ground, grass prickled my fingers. I felt around and I opened my eyes, recovering from the pain and was shocked to find myself in a forest. Had it worked?

I stood slowly, supported by a tree bark. I saw people appearing all around me and walking towards a crowd. Men, all of them dressed the same as Ansgar, with the same model of flax pants and shirts. Oh my god, it had worked. I was in the faelands.

I searched for my composure, trying to look casual amongst the people that appeared through that forest. Finding courage, I walked towards one of them and started speaking.

"Excuse me, would you be able to tell me where I can find Prince Ansgar?" I forced my voice to seem cheery, relaxed. The tall man with ginger hair just looked at me, sizing me up and down and huffed, then blatantly ignored my question and turned towards the crowd.

Well, thank you for the warm welcome, homeboy, I sneered sarcastically and went onto another man that appeared just to my right side, a few trees away.

"Excuse me," I hurried my step to reach him, "Would you know where Prince Ansgar is please?"

He scanned me in disgust, sizing me up and down and replied dryly, "Is there anything you wacky females won't do to get him? Leave the poor male be!" he reprimanded and strode away, hurrying his steps farther from me.

Something felt very wrong, this had been the worst idea in the world! Not only that, but no one was willing to help me find Ansgar and I couldn't really tell them why I wanted to see him without causing a scene. I was now trapped in this place with no way to go back home. Stupid, stupid idea! I heaved while bouncing my leg up and down into the dark soil when a hand abruptly seized my left arm.

"What in the name of all the goddesses are you doing here?"

I turned towards the man who pulled at me with anger, ready to slap him, but as soon as I saw his beautiful dark face, I wanted to hug him instead. Relief flowed over me as I gazed upon Vikram's angry face.

"I just need to talk to Ansgar real quick," I announced, not wanting to tell his brother everything that happened since we'd last seen each other.

He raised his eyebrows, scanning me with a look that clearly declared his need to know everything.

"There's history of fae mated with humans, I can prove it. So I came to see Ansgar and to tell him that I love him and I will fight for this, if he still wants me. And seeing how he chose my favourite flower as his mark, I think he does."

355

Vikram's frown deepened so I added, "Plus I'm stuck here, I need Ansgar to take me back home."

"How did you even get here?" he asked through his teeth, his grip sure to leave a bruise on my arm.

"I drank this horrible tea, it made me sick and I woke up here. And I asked people to help me find Ansgar but they all look at me like I'm some kind of crazy," I explained.

"You think?" he growled.

"Nobody is supposed to know I'm human," I replied below my breath. "That was the whole point of this. Not to draw attention. And everybody speaks English here?" I enquired with both shock and relief.

"And showing up in a wedding dress is casual for you?" Vikram sized me up and down, same as the other man had done.

"This is a ball gown," I corrected but he did not seem to care.

"It's a sea-foam green dress and you are all adorned," he returned my gaze. But when he saw the stunned expression on my face, he added. "We get married in sea-foam green. It looks like you are chasing Ansgar in a wedding dress."

"Shit," I replied. "That was not my intention."

"Intention or not, keepers came to me to report it. You are already drawing attention upon yourself," he reprimanded as he let go of my hand.

I mumbled a low "sorry" but he seemed to be having an internal debate with himself. "Fuck... Ansgar's marking... Damaris... blessing... shit... silly human."

"That would be me," I pointed a finger at myself to draw back his attention. "Help me?"

He huffed, then grabbed my arm once again, pulling me away from the gathering crowd outside the treeline as I heard him mumble another "Fuck," through his teeth.

Vikram walked me through the outskirts of the town, making sure to stay far away from the massive gatherings and continuing to swear through his breath from time to time, until, about half an hour later, we were standing in front of the palace doors. A massive conglomerate of stone and expertly carved wood, all filled with gardenia decorations—identical to the ones in Evigt—rose in front of us. But I was not given enough time to admire my surroundings. I was shoved through gigantic sculpted wooden doors and up towards a staircase, all while Vikram held my arm tightly and pushed me in front of him as quickly as he could.

Only when we stepped through another impressively decorated set of doors, on the second floor, did he let go of his hold and allowed me to take a break. He had dragged me so much that I had almost been jogging alongside him for the past half hour. I was sweating and dirty and needed to catch my breath, so I sat on a chair, completely uninvited and grabbed a crystal glass from the table, pouring myself a drink of whatever the amber liquid was.

"Stay here," Vikram ordered, the first words he had deigned to address me with during our hurried tour through the town—or city, I didn't exactly know what it was.

Sylvan Regnum, Ansgar's voice trembled in my mind. This was his hometown. *His home.* A wave of warmth dropped in my stomach, and I knew for a fact it was not from the liquid I drank, which turned out to be some kind of brandy or whisky, I never knew the difference. They all burnt the same.

I looked around at the room, several ornate doors opened various chambers from the sitting room, one displaying a very large baldaquin bed, covered by dark silk and chiffon curtains. All around me, weapons and maps decorated the walls, swords and shields, all carved and wonderfully designed in such a way to not only adorn the chambers but offer the room a commanding stance. These were Vikram's chambers, I realised, as I took in the pieces of silver armour distributed in one of the rooms, along with dozens of swords and shields.

I wanted to make my way into the chamber that had been converted into an armoury, when the big doors opened and Vikram's voice echoed, "Make sure this...female," he forced the words out of his mouth, "gets something suitable to wear, arrange her hair and have her ready in half an hour. I will collect her myself."

The two faeries that accompanied him nodded and quickly made their way towards me. "She does not go anywhere else, and she is not to be asked any questions," he continued, the females only nodding in agreement as they started picking at my dress. "If she tries to engage in conversation, she is not to be answered," the prince finished before closing the door with a hard slam.

Well, that made it clear, I had to shut my mouth until he came back for me. Point taken. So I allowed the ladies to undress me and undo my hair, combing at it to destroy every single wave I struggled to create and support with hairspray, while another grabbed my face and wiped away the makeup. They brought to me three dresses, one light blue, another dark green and a soft purple, all of them more similar to cropped pieces of fabric than actual designs. I pointed at the light blue one and lifted my arms while they wrapped me in pieces of silk and chiffon, tying intricate knots and sutures until one of them made me step in front of a mirror.

I looked stunning, they had made me truly look like a princess and I scoffed at my previous effort. Compared to the ball gown I had brought with me, now discarded onto the marble floor, this dress had a deep cut décolletage that made its way to my stomach, my breast supported by wide interweavings of chiffon that decorated a path up to my collarbone. The waist was high and tight, allowing an influx of chiffon to create waves all the way to my ankles, arranged in such a way that the fabric fell over the silk underneath to create different hues and shades of blue, all intricate and glinting in splendour. My hair was loose, slightly curving onto my shoulders with only two braids at the sides that had been pulled in some sort of flower design at my nape, held together with a small green broach.

"That's more like it," Vikram's voice announced his return. I thanked the ladies who helped me. They nodded and made their way out, bowing to the prince. He closed the door and stepped towards me, stopping mere inches away and glowering at me. "If you want to have any chance out there, you will do as I say."

I nodded, silently awaiting his command. "You are Anwen of Amethya—a small town in the West. You came here for the celebration. You will stay with the crowd until the ceremony is over. You will engage in small talk only and not give any personal details about yourself. You can ask questions about the city as this is your first visit. And yes, everyone speaks the common tongue at gatherings, so you'll be able to converse at will."

He paused to make sure I was capable of collecting the information in my human brain. "Go on," I pushed.

"Only when the celebration is over, that is when Ansgar's mark will appear into the kingdom, will I come find you and take you to him." He paused as my face relaxed and a smile curled my lips. I was going to see Ansgar.

"You are not to address him directly or search for him until I take you to him," he emphasized. "When and if you are talking about him with the others, you are to keep your personal relation hidden and refer to him as 'the young prince' or 'His Highness Prince Ansgar', not 'daddy' or 'baby' nor 'booboo' or whatever things your human customs make you call him."

I snorted. "Women call you 'booboo'?" I asked, unable to contain my laugh.

He didn't seem to find it funny, but asked, "Am I to understand you just call him by his name? When you humans are so passionate about changing the word meanings to refer to your lovers?" he admonished.

"I cannot take credit for what the human race does, but yes, I call him Ansgar." Vikram looked at me incredulously. "We'd been together for like a month when you came in and destroyed everything. We didn't have time to pick names." I paused. "Well, he has one for me. He calls me fahrenor. It means my starlight," I exclaimed proudly.

Surprise flourished in Vikram's eyes, only for a moment, before he grunted. "I do not care what my brother calls you, you are still human."

"And his mate," I urged. "I can prove it."

Vikram snorted and started walking towards the door, so I followed his trail.

"Hey, could you translate some things for me so I can tell Ansgar and surprise him?" I asked it more as a joke but it made Vikram sigh deeply. I followed him to the massive, sculpted doors—they were battle scenes, I realised—when he paused and turned back to me, throwing me a look that said, 'don't do anything stupid.'

"Tell me again," he demanded.

I knew what he meant, so I repeated the information back to him for a third time, "I am Anwen of Amethya, first time visitor, small talk only, no personal details, eat and drink with the people. Once the mark is visible, the party is over and you will take me to see booboo."

He grunted in annoyance so I corrected, "Apologies, His Royal Highness Prince Ansgar Booboo."

"I am the middle prince, older than your... mate," the words ripped through him mockingly, "You should show more respect when you address me."

"Hey, you made me break the relationship with your brother, without giving me a chance to prove myself. You discriminated against me just because I am human and made me cry myself to sleep for a month. Consider this payback," I snapped at him and he sighed deeply, opening the door and holding out his hand for me to take, as we both made our way outside the palace doors.

Chapter Thirty-Six

The crowd cheered when I reached the podium, the king's throne prepared for me to claim. The greatest honour Father could do for me. To my surprise, he had received me with open arms and countless apologies, both he and the Queen overly concerned with my wellbeing—I assumed Damaris had told them about my weeks drowning in alcohol—and promised to do what they could to help me achieve prosperity and joy.

I hugged them both and apologised as well, for dislodging the news in such a way, especially since my mate had decided to continue with her human life and had ruthlessly dismissed me. We spent the evening together, as a family, both of them crammed in my chambers, offering advice and talking me through the proceedings of the evening and treating me, to the best of their abilities, as if nothing had changed. As if I hadn't been rejected, lost my will to live, abandoned the district and my duties and behaved like a green youngling, unable to control emotions. Mother made a point to sit with me and tell me her findings regarding the situation I presented to them a month ago. She had searched the libraries of the entire kingdom, rewarding each and every scholar who brought information regarding mating bonds and human connections.

"All letters came back the same, my son," she announced while patting my shoulder. "There are no documented cases." It was a compassionate way to tell me my feelings had been overwhelmed by the woman and made me imagine a deeper bond. In any other situation, I would have fought her, arguing that what I felt was true, that I had found my mate and insisted on it being the first connection of the kind. Insisted that Anwen be allowed into the kingdom and into our lives. Yet it was to no avail. Why waste breath and upset Mother, if said mate did not want anything to do with me?

Before dinner, Damaris and Takara made their way into my chambers—it seemed to become the assembly location of the evening—and as soon as I saw her, I rose from my seat and ran towards my sister, holding her tightly in my arms and lifting her up to swirl her body across the room. She laughed joyously and kissed my forehead, asking me to put her down. My nephew did not like pirouettes or any kind of sudden off-ground movements, it seemed.

I smiled at her and quickly put her down, careful to sustain her weight long enough to make sure her soles were fully planted on the floor. I kissed both her cheeks, then kneeled in front of my nephew—or niece, I smirked, gaze pointed at Damaris—and placed a kiss on her tummy. Only after that, I reached my brother and offered him a tight hug, thanking him slowly when our faces stood close together. No other explanation was needed, he knew what for and nodded.

"So," I asked as all the family gathered together, apart from Vikram, whom we had been waiting for almost an hour, "Are we ready to do this blessing or what?"

They all smiled, Takara bowed in thanks while Father started explaining the order of events and process of the evening. They apologised for adding another event into my marking celebration, since the holiday was supposed to be about me and my chosen symbol exclusively, but I confessed my excitement to share the spotlight with my niece or nephew.

"If you do your job right, the goddess will bless us with a son," Damaris voiced, always the supporter of tradition.

"If you'd bothered to read some more anatomy books, brother, you would know by now that the goddess' blessing has nothing to do with gender."

"You do," Mother pointed out, much to Takara's delight.

"One can hope," my brother defended himself. "Make sure to put enough energy in that drop, brother," he urged.

"Drop? I will drown your mate in blood if I have to."

Both Damaris and I started laughing, while Mother and Father rolled their eyes.

"One drop will be enough," Mother's voice resounded as Vikram made his way into the chamber.

"Well, well, well, if it's not the male of the hour," he greeted with a grin, and instead of turning his gaze on me, he stepped towards Takara and petted her stomach gently.

"They just finished that argument," the healer announced as

Vikram made his way to me and trapped me into a hug. Instinct forced me to sniff at his clothes as a familiar scent emerged from them, both frequent and distant, changed yet awakening memories. I scanned his face, but he walked away from the closeness we shared.

"I need to sort out some things, see you at the party?" he announced more than asked and made his way out without even looking back at any of the family members.

I greeted the gathering of faeries and settled onto the throne. I expected it to feel unwelcoming, uncomfortable even, like it could sense its rightful owner, but to my surprise, the energy surrounding the sculpted royal seat responded positively to my own, wrapping me in a veil of power and strength as I supported my back onto the wide spindle. The King and Queen each occupied a smaller throne, Father to my right while Damaris, Takara and Vikram, who made his way in a hurry to catch up to us just as we stepped onto the dais, remained standing behind us, their energy towering my own.

I felt ripples of it scatter across the land, into the crowd, almost uncontainable, urging me to release it into the ground and force my chosen mark to spring free. I only dared a small look at the King, with the corner of my eye, who nodded encouragingly, ushering me to proceed. As I allowed the blast to expulse itself out of my veins, my pores, my body, Anwen's smile creeped into my mind.

A pinch of sadness unleashed itself from that deep corner I had buried my feelings into. It did not have time to linger, as thousands of faeries started clapping and hailing widely, overpowered by the emerging marks that materialised everywhere into the kingdom. Wherever the eye could be set upon, there was a gardenia. In Mother's hair, my own, forming a carpet under our feet, pouring from the sky, flouring onto the tables and falling onto people's drinks, sprouting from the forest and every living plant and growing across the walls.

I felt a tide of relief surging through and knew that it was done. The symbol was marked. The energy was bound. She will be my undying source of energy.

"My chosen mark is the gardenia flower, known around the realm to symbolise gentleness and joy." It also represented secret love, a private meaning to keep me warm in the moments I dreamt of her. "As I continue the passage through life, I claim this symbol and bind it to my energy, I vow to draw power at my most dire junctures from its existence and create a family that will honour and protect this organism for the next generations."

I then stood from the throne and placed my right fist across my heart, bowing slowly at the mass of beings gathered in celebration. Some of the males conjured their own marks as a greeting to mine, a way to receive and welcome it into their ranks while the females and younglings clapped and whistled in content, some of them dancing or grabbing bunches of flowers to throw them once more in the air, to continue the downpour of petals I had summoned.

366

Each member of the family bowed and saluted me, the King and two commanders placing a hand over mine and the Queen and healer offering me a soft kiss on the cheek.

"All hail Prince Ansgar!" the King encouraged, making the crowd erupt into a cheer so loud it made the soil tremble under our feet. I shifted from the throne and stepped to the left side of my father, eagerly awaiting the announcement that, I felt, was more deserving.

"Since we are gathered this evening in joyous celebration," the King started speaking once more and I felt Takara and Damaris vibrate with excitement, "it is only fitting that we make this evening even more memorable." The crowd stopped in wonder, not knowing what else to expect from the royal family. A marking celebration was almost as important as a wedding. "Prince Ansgar was kind enough, as he always has demonstrated," Father turned to me and placed a proud hand on my shoulder, "to share his marking celebration with the rest of the family, mainly with the heir to our throne, Prince Damaris and our wonderful healer and new daughter, Takara." Father removed his hand and beckoned the two to step forward, "Who, in seven months, will bless us with a grandchild."

A burst of noise followed the announcement, with cheering, tears of joy, whistles and claps, each of the faeries using their power to show their excitement and happiness, some even made sparks in the sky and others started fluttering their wings so fast, a slow hum echoed in the air.

"Prince Ansgar will do the honours," Father announced as he took a step back, joining Mother and Vikram, leaving me in front of the dais with the couple.

A goblet of the blessing liquor passed into my hands. I took a moment to analyse the content whirling in the silver cup, I had never seen it before and its list of ingredients was kept sacred and passed from healer to healer. Only females were allowed to help and participate in the making of the elixir.

My inner scholar took a few seconds to analyse it, but my nostrils, although well trained, could only sense honey, moon rock water, waterlily and silverweed seeds, though the list of ingredients contained, probably, the sum of a hundred. Only one left to complete the potion, so I pulled out my dagger and made a cut in my palm, only about an inch wide. I clenched my fist and allowed the blood to drip into the brew, all the while willing my energy to accompany the drops and flow into the goblet.

Mother had asked for a drop, two to make sure, but I would not gamble my brother's child's so I made sure the glass was full when I passed it to Takara, more than half of the mix containing the essence of the last born of the family.

"Princess Takara, sister, I offer the mark of our generation, and with the blessing of our mighty goddess, I welcome your offspring into the kingdom," I uttered the words both Takara and Mother had asked me to say back to them about a hundred times as we walked into the crowd. She thanked me and took the silver finished goblet from my hands, surprise flickering her eyes at the amount of blood I had dripped into it, then nodded in appreciation and eagerly drank the whole thing, taking big sips as she breathlessly finished the mix.

"Let the celebrations begin!" the King urged. He stepped

forward and woke the crowd from the trance they had been enveloped in, witnessing the ritual.

The rest of the family joined us and congratulated both Takara and I for the brilliant execution of the rite and the powerful marking of my chosen symbol. We hugged and joined the festivities, held a toast for the newest member of the family and admired the dancing crowd from our selected seats at a table placed on the podium.

"Are we going to have some fun or what?" Vikram finally spoke. It was unusual for him to refrain from comments, especially snarky ones on special occasions, but tonight he had been reserved and kept to himself most of the time, more concerned with the crowd than the evening's events.

"You go first," I invited, reading fascination on his face.

"Seen someone you want already, brother?" Damaris joined the teasing while Takara remained very engaged in conversation with the Queen.

"I am more concerned with finding our little brother a special someone tonight," Vikram teased.

"I don't feel like dancing," I pointed out and turned to Takara, trying to infiltrate myself into the conversation.

"You must dance at least once, son. It's tradition," Father insisted and I sighed, knowing he was right.

"Come, I know someone you'll definitely like," Vikram snatched my arm and pulled me from my seat.

I wanted to pull away and reclaim the position, but Mother urged, "It's best to get it over with, son."

"It's one dance, Ansgar. Five minutes and you're back. I promise not to eat all your peach goodies," Takara prompted, taking another bite of the pastry for emphasis.

"Come, brother," Vikram continued to drag me from the podium and into the crowd, as I muttered my disagreement. By the way he had been piercing through the mass of earthlings, he seemed to know exactly where he was going, though we had to stop many times to greet faeries, lords and ladies, friends and former tutors and were asked to dance by many females. Vikram politely rejected them and continued to drag me to the farther tables, those occupied by visitors and distant families.

"Why can't I just take one and dance?" I asked Vikram, who continued to drag me through the cheerful crowd.

"Trust me brother, when you see this one, you will thank me."

"Aha," I muttered in disbelief but continued to follow him until we reached a table where a few females gathered together around a fruit sculpture, laughing and picking at the pieces.

I stared at them, then at Vikram, throwing him a surprised look that said, *Why does it have to be this particular table?* until he introduced himself and broke the crowd.

"Excuse me ladies," he made his presence known and all of them turned their attention to us. My spirit trembled, my attention fixated on her, scanning her from head to toe to make sure what they were reflecting was indeed, real.

"Lady Anwen, meet Prince Ansgar," Vikram announced as Anwen, *my Anwen*, stepped closer to us and bowed.

Whatever this was, whatever she and Vikram had done to infiltrate the party, I did not care as I took her in, my breath skipping.

I looked from her to Vikram, who threw me a self-satisfied grin, then back to her, not believing my eyes. My brother cleared his throat, reminding me of the need for a private conversation.

"Dance with me," I addressed Anwen and before she could even breathe an answer, I took her in my arms and started swirling her around, her blue dress forming waves of colour in our way, until we reached several couples that were already engaged in the song.

I pressed her body tightly to my own. One of my arms took hers and the other remained draped on her back, making sure to feel and reach for her, without raising suspicion from the crowd. Even though I saw and touched her, some part of me remained wary, urging me to hold her in place from fear she might evaporate into thin air.

"How?" I whispered into her ear, ignoring the music and the dance steps we were supposed to follow.

To my surprise, she fitted quite well into the multitude of faeries, considering this was her first visit. She looked almost regal, dressed and adorned in finery, chatting politely with the other fae and able to hold conversations without unveiling herself to them. The only part she struggled with was the dance, her feet stumbling more than floating and stepping on my toes on more than a few occasions. I was not much help either, since I held more concern with her presence than the actual movement.

"Follow my lead, relax your feet," I whispered, completely disregarding my first question as I spun her around and took charge of the dance, joining in the other couples and performing the intricate movements Mother had forced us to learn since we were

371

younglings. At first, Anwen's eyes widened, a shocked and slightly scared expression built up on her face, probably confused by my sudden decision to actually move. She stared at my feet, focused to copy my every step, until I released her hand and gently touched her chin, raising it to face me.

"Your attention is more appreciated here," I said and smiled at her, taking her hand back into my hold. She chuckled, losing a bit of the tension and allowing her figure to be swayed.

"My feet have missed you too," I added, "but not more than my eyes." I felt the need to continue. "Who am I kidding, every single part of me has missed you," I voiced and she laughed, her feet now following after mine onto the dancefloor.

We continued moving in silence, Anwen pressing her lips tightly together. She wanted to hold back the words before they could erupt from her mouth. There would be time, once the song ended. For now, all I wanted was her. Her breath on my neck, her hand in mine, her body spinning by my side in that dance. We were wrapped together in a moment, one that felt like an outburst of sunshine after a full month of terrors. She was here. And I swore to never let her go again.

Anwen

Chapter Thirty-Seven

I leaned into his shoulder as I craved more of that touch. We had been dancing for so long, flowing through songs both cheery and slow, each allowing us to lean into each other in a different way. Even though I had him back, that, through some miracle I ended up in his arms, I found myself unable to let him go. Each time a song ended and he wanted to walk away from the the dancefloor, which was more a mixture of moss and petals rather than an actual floor, I would stop him and ask for one more dance. He always accepted with delight, as though that part of him that was connected to mine shared the same fear. We couldn't let each other go.

"The King and Queen are retiring for the evening," a voice announced. It was close, right next to us, invading the trance we had been caught in. When I turned my head to follow the sound, I met Vikram's gaze and to my surprise, it was not as harsh as I remembered it. A smile curved his lips and stared at us, with pride.

Ansgar barely acknowledged his brother, his look still caught in mine, captivated by my gaze when he replied, "We'll be there as soon as the song ends." Vikram nodded and made his way back, sensing that we were too absorbed in each other to be able to simply halt our connection. So there I remained, basking in his touch, his warmth, the feel of him that both my body and spirit had missed so much, too much.

Once the final notes of the flute turned into a whisper, Ansgar's feet paused, forcing me to imitate the gesture. Then he smiled and without letting go of the hand he had been guarding into his own like a treasure, he invited excitedly, "Come meet my family."

I did not expect him to utter those four words, I thought that he'd rather ask for me to wait until the members of the royal family were gone, not go and introduce me to his entire family, whom not only were celebrating their youngest prince, but also the arrival of a grandchild.

"Ansgar," I murmured softly, just as he started leading me into the crowd and back towards the dais they had been sharing for the evening. "Do you think it's the best idea?"

I followed the trail Ansgar drew for me, squeezing his hand tightly, since any form of protest was in vain. I was going to meet the Earth Kingdom's royal family, and my only explanation for being there was that I'd crashed their son's celebration. That would go well.

I tried to act normal, but the young prince passing through, holding hands with an unknown woman, was no common news and all the faeries turned their eyes on us within an instant. They even parted the gathering for us, to allow the prince and me to squeeze through easily, more to their benefit, so they'd have a better view at our passage. I kept my head low, thinking that my face would give me away if they had enough time to study my human features.

We rose straight onto the podium, Ansgar planting determined

374

steps towards the thrones and the table that had been prepared for them, but I knew that all the attention focused on me. I wondered if they knew who I was, if Vikram had broken the news and tried to reason with them to avoid confrontation. By the way he sat carelessly at the table, drink in his hand, I thought not. That's what I got for stepping on his toes.

"Mother, Father," Ansgar started speaking as soon as we reached the table, "this is Anwen." He allowed a second for the King and Queen to find me, study me from head to toe, before adding softly, "My mate."

The braided strands of his beard jiggled lightly as the King moved his attention from his son, then back to me and as he studied me, I felt forced to do the same. I saw parts of Ansgar in him, the elongated jawline, that brash way their eyebrows connected when they were caught too deep in thought, even the way he curled his fingers around the rim of his glass.

"Is this the human you told us about, son?" the King's voice echoed in our ears, rough and commanding.

"Yes, Father," Ansgar replied, no sign of unease in his tone.

"Did you bring her here?" It was the Queen's turn to ask questions. As I shifted my focus to her, her gaze pierced so deep into me she would probably know everything I've done today, I found something unexpected in her eyes. Understanding. Her onyx contemplation brushed through every part of my body, my attire, my stance, scanning me, trying to attribute my existence next to her beloved son.

"If I had, she'd have been by my side every moment, Mother,"

Ansgar replied, pressing his meaning.

The Queen did not respond, her attention fully focused on me. I knew she was the one to make the decision that would either bind or break us. She was queen over the magic reigning the earth, so when she took a breath in, preparing us for her decision, composure not leaving her features for a second, I squeezed Ansgar's hand tightly. To tell him that I would fight. Whatever may come, I would not cower, I would not falter, I would fight for him. For us. His gentle squeeze was the reply I needed, a sign of understanding, as the Queen finally spoke.

"When Ansgar told us about you, we did not believe it." Her onyx eyes stood fixed on mine, and I wasn't even blinking from fear I might sway her decision. "No one has heard about this kind of binding energy you claim to be experiencing…"

There it was, the rejection I was dreading, yet knew it would come. The Queen continued, "Yet, we trust our son's knowledge. There is much to discuss, much to assess, and we want Ansgar's happiness above all else," she said as I released the breath I held.

"Tonight is for celebrating, we will have the talks another day," the King added, placing his hand over the Queen's, offering her, and us, a sly smile.

I murmured a "Thank you" and curtsied to them both as I greeted them by title. "King Farryn," I bowed low and he nodded his agreement. "Queen Bathysia." Her stare didn't leave mine, an unspoken warning.

We wished them a good night as they joined the crowd and made their way through, disappearing into the multitude of faeries.

Ansgar was beaming, as he invited me to the table, in the chair the Queen had sat merely a minute before and introduced me to his older brother and his wife, Damaris and Takara. I understood what Ansgar had told me, that he was the King's son along with the heir. They both shared the same sun kissed skin and golden locks, whereas Vikram was the embodiment of the Queen, both of them choosing to ornate their adamant skin with silver accessories, making them shine like the stars swirling in the night sky.

"It's good to finally put a face to a name," Takara was the first to break the silence as I took the opportunity to congratulate them both. Damaris smiled and nodded in thanks, showing more reservation towards me than both his parents had. After a few minutes of small talk, during which we covered the celebration, the story about gardenias and their meaning, and I took the opportunity to taste some of Ansgar's favourite cakes, he grabbed my hand and squeezed it gently to catch my attention.

"We'll let you rest, Takara. Brother, take care of your precious wife," he said and stood from the table, placing a small kiss on her cheek, making her giggle.

Damaris did not abstain from showing his distaste towards our early departure. The party remained still in bloom and Ansgar was meant to celebrate with his people, but he politely bid both of us a good night, then invited his wife to a dance, leaving us alone at the marble sculpted table.

"We're leaving?" I incredulously asked Ansgar as he rose to his feet and urged me to do the same.

"I would very much like to kiss you now, and unfortunately it is

377

not something I can do in public yet. Unless you want to continue dancing?"

"Kissing is good," I jolted at the thought and nodded eagerly, almost flying from the seat I had occupied and reached for his extended arm to follow him into the crowd. We made our way through the dance, acting as though we planned to join in at any moment. Instead, Ansgar led me to a narrow pathway through the tables, then towards the tents where the food was prepared to then make our way into the main kitchens and escape the party through there. I wanted to say how surprised I was that he knew his way so well around the castle, when I had found it labyrinthic.

But this was his home, he had grown up in these halls, under this roof, in this kingdom that was fascinating and scary in equal measure. I took a moment to analyse my surroundings, the tall doors, the sculpted columns, the way each wall was organized in such a way that it looked like a portrayal of a forest. Even the staircase dazzled with leaves and flowers of so many different kinds, I doubted even a scientist would be able to name them all. At last, we reached a door that Ansgar pushed open as he grabbed my hips and raised me up onto him, catching my lips in a kiss, then twirled us inside and kicked the door to force an abrupt closure.

How I missed the feel of him, the taste of those delicious lips, the way his tongue curled up into my mouth, making me taste him. Within a second, my hands were stroking his hair, burying themselves into those beautiful golden locks while his torso supported my hips, as he kept his arm wrapped around me with determination. We were finally here, finally together, alone and able to do this again. His lips slammed into mine over and over again, claiming them, claiming me. Words made way to moans.

Both our bodies demanded closeness, more and more of it, so much that without warning, Ansgar clutched the inside of my cleavage and pulled hard onto the fabric, ripping the material in his path and forcing my breasts to spring free. I did not care, did not shy when small tremors sparkled on my skin, begging for more of his touch. The prince slowly put me down, my bare skin brushing against his shirt. Little did he know that were it not for him supporting me, I would have already fallen from the wave of emotion, from the sweet encounter with his body. Mercifully, he did not let go, his strong arms still pressing tight against my back, upholding my weight with his own. His gaze moved over my face, searching, analysing. I had come for him, he understood and his next words portrayed the feelings both of us forced into hiding this past month.

"I love you," he said. Slowly, gently, like a hymn, one that would mark our union, our mating.

I threw myself deep into those ashen eyes that had become both my salvation and my doom, and whispered, "I love you, Ansgar."

He paused, his entire figure tense, taking me in. Then, with a breath came a single question. "What did you say?"

"I love you, Ansgar. Above all. I love you." A small tear made its way down my cheek from the memory of the past month, of the devastation I had caused both of us. His thumb brushed it away. His palm cupped my cheek and placed a gentle kiss on my eyelid, isolating the source of the tear. Then he moved to the other one, then to my forehead, my nose, both of my cheeks and finally, to my mouth, where he placed his lips over mine in agonizing slowness, to seal our words, our promise.

"I am yours. Completely, fully, eternally," he declared with a vow, "if you will have me." The prince paused. For me, for my reaction. And I knew that whatever I was about to say, would become my vow to him.

"I am sorry that I am not what you expected. But know that I love you with everything I have, with everything I am."

"Anwen," he barely let me finish the sentence, "you are everything."

With that, we unleashed onto each other, not caring, not wanting to know what was happening around, who could hear us or if someone could come in at any time. Ansgar continued ripping into my dress and with two strong tears on his part, the entire thing fell off me, a river of chiffon laying at my feet as my bare body presented itself in front of the prince. Since I was not allowed to keep the corset I had arrived in, my underwear set remained discarded into the folds of the dress and I did not dare ask the three females who came to prepare me for a new set of panties. So, much to Ansgar's delight, I found myself completely bare underneath that dress.

"This is the best marking present I could have asked for," he replied with a smirk and stepped closer to me, after he took a moment to admire my naked self, and placed a kiss on my shoulder, then one on my clavicle, his lips slowly trailing down. Down to the valley of my breasts where he started licking my skin as one of his hands cupped my breast, his fingers teasing the nipple. Then, within a moment, his mouth made its way onto the other one, teeth scraping around, teasing until his tongue started licking again. I took deep breaths as he worked my breasts, moving from one to the other, cupping them and licking and biting until I was ready to burst out of my skin.

"Ansgar," I barely breathed, barely managed to untangle my hands long enough from his dishevelled hair to demand my prince's attention.

"Let's play, fahrenor," was his reply as he pulled me in his arms again and stepped towards the closest furniture object he could splay me on, a dark green settee with metallic decorations. As soon as my body was placed over it, Ansgar retook his teasing, only this time his mouth headed downwards, past my navel, kissing and licking onto my skin as he descended on me, a hand gliding between my legs.

The first stroke of his tongue made me want to explode with pleasure. I had missed this so damn much and my body already positioned itself to give him better access, already expecting his touch, his fingers inside of me, and God, I hoped he still did that thing with his tongue, where we twisted my clit in such a way I would always gasp and moan until my throat became rugged. To my excitement, that was exactly his plan, as though he was able to read my thoughts. His tongue expertly grabbed me the way he knew I liked it most, his fingers scraping and twisting. He had done this many times, back at the mansion, teasing and tantalising my inner thighs and my core until he learned what I wanted and responded to best. It was no surprise that I shattered within a minute, hands digging into his back muscles as I screamed his name loud enough for whomever lived in this castle to hear.

This time, however, he did not stop, did not even pause. He kept devouring me like a starving man, licking, taunting and teasing until a second orgasm rushed out of me only a few minutes later. Still he did not stop, would not stop when I tried to pull myself away from his tongue, the area much too sensitive to be able to take even the slightest touch. But he kept me in place, forearms pressed against my legs, opening me up to him and pressing enough weight onto my hips that it proved impossible to move them. He feasted on me like a man possessed, as though he wanted to make up for all the time we had lost and did not know, or care, that my core was exploding under that mouth of his.

"Ansgar, please," I begged, trying to move my hips again for emphasis, yet he held me in place, both his fingers pumping in and out of me as his tongue teased and tormented, inside and around until I broke and screamed. A third, unexpected and unrequested wave of pleasure flowed through me and expulsed that accumulation tension that had almost driven me crazy.

Only then, when I was left shaking, legs trembling hard, did he ease his hold on me and allowed me to escape from under him. He placed gentle kisses over me, on all the places he had so deliciously tortured. To soothe, to relax the area that he was most certainly not done with for the night. Ansgar sat on the settee by my side and pressed my body to his own, my head resting on his shoulder while he sowed kisses into my hair.

"That was…" I stopped, realising I did not have words to

describe what had just happened, the agony and delight my body had experienced. But as I was a trembling pile of limbs, his shape had become rough, muscles tense and strained, a general unease overpowering him. I looked inquisitively at him, trying to place the sentiment. He noticed and a sad, worried smile curved his lips.

"I wanted to make sure it felt good for you. Now," he said, leaving the unspoken meaning for me to unveil. Now, before something else happened.

"I wanted tonight to be good for you," he repeated, stopping my line of thoughts. "I am sorry if I overstepped, pushed too far. The wonder of your body is an encyclopaedia I plan to get very acquainted with," he transformed that worried smile into a proud grin.

I giggled and kissed his lips. "You have creative credit," I snickered. That made him chuckle, but his eyes remained serious.

"I am sorry if tonight won't be as you expected. I'm told it improves each time you do it." His eyes pierced my own and I finally understood what was happening. His push to force me into pleasure, his worry. It was not worry at all. It was nerves. Because tonight would be his first time. With me. With his mate.

"My first time was awful," I tried to ease the tension and help him relax, just as I would have wanted someone to do this for me ten years ago. "It was quick, messy, painful, and the guy turned out to be a jerk."

He huffed, anger lining his features.

"We'll make it work," I encouraged. "And the second time will be better," I urged as I placed a kiss on his shoulder. "And the third," another one on his neck, "and the fourth…" This kiss landed on his lips. Ansgar smiled and whispered the words he knew would be my undoing.

"I love you."

"Hie vaedrum teim," I murmured the words I had made sure to learn during his marking rituals. Words that I remembered his low voice whispering into my ear the morning after he returned from his visit.

"Hie vaedrum teim aldig, Anwen. Satrem vaed unde vahr teim," he breathed back into me.

"Should I go back and ask the girls what that means?" I giggled, waving slowly at myself to remind him that I was completely naked while he still had all his garments on. Seemed pretty unfair.

"I love you too Anwen. I will love only you," he translated for me, caressing the figure he also seemed to realise was too naked compared to his own.

"You need to teach me," I demanded. If I was to be his mate, I needed to be able to at least speak their language.

"Not before you teach me," he murmured and moved away from my closeness only long enough to remove his shirt. Then he held a hand out to me and as I grabbed it, he beckoned me towards his lap. A silent invitation. So I placed myself on top of him, legs spread on each side of his hips, my body wrapping around his own. His hands travelled down my spine and cupped my rear, holding me in place on top of his hardening member. I allowed my folds to linger on top of the fabric of his pants, the only thing that came in between us and moved my hips up and down across his erection, the anticipation forming goose bumps on my skin, my legs.

Ansgar breathed hard, as though he remembered the need to control himself, his own desire. He hadn't allowed himself to fully fall into the abyss I was about to take him into. But he trusted me, he had chosen me. So I slid a hand down into his pants, gently scratching that triangle of muscles of his pelvis, tantalizing him until my hand fisted around it.

Thick and hard, awaiting my touch. Ansgar hissed heavily and I continued my movement across his member, caressing and teasing it, allowing it to spring free from the trap his pants had been. I almost wanted to throw myself into it, impale myself into that thick, long hardness of him that had kept me wanting for months. I almost did, my instinct thriving for a mere second.

"Where's the bed?" I barely stopped myself, though my hand refused to let it go, stroking it with gentle movements, barely able to contain it with just the palm of my hand. I did not know if all fae were this blessed with their length, but damn, it will be a memorable night.

He did not reply, but he tried to stand, shifting me from my claimed position. As soon as my legs touched the floor, he placed an arm on my back and the other under my knees and lifted me in a single movement, his nakedness pressing onto mine as he carried me into his bedroom. Which, to my surprise, was identical to the one he had been living in back in the forest.

"How?" I asked in amazement, holding onto his general warmth.

"Energy. It copies things," Ansgar replied, holding me in place to allow me to take in all the details. Details I knew, that I had

385

studied, a mere copy of the ones in his bedroom. His original bedroom.

"When we wake up tomorrow, will we be transported back to the forest?" My enquiry, or naivete made him chuckle.

"It doesn't work like that. We'll have to go through the trees." Before I could say something else, he continued, "Also, no one said anything about sleeping tonight."

Ansgar widened his grin and placed me gently onto the bed. My entire body fluttered and I stopped to take him in, his sculpted form, bronze skin and that hard member, towering over the bed, over me. I shifted, positioning myself into the centre of the bed to make room for him. With two sly movements, he was propped up on his forearms on top of me, our bodies touching in so many places that the building sensation was driving me mad. My breath accentuated as I spread out my legs to make room for him, allow him to situate himself at my entrance.

"Do you need me to…" he wanted to ask but it was my turn to stop him. I knew what he would say. What, even now, in this moment, the one he had been waiting so long for, was willing to do. To care for me, to make sure I was ready and prepared to receive him. Little did he know that one look at his cock and I was already dripping wet, wanting it, needing it inside of me.

"No, I'm ready," I replied eagerly, trying to make his first experience memorable. I had expected him to jump at the opportunity with one swift movement, yet he remained unfazed, gazing into me with so much love, it almost made me feel unworthy.

He was nervous, some of his muscles tensing and he seemed shy.

I placed my lips on his, urging him to kiss me, to lose his focus into me and forget about any expectation, any advice he might have received that was undoubtedly coming back to him. It was just us, two lovers, a couple ready to join together and celebrate love.

Just as his tongue swept in, so did he. During our gathering of lips, he had found my entrance and now, he was slowly, so slowly allowing himself to claim me. Inch after inch, he pushed in, all the while his attention was on me, on my face, scanning me for any signs of discomfort even as he kissed me. I placed my palms on his back, urging him on, leading him.

A moan escaped my mouth as I forced my body to relax, my lungs to breathe and my core to split wide enough to receive him. Luckily, it did. Up to the hilt and I sighed with relief as I realised my body was made to fit my mate's. Perfectly. There was no room inside of me that was not completely filled by him and the sensation was mind blowing, like nothing I'd ever felt.

Ansgar's face was grim, his brows furrowed, breaths uneven as he continued to gaze into me, his eyes wide with the experience, the sensation of being inside. He retracted a few inches, with the same gradual movement, then back into me, burying himself even deeper this time, if such a thing was possible. When he did, his face illuminated with surprise. He did it again, retracting even further, then slamming back, harder this time, until he built a steady rhythm which he followed as sensation kept building.

God, this felt good. Unbelievably good, so good that I needed to contain myself and without thinking, I grabbed unto his back, my fingernails marking his skin as a moan evaded my mouth. A few seconds later, Ansgar's throat escaped rhythmical grunts and the movement of his hips halted, his face contorting with pleasure, his breathing jagged and irregular, leg muscles tensing. A blanket of pleasure was thrown over him, nothing else existed but that moment, that sensation. Only when he opened his eyes he seemed to remember I was there, even though he was still inside me. His features immediately shifted into regret.

"No, no, no," I immediately raised from under him, the movement letting his member slip along with a trail of his pleasure. I cupped his face and forced him to look at me, even though he seemed to want to escape me, something like shame starting to mask his face. "I love you," I said, hard and determined. "It was amazing."

He nodded in agreement. "For me," he trailed. I kissed him and forced him to lay on the bed, placing myself in my favourite position, atop his chest.

"I love you," I whispered again, listening to his heartbeat become steadier and forming lazy circles on his abs.

"And I love you," he murmured.

We remained like that for a few minutes, basking in each other's warmth, enjoying the feel of our connecting bodies, our naked skin savouring each other's touch.

"Thank you," Ansgar breathed. His fingers lingered on a caress down my hips.

"What for?" I asked, not understanding his meaning.

"For this," he replied, cupping my rear for emphasis, "for coming here, for accepting me."

I waved my head. "I should be the one thanking you. I'm so sorry for…" I paused.

What would I even apologise for? The list was so long it would probably take me all night to explain everything I had done, every lie I'd told, the reasoning behind it.

"You chose me, in the end," he responded. "That's what matters."

"Ansgar, everything I told you was a lie." I needed to clarify, let him know that it had always been him, ever since we met. "I just told you that because I didn't think it was possible, this relationship between us. I thought freeing you was the best option."

He raised his brows in surprise, so I told him everything that happened. How I wanted to see him that morning, but I received a visit from his brother, how he'd explained that there is no such thing as a mating bond between us. That I thought I was getting in the way of his happiness. That I thought I would not, could not be enough. He tensed and wanted to rise from the bed in anger, probably to chase his brother for an explanation but one look at my naked shape and he decided the rage fit could wait for another day. He relaxed afterwards, and had a laughter fit when I'd told him about the dress I'd arrived in and how Vikram was the one to save me.

"I need to find that dress," he said in between chuckles. I told him about how one of the forest guards knew about the fae because his human grand aunt was mated with one, how he'd given me the root to make tea and how I'd ended up here, not wasting a moment away from him.

"It's been only you," I said again. "Since that kiss we had on the plateau. If I am truly honest with myself, even ahead of that, probably since that sunset we shared together, when you held my hand. My heart knew before my mind even began to understand it," I stated as he lunged for me with another kiss, his body crushing mine.

"Let's do it again." He pushed his growing hardness into me, penetrating deep inside with two strokes. As he sheathed himself, he paused, as though he could sense that my body needed to adjust to fully receive him. He started moving with excruciating slowness, allowing me to feel every inch of him, those thick veins on his cock scraping at my insides in such a way that I knew I could not last long and I'd start begging him for more. When I started moaning, he obliged, moving in and out of me faster, deeper, pressing my hips hard into the mattress as my core started building up pleasure from the feel of him.

Within minutes, I was squirming under him while tingles shimmied across my body, from the waves of pleasure accumulating in my core. He would not stop, would not slow down. Possessed by the pleasure, by our union, Ansgar pistoned in and out of me with abrupt strokes, hands gripping my hips tight enough to bruise and when he bent down to bite my shoulder, the pleasure rippled through me and I shattered around him, clenching him tightly with my legs as spikes of desire erupted from that spot he was hitting so well.

A satisfied lover's smirk cropped on his lips and he allowed himself to find pleasure with a few more strokes, deep enough that I felt my stomach tighten. He finished with a groan, his gaze penetrating my own, a perfect portrayal of our bodies.

"The second time is better," he announced between pants, voice roughened by sex.

I smiled lazily in approval. To my surprise, not even a minute later my lover was ready for round three and without even announcing his desire to continue our sex marathon, he just spread my legs wide enough to allow his body to fit in between them, his hardness already pointed to my entrance.

"Already?" I scowled, eyes wide with surprise.

"This feels excellent, I want more of it," he murmured as he nudged at my entrance, a silent request to let him in. And I did, I allowed him to explore our bodies, our union, the build-up exquisite sensation that our friction created and we groaned and shuddered together.

I knew it was going to be a long night when, just an hour after we decided to go to sleep, Ansgar's hardness poking at my rear woke me up to find him smiling and hungry for me, so I obliged. This time, I laid him on the bed and speared myself into him, moving up and down, grinding on him until we were both a sweaty mess of limbs and tongues and he roared, actually roared when he found his release, his fingers digging into my hips so hard that deep scratches were left behind and we were forced to stop so he could clean the almost-bleeding marks.

He felt so bad afterwards that he made it up to me again and again, worshiping my body with his hands, his tongue and all of him, until wave after wave of pleasure left me a pile of trembling mess. Only when dawn rose, its light shining over the sweat of our bodies, did we stop, Ansgar bringing me close to him and placing soothing caresses across the skin he had tantalised all night long.

"Let's sleep for an hour or two," he murmured into me, "then we'll go home and do it all over again." The perky smile remained on his lip and he instantly fell prey to sleep, the exhaustion of the night leaning heavily on top of his eyelids. I kissed his jaw, the only part of him within reach, without having to change my position and rested my head on his shoulder, my body shivering with the rivers of pleasure he had left behind.

Autumn

Chapter Thirty-Eight

The chirrup of the canaries in the garden woke me up to find Anwen clutched to my shoulder, her skin bearing the marks of last night. She was nestled into me, enjoying the warmth of our bodies while her hair formed waves of hazel onto the white silk pillow. She was mine, she accepted me, joined with me and together we made our energy whole, new again, like a star that was reborn into the night sky and had now the ability to outshine all its sisters.

I carefully moved her head and made sure to cover her with the blanket that was more wrapped around her feet than on top of her. As I pulled it up across her body, I saw the marks of what we'd done, remembered how I dragged my fingers down her hips where dark scratch marks remained, along with a growing bruise on her hand. And a bite mark on her lower neck where my teeth had ripped into her when she moved with such veracity on top of me it made me explode inside of her. I needed to be more careful, I decided, as I shimmied from the bed and pulled last night's pair of pants from the settee. I tried to make my way into the kitchen and prepare a platter for Anwen, but as soon as I stepped out of my chambers, Vikram intercepted me and dragged me into the breakfast room, where all the family, apart from Father, seemed to be eagerly waiting for me. No matter how hard I tried to protest and explain that a pair of dirty pants and nothing else was not the way to present myself in front of Mother and Takara, he did not seem to care as he physically shoved me in the room. They all stared in surprise. Damaris even had the good sense to choke on his juice.

I lowered my head and puckered my lips, not feeling at all comfortable and as I looked down at my stomach, I realised that I was not the only one to leave proof of my pleasure on my lover. Two big scratches marked my pecs and the left side of my abdomen, clearly Anwen's way of letting me know she had enjoyed our late night activities. I shifted my gaze to Vikram to find him beaming behind me, making an effort not to bounce up and down with excitement. I was the first to speak.

"I only came for some food, Vikram had the poor taste to bring me here in this state," I explained my apology to the two females, both of whom pierced me with frowns. Damaris' face remained plain, though he visibly struggled to do so. Vikram, as expected, had to say something.

"Breakfast in bed after an entire night of sex? Brother, you are a very attentive lover," he smirked like a cat who had just eaten a full jar of cream.

"Seeing as you are here and not in your bed with the latest conquest, you are clearly not," I replied and proceeded to pick an empty plate and fill it with a bit of everything displayed on the table.

"If I'd known she was staying overnight, I would have arranged rooms more suitable for her," Mother pointed out, unable to keep her eyes away from the big scratch on my lower abdomen.

"Thank you Mother, but there is no need, my mate will share my rooms from now on." She opened her mouth to protest, but I anticipated the question and continued, "We will of course have much to discuss, I will bring her next month and we will have dinner, talk things through." Then I paused and placed the plate back on the table in order to give her my full attention. "I will do whatever is needed, whatever is asked of me, serve in any way I am required, but she stays," I demanded, my gaze burning into hers, a clash of shadow and adamant, both determined, both ready to fight for our stance. To my relief, she nodded and lowered her eyes in defeat.

"Now that we have established how my brother is ready to die for love, can we please talk about the sex?" Vikram served himself another chocolate pastry and occupied the chair next to me, biting into it with excitement.

"There is nothing to talk about," I replied and grabbed a glass to pour juice into.

"Well, brother, judging by the marks on your chest, your abdomen and your back, the lady liked it. A lot," he grinned.

I huffed, surprised that Anwen had the chance to mark so many parts of my body and wicked delight poured through me. The things I would do to her, Goddess save me, I planned to devour that woman every day and night until either one of my organs would fail.

"Mind your own business, brother," I uttered a belated reply.

"Oh, I would, but considering both our living quarters are on the

397

Eastern side and you kept me up all night, I think I deserve details," he insisted as he took another bite of that pasty.

"If you are going to talk nonsense, I will go before my stomach turns," it was Takara who retorted and I nodded gratefully in her direction.

"No need, I'll be on my way," I announced, holding the plate and the glass and made my way to the door.

"We'll see you all next month. Mother, thank you. Takara, hope you have an easy month, Damaris, take care of her, Vikram..." I stopped as my brother threw me a seductive smirk. "Shut up. May you all have a blessed month."

I made my way back into the chambers and found my mate sleeping in the exact same position I had left her in, so I grabbed a small table that I usually filled with books and placed the plate and glass on top of it, then dragged it by the bed, next to her.

"Good morning beautiful," I whispered, my breath tickling the shell of her ear. She smiled softly, lazily, tired from the eventful night. "Breakfast for my lady," I announced. It seemed to persuade her a bit more as she opened her eyes and excitement flashed through them at the assortment of pastries, quiche and fruit I had gathered for her.

"Mmmm, delicious," she murmured and stood slowly, pulling up the sheet a bit more to cover her breasts as she rose, but instead of the plate, she looked at me.

"Good morning," Anwen greeted with a smile and I did not abstain from kissing her, long and hard. The first thing I wanted to taste for breakfast.

I forced myself to stop after a while and let her eat, while I changed and packed a few more things I needed from other chambers and supply cabinets and placed them in their rightful place back into the bedroom, to be copied into Evigt. Once Anwen was finished, I gave her one of my shirts and pants, seeing how the dress she had worn last night was destroyed and unusable and we made our way down to the stables. I normally enjoyed walking back into the forest and through the portal but seeing how we were both in a hurry, in need of a shower and my mate did not have suitable clothes, I decided a horse ride was the easiest thing to do, apart from a carriage but I was sure she would not like the attention.

Anwen seemed reluctant at first, protested a bit, but when I explained that it was either ten minutes on the horse or an hour walk, she allowed me to hoist her up into the saddle. By the way she grabbed onto me and did not reply to any of the explanations and details I offered when we passed different buildings or streets, she was uncomfortable and scared. I held her tighter, making sure to point out the remaining distance every other minute.

Luckily, she started relaxing when the forest became visible and almost kissed the ground after I placed her down from the saddle. I smiled and scratched the horse's mane before sending it back to the palace, then grabbed my lover in my arms and stepped into the portal that would take us both home.

She only spoke once we made it through the door of her mansion, when I finally put her down, since in between swapping portals and jumping matter, it was clear her mind and body felt dazed. The first thing she did was go into the kitchen and press the button on the coffee maker, filling the sitting room with a toasted-nutty aroma.

"Coffee?" she asked sweetly while she came out of the kitchen with two steaming mugs, then passed one to me and proceeded to sit on the sofa. I took a moment to breathe everything in, take in the details of the place I had seen so many times.

Once Anwen had announced the ending of us, I'd spent nights thinking about the surroundings, missing the royal blue rug on the entrance hall, the ficus pot hanging from the bookshelf and the crystal lamp that sent small rainbow projections onto our bodies when we watched stories on the sofa. But what I missed most was this, the small gestures, the inconsequential movements our bodies shared that proved nothing but that, a shift of the muscles, a gesture we had done millions of times through our lives. When she extended her hand to me with a cup of coffee, when she patted the seat next to her with a silent invitation for me to join, the way she rested her head on my chest and allowed her hair to release strands on my shoulder. The gestures that united us, that made us one.

I kissed my mate's brow and she sipped lazily from her coffee. "I need to visit the district," I announced and as soon as the words were spoken, she shifted. Something had startled her.

"You're leaving?" Anwen threw me an incredulous look.

"Just for a few hours, fahrenor. There are things to be sorted, faerie homes to be visited, it's a marking tradition," I explained.

"Can I come?" she tried to look excited but I saw through her mask. Even so, the fact that my mate did not want to sever our connection this quickly brought me enormous joy. I kissed her slowly, refraining myself from going too far, joining too deep because I knew that one bit of her taste would set me ablaze, so much so that I would not be able to leave until I'd fucked her to my last breath.

I was desperate, my spirit begged to be reconnected with hers and now that I felt how her body opened up so perfectly to receive mine, I was about to burst out of my skin so I could feel her again, and again and again, hear those little squeaks she made when the sensation was too much. Goddess, this woman would be the end of me.

"Why don't you relax for a few hours? Sleep a while, rest up," I suggested and her face brightened at the thought. I knew she was tired and I had better ideas than to drag her across the district for hours on end. By the time I left, she was already in bed, comfortable in her mountain of pillows.

I spent the day visiting and greeting each and every faerie I found, making sure to visit the families of those who had been affected by the fire, offer my support and check on their healing and progress. All of them congratulated me cheerfully, some asked about the mark's meaning and others, the ones Anwen had met during her stay, already knew and wished me, some in a more reluctant than cheerful tone, a fruitful mating. I listened to the reporting, did the necessary healing in the Western side of the district, the one that seemed to be drying out the roots in the past month, for some unknown reason.

By the time I finished, it was almost dawn, so I headed back to the cave for a quick shower and a set of fresh clothes and appeared straight on her doorstep. Even though we had been separated for less

than a day, I could feel the effect on the intertwining of our energies. I did not know how long the mating effects lasted, or if they would be completed in our case, seeing how Anwen was human, but something had banded in between us last night and a steady stream of new energy flowed through my veins, alimenting my power. Anwen's energy.

I knocked on the door. It did not feel right to enter without her permission, especially since I had not been allowed in this place in the past moon cycle, but I took the time to grow a crown of gardenias and white roses. When my starlight opened the door and practically surrendered in my arms, I placed it on her head, crowning her.

"Finally," she reproached my tardiness and placed a hand on her head to keep the flowers in place. "I was starting to worry you forgot about me."

"I could never," I smiled and placed a kiss on her brow, then closed the door behind me and headed into the kitchen where some kind of pie awaited.

"You cooked?" I was surprised. "For me?"

"Tried to cook," she raised her shoulders to say she was not very pleased with the results. "I noticed how you fae love your pies, so I tried to make you one."

I approached the plate and took a cautious sniff. I sensed pumpkin, some kind of salty cheese and ash. Lots and lots of ash. I even raised my brows in question, making Anwen confess.

"I burnt it. Cressi wrote to me and we stayed all day talking and I didn't hear the beeping. By the time I got to it, it was burnt."

402

"I'm sure it's still delicious," I encouraged with a grateful smile, picking up the fork by the plate as I took a generous bite.

"You hate it," she huffed and crossed her arms in offense, before I even tasted the food.

"I do not!" I tried to defend myself while the clumpy piece of burnt crust scratched my throat. "It's good."

She stared at me incredulously.

"It's okay," I rectified. "A bit crunchy."

She continued to stare for a long minute, and then Anwen fell prey to a laughing fit so big that she almost suffocated. I allowed myself to laugh too, not knowing if it was her hysterical laugh that made me chuckle or the situation itself. Either way, I loved it. Loved her.

After she wiped away the tears from her cheeks, my mate grabbed my hand and dragged me to the sofa. As soon as I sat, she positioned herself on top of me, both inhaling heavily from the closeness.

"I missed you today," Anwen hummed in my ear, her warm breath tickling my lobe.

"I missed you too," I murmured, barely able to contain myself from taking her then and there. "So much that I decided I'm taking a few days off," I said tentatively and her eyes gleamed with joy.

"You are?" her laughter exploded in the room, illuminating it brighter than the sunset pouring through the window.

"I think we need a few days to…" I started drawing lazy shapes on her thighs,"enjoy ourselves," I replied and kissed the side of her neck. "Enjoy each other," I added as I kissed the other.

"I very much agree, my prince," she replied half mockingly and removed herself from my lap, my insides screaming from the loss of her. But before I protested, her hands gripped my pants and dragged them down, my obvious desire for her springing free. Instead of claiming her place back onto me, she settled herself in between my legs, her fingers slowly scraping my thighs.

"Anwen," I murmured in warning.

"Ansgar," she imitated the tone of my voice and without warning, grabbed me in her hand, squeezing and stroking and before I could even grunt from the building sensation, her tongue was on me, circling around the tip.

"Anwen," I whispered, voice so rough it could barely escape my throat. She moaned with satisfaction as she took me in her mouth, her tongue swirling around the veins, teeth scraping slowly, carefully as her mouth received me deeper and deeper.

"By the goddess, Anwen," I cursed, or I think I did, as she worked me with generous strokes of her tongue, the building pleasure so rough that I had to grab onto something to keep myself from falling over an imaginary cliff.

One of my hands found a pillow and squeezed the fabric so hard it ripped through but the other found my lover's shoulder, the nape of her neck and instinctively, I snatched her by the hair. She did not seem to mind as she bent down further onto me, so much that I practically felt myself poking through the back of her throat and I couldn't...

"Anwen, stop," I tried to say but she did not care, would not listen. She continued to torture me so sweetly.

404

"Anwen!" I heard my raspy voice but by the time I finished releasing her name it was too late. I felt myself spilling into her, down her throat and a flood of relief poured through me. I realised what had happened, what I had done and immediately let go of her hair and tried to remove myself from her mouth and help her sit back up, by my side.

I panted heavily, the marvellous sensation still sending waves through my body and as she looked at me, she smirked proudly. I exhaled, another wave of relief inundating me.

"That was..." I waved my head in awe, I didn't even know if such a word existed.

"A thank you," my mate replied with a grin. "For taking a few days off."

"Then I think I need to thank you as well, my lady. For allowing me to stay here and devour you," I grinned and, not letting her react, I lunged at her and hoisted her legs up on my shoulders. She snickered with excitement as I pulled her tiny shorts to the side, giving me free access to something I craved more than dinner.

A knock on the door woke me up and had my mate bouncing from the bed.

"Shit, it must be Friday."

She grabbed my shirt to cover herself, then realised it was mine and threw it back on the floor, searching desperately for a garment of her own.

In the past few days we had done nothing but eat, sleep and mate. I took Anwen in so many ways and so many places I had lost track, though I was now perfectly acquainted with each one of her moans and knew exactly how she wanted me to satisfy her. It became impossible to control ourselves, if one of us suggested another activity that was not bodily-exploration related, like watching a story or going for a walk, or even taking a bath together, it only took us a few minutes and desire overpowered everything we did.

So we allowed ourselves to relish in it, to explore our bodies inch by inch, to hold competitions on how quickly we can make the other shatter and to relish in each other every waking moment we had. Even now, seeing my mate's breasts bounce up and down in her desperation to find something on the floor stirred my desire and were it not for someone knocking on the door, I would have probably jumped up from the bed and fucked her until she screamed my name over and over again.

"Don't make a sound, they never come in here," she warned and closed the door behind her. I heard her steps onto the staircase, her sweaty feet slamming on the hard wood and a few moments later, the door opened and my mate greeted the guard.

A chill went through my body at the surge of energy that walked through the door and I knew something was wrong. It felt as though the room was ablaze, the air pressing in so hot and ready to burn, ready to wound and destroy. And Anwen was in the middle of it.

Caution aside, I moved out of the bed and got dressed, then searched for the only dagger I had brought with me which luckily was thrown somewhere in this room, then I pushed the door open carefully, mindful to not make any noises that could attract the guard's attention. I knew it would get Anwen in trouble, so I only stepped into the corridor and walked by the staircase long enough to eliminate any threat. After that, I was determined on going back and staying hidden until the man left.

As I creeped into the sitting room, I spotted a dark haired man in a green uniform, he was facing Anwen and passing her some bags, the two chatting casually. She looked relaxed and trusted the man. She even smiled at him and they shared familiarity. Maybe I was wrong, maybe the mating instinct got the better of me and the threat I felt was simple jealousy. He looked and acted like a guard, I had spotted them several times around the territory and they all wore the same stance and green coat. Until I saw his face.

Every cautionary impulse vanished and I lunged for him, dagger in hand, ready to wound, ready to kill. The bastard sensed me, or maybe it was Anwen's scream that warned him when I tried to thrust the weapon into his neck. He turned just enough to shift the blow to his shoulder, where I left a deep cut that instantly started bleeding and staining the polished wooden floor.

"Ansgar, stop!" Anwen ordered but I pushed her out of the way and into the kitchen, making her tumble on the floor.

Protect your mate. It was all I heard in my mind, all my instincts screaming, demanding me to do so. I lunged for him once again, aiming for his throat, his kidneys, anywhere I could fatally wound. Again, he shifted out of the way and jumped over the sofa, so I followed him, pushing him further away from her as one of my knees found its mark and shoved a blow at the back of his head.

Anwen shouted again, screaming at me to stop, ordering me to, explaining that this bastard was her friend. It only took the second while I glimpsed towards my mate for my throat to be wrapped in iron. He had found the chains Anwen used on me that time and sent one of them flying at my head, squeezing hard enough to remove the air from my lungs. I heard Anwen's voice again, distant, screaming and through some miracle, she reached him and pushed him away. To my surprise he let her and just as everything was turning dark, my mate released the chain around my throat, allowing me to breathe.

"Ansgar," she cupped my face and scanned it, needing to know I was okay. From the corner of my eye, I saw Fear Gorta picking up the dagger I'd used against him and making a sign of throwing it into my mate's head. I grunted, the message crystal clear.

"Ansgar," she softly, lovingly caressed my face, tears flowing, "it's okay, he is a friend," she tried to explain and I could not bear the innocence in her eyes. She had been cheated, we both had. All the while I thought he had vanished, that I made him disappear the first day, and in turn he had infiltrated the guards to get to her. To befriend her, make her trust him.

"Why?" I grunted, still on the floor with Anwen on her knees, by my side.

"Where's the fun in that, tree princeling?" he mocked and hovered over us, stepping slowly and playing with the dagger, able to launch it any second. I could do nothing to stop him, except throw myself in front of it. I would do it, for her, I would do it.

"This is between you and me, she has nothing to do with anything," I threatened and tried to stand but as soon as I made my intention clear, his hand tensed on the hilt, so I stopped.

"Ansgar, he is a member of the guards, he is a friend," Anwen tried to clarify, still thinking the whole situation was a misunderstanding. "His name is—" she tried to tell me but I stopped her. I already knew.

"Rhylan," I continued for her. "He calls himself Rhylan now, correct?" I asked the fireling.

"Yes," he nodded with a smile, introducing himself to us all over again.

"You know him?" she asked incredulously.

"He is the one who attacked you, the day we met. He is a fireling."

"No," Anwen shook her head in disbelief. "No, it can't be. He is not fae, he can touch iron." She continued moving her shocked gaze from me to Rhylan, then back to me, expecting, hoping that one of us would tell her it was all some kind of joke. She seemed to realise it was not and rose to her feet, shoving Rhylan. Once again, he let her, to my surprise.

"How dare you lie to me? I trusted you! It was all a ruse to get to him?" she pushed her fists into his chest again, only this time he lost patience and shoved her on the sofa. I took the opportunity to regain my stance.

"Now, now, sprout, no need to get sentimental. You don't like pain, remember?" Rhylan smirked darkly at my mate, then shifted his attention back to me. "How was the visit?"

409

"What do you want?" I pressed and tried to take small steps towards the sofa, trying to cover Anwen.

"The entire forest heard you two fucking, so I assume it was a pleasurable encounter?" The words rolled off his lips with distaste.

"That's none of your business, you freaking jerk!" It was Anwen who replied.

Fear Gorta huffed, placing a theatrically offended hand to his chest. "None of my business, sprout? It was I who helped your joyous reunion, was it not?"

My mate rose from the sofa and as she did so, I immediately gripped her wrist and pulled her behind me, protecting her with my body, away from the weapon resting in Rhylan's hand.

"What do you want?" I pressed again, this time emphasizing the hate and anger rising in my throat.

"It is quite simple, I want payment," he replied as though it was as clear as child's play.

"What for?" I grunted, all the while stepping back and almost shoved Anwen against the wall, expanding my arms as much as possible to form a protective shield in front of her.

"The journey, of course. What, did you think it came out of my charity funds?"

I frowned as I tried to decipher his words, but it was Anwen who replied from behind me, "Fine, I'll write you a cheque."

"Humans and their petty cash," Rhylan replied annoyed. "What you received, silly sprout, is worth a lot more than your paper."

"What did you give her?" I demanded.

"Cloutie root. Burnt Cloutie root," the bastard replied with a proud smile.

Fuck. My brain stopped working, my heart stopped pumping...

Fuck.

"Anwen," I asked her without breaking eye contact with the fireling, "tell me everything about that tea you drank. What did it look like?"

A shred of hope lingered, the assumption that Rhylan may be bluffing, but as soon as she started talking, I knew we were both doomed.

"It was a small vial, with some kind of a black root. When I cut it, it had silver-blue strands, like... like cerulean, the tea was black and smelled horrible and when I drank it—"

"I think that's enough, sprout," Rhylan announced, not giving up his satisfied smirk. "You've convinced him."

"No!" I responded, feeling how my heart was about to stop beating any second. He would not have her, I would not let him. Whatever I had to do, whatever he asked for to prevent this, I would do it. "Pick something else," I urged. "Anything else." Tears formed in my eyes but I would not let them fall, I was not defeated yet. Not yet.

"No, no, no," Rhylan shook his head. "You know that is the only payment, princeling. You are a smart one. One root, one household, one—"

"I live here too," I uttered, expelling the phrase without a second thought, pushed through my lips more by my heart than my brain.

"Are you willing, tree princeling?" he purred. And I knew. I knew this had been his plan all along and I had fallen into it.

I nodded and the bastard clapped his hands in excitement. "To prove my kindness, one last time," he pressed those words with delight, "I'll meet you by the river in ten minutes. You know the place."

With that, he vanished.

Anwen, who had remained silent as a grave, started crying slowly, holding me in a tight embrace from behind. I took a few deep breaths, steadying myself for what was to come, then held her in my arms tightly, inhaling the smell of her hair, the softness of her skin, her beating heart.

"Anwen, you need to listen to me carefully." I cupped her face and raised it high enough to force her to look at me.

"I didn't know... he can touch iron... we had cake... I'm sorry," she continued crying and mumbling things that probably made more sense in her head.

"Anwen!" I raised my voice and she stopped, from instinct or fear, I did not know, did not care, as long as she listened.

"You need to call the guards. Tell them to come stay with you. At least three or four. Then call your father and ask him to take you home as soon as he can. Today, in an hour, now. As soon as possible," I ordered but she shook her head, dismissing, denying what I had asked.

"No, Ansgar, I'm not leaving. Not calling the guards, they will know, they will find out." She started crying again, shaking her head. "I won't do it."

"Anwen, I am begging you. You need to leave; he can't find you again. I cannot go without knowing you will be safe."

412

"No!" she sobbed. "We'll leave together." But even as she uttered the words, she knew the truth, part of her understood that this was our last moment together.

"I love you," I told her. I pressed every word, every letter trying to carve it into her mind. "I love you," I repeated and kissed her deeply, slamming my lips onto hers, our faces covered in tears.

"I love you too," she murmured between her parting lips, as our tongues caressed one more time before separating. Just as we were about to.

With a last look at my beautiful, beloved mate, I disappeared.

Anwen

Chapter Thirty-Nine

I fell to my knees. What had I done? My entire body was violently shaking, from the fright, the need to find Ansgar, who had just vanished in front of me. I knew where he was going, where he had to go, because of what I had done. Something as innocent as drinking a tea turned out into whatever payment Rhylan claimed and I only feared the worst.

I had to listen to his words. I hurried to the phone from where I was supposed to call the guard in case of an emergency. I had never done it before but the contract stated it would connect automatically and someone would pick up. I did not know what to say, what to tell them, I did not know if Ansgar would come back here or if he was injured somewhere, but none of it mattered because there was no answer, no matter how many times I rang. Probably Rhylan's doing again, if he managed to infiltrate the guards and visit me so often, he might have also tampered with my emails and phone.

I tried calling Dad, the only other number I knew by heart, but a robotic voice told me I could not make an international call. So I hurried to the laptop, wiping tears from my face that I didn't even notice, until I couldn't see the screen through the watery mess.

The video calls were down, of course, I tried every channel and every person, all of them cutting out so I did the only thing I had left, emailed my father. I knew he would see it in a few hours from now, but it was the best option I had, and I hoped that by that time, Ansgar would be back.

'Dad,

Something happened, I need you to send the jet to get me out of here immediately. Talk to the royal family, the guards, anyone, please get me out of here as soon as you can.

It's urgent, I need to come back home.

Please.''

I did not add more information; I did not have any more myself. I didn't tell him not to worry because, from Ansgar's face, from the shock at the news and the way he agreed to meet that bastard Rhylan without any protest, I knew something had gone wrong.

By the time I finished wandering around the house to find anything that was suitable enough to use as a weapon, all the while trying to regain control over my shivering body, twenty-five minutes passed. I had set myself an hour, hoping that Ansgar would be back by that time and then I planned to run to the river, cross into the faerie-inhabited part of the forest, and walk along the bank until I found them.

That was the end of my plan because I had no idea what to do once I'd found them, since Rhylan seemed invulnerable to iron, and I was not one to know a lot of self-defence. But I packed all the knives I found in my backpack, including the dagger I used at the beginning of my walks, rubbing alcohol and matches. Along with a first aid kit and a bottle of water.

"Thank God!" relief inundated me when the door opened and Ansgar walked back inside.

I rushed to him, happiness flushing through my veins as I hugged him, kissed him excitedly, my hands running through every inch of him to make sure he was safe, unharmed. Apart from a sorrowful expression on his face, he was perfectly fine, I thought.

The memories of what happened, the guilt, my stupid ignorance pressed over me and I started crying, yelping, asking for his forgiveness. Whatever I had done, whatever I had put him through with my blind trust and stupidity, I promised to make it right.

"Fahrenor," he lifted my chin gently to make me face him, his gleamy ashen eyes. "There was no way for you to know. I should have taught you, prepared you better. Kept you safe." He pressed a kiss on my hair, then another on my brow. "Did you call anyone?"

"The guard would not answer; I don't think the phone is working. I emailed my dad, asked him to prepare the jet."

He nodded approvingly. "Write to him again. Tell him Sunday morning."

I raised my brows in surprise. "Why?"

"It's the best time," he said and walked into the kitchen to allow me the time to do it. I heard him drinking a few glasses of water straight from the tap, not bothering with the cold one we had in the fridge. I wrote back to my dad, with the details Ansgar provided. He walked behind me and read the email, whispering his approval when

416

I pressed send. I told dad not to worry, that I was fine but I needed him to pick me up on Sunday morning. Due to Ansgar's insistence, I added another line to tell him that it had to be Sunday, as early as possible. When I asked about it again, he avoided the answer and started kissing me.

"Ansgar, what's happening?" I shifted back from the chair to look at him, tried to decipher whatever he was not telling, whatever he was trying to concede from me.

Something was not okay, but he didn't seem angry with me, even though I deserved it. He would not tell me what happened, but he seemed more relaxed at the thought that my father was coming to pick me up on that particular day. A day and a half from now. That was all we had left.

I had so many questions, things to say to him. We needed to form a plan, I needed to know how we could meet once I returned to New York, how I would find him, but everything faded into nothing as he pressed his lips on mine once again, willing my mouth to open and receive the taste of him, his hands caressing my skin like a soft wind did the surface of a lake.

I needed him as much as he needed me, I wanted to feel him inside of me, know that he was there, back and safe in my arms, so I let him. I let him carry me back into the bedroom, where he removed my clothes with such gentleness as though he was unwrapping a precious gift. He planted a long line of kisses from my neck, down the valley of my breasts, stopping to grab and tease each one with his tongue and teeth, then down to my navel and lower, towards my inner thighs.

"Ansgar, please," I begged, the need to feel him in me too great to care about anything else. I covered my core for emphasis, hoping that his face, now situated in between my legs, would be replaced with what I wanted the most.

"We have all night, my love. Let me enjoy you." He delved between my thighs with his mouth, his lips sucking and tongue brushing me like an easel in the hands of a madman. I gasped, my breath stopping when his tongue slid inside of me, tasting and tormenting and even so, I wanted more. More of this, more of him. "Please," I whimpered again and this time, my breaking voice had him convinced because he slid into me in one determined stroke, making me scream at the sudden sensation, the way my body had to part so abruptly to receive him.

"Mmmhmm," he moaned at the tightness, the way my thighs squeezed him. "I will never get tired of this fahrenor," he murmured and started to move, forcing me to feel every tick inch of him as he retracted, then pushed back in, each time a little faster and deeper until I was so full of him, I wanted to blast out with pleasure.

The thrill of Ansgar inside of me, of our bodies connecting in such a way had me whimpering and almost sobbing as wave after wave of pleasure ripped through me, over and over until I became a trembling mess, begging him.

To stop, to give me this, to give me more, I did not know.

The only thing my mind could focus on was the way he felt, the way he forced my body and lower muscles to contort in such ways I did not think possible, making them expulse every shred of pleasure they were capable of. By the time we finished, both our bodies shaking from the magnitude of pleasure and effort we had pushed them through, a blanket of night had fallen over the horizon. I shifted, awakened from a trance to check the alarm clock. It was almost ten in the evening.

"I need to call my dad," I announced to Ansgar, who rested lazily on the bed sheets, his head tilted to one side on the pillow. Sleeping. He had fallen asleep in the ten seconds it took me to raise from bed and check the time. I smiled at him and placed a kiss on his cheek.

He looked peaceful. Tired, but serene features lined his face. I pulled a blanket and tucked him in, gently caressing his jaw and planting a few more kisses on his lips, which, to my surprise, he did not react to. Very tired indeed.

I cracked open a window, just an inch or two, enough to let fresh air in, along with the songs of crickets and birds I knew he loved, then headed downstairs and placed two pizzas in the oven, realising we hadn't eaten anything all day, apart from each other. I grabbed the laptop to see my father already connected and waiting for me to call.

I sighed, knowing I had lots of explaining to do. I had hoped Ansgar would be awake and by my side for this, but I did not have the heart to wake him up, especially after all the events. I would keep details to a minimum and once he and I talked and formed a plan in the morning, I could give my family more details.

So I pressed the video call button and in only two buzzes, I found both my parents sighing with relief to see me safe and well. I told them I was going crazy with boredom and I needed to go back on Sunday because Cressi had an event I needed to attend the next day.

Even though dad scoffed at all the paperwork and fines we had to pay, which I offered to do so from my trust fund, an idea that he immediately rejected, my mom looked relieved to have me back earlier and started telling me about all the event planning she had done and the people she had already hired. The oven dinged and I said goodbye to them, thanking them for the support and understanding, then headed back into the kitchen to search for two plates and bring my fae prince some food.

As I climbed the stairs carrying two plates and two cans of coke, I heard him being sick in the bathroom and immediately hurried into the room. He had closed the door, a silent request for privacy. I wouldn't want anyone to hover above me while I was spilling my guts either, so I went back into the kitchen and grabbed a bottle of water and an apple, ready for when he came out.

I hated everything after a session of retching, but my mother always forced me to bite into an apple, even though I would spit it out afterwards. The sweet taste worked wonders for removing any lingering disgust from my mouth. I waited a few minutes, pacing the room and listening to him struggling to breathe in between vomiting sessions. I did not know what made him so sick, and part of me feared it had something to do with Rhylan or whatever had happened by the river.

I knocked on the door to make my presence noted and pushed it open to find him kneeling in front of the toilet, head shoved midway through as the last remnants of his stomach were emptying. As soon as he sensed my presence, he pressed the flush and quickly wiped his mouth with the back of his hand.

"I'm done," Ansgar announced before I even had a chance to ask, so I handed him a face towel and the bottle of water I had brought with me. He took them both gratefully and hurried us out of the bathroom and back into bed, where he stretched fully, allowing only his head to be raised just a bit higher on the pillow. His breath sounded low and dragging, muscles tense, as though cramps still coiled inside his stomach. I knew better than to offer him food, but when he saw the pizzas and the coke, he smiled lazily and asked if we were watching a story.

"Only if you want to," I replied and when he nodded with a bit more excitement than natural, I headed downstairs to bring the laptop and arranged it on top of a hard pillow on the side of the bed, while Ansgar and I sat close together, watching the screen from our pillows. I asked if he had any preference, but he only asked to watch one of my favourites, so I selected 'Coco', hoping he would like it. I chuckled at the memory of how he had laughed for hours after we'd watched Peter Pan and I admitted that Tinkerbell was my portrayal of faeries until meeting him.

I had a few pieces of pizza, then placed the plate on the nightstand and shifted more onto him, meeting his warmth. Ansgar wrapped an arm around me and pulled me tightly to him as he planted soft kisses on my earlobe. A few minutes into the movie, his breathing had evened and his hand relaxed enough on top of me to know he had fallen asleep again. So I flipped the screen shut and snagged a close by blanket to cover us with, then let myself drift into sleep caught in my love's embrace.

I woke up to daylight and when I shifted in bed, I was surprised to find Ansgar still sleeping next to me. He was usually the one who woke up at the crack of dawn and by the time I normally rose from bed, he'd done part of his duties and made breakfast.

"Morning," I turned to him lazily and greeted, pulling myself up enough to reach his face and give him a kiss. "Ansgar," I shook his body, forcing him awake. He was burning up so badly that the covers were wet underneath him, his face flushed and lips cracked.

"Baby, wake up," I shifted into him, shaking him hard, forcing him to react. He slowly, so slowly opened his eyes, as if it was the most effort consuming action.

"You have a high fever," I stated the obvious, but his eyes, those beautiful eyes that normally swam with shadows, looked dried out. Only soft silver irises remained.

"Hhmm," was all he said, a murmur he put so much effort into that he fell back to sleep.

I was instantly up and ran into the kitchen to find whatever I could, whatever I had back in this cabin to bring his fever down. My first instinct was to call an ambulance, but I had no phone and we were in the middle of nowhere. Then I tried to call the guard again but no one answered, so I took matters into my own hands and headed to the medicine cabinet, trying to find anything that might help.

I found paracetamol and ibuprofen, I didn't know which one helped with a fever but those were the only names I recognised and everything else was in Swedish. I blended them up along with some almond milk and strawberry, found a straw and went back into the bedroom, lifting Ansgar's head enough to make him take a few sips of the drink. He reluctantly did. I removed all the covers and his shirt, then opened all the windows to let fresh air in.

The forest, I discovered with shock. My eyes did not stumble upon the usual sea of green that shifted in the wind. Instead, the leaves had turned brown and amber overnight, similar to that day of the storm, only this time it looked to be across the entire district. Not only the trees but the moss, the grass, everything changed into a million shades of brown, just like... autumn.

The leaves were dying, Ansgar was sick, they had to be connected.

I hurried into the bathroom and grabbed a full load of towels, threw them all into the bathtub and opened the tap to cold water, making sure they absorbed as much coldness as they were able to, then I hurried back in the kitchen and took out an entire bowl of ice cubes which I brought into the bedroom and rested it on the night stand. I wrapped Ansgar in the cold towels, placing one on each of his arms, one on his chest and one on each leg, while I wiped the sweat from his forehead with another one, a smaller one nestling a few ice cubes, and gently pressed them on his face, his cheeks, his lips and down his neck every minute or so.

I repeated the process for two hours, until there was no ice left and the towels were soaking wet from his still steamy sweat. It was not working, every time I touched his face to check his temperature, I felt it getting higher. Every few minutes I went back to the window to study the forest and my heart sank when I saw the leaves had started to fall, creating an amber carpet on the ground. I needed help.

"Ansgar," I tried to wake him again to no avail. His skin was turning clammy and his lips were chipped from the fever, from dryness. "I'll be back soon," I whispered, though I knew he would not, could not hear me and I went outside to try to get help.

I ran towards the river as quickly as my feet could hold me, I felt my calves burning and twitching in pain but I did not care, I needed to find someone, anyone that could help. As soon as I reached the river and crossed to the other side following the path downwards to the cave, I started screaming for help, forcing my voice to echo and penetrate deeper into the woods.

The trees were dying all around me, the moss looked dry and blackening and the leaves of grass looked scorched, no flowers in sight.

"Help!" I shouted for what felt like the millionth time until a figure appeared into a pathway in between the barren willows. "Please, help!" I ran towards the creature, a tall male, as wide as a tree trunk with branching hands instead of fingers. He paused, taking me in with a curious look, his yellow round irises moving up and down my body.

"Please, help!" I retook his attention.

"What do you need, human?" he pressed the last word like an insult.

"The forest is dying," I shouted, pointing out around me as if he could not see for himself. "Ansgar is sick!" I announced while tears made their way to my eyes. "I need help," I urged, defeatedly, not knowing what else to do.

"The prince signed his deed, little human, and took us all with him," the faerie replied repulsed, no compassion in his voice.

"What do you mean? He needs help, he's got a high fever, I don't know what to give him to make him better. You need to help me, please!" I kept saying that word. *Please, please, please* even though it seemed to have absolutely no effect on the creature. I stepped to touch his branched arms, to grab him and drag him with me, hoping that once he saw Ansgar's state, he would understand my desperation. I don't know if he took pity on me or of he wanted to torture me even more, but he continued.

"There is no cure for what the prince did, girl. He doomed us all."

"What are you even saying?" I reprimanded. "I am telling you that your keeper is sick, so he can't heal the forest today. You need to help me make him better, so he can make your home better," I tried to make it sound like a trade, but he huffed.

"It is *because* of the keeper that the forest is dying. It's dying along with him. The prince chose to save you and doom himself."

He looked at me, scanned me, as though calculating my unworthiness.

"What?" A wave of a breath barely escaped me.

"He gave his energy to the Fear Gorta to save you, silly human. He told us so yesterday, before he went to die at the queen's mansion. With you," he pressed the words with disgust as I fell on my knees, my chest barely able to contain the aching rasping in and out of me. "Better get back and at least stay by his side. Give him an easy death since the fool cannot have an honourable one."

No, it could not be. My chest heaved and bile rose in my throat, it could not be.

Ansgar.

I ran.

I ran until my soles felt like they were detaching from my feet, until every muscle broke from effort, until I got home and hurried back in the bedroom, falling onto my knees by the bed.

I found him still breathing, slowly, desperately, his lungs appearing to inhale lead, but he was still alive.

"Ansgar," I cried and caressed his cheek.

Cold.

Cold as ice.

Cold as death.

Within the two hours I had been away, his entire body shifted from scorching hot to shattering cold.

"Ansgar, please," I sat by his side and cried, covering him with my body, trying to give him whatever it was that his own needed to recover. He could take it from me.

A hand caressed my hair and I shifted, to find his eyes open.

"Ansgar," I cried, my throat heavy from screaming.

"Anwen," he murmured, so slowly, his lips barely forming the words.

"What did you do?" I accused, though I knew.

He had given his life for mine.

That was the payment Rhylan required. Me or Ansgar, and my mate had made the choice.

"Stay with me, fahrenor. Guide me home." If his words were not enough to convince me, his pleading look was. I would not abandon him, not now.

"I love you," tears flowed freely down my cheeks and he stretched out an arm to caress them, but the movement must have been too painful and his hand fell on the bed halfway through.

I laid by his side on the covers, hugging him into me, desperately trying to take from me that part that he was missing and give it back. I did not know how this flow of energy worked but I hoped that if I stayed close enough or did something right, I still had a chance to save him.

Bolts of pain rushed through him as he used every remaining shred of strength to shift into position and hold me in his arms, my head on his shoulder and his arms around me, the position we used to fall asleep in.

My heart crumbled into a million pieces and I was slowly shaking, shuddering in pain when I understood. He wanted it to feel as though we were falling asleep.

Only that, this time, he would not wake.

"I love you," I whispered and shifted my head upwards to be able to catch his lips in mine. Smoke swirled in his vision as a wave of pain coursed through him, stealing his breath for a few moments, but a heavy inhale ignited from him again, barely strong enough to keep his heart beating.

"I love you," I repeated, caressing his back, just like I always did when we went to sleep, focusing my every muscle to listen to me, to give me these last moments with him. Even though my eyes escaped a constant flow of tears that streamed down on his shoulder, I felt grateful that my mind was strong enough to force the rest of myself to remain still and not break. Not yet.

His body started trembling next to mine, uncontrollable movements shifted the bed and I saw him clench his jaw against the agony.

This was it. I knew it as his eyes opened wide, empty, the bare remnants of what he once was. The last shred of him, willing to gaze upon me one last time.

"I will always love you," I promised, an oath that I planned to keep for the rest of my life.

"I...love...you," his lips barely formed the words, inaudible while his body convulsed by my side and I placed my lips to his to catch that last breath, threatening to come out.

As soon as my lips joined his, it stopped.

Everything.

Him, the world, every dream I ever had, it all disappeared in a moment.

Instead of the lips I kissed, instead of the body I hugged and loved, remained a pile of dead leaves, flowing onto the bed, as my love turned into nothing right in front of me.

Epilogue

"Six months ago, our wonderful volunteers and members of staff fed Mother Earth a handful of seeds. Today, those sprouts stand as one, proud and tall to form a labyrinth of firs, one of the many projects we plan to re-establish in the most damaged areas of the Carpathian Mountains. It is with joy and honour that I find myself here today, to support a project dear to my heart."

"It is time to look at nature with a kinder eye, to understand our history as human beings, as part of the creation and find new ways to cohabitate with the forest."

"As founder of the Fahren Foundation, I find myself proud and honoured to be witnessing the growth of a new forest, a new landmark. Dear forest of firs, may your roots be strong and steady," I raised my champagne glass and, as I drank, I recited the same verse I did every time we inaugurated a new project.

May the Goddess hold you and accept you.

I strolled through the press, greeting everyone, smiling robotically at my picture taken over and over again, already knowing what titles they were going to use. 'Rebel heiress debuts new project' or 'The new life of Anwen Odstar: changing the world one root at a time'.

I did not care, I did not read them, nor went on social media anymore. Or parties.

The only times I went out in public was during the inauguration of a new forest. We had already planted nine, in areas marked by deforestation around the globe and the foundation, although started with my trust fund, was now receiving substantial donations from large companies, who either cared or wanted to look good.

I did not mind either way, funds were funds and in only a year, I hired a team of biologists, geologists, zoologists and many other scientists, along with hundreds of local staff and volunteers. They analysed the best plant for each kind of soil, found the locations most in need and travelled to supervise the plantation and growth. I usually stayed in the garden back at home and planned campaigns, or researched, keeping myself to myself, when I was not forced to interact or received visits from Cressida.

Isolation trauma, the doctors had called it. Little did they know.

When Dad arrived with the guard and found me crying hysterically in a bed of dead leaves, he thought it was some kind of phase that would pass as soon as we came back home. When two weeks later I refused to get out of my room or eat more than the bare minimum to stay alive, they called doctors. Specialist over specialist, none of them could find what was wrong with me, so they had called it depression. Because I had spent so much time isolated in the woods, grieving my deceased brother.

Cressi was the only one allowed in my room at any time, and to her credit, she gave up several contracts to babysit my sorry ass. She did not mention Ansgar to anyone, she did not ask about him, but she knew. It must have been the only logical explanation for my state. The last time I'd called her, I told her how happy I was, how we were going to sort things out and be together. Then, a week later I was hauled into a plane and brought home, unable to stop crying for days. She knew. And I loved her all the more for not pushing me.

In the first few weeks, I dreamt about him constantly and during those hours, I found a shred of happiness again. I faked having trouble sleeping and asked for pills, forcing myself to sleep longer hours, forcing my mind to imagine him so we could meet in dreams. Where he smiled, laughed, kissed me, drank my cocktails and hugged me tightly.

But even those started to fade away. I knew there would be a moment when my brain would start to forget him, his features, the way the sun kissed his skin, the shadows dancing in his eyes and there was nothing to do about it. I did not even have a picture to remember him by.

Everything was missing, a part of me was missing, the love of my life was missing, and there was absolutely nothing I could do about it. So I laid in bed and cried, woke up and cried, saw Cressi and cried.

My belongings were returned from Evigt three months after my arrival along with an apology, explaining that the state of the forest was so damaged after my departure, no one was permitted to enter until the woods found their balance again. I felt relieved they did, it meant a new keeper had been dispatched into the district. I pitied him for the amount of work he probably had to do after the devastation left behind, and was grateful to him for bringing the woods back to life. For fixing my friends' homes.

I left the boxes and suitcases untouched for a while, until Cressi offered to go through them with me. There were notebooks, clothes, shoes, creams, perfumes and cosmetics shoved in each and every pocket and case we could find, but the treasure rested in a black box, one that had contained the shoes I wore when I visited the Earth Kingdom.

I opened it and found one of Ansgar's shirts, neatly folded inside. I shrieked at the memories, grabbing it to my chest to discover his scent once again. For a moment, I felt him, still with me and I shuddered as tears pooled on my face, onto the fabric tightly pressed over my heart. Cressi came by my side in an instant, and I started screaming about how much I missed him.

She hugged me tightly and caressed my hair, for hours on end until there was no more feeling in me to expulse. That shirt became my most precious possession, I slept hugging it, travelled holding it in my bag and every time I needed a little push, I found the fabric and caressed it gently.

If I didn't have something to remember him by, I would make it myself, I decided one day and so, ten months later, I was the founder of a foundation that saved and planted new forests around the world. I did not think of a better way to honour my mate.

"Time for your stroll, Anwen," one of the first biologists I had hired, Michael, announced. He knew the ritual; we had done it many times over. Once the inauguration was done and the press left, I liked to take a walk through the woods by myself, feel the soil underneath my feet, smell the new life, and dedicate the location to my fae prince.

"Thank you, Mike," I nodded and went back to the car to change my pumps for running shoes. I always arrived in a shirt and jeans to these events, just so I would not have to change afterwards for my walk. The only thing I took with me was my bag, Ansgar's shirt neatly folded in a velvet box. My most prized possession.

As I walked through a pathway my feet created for the first time,

433

I took in the trees, rejoicing in the scent, I heard rustling. The trees had grown tall enough that I could not see past them, and the noise came from deeper into the woods. I followed quickly, thinking that one of the volunteers or press snuck inside and got lost. I hurried my step when I spotted a silhouette forming. By the time I approached it, I distinctly saw a tall man in a black outfit.

"Hello, sprout," the voice greeted cheerfully and I froze. It could not be. Not him. Not again.

"What do you want, Rhylan?" I replied, disgusted, barely able to speak from the hatred towering in my muscles. "Haven't you had enough?" I wanted to kill him, find a weapon and murder him. The bastard deserved it.

"Now, now, sprout, no need for such violence." He stepped closer, lingering only a few metres away from me. I had researched enough about him to know he was capable of reading thoughts, and could not die, but it was still worth a shot.

"What do you want, Rhylan?" I repeated, remembering the last time I had seen him.

"Initially, I wanted to know if you liked my present," he smirked slyly, "but seeing how you take it with you everywhere you go, I would say yes."

I didn't deign him with a reply.

"Still upset, sprout?" he cooed just as a child would. "Hate me so much you won't even talk to me? Want to kill me even though you are now aware of my powers?" Rhylan teased.

"I want to kill you, you disgusting son of a bitch, every single night as I cry myself to sleep," I rasped.

"Aaaww, baby sprout is missing the tree princeling because you loved him so much?" he mocked.

"You wouldn't know what love is if it hit you in the face and wiped away that disgusting, horrible grin of yours," I retorted.

"Hmm..." He paused, faking to be caught in deep thought, though I knew him enough by now to recognise his theatrics. I spent a long time remembering every single conversation we had, hating myself for not questioning him when I should have.

"Tell me, little sprout, would you like to make a deal with me?" Rhylan returned to his dark tone, the one he had used in the cabin.

"A deal with you?" I fought the instinct to spit in his face. "You have nothing I want."

He paused, thinking again. "No? Are you sure?"

"Very," I groaned and turned to leave.

I wanted to find a weapon and shove it straight through his brain, make him suffer. I hurried back on the pathway my feet had created, not even wanting to turn and see if the bastard had disappeared. His voice sounded in my ear, a deep whisper shaking my world.

"Tell me sprout, how would you like to see your princeling again?"

Follow Anwen's journey in Tales of Fire and Embers.

For a new author, reviews are everything, so if you enjoyed this book, feel free to give it some stars!

More from the author

Discover the Tales of Earth and Leaves series

Tales of Earth and Leaves

Tales of Fire and Embers

Tales of Forever and Now

Tales of Wind and Storm

Discover *Love, Will, an LGBT historical fiction*

If you enjoyed this book, you'll love the FREE bonus story *Tales of War and Fire.* Subscribe tc ..., newsletter and get your copy, along with bonus chapters and fun content.

www. xandranoel.com

BOOKTOK THANKS

I would like to place a very special thank you to the booktok community, the amazing people I met on tiktok who dedicated their time to read and cuddle me with words of encouragement. I never thought such a wonderful community could be found online, and I am so lucky to experience it and to be supported by so many book lovers. This one is for you!

Special thanks to the following accounts: itsmiaregine, snowinjulywriter, voldyspatronus, jmarie423, kayleec611, a.taurus.reads, bettyrodz11, itsemzherexx, tonicameron4, dearlybookish, kysrinaria, daniellepeterson43, christinagizzi, moonwatcher513, feline_fatalistic, scout.ticklequeen, resinrehabbystacey, user012923354, viki2802, rstephie.jade and jessikadarkstar.

Also, a special thank you to my critique partner and future author Rachel Metters for reading my manuscript numerous times and all the useful advice, for staying up late to talk about our author doubts and sexy faerie males.

See you all in the next book!

Printed in Great Britain
by Amazon